BORN
OF WAR

ANDERSON HARP

BORN OF WAR

He who is brave is free.

—LUCIUS ANNAEUS SENECA
4BC–65AD

PINNACLE BOOKS
Kensington Publishing Corp.
www.kensingtonbooks.com

*To all those who served with the Army's 96th Infantry
Division and the Marine Corp's 1st Marine Division
waging the battle of Okinawa in spring 1945. And to
Tech Corporal Bert Harp, who was one of them.*

PINNACLE BOOKS are published by

Kensington Publishing Corp.
119 West 40th Street
New York, NY 10018

All Kensington titles, imprints, and distributed lines are available at
special quantity discounts for bulk purchases for sales promotions, pre-
miums, fund-raising, educational, or institutional use. Special book ex-
cerpts or customized printings can also be created to fit specific needs.
For details, write or phone the office of the Kensington sales manager:
Kensington Publishing Corp., 119 West 40th Street, New York, NY
10018, attn: Sales Department; phone 1-800-221-2647.

This book is a work of fiction. Names, characters, businesses, organizations, places, events, and incidents either are the product of the author's imagination or are used fictitiously. Any resemblance to actual
persons, living or dead, events, or locales is entirely coincidental.

PINNACLE BOOKS and the Pinnacle logo are Reg. U.S. Pat. & TM Off.

ISBN-13: 978-0-7860-3423-9
ISBN-10: 0-7860-3423-8

First printing: April 2015

10 9 8 7 6 5 4 3 2 1

Printed in the United States of America

First electronic edition: April 2015

ISBN-13: 978-0-7860-3424-6
ISBN-10: 0-7860-3424-6

PROLOGUE

William Parker's hands were covered in blood.

It will wash off, he told himself, half asleep.

He stared at his hands in the dim light and knew it wasn't true. This was the kind of blood that woke him up in the middle of the night, that pulled him out of bed soaked in sweat.

Parker had been raised on hunting. A deer shot on a cold November morning bled, but that blood washed off easily. The deer didn't deserve to die. It didn't have a name, but it did have a purpose. It provided food.

"Neither wound nor kill for no reason," his father had said.

William Parker's father had been killed aboard Pan Am Flight 103. Taken by a terrorist's bomb. The men who'd killed him deserved to die. Their blood washed off.

His wife of only a few days had been killed when a maniac drove his car into a crowd. Another easy kill whose blood would wash off.

And there were so many others. . . . Like the ones who'd taken his father and wife. The men who believed the innocent should die for some strange, irrational reason. The monster that somewhere, in its past, crossed the line. The quiet student in the back who used a line out of a religious text to authorize the slaughter of hundreds. Thousands. The one who initiated a search on the Internet for fertilizer and bombmaking materials.

What is his name? Parker looked at his hands again. The blood was gone. It was dawn.

Somewhere, not far away, lurked a monster that sought to bloody its own hands. For now, it remained nameless. It waited, lurking, seeking its fame. It rose from the same bottomless muck. It would do whatever it took to kill for no purpose.

His bedroom remained cold in the summer only by virtue of its dark shades and air-conditioning. By late afternoon, the heat would brew up black cells of storms painted red on the radar. The storm cells would churn up winds that could cut through neighborhoods like some horrific chainsaw.

Someone who will deserve to die is out there. He sat up in bed. The house was silent.

A red cell like the ones on the weather map when a bad storm's coming. He felt it.

William Parker didn't know where.

But it was coming.

CHAPTER ONE

School starts in three weeks, Cathie thought. Just three weeks.

The new kindergarten teacher of the Mountain View Baptist Church had worried about the start of the full-time school schedule for some time.

Late July already? Vacation Bible School was coming to an end next week. Then parents would get one last trip to the beach before the children returned to the full fall schedule.

It is important that they feel okay. They need to feel safe. She had considered the matter for some time but particularly now as she stood at the entranceway waiting for the kids to arrive for Bible school. *My first year as a real teacher!*

The building that housed the new elementary classrooms was barely a year old. The Mountain View Baptist Church named its school after the preacher who had formed the church only a decade earlier. The Reverend Patton School was the pride of the nearly thousand members who made up the church's congregation. Large panes of glass and wide-open hallways were bathed in bright light even on dark days. The small classrooms lined with unmarked desks still smelled of fresh paint. The walls of the corridors, especially near the entrance, were covered with the poster board colorings and drawings of the kindergarten students. The church and its main chapel were connected to the school by an open, covered walkway where, after the children reported to their classes, they would line up before marching into the main chapel for the beginning of the day. Each day started with a congregation of all of the students from the summer Bible school and a reading from Reverend Patton.

But for now, Cathie had the duty of meeting each of her pre-kindergarteners at the front as they unloaded from their parents' cars. She stood at the double glass doors that led into the school's main foyer. The Yukons and Ford trucks streamed through the covered access, lined up bumper-to-bumper, one by one, as if being cleared for a landing at O'Hare.

She didn't mind door duty. It was fun seeing the little ones, still half asleep, climb down from their trucks with their pink and red backpacks. They were so innocent. Cathie held the car door open with one hand while she helped a little girl slide down with her backpack rising up over her small shoulders. It surprised her that the load often weighed as much as the child.

She had the job of being the protector.

"Wow, that's a big one, little girl!" she smiled. Cathie was known for her infectious grin that filled up her round face and showed the slightest gap between her two front teeth. That gap had always made her shy and reluctant to smile until she got to know someone. Her dark brown hair was always perfect. The freckles confirmed the look of a girl raised in Mobile on salt water, more used to being on the bay in a skiff with her grandfather checking the crab traps, rather than wearing a dress and being a schoolteacher. And now she was responsible for the twenty-two pre-kindergarteners of Room B-1. In three weeks they would become her first kindergarten class.

"How are you feeling?" The child's mother leaned over the steering wheel, putting her cell phone down on the center panel for a moment.

"Good, good."

No announcement had been made, but mothers could read her face. They instinctively knew. And Cathie was embarrassed as to what the mother's smile meant. She had only been married to the police officer for a year. Marriage and a child seemed to be a lot for one year.

"How's my little killer doing?" the mother changed the subject, asking about her own child.

She had a dry sense of humor that Cathie knew was warranted. The little girl was one of four and the only girl. The brothers bled more than the Red Cross when they messed with their sister. The child loved her pigtails and always wore a well-used and oversized Atlanta Braves baseball hat.

"Are you kidding? She loves B-1!" Cathie adjusted the backpack on the little girl's shoulders. "Your daughter is doing fine." Even the parents needed to know their children were safe.

She had already learned, even as the newest kindergarten teacher at Mountain View, how important it was to reassure them all.

After the little girl pulled up the backpack, she bent over to tug on one of her boots that had started to slide off in the descent. Again, Cathie helped adjust the backpack. A summer rain had lasted for more than a day and carried with it a persistent and strong wind. Each of the children wore a different colored raincoat, which always amazed her. The coats were fire-engine reds and banana yellows and when bunched together at the end of the day getting ready for pickup, they filled the hallway in what looked like a gigantic bag of Skittles.

The next truck pulled in and another child hopped down, stopped, and tugged on her rubber boots.

"My, you look stunning!" the teacher said to her little charge.

Cathie patted the child on her head lightly, noticing in the flick of her eye that her wedding ring still sparkled even in the cloudy, dull light. *It's been a year!* She turned it lightly on her finger.

The Yukon pulled ahead, followed by a lifted Ford pickup. The trucks moved slowly as they passed through. It was not like when she was a child. Then the drivers were all mothers, favoring Toyota vans. Now the occasional father would drop off his child. The fathers drove big trucks, well off the ground, and were so careful in the line of traffic. They seemed to be aware that small things could get out of sight quickly.

Their trucks moved slowly as they passed through.

In the brief second between vehicles, she looked up to the line of trucks and Yukons that circled the parking lot.

Something caught her eye.

On the far end of the line of vehicles and the parking lot, near the highway and a row of trees, was the figure of a man standing next to a pine. He stood alone.

The pine trees had only been planted about a year ago, when the new school was completed. The church had started downtown as a dedicated group of followers of a Southern Baptist preacher who pulled his people together through hurricanes and layoffs at the shipyard. Cathie's father was one of the first to join. Back then, the congregants met at a school gym rented on Sundays. Now, the chapel was almost always packed.

It struck her as odd. He stood behind the small tree almost like a bad joke. She had heard of a father whose anger from a bad divorce caused him to show up every day until the police talked him into channeling his hate some other way, but this figure was different.

Something doesn't seem right, she thought. She felt in her pocket the thin shape of a cell phone. Her husband had affixed a small cross to the cover. Cathie could always feel the shape with the tips of her fingers. She held it for a moment, hesitating. The next truck pulled up in front of the doors and as it did, the side mirror pulled just above her head. Again, she helped open the door, seeing two pairs of little hands push it from the inside.

She looked over the side of the truck as she opened the door. The man was missing.

The two girls who climbed out were twins who didn't seem to mind at all that their mother dressed them up in identical outfits and their father carried them to the church school every day in a truck loaded down in back with crab traps. Everyone on this side of the bay had salt water in their veins and crab traps in their trucks.

The vehicle carried with it the smell of the bay.

"Hey, there!"

"Not the perfect day for a Monday," the driver yelled the words over the rumble of his truck. "But summer's making the bend. Already the end of July."

"Yes." She paused. "But it will be a great week!" Her words always bubbled out. She waved at him as the two little girls passed under her arm, and she held open the glass door for them as they walked into the school. The wave was a brief flick of the hand, but it meant much more. It meant "your children are under our care now; I will protect them as if they were my own."

The father waved back, with a cell phone in his hand, expecting to see them later that day when the same routine would occur in reverse.

But she stood on her tiptoes, unconsciously, as the Ford passed and cleared an empty space between vehicles.

The shape on the other side of the parking lot was still missing.

Another vehicle was in line with the next drop-off. In the brief space between the two, she scanned the edges of the parking lot. Nothing.

Worry comes often when there is a lack of information.

"Pops!"

She stepped inside the door and yelled down the hallway to the old man who was the church school's entire security force.

He was at the far end of the hallway standing in a corner dressed in a starched, well-pressed white shirt with a security patch on his shoulder and blue well-creased cotton pants. The school had engaged in much debate after Sandy Hook about whether to arm him. In the end, the council reached the judgment that this was Mobile, Alabama, and risks such as what happened in Connecticut didn't exist here.

She knew his reputation. Pops was kind to the children but with a glance could stop a playground fight as soon as he arrived.

However, he was hard of hearing and often forgot his hearing aids. She heard the older students laugh at him as he passed them by in the lunchroom.

Yet Pops came with credentials. He had served in the Navy for twenty years and rumor had it that he served as a senior chief on a nuclear submarine. He would tell stories to the children, which the teacher would occasionally overhear, about living under the sea for months at a time.

But now he moved slowly and with a constant limp.

"Pops!"

She hollered the word louder this time, causing the children coming into the school to stop and look back at her, as if Cathie's calls were directed to each of them.

"No, kids, go on in. Take your coats off and go to your rooms." Her voice was tense. "I'm just looking for Pops!"

She smiled, unconsciously letting the glass door close on a child standing just outside. She quickly pulled the door open, looking beyond the child.

"I am sorry, Matthew, that was not very nice." The boy was big for his age, as tall as the teacher, even though only in fifth grade. He would play football one day at Daphne High. The school, on the eastern shore of Mobile Bay, was known for state championships and winners. And she would look up to him.

"Matthew, do me a favor and go get Mr. Ellison." Pops's real name was Thomas Ellison.

"Yes, ma'am."

He had speed. Matthew won every race on the playground.

Two more vehicles passed, both white Yukons. It was the popular color now.

The church was built around a pastor that had a strong following, but Mountain View was the church of working people. Most were well paid and drove the sixty miles to the lucrative jobs of the Pascagoula, Mississippi, shipyards.

"Where did he go?" She spoke the words to herself unconsciously, pulling the two glass doors together with a bang as if closing the castle gates.

She pulled out her cell phone and hit the direct dial

for the first name on the list. It began to ring. Voice-mail came on. She held her hand over the phone as she whispered a few words.

Two of her children heard the banging doors, saw her on the cell phone, and ran from the hallway towards her.

"Children, go back to your room."

Their small faces showed fear.

Cathie waved her hand towards the two as she turned back to the parking lot. She continued to scan among the parked cars as she saw the last truck pull off, back onto the highway, its driver off to work. In the corner of her eye she saw the security guard scurrying towards her and felt the tug of a child's hand from behind.

And then she saw the figure moving towards her. It was how he moved that scared her. He came at her like a mad dog with his head down low but his eyes fixed.

"Oh, my God."

CHAPTER TWO

A man stood on the edge of a small one-lane highway deep in the woods of northern New Hampshire. He stared at the sign that said DEER MOUNTAIN CAMPGROUND as he walked back and forth. He held a cell phone to his ear as he pulled his long black hair back behind a sweater cap. His hair extended down below his collar and was stringy, matted, and oily. It had been days since he'd had a shower.

He was both short and small. He had been on the road for days without stopping for anything but gas, chips, and Cokes. He would remain on the move for the next few days. Movement was survival.

"Yes, that is right."

The signal was weak and, like an old television antenna, he turned and turned again trying to hold on to the words.

Omar pressed the cell close to his ear. He could feel the heat of both the pressure and the warmth of the telephone as he unconsciously squeezed it tighter.

"Yes, my brother, the front doors. The glass ones. No one will stop you."

He had a vision in his mind of the days that he spent

at the same church. His mother secretly took him on Sundays to the rented school gym. Later, his father screamed with disapproval when he learned that the boy and his sister were going to a Christian school.

It took another relative to give him the reason to reject his mother's Christian world. It wasn't that he accepted his father's religion. His father was weak and failed to accept the true teachings. He was determined to take a different path.

"The last one has left." The voice was clear. Omar could see in his mind the clearing of the parking lot, as each of the "redneck" trucks left. Omar had taken pride in his Honda Civic being much smaller than the trucks. It was old and smelly but it meant that he didn't need transportation from his mother. They had laughed at him at Daphne High School but his humor always saved him.

Omar was, from the beginning, an outsider. He knew it and had adapted himself well over time.

"Now. Strike now!" he yelled the words, catching himself, looking around the woods to make sure that no one heard his scream.

Omar had left Mobile the day before, driving through the night. It was nearing the end of Ramadan. He knew that Allah would give him compensation for helping kill the nonbelievers. Once all was in place it was critical that he leave his brother behind. They had planned it this way for months. He had left the car he stole from his mother in a campground parking lot. It was the last one near the most northern entrance to the Cohos Trail. The pathway went deep into the dark woods turning west and then north towards the Fourth Connecticut Lake.

She will get it back. He dismissed the thought as

quickly as it came into his mind. *I will get word some-how to my sister.*

The car could remain there for days without question—people would think he, like others, was out hiking the trail or camping in the shelters and lean-tos that were spaced near the lakes.

As its name suggested, the Fourth Connecticut Lake was one of four lakes that formed the headwaters of the Connecticut River. Each small body of water, something slightly bigger than a pond but still classified as a lake, was part of a chain that went deep into the forest of northern New Hampshire. The trail followed the stream to the north and to the Fourth Lake, and then, only a short distance beyond, it crossed an opening. Omar had been here before. He was looking for the small disc embedded in a concrete marker that had a line through its middle. With one step over the disc he would be out of the United States of America.

"Come on, my brother. You will be entering into a special place. You will pass through the gate! Your bravery will be spoken of by the most fiery of warriors and the smallest child will scream out your name!"

It would only be a flash of a moment. Omar was actually jealous.

I must be a true believer. Once faith overcame fear, it all became easy.

Omar had been Eddie's cheerleader for several years now. They had become friends early on. Both would hide in the woods near the shoreline of Mobile Bay where they had a secret camp. It was a refuge, especially when their parents would start waging war with each other. They had this in common. Eddie's parents eventually had a bitter divorce. His father quickly remarried while his mother filled the trash cans with empty vodka bottles she hid in brown paper bags. The can would rattle when it was moved.

With Omar there was the bitterness but never the divorce. His parents were bonded by the anger they carried from the yelling.

But there were good times. Growing up on the bay, the two boys would hunt squirrels together, and fish, and wait for the red tide. The water would suddenly change and the shore would, in a matter of hours, be covered with fish struggling to breathe.

They would bring plastic buckets that they would fill with fish and cook on the campfire at their hiding spot surrounded by stones pulled from the shoreline.

The church was no better than their homes. They were the odd ones, often bullied by the jocks. Omar was small, always thin, but with a certain amount of strength. Eddie was the opposite, always round but never strong. Omar was also foolhardy. He was expelled from the Vacation Bible School once for jamming his finger into another child's eye. Blood ran down the child's face as he wailed away. Omar was known for his ability to go beyond.

They both had been students at the Baptist school. Omar was the first to doubt the teachings. He would ask questions that were meant to push the teachers to their limits.

It was there, at the school gym, in fourth grade, when a larger fifth grader had cornered Eddie and started pounding him with his fists. Omar, no more than half the size of the bully, had jumped on his back. Omar reached for the eyes but the kid shook him off like a bear, slinging him against a wall of lockers. It didn't matter. Omar didn't quit. He was born to be a great fighter.

After the fight, Eddie followed Omar wherever Omar led. Later, he would be the first one that Omar converted to Islam.

Thereafter, they both were in the same grades at the public school and then at Daphne. After graduation, they started college in nearby Mobile. And, as students together in the small college, they joined the madrasa at the same time, each working late, mopping the floors, and learning the Koran, sleeping on mats on the cold linoleum.

A short time later, two others joined the group. But the older ones at the madrasa made fun of them, accusing them of having a false belief and not being dedicated enough to the teachings. Those were the older Muslims, virtually none born in the United States, often brought to Mobile by the shipping work. Like a fraternity, the older ones from Qatar and Iraq and Iran would never let the younger converts into the inner order.

Omar and Eddie were two of the first on campus to have full-grown beards even before it had become popular with the other non-Muslims. Omar's was always straggly, with bare cheeks that took away any uniformity. Eddie had a full beard that swallowed up his already round face and made him look much older. Omar laughed at him.

"You look like you pasted it on." He tried to pull on Eddie's beard. "Bought it at a beard store!"

But that was all some time ago. And now Omar was tired.

The leaves were changing color in the mountains of New Hampshire even though it was only the end of July. He had made this trip before, several times. He knew it well. The crossing allowed him to visit the others in Toronto without the government of America knowing he had even left the country. It was the other fellow Muslims that shared his hate for America's society. The border crossing had become more difficult after September 11th for someone with a beard. Every piece of luggage had been torn apart, the car stripped down to its bare metal. So he found this other route. He had crossed over and back again several times.

The letters never knew I was missing!

The letters, he often joked, were the CIA, the NSA, and the FBI.

Omar had spent the last few days at Eddie's apartment shaping the charges so that all would fit into the vest, and running a wire down the sleeve of the long black trench coat that Eddie would wear. In the weeks leading up to the plan, they stayed up late at night, praying and talking, often sleeping for no more than an hour or two just before daylight.

When last together they ate a simple meal, prayed, and then hugged.

"You know it is important that I leave." Omar said.

"You will make it." Eddie didn't seem sad or doubtful.

"You will step in and scream out the words of praise." Omar's instructions were well rehearsed. "Allah be praised!"

Omar had spoken to Eddie often of who should be the first. He knew that Eddie did not think that being the first meant being less. Both of their journeys would lead to the same place but Omar's would be longer and far more painful.

"I am walking across the parking lot." Eddie's voice shook through the phone.

Omar could sense the movement as the voice wobbled. He saw, in his mind, a teacher inside looking up. It was the new school. Omar knew of the pride that the church had in opening the new building. And Omar could see the old security guard running towards the door.

There was a moment's silence.

"I am here," said Eddie.

The teacher looked into the round face of the man, at his beard and chalky white skin, just beyond the glass doors. But for the doors, they could touch one another. His eyes were cold, brown, and focused. It was as if he was looking through her. He was that mad dog with his head tilted slightly down, but his eyes bored a hole through her.

The guard was still on the far end of the hallway and the children were shuffling towards their classes. Cathie felt the continuous tug of a child behind her.

"Go to your class now!" Cathie glanced backwards and saw the twins. They started to cry.

Cathie grabbed the two doors, shoving her hips into the center where they pivoted open and wrapping her arm through the loop of the two handles. With her other arm, she shoved the one child backwards.

"No!" She yelled. "No!"

The stranger yanked at the doors but she did not budge. He shoved his shoulder against the glass and bounced back in almost a comical fashion, like a tennis ball caroming off a practice wall. He bounced once, and then again. And just as he did so a second time the wire was tripped.

The flash pushed everything into darkness.

* * *

"Hello?"

The cell phone went silent. With the silence he knew it was over.

Omar made one other call overseas.

"As I said, it is done." He spoke only those words and then hung up. They would know all the details later. It was important that they heard something from him directly. It confirmed what he had been saying for months by the Internet.

Omar looked at the cell phone briefly again and then tore it apart. He searched for a rock and pounded the phone into fragments and then threw it all, except the chip, as far as he could, into the woods on the other side of the trail. It scattered across the forest floor like a handful of gravel. He carried the chip with him on the hike and when he came to the Fourth Connecticut Lake, he took a handful of mud from the shoreline, wadded it up around the chip, and tossed it as far as he could, deep into the center of the lake. Two ducks were startled by the splash of water and took off in flight. He washed his hands off at the edge of the lake.

His wife, Fartuun, would meet him at an opening on the other side of the border. She was a Somali from the Toronto community. Fartuun looked like her father. They had such thin faces that it appeared their skin was stretched over their skulls. Their eyes were sunken. She had a light complexion, smooth hair, and a small pointy nose. She was a descendant of the first of the human race, thought to be over a hundred thousand years old. The bones of her ancestors were found in the hills of Ethiopia.

Omar had decided that he needed a wife, as it was the custom and charge of the Koran. He had met her father during one of his trips north, and Omar and Fartuun had married a year ago.

Fartuun would support him and follow his edicts. The only world Fartuun knew consisted of several city blocks in Toronto. She would not know everything. She was to bear his children. His jihad was his and his alone.

His journey had always been planned.

CHAPTER THREE

Zip! Pop!

The round tore through the mud wall, causing a puff of red and orange dust to explode on the rear side with the speed of a pin being stuck into a child's balloon. "I told you not to cheat!" Gunnery Sergeant Kevin Moncrief growled at the taller man braced against the wall in front of him. Moncrief was the monitor standing to the man's rear, holding the man's body armor jacket with his thumbs tucked under the arm openings. It was mainly a place to put his hands, as they felt useless without a weapon in them. A stub of a two-dollar cigar stuck out of the corner of Moncrief's mouth.

"Sometimes!" The cigar slanted Gunny's grin. Jet-black eyebrows accented dark skin he inherited from his father. Unlike his father, however, his hair was cropped close in a Marine high and tight. It was a significant change from his heritage. Moncrief was a descendant of Taza through his father. Like Taza, he had a pleasant and open countenance that the people of the great mountain shared. Taza was the father of Cochise, from a tribe of Indians that eventually settled in Waco,

Texas. Gunny was born in Waco and raised in the Texas sun.

A target vibrated behind the wall. At first glance, it appeared to be a man. The bullet had ripped through the center of its head, knocking it backwards on a hinge. It was supposed to move into a firing position just around the corner of the mud wall. But it had not made it as of yet.

The moving target was called a T-20. An armed terrorist would roll out, around the wall, within the specific time set in the system. The top half of a man, dressed in the clothing of Al Shabaab, with a beard, head wrapped in a black cloth, and wearing an old version of a camouflage utility jacket, would appear. This guerrilla torso was mounted on a computer-controlled Segway. It was a sophisticated moving target meant to act like the real terrorist it simulated.

The shooter, in a well-worn desert camouflage tactical shirt, stood still behind the wall with his Heckler & Koch P-30 automatic pistol raised. Its hammer was still cocked, the slide still forward, indicating that another round was chambered. It also meant something else.

Parker smiled. It was the first time he had smiled in some time. It was a smile tucked behind a short brown beard. His long brown hair, topped with a frayed baseball cap, was flecked with gold from days upon days in the direct sun. The blue eyes could not be seen behind the tinted protective lenses of the Wolf Peak Edge wraparound sunglasses. He was much taller than his monitor standing behind him.

"You said do it with less than a magazine."

Parker held the pistol in front of Moncrief with the barrel pointed away and up, prompting Gunny to hold out his hand and Parker to drop the magazine into it. The gunny held it up to look. The sun reflected off the two shiny .40 caliber brass rounds still in the magazine.

"Two left."

"No."

Parker pulled the slide. Another round popped out of the weapon and Moncrief caught it as it flew through the air.

"Three. You know better."

"But you aren't supposed to shoot them through the wall!"

Parker shrugged.

"Let's do it again."

"What the hell?"

Skip Neave looked up from the clipboard lying on the hood of his pickup truck. A cloud of red dust was cutting across the open field of the training center. A dirt road curved across the mostly grass field, but it was a clay-based soil and, without rain for well over a month, the clay had turned to powder. When the Polaris Ranger drove down the road with its knobby tires, a whirl of orange-tinted dust rose into the air.

Neave watched the cloud come closer, gauging the speed of the Ranger from the spin of the dust.

"He's going to flip that damn thing."

Neave hadn't worry about a flipped Ranger when he was the command sergeant major of the elite 75th Ranger Regiment. In war everything was expendable except a fellow Ranger. He didn't give a damn about breaking equipment unless it resulted in the worst duty possible—writing the letter.

The Polaris Ranger was a safe bet. It had been specially fitted with brush guards and roll bars. It had extra rigging for the lights used by the Operational Training facility during the nighttime running around that they often did. But now he was retired, after eighteen combat tours and twenty-four years of Ranger duty, and working with a contractor. And the contractor didn't like replacing totaled Polaris Rangers.

The ATV pulled up short of Neave's truck, slamming on the brakes and, even with the knobby tires, sliding within arm's length of Neave's own brush guard.

"You got to see this shit!"

Neave didn't have a chance to start cussing his trainer. They had both worked together for nearly a decade running hard, long, deadly combat operations in both Iraq and Afghanistan. The trainer could be loud, while Neave was quiet, but both could be dangerous to the wrong people. They were both craftsmen, trained and experienced in their trade. The trainer used cusswords as nouns, vowels, adjectives, and everything else.

Neave didn't have a chance to start cussing his trainer. He knew the man couldn't communicate without the famous three interlinked words.

"What the hell?"

Neave's look translated into "it better be important."

The trainer understood the stare. "No, really—you got to see this shit." The trainer never wanted Neave to come see a shooter. This had to be something very special.

"Is it that Marine and his buddy?"

A retired Marine gunnery sergeant had recently been hired to work with some of the training groups that were cycling through the OT. The operational training facility, a farm that had been converted into a warriors' training camp with several million dollars, had first become popular with Army units in the region, and then with FBI Swat teams. Recently, the Marines had gotten on board, as it gave them a special place to fly in on the OV-22 Ospreys, always at night, from Camp Lejeune several hundred miles to the north for an assault on a building that OT had constructed on the far end of the farm. It was meant to be an embassy. It was meant to ensure that there would never be another Benghazi.

The O.T. wanted a Marine on staff to ensure that they cross-pollinated with the right language. O.T. wanted to be multiservice, whether Army, Navy, Marine, FBI, or the Los Angeles Police Department.

The gunny came with the credentials. He had served in Force Recon and was one of the few who had helped set up the training for transitioning some Force Recon Marines into the Special Operators that formed the new Marine Corps Special Operations Command.

However, there was a rub. With the Marine Corps' creation of a Special Operations force, it had two high-speed units. Force Recon had the mission of being dropped deep into enemy territory. A Force Recon team was a lone-wolf operation that survived on its own. In Vietnam and Iraq a Marine Recon team would be dropped on a hilltop, in the dead of night, and the helicopter would come back for them a month later. If the team was at the hilltop when the helicopter returned, they would be picked up. Some teams did not show up and were never seen again. A Recon Marine was the definition of a lone wolf. Parker and Moncrief were trained as Recon Marines and fought in Iraq with a deep insertion team that radioed in the location of targets well behind enemy lines. Their Air Naval Gunfire Liaison Company slipped near to the Iraq tanks and then obliterated them with a two-thousand-pound GBU bomb dropped from a B-1 bomber. The Iraq National

Guard had placed a bounty on both Parker and Moncrief's head.

Force Recon wasn't sure, however, that Special Operations was needed. The special operators were trained to be lone wolves as well, but Special Operations got one thing that Force Recon didn't get. It had the money. The Secretary of Defense wanted a Special Operations type of force. If the Marines didn't have a designated Special Operations force it missed out on the Special Operations funds.

And Special Operations got another thing that Force Recon didn't get. It had been given a name. The battalions would be called Marine Raiders. The Raiders were given the funding for Heckler & Koch German-engineered automatic weapons, suppressors, satellite radios, and combat-driven iPads. All of the high-speed units like the SEALS and Delta received the same type of funding. If the Marines wanted part of the Special Operations dollars they had to have Special Operations units. And they had one advantage over the SEALS. Like the Marine Corps, what was different was that a Marine unit had everything in support whether it was airpower, or artillery, or logistics. They didn't have to outsource anything. They were self-contained. And they could move, and move quickly.

But Gunny was a special contract at the training center. He came only when needed. He was, however, invited to use the farm whenever he liked. The ammunition and ranges were unlimited. Neave had seen him shoot.

This time he had brought a friend.

"I have all this shit to do before that Chicago SWAT team gets in tonight." Neave preferred the military visitors. The farm had the creature comforts for the city boys. The woods had several villages of prefab cabins, all two to a room, which had been brought in by a convoy of flatbed trailers. Each cabin was simple but well equipped. The walls were made of unpainted plywood sheets, each room had two bunks with sheets and blankets, pillows, a closet-sized bathroom with a prefab shower, and even a mini-refrigerator. There was no time for a television, as the days were intended to be long, from dark to dark, and the nights very short. Still, for most of the visitors, it was a luxury to have something softer than dirt, and something dryer than a space under a pine tree. The Rangers and Marines were embarrassed to use them.

"Take a minute." The trainer was persistent.

Neave hesitated. He did, however, have ultimate faith in his friend. They had spent too many tours, on too many missions, for Neave not to know when it was something important.

"We will take my truck," Neave said. He wasn't going to eat dust in the Ranger or, even worse, follow it as it kicked up a trail of red and orange smoke.

"Yeah, yeah, yeah."

They drove more than a mile across the farm to a valley on the far back end. It was meant to be remote. The entire farm was encircled with two rows of fences, the first a simple multistrand barbed-wire fence with No Trespassing signs. The second had the more serious Warning Imminent Danger sign that was meant to stop even the most casual deer hunter making the wrong turn or being too curious. Deadly Force Used.

The road went through a small forest of planted pine trees, now grown to a height that shut out virtually all of the light below. On the other side of the forest, the road descended into a shallow valley. Large mounds of dirt formed a wall with a road cut into the side of the formation. Just short of the top of the mound, a parking strip had been laid down and surfaced with gravel. The roofs of the trucks remained below the crest. Another pickup truck, white with a red-orange coating formed by the dust, was parked there. Neave pulled in behind it.

"Good, no shooting." There was no sound of gunfire. The trainer closed the door to the truck and the two crossed to a wooden stairway that topped the berm. The man-made ridge of dirt served as an insulator for wayward rounds. A platform with a long-planked wood table ran the stretch of the lookout. It had a framed tin roof that took the operators out of the sunlight. Sandbags were stacked on the range side so that it would take the oddest of ricochets to hurt an observer. On the other side and below, a mud village complete with walls and roofless huts stretched for fifty yards to both the right and left.

"Hey, boss." Another trainer looked up from a portable computer.

"He wanted me to see this." Neave was impatient.

"Yeah, this is pretty good. He is setting up right now for another run."

"How many does this make?"

"This will be the third."

"And?"

"Each one is faster."

Neave watched two figures enter the village from the left. One followed the other. He looked at his watch as he saw the lead shooter lock and load his weapon.

The two moved in a methodical snake-like path with the leader cutting around the corner. Neave could see the T-20s lined up behind the different locations.

"You change them each time."

"Yeah, none the same."

The shooter moved, stopped, and shot. The target dropped. He had an instinct.

"Damn, is this Doc Holliday?" the trainer spat. His cheek was swollen with a pinch of snuff.

Neave didn't say anything. He glanced at his watch again. Another shot was fired. Another target popped backwards.

"What type of shots?"

"All head. Center of mass." The trainer on the computer looked at the sensors.

Another pop and another target dropped.

"He put two through the walls."

The shooter worked his way across the village, moving and shooting.

"How about a reload?" Neave asked as he glanced up to the range.

"Yeah, we did that on the last round."

One round had added a few extra targets so that the shooter had to load another magazine. It was an additional test of concentration and aim.

On this round, like the first run, it took Parker only twelve rounds out of fifteen. He had finished working his way through the entire village.

"He passed two innocents." The trainer looked at the T-20 targets as the computer reset the plastic jihadist warriors. Two dummy targets had been set up as innocent women.

"He was born for this shit." The monitor spat over his shoulder as he mumbled the words.

Neave looked at his watch. A new record had just been set at the farm. *This guy was dangerous.* Neave knew what he was talking about. He was one of the few who could shoot like this. The smell of burnt rounds filled the air.

CHAPTER FOUR

A white man walked quickly along the side street of the city of Sana'a. He stopped to inhale his cigarette, at the same time leaning against the wall of the old building as he tried to regain his breath. The old men in the side street stared at the Yankee dressed in his brown laced-up shoes and khaki-colored suit. He wore an open-collared, silk, white shirt. He looked out of place and he didn't care. Everyone in the city knew when he had arrived and why he was there. He was safer in Sana'a than in Detroit.

This damn, bloody altitude.

The capital of Yemen had two unique features. The first was that the nearly two million people who lived in the maze of fortress-like buildings, all connected by an endless run of alleys, tolerated living in a city nearly a mile higher than Denver. And the city was founded before Christ. The old men said that the son of Noah came to this desert spot over twenty-five centuries ago. The men of Sana'a moved like ants on an active ant-hill stirred by some imaginary stick. Few women were to be seen.

The visitor pushed up his glasses on his nose as he

inhaled the cigarette again. He had been smoking since his twelfth birthday and on that particular date finished off a pack of Camels he had stolen from his father. The habit had lasted for three decades. He had a weasel's smile and brown hair that went over his ears, combed to a high part. He spoke his words too fast, in a frantic pace, which caused people to doubt his sincerity even further. The man tilted his head slightly as he spoke, which only caused one to notice how he squinted his eyes.

The eyes were particularly a problem as he wore glasses that had a changing tint from sunlight to dark.

But he had always delivered what he promised.

The café was just inside the gate to the old city. The ancient clay walls of the city gave a brown look to the stacked, tall blocks but the people had white-washed the frames of the window. All of the buildings were flat topped like some big, brown stack of Legos made out of clay.

He put his hand on the wall of the old Bab al-Yemen gate to steady himself. The altitude had taken its toll. The journey had not helped. He flew into Salalah in nearby Oman, rented a Land Rover, and drove across the desert border to leave a less obvious trail. He pulled his hand away from the wall, looked at the chocolate coating of dust on his palm, and pulled out a white silk cloth to rub the dirt off.

The men who walked by gave him looks and then quickly turned away.

Bertok Genret was there because he loved his Canadian Golden Maple Leafs. The gold coins each contained an ounce of pure gold and he enjoyed just holding one of the coins. His one locked room in his Swiss villa had a false front of a door that led to a vault. He didn't keep everything in this one vault. He knew that it was important to spread the load, but the one room no bigger than a closet held canvas bags of his precious leafs.

"No one reads the words on a leaf," he often said.

He meant that no one cared how he acquired his gold.

Genret walked to the café and took a seat at a table well to the back. It wasn't just the villagers walking in the tight alleyways that he was concerned about. Sana'a and even its smallest alleyways were under near constant watch from the sky above.

"*Qahwa*." He had grown fond of the dark coffee served in Sana'a. The old waiter wiped the table with a brown rag that looked like it only added to the dust and grime of the surface.

"One?"

"Yeah." He spoke the word sarcastically as he sat alone at the table.

The old man understood the sarcasm and walked away. He returned with a chipped cup, making no offer of milk or sugar.

Genret lit up another B & H Gold.

Got to get out of this hellhole. He looked down at the dwindling pack of Benson & Hedges cigarettes.

"Mr. Genret."

The man standing in front of him wore robes more in keeping with others in the café.

"*Al-salamu alaykum*." Genret did not stand. He liked being rude.

"*Wa alaykum s-salam*." The man stood over the Brit as he continued to smoke his cigarette and put the coffee cup to his lips.

"Sit down, Musa."

"Someone else wants to talk to you."

"Oh?" Genret had dealt exclusively with Musa now for nearly a decade. He noticed movement in the entranceway to the café. A small man with a round bearded face dressed in white robes and an odd-looking leather jacket walked in. Only the top of his beard just below the nose was visible. His face was mostly covered by a red-and-white checkered keffiyeh. The silk headdress was often worn in Sana'a but rarely was it wrapped so tightly across the face. It was as if the winds of a storm had kicked up the dust and the man was using it for what it had been intended. It was, however, so tightly wrapped that it looked odd. He stood out among the hundreds of others with the same keffiyeh. He had two large bodyguards, AK-47s held tightly at their sides, trailing behind.

The jacket was unusual, in contrast to the white robes common to the city, but not overly exceptional. Even though a desert town, it was at nearly eight thousand feet, keeping the temperature constant. Often, Sana'a would be cool. And at night it could be bitterly cold.

"So, you are our famous Mr. Genret." The man pulled the wrapping from his face as he spoke to reveal the angle where his beard followed the outline of his jaw. His combed-over hair, along with the beard, gave the impression of a large brown ball with hair glued to both the bottom and the top. Unlike Genret, he had a muscular frame. It was not clear to Genret whether the man spent his life in tents or on the top floor of the Ritz. Although in Sana'a he was certainly not staying at the Ritz.

"And you are?" Genret leaned back in his chair with his arm to his side, flicking the cigarette ash on the floor.

"Sheikh Muhammad Al Faud."

Genret dropped the cigarette to the floor and sat up in the chair.

"Faud Mohammed Khalaf?" Genret used his other name. His body tightened up like a rattler. He looked around, keeping an eye on the café's arched opening. This man was known to be very dangerous. He could kill and, more important for Genret, Faud was a target to be killed. A Predator would not hesitate to drop one on the café, even in the center of the capital of Yemen, for this target. Genret would be a casual side player in a CNN news story the next day. It would take a week or more for his fate to make it back to his wife in Switzerland. The story would simply read that the financial mind of Al Shabaab had been killed by a Predator strike in Yemen.

"Don't worry, Mr. Genret." The man sat down opposite Genret and waved his hand at the waiter. "*Qahwa!*" he yelled over the high-pitched music that played from a box behind the bar.

The waiter brought another cup of coffee; however, this time he acted carefully, cautiously, wiping the table with a bright white cloth. It was clear to Genret that the waiter also knew who his customer was. Again, Genret was scared.

If the waiter knows, who else is aware of this meeting?

The answer was that the meeting needed to be short. The only safety for both was to remain constantly moving.

"So you know me."

"Head of finance for Al Shabaab." Genret knew of Faud. He was an Arab with a price tag on his head that might have exceeded the Leafs in Genret's secret room.

"Yes." The man smiled as if he had been introduced as the founder of Facebook.

Genret offered the pack of cigarettes to his seatmate at the table.

"The habit is deplorable," said Faud. "It is a Yankee

addiction that is far more harmful to you than the bullets of those AKs." Faud pointed to one of his guards sitting at the table behind and looking out, constantly, towards the alleyway. "If America wants to kill, they have done it best by tobacco."

"You want arms?" Genret asked the obvious; however, Faud didn't need to leave Somalia to place an order for several crates of AK-47s. "I assume that is why you have come?" Genret had never dealt with anyone from Al Shabaab at this level. He was somewhat stymied by his visitor.

"We want something very special." Faud paused.

He drew with his finger a shape on the table. There were no markings. Only the movement of his hand. Genret noted that his hand was brown and tough like a piece of leather exposed constantly to the sun. The fingers were short and stubby and fat. He was a Saudi by birth.

More difficulty, more profit. Genret pondered the idea. A truckload of Russian rocket-propelled grenades was less profitable but just as marketable. The penalty for something more deadly was rarely worth much more than what Interpol would have given him just for the RPGs. Ten years in prison was ten years whether it be for cases of RPGs or a missile. And that required his staying in the same jurisdiction long enough for Interpol to catch up to him. And then there were always the jailers. Money, especially gold ounces, helped many cross through borders.

"Semtex-H? Is that what you want? I can get a shipload on sale." Genret felt slightly repelled. The plastic explosive would take down the roofs of malls in Ethiopia and Nigeria, crushing the children underneath.

"You have children?" Faud asked the question.

"Yes, I have two."

"In your Geneva?"

"Yes."

Genret knew that Faud and the world kept track of where the arms dealer's ties were. But it didn't sound like a threat. It would have been a loss to Al Shabaab for Genret to leave his trade.

"I have two wives. One in Somalia and one here in Yemen." Faud looked away for a moment. "One wife is from Saudi Arabia, like me, but we can never go home."

"Yes."

"No, you don't understand. You never will." The Saudi turned deadly serious.

Faud leaned over the table and looked directly into Genret's eyes. Genret felt the stare through his tinted lenses.

"It is Allah's will. Those words mean little to you nonbelievers. You see no more than your present world. You never will."

There was silence.

It was true. Genret made money as a necessity. His children would fly with their mother to New York at Christmas, but he never considered that the same flight might be carrying a laptop loaded with Semtex. The sin was that his wife and children knew him as an exporter. The wife never asked for the truth and he never provided it.

"Mr. Genret, we want a Dong Feng 21."

Genret rolled back in his chair, catching the news like a baseball bat to his chest.

"I am not sure." He hesitated with his choice of words. He wasn't trying to be dramatic. He had nothing else to say. A nuclear core was probably easier to obtain. The Dong Feng 21 was the only weapon in the world that would have caused Genret to roll back as he did.

"We have a weapon identified."

Genret thought that every intelligence agency in the free world would pay, dearly, to hear what was said next.

"You know what they call it?"

"Yes." Faud paused. "And it is well suited to our little land with such a long coastline. Don't you think? We have too many American ships off our coast."

A mobile, well hidden, protected DF-21D would tip the balance of the scales in the Gulf of Aden. Shipping had to use the tight waterway as they exited the Suez Canal, but it also meant that military ships were likewise squeezed into the same narrow corridor.

"Is it China?" Genret had had little dealings with the sale of weapons from China. It was known, however, as the creator of this new weapon, or at least what was considered to be the newest and most capable variance. The DF-21D's software was known to be able to track and kill the fastest of America's military ships. It was a "carrier killer." The rocket would climb and then sink to surface level as it tracked its target. A ship of nearly five thousand men and a deck of aircraft could be at risk.

"China is not the only one. Although they have been most generous in offering our brothers the skills needed." Faud had said much in one statement.

Iran has created a knockoff! Genret pondered the thought as he nervously lit another cigarette. *God, MI-6 would drop me in the Gulf Stream with my brains like mashed potatoes.* He would be drugged and gagged until they could get him to some stone shack in the highlands. He wanted to shut his ears. The knowledge burned through his chest. A leak would cause the free world's intelligence networks to grab him for any chance of this information. Israel would pay a bounty for even a hint of this information.

And if he told anyone, Al Shabaab would follow him to the driveway that led up to his Swiss hideaway and kill him. With one sentence, Genret had been pulled in whether he liked it or not.

"We need your skill in transportation. What price to get this across the Gulfs of both Oman and Aden? What price to get it to Somalia without being detected?"

"Will the Iranian Navy help cross one?" Genret asked.

"Yes."

"And what will Oman do if a truck passes across its lands?"

"They will look away."

"Do I have to pay for that?" The cost of bribes carried an extra expense that had to be planned for.

"No."

Genret didn't believe what he was hearing but took another sip of the coffee.

"10,000 Leafs at one ounce per," said Genret.

The job had the makings of being that final push that he and his competitors always were looking for. Genret knew that if he passed on the job he would never leave Sana'a. But the thought of death didn't enter his mind as much as the fact that the other arms dealers would be sick to know that he was the chosen one.

I can insulate myself. With enough money, I can layer the job.

Genret thought of the many go-betweens who never had to know what was in the back of the trucks. It would take several trucks to split apart the device to lower the suspicion, but it was doable. The parts would be separated and shipped in "layers" of cover trucks.

"Your price is reasonable."

Genret was shocked at the response. He should have asked for more.

"Plus expenses. We have to pay many," he said.

"We will raise the money," said Faud. "You may begin the plans."

"It will be a target." Every agency in the world would jump and act on it.

"Yes, but it will have a brother and sister soon thereafter. And with the Gulf of Aden and the Indian Ocean unsafe they will have to disperse their fleet. With their ships spread out our pirates will be able to roam."

"It is a game changer."

Faud pulled the keffiyeh around his head before he stepped out into the sunlight. He glanced quickly up to the sky and moved in the shadows of the clay buildings to a Toyota truck waiting on the other side of the city gate.

My new friend will be more help than he realizes.

Faud felt the cell phone in his pocket. It was one of many that would be used for only one call and then crushed and tossed. The chief financier of Al Shaabab had worked at his trade well before Somalia became a known word. He was linked to the entire network.

When will our American arrive?

Omar was more than just a new jihadist. He had become a source of Internet popularity, and with his popularity came much-needed money.

CHAPTER FIVE

"Let's stop for dinner." William Parker leaned back in Moncrief's truck as they headed north from the Farm.

"The usual?"

"Yeah, my treat." Parker pulled the sunglasses down around his neck as darkness started to set in. The glasses had a strap that held them on and as he pulled them down he smelled the familiar scent of what others called "gunpowder." It was really a more complicated chemical formulation that included nitro and graphite.

Most of the Special Operations guys wore some type of gloves, which also carried a unique smell. Parker, however, refused to wear them. It was important that he was able to feel the weapon. He needed the sense of the trigger pull. Each weapon, whether a rifle or pistol, had a distinct squeeze that caused the round to go high or low or on center. The farther the distance, the more the pull would send the round high or low and right or left.

It was also the consistency. A well-aimed round went on target when the shooter was consistent. Arnold Palmer was the best example in the game of golf. His style of swing was unique, but since he was consistent, the ball was always on target.

They drove for several miles to the north, turning on the cutoff to the small rural town of Cuthbert, Georgia. The truck passed open fields planted with green rows of peanuts and forests made up of perfectly lined pine trees. The pines grew in rows similar to the Marines in formation on the parade deck at Parris Island.

"Everyone is getting a lot of time." Parker spoke as he looked out the window. He was referring to the constant rotation of Marines. For every combat tour of duty, the time back in the states was getting less and less. Only the lucky ones got a year between the times spent in a combat zone.

"Did you hear the news of E's brother?" Moncrief was referring to another member of their past team, Enrico Hernandez. He had a younger brother who was a staff sergeant on active duty with the Marines.

"No."

"Just was RIF'd."

"What?"

A "reduction in force" was shaking all of the military to its roots.

"A third of all the E-6s were sent to the house." Moncrief used his somber voice saved for the few military funerals he had attended. A drop in staff sergeants was significant but that was not the only rank that was targeted.

"Didn't you have him when you were on the parade deck?"

"Yeah, little bastard, I saved his ass." Moncrief had done a tour years ago as a drill instructor at Parris Island. An Apache warrior descendant as a drill instructor was not a good day.

"The fool told me his birthday." Moncrief laughed as he spoke. "And we celebrated."

"I don't think I want to know."

"I covered his butt. I already had served with E."

"I'm not sure how kind you were." Parker didn't smile despite how Moncrief was trying to provoke him.

"He did three combat tours." Despite combat experience, the young staff sergeant was being put on the street.

"Gunny, not your fault." Parker knew it needed to be said out loud.

"So, same time next month?"

"Maybe."

"The MarSOC guys are coming down to the farm next month."

"Yeah."

"They'll run down on Ospreys. You need to come see the new toys." Moncrief looked ahead as they drove into the center of town.

An old brick courthouse was just off the town square. It had a chain-link fence that encircled the building. For years now, the old courthouse had been on the verge of falling to a homeless man's match or a random lightning strike.

"There's the Subway."

The yellow sign marked a quick stop for food.

Moncrief's truck radio was set on a low volume. They pulled up to the front and he shifted into park. He reached for the key to turn off the engine.

"Wait a minute." Parker stuck out his hand. He turned the radio volume up.

". . . . blast killing four in Mobile." The voice was a news bulletin.

"What the hell?" Moncrief leaned over the steering wheel as they both listened to the news.

"The FBI has confirmed this was an act of terrorism. The bomber was killed in the blast. He is suspected to be linked to an alleged terrorist cell in Mobile, Alabama." The two men stared at the radio as the broadcast continued.

"Wasn't your wife from Mobile?"

"Yeah." Parker continued to look forward into the dark.

"Hey, Gunny, how about we skip eating?"

"Sure."

Moncrief shifted the truck into reverse, swung his vehicle around, and headed north.

William Parker's farmhouse was dark. It had been for some time. The truck pulled up to the front door. In the vehicle lights one could see the weeds that reached up to a man's waist. It appeared abandoned.

"You want something to eat?" Parker swung open the truck's door and grabbed the plastic case that held his pistol and his rifle bag from the rear. He also took his water bottle from the console. It wasn't as if there was much in the farmhouse. At best, the kitchen held a Coke and a can of Vienna sausages.

"No, boss, I think I'll head north. Should get to the house around midnight."

"Got it." Parker had been quiet for most of the time since they left Subway.

"An American terrorist." Moncrief spoke straight ahead to the windshield of his truck.

"Mobile." Parker shifted the two weapon containers to his left hand. He reached across the truck's cab and shook his friend's hand.

"Thanks, Gunny."

"I'll just show up at the same time in four weeks." Moncrief didn't say more. His friend had become a loner. Parker's telephone landline had been pulled for some time now. He'd tossed the cell phone and with it the last form of communication. The house did not hold a computer. His house and farm had been sold to a small corporation with an attorney in Atlanta as the agent and registered officer. Cash from the attorney to the county seat paid the taxes regularly. The people in the courthouse knew who the owner was but no one talked about it. It had become a part of rumor. Parker had gone off the grid. They all left him alone.

"Yeah, I got it."

But Parker wasn't thinking of four weeks from now. He was thinking of what had just happened in a city farther south.

William Parker watched Moncrief's taillights as they crossed over the ridgeline heading back to the county highway. He stood there for a minute in complete darkness on the front porch. The disappearance of the truck left a silence and then, as if it were a machine spinning up, he heard the woods become alive again. He opened the heavy wooden door and turned on the lamp on the table. The door was never locked. It didn't need to be. The room had that smoky smell from the stone fireplace. It was brutally quiet. The absence of someone lay over the farmhouse like a soaked towel covering a face.

He hesitated for a moment before putting his pistol case and rifle bag against the wall. Parker took a swig of the water from the bottle and then went back outside. He walked around the lodge to a large shape barely visible in the darkness. A motion detector caused a light to come on revealing a blue tarp. He pulled the cover off to reveal a black truck. It had not been used often but was built for the country. It was a GMC Sierra off-road that had been brand new only a year before.

Parker reached under the edge of the Ranch Hand bumper and pulled out a key. He climbed into the front seat and turned on the engine. It was his only link to the outside world. He pushed the scan on the radio, turned up the volume, and listened to it travel through the stations until it hit on a news channel.

". . . an act of terrorism has again struck on American soil."

Parker wanted the facts.

CHAPTER SIX

Omar heard the news as he headed across Canada and neared Toronto. *I am a Banu Najjar.* Omar considered the thought. He learned of the importance of his tribe from his uncle. It was his uncle who taught him the importance of the faith. It was his uncle who taught him that death meant little if one died for Allah.

The elder was to be followed without question and only the bearded ones were to be respected. His branch of the tribe came from Syria and before that from Yemen. It was said that Muhammad spoke of his tribe. As soon as he returned from his first trip to Syria as a young man Omar began trying to grow his beard.

His beard left a patch of bare skin on his cheekbones so it was neither uniform nor attractive. The beard was important. It carried with it the sign of manhood and leadership.

A clean face. Omar thought of how repugnant that was as he looked back on his high school days in Daphne. It would make the journey much safer if he shaved before he passed through the Western airports; however, it would create the opposite effect when he reached his destination.

*   *   *

He tuned the radio while his wife drove the Nissan.

Toronto. He stroked his beard as he thought of the past.

"Will we see my family?" Fartuun spoke over the sound of the radio.

He put up his hand to silence her. Omar had changed his clothes and put on a Toronto Blue Jays hat. He wore sunglasses. She was uncovered, which was what the infidels did; however, it was important that they blended in as they neared the city. On other trips the customs would be followed; however, this was an escape—not a regular trip.

It was the beard that worried him the most. But he had a plan.

"At that next gas station stop and I will change." He had bought a dark, pinstriped, vested suit with a white button-down collar shirt. The tie was important. It was crimson and blue. The dress would break him out of the "profile."

"You can stay for an extra day or two but first you must take me to Pearson," he said. "They will be knocking at your door if you stay too long. You must follow me to Egypt as soon as you can." Pearson International Airport in Toronto had a flight to Europe nearly every other hour.

Omar was correct about the time. It would be an easy trail to follow. Everyone knew that Eddie was a friend of his. As soon as Eddie was identified as the bomber, Omar would be next on their suspect list.

They will be knocking on my parents' door tomorrow.

He could see his father's rage when the news hit. The first wave would be the coworkers turning up their radios when they heard of a bombing in Mobile. Then they would learn that the suspects were two young Muslims. The knock would only confirm what his father suspected.

The mosque in Mobile was the first place where he had heard of the Islamic conference in Canada. Eddie had gone before him. But Omar had followed quickly after that.

Then Omar had traveled to his father's homeland of Syria for the first time when he was in ninth grade.

"You have not been to Syria." He spoke to his wife as if he didn't really know her.

"No."

"I have many cousins there. I joined my uncle for prayers. Five times a day!"

She nodded her head. The wife only listened.

"Syria changed me. I went back to Mobile and it was a different world." Omar watched a Yukon truck pass. A young blond woman was behind the wheel. In the instant he saw her he was reminded of why he took this different path.

"I hated Mobile after that. The drugs, television, the stupid people. They had no direction."

High school became miserable. And he fought it and everything school and his broken family stood for.

"I wore Islamic dress to school." He laughed. She smiled.

"They all laughed at me." His tone changed again as he remembered how quickly his world had changed. "My teacher changed. Mrs. Hughes taught me to be liberal in thought, but when I confronted her with the teachings of Muhammad she became angry."

Another person in his world who had pushed him further away. His faith became his anchor.

But Mrs. Hughes wasn't the only problem.

Omar looked out on the buildings of Toronto in the distance.

He had lived there, on and off, for years. He reached behind his seat for the suit jacket and pulled the Air Canada ticket out of the front pocket.

They had driven through the night stopping only for gas. "The flight leaves in just a few hours."

The flight was direct to Barcelona leaving at 1:00 P.M. It would stop in Montreal and then Zurich. It was intended to go on to Barcelona, but he would leave the airport in Switzerland and take a train across the border to Milan. From Milan, Omar had another plane ticket, which would take him on to Cairo. It was only in Cairo where he could wander into the crowd and feel safe.

"They probably are tracing Eddie's trail to me by now."

Eddie and Omar used a patch of grass near the high school parking lot for their prayers. The one thing his father had done was go to the principal and insist that his Muslim son be allowed to do his daily prayers. It was the only thing his father had done on behalf of his son's Islamic beliefs.

"If I hadn't gone to Toronto I would be in medical school by now." He was talking out loud to himself. "It was what my father wanted me to be. It was his dream. An American Muslim and a doctor but not a Muslim of the true faith. He wanted a Muslim for show."

Omar looked on his past like turning the pages on a family album.

"He will hear of the bomb and soon realize it was Eddie." Omar was correct. A photograph taken from the church's parking lot security camera had already been downloaded, enlarged, and cross-checked. It would not be a hard crime for the FBI to figure out.

Faud had promised at least forty-eight hours before Al Shabaab would announce to the world that their soldier was responsible. A terrorist plot deep in the American South, masterminded by an American jihadist, would spin around the world's news networks a million times. And with it, donations would flow in just like the Americans' sudden loyalty to a football team that had just won the Super Bowl. Omar was proud of his role in this plan.

"Do you remember my first winter here?"

"Did I know you?" his wife asked a fair question.

"My father was livid. I quit college in Mobile and called him from here." Omar chuckled at the memory. "I don't think I had ever had a cup of coffee until my first winter delivering milk to Somalis."

"Yes, that is where I heard of you." His wife smiled.

"Milk and eggs." He thought of the crates he tried to move on the dolly over the snow and ice. "And milkshakes. Always milkshakes. They would say '*Ya Waaye!*'"

"Who's there?"

"Yes, who's there!"

"There is the gas station." She pointed to an exit in a dismal part of Toronto. It was a safe place to stop and change.

"I covered all of the Westside that winter."

The Westside of Toronto would hear of the Muslim boy from the South that caused an attack to be carried to the American heartland.

"The Somalis will be proud of me when they hear that I have joined the fight!"

CHAPTER SEVEN

Paul Stewart studied the most recent email he had printed out as he spoke to the computer. The email had distracted him despite the importance of the conversation he was having with the woman on Skype.

"Are you ignoring me?" A woman in her mid-twenties, with a natural, simple beauty was on the screen. She had black eyebrows that set off a near perfect face. Her hair was pulled back tightly just like her mother would often wear it.

"No, of course not." He was, in fact, ignoring her. The email was from his boss, the director of the CDC. It spoke of the smallpox vials that had recently been discovered in a back storage room after being lost in the complex. The CDC was in the center of a firestorm.

The complex campus of buildings held the most dangerous organisms in the world. It was close to Emory and in one of the most affluent neighborhoods in all of Atlanta. Many who lived nearby had always worried, but until now there wasn't a well-known reason for the worry.

"Yes, you are." She would catch him on occasion and pull him back to earth.

Paul knew this weakness about himself. More than once in the lab, he looked up at the clock and made a mental note that he needed to start closing down the test for the day. In what felt like a few seconds, he glanced up at the clock again and saw that it was one in the morning.

"They are going to name a senior scientist to head up a complete revamping of our security system." It would become the most important and unlimited job in the most well-known laboratory in the world. The chosen one would have access to every experiment, know all that was going on, and eventually be irreplaceable. He had been pushing for such a job for nearly a decade. Scientists were the worst for being told what they had to do. Protocol and systemic approaches to problems were the heart of science until a system was being imposed upon a team of MDs and PhDs.

"You have that job."

"I don't think so."

"Oh yes. If you want it."

He wasn't sure if his daughter wanted him to get the job or was warning him to stay away from it.

"So, where are you now?" He tossed the email across his already overcrowded desk.

"Still in an airport waiting for an airplane."

"I am not sure of this." He squinted over his glasses as he spoke.

"Again?" She gave him a stare just like his wife would. She had her mother's same blue eyes. They weren't clearly visible on the remote computer hookup, but he knew them well. And he knew the blouse she was wearing. It was the same one she had on at Hartsfield several days ago when she left. It was a wildly colored blue and gold blouse, much larger than her petite size called for, made of cotton and bunched up in wrinkles after several nights crossing the Atlantic and sitting in airports waiting for airplanes to arrive. The farther that one went in to Africa, the less reliable the mode of transportation.

"You did this twenty years ago!"

"Yes." He had heard this argument repeatedly since the idea first came up.

"Fieldwork helped you understand how these diseases spread."

He couldn't fight the logic of her argument.

"I get it." He understood, but that didn't make it more agreeable. This was his daughter—not just some bright young medical graduate from Harvard.

"I didn't go to Boston so I would spend the next twenty years in a lab killing mice," she said

"That's unfair!" He smiled. "I like my mice."

"Ethiopia will teach me more than anywhere else." She had to be given credit for her stubborn Scottish background. The Stewart family did have a history of digging their feet into the ground. She had been raised by demanding parents who often sent her off during the summers to camps such as Camp Skyline in the Georgia Mountains. Both parents were professionals. Her mother had been a pediatrician until breast cancer killed her. Paul was the scientist. Somewhere in her past he became "Paul" to her and not "Dad." The summers at Skyline created self-reliance. When the others would go home from a session, Karen stayed for another round. It was better than an empty house near Emory. She didn't mind.

"MSF's work is invaluable." It was obvious she knew this conversation was coming and had rehearsed her argument for months. Doctors Without Borders, or Médecins Sans Frontières, provided what little help could be offered in the most remote places on the planet but also shared scientific knowledge with both the World Health Organization and the CDC. It gave the CDC some chance of staying ahead of the risk of death that now traveled regularly in airplanes and through airports.

"You have said too many times that international flights are capable of pumping everything into our world."

"Do I need this lecture?" he said.

"Plus, you would never have made it at the CDC without your tour in Africa."

"What else?" He loved his daughter but was losing patience. "I need to go play with some nasty little friends."

She laughed.

"Well." He didn't like to say it but he did. "Get your damn experience and get out of there."

"Gee, thanks, Dad. I love the vote of confidence!"

Unfortunately, it wasn't the risk of infection that Paul Stewart needed to worry about.

CHAPTER EIGHT

William Parker left the tarp off the truck that night. The next morning he drove north to Atlanta. The vehicle bore a tag from Stewart County that was registered, like everything else, to a small, closely held company that defined its purpose with the Secretary of Corporations as doing fieldwork.

He pulled into the parking lot of the SunTrust Bank on the south side of the city, near the airport, and headed into the bank lobby. It was purposeful that he used a bank some two hours north of his farm. Few visits were required and it was closer to his Atlanta attorney. While serving as a district attorney years ago, Parker had given his friend his first job. As Parker made fewer visits and only when in need, it made sense that the chosen bank would be one closer to his friend. It was one of several banks across Atlanta where he had the same type of account.

"I need to get into a box."

The bank secretary recognized him. It was easy, as his bearded, long-haired, and lanky self stood out from the bank's run of customers, particularly in the South. The teller did not know another customer who had the combination of a beard, long hair, and a safety deposit box. She only knew that his name was "Mr. Berks" and he was allowed to sign into the safety deposit box vault with a weak-looking driver's license. It would have barely passed examination at a local bar. But she had been told to not ask questions.

"Yes, sir."

They headed downstairs to the vault room.

He walked behind her, intentionally so, as he pulled a chain necklace from around his neck and unsnapped the safety deposit box key without being obvious.

"Box 1969?"

"Yes." He didn't particularly like the idea that she remembered the number.

I need to change banks. It wasn't so much that she made him mad; it was just important that everything remain in flux.

Parker signed the pass slip with the same "Phillip Berks" he had used before. He signed it awkwardly with his left hand. It would slow down anyone making an effort to compare signatures with another record.

"Do you need a room?"

"Yes, please." He lifted the box out of the drawer. It was minor but important that she had no sense of its weight. He carried it into the small room, closed the door and opened the box. It was crammed with stacks of used fifty-dollar bills. The box contained more than a quarter of a million dollars, and his friend the attorney had another key. It was resupplied as often and as necessary as he directed Moncrief to contact the attorney.

Parker put two thousand dollars into his shirt and then rebuttoned it. He preferred twenties as the fifties were more noticeable but were likewise less obvious than hundreds. It was important that they were all well used. This was his traveling money.

The truck headed south out of Atlanta on Interstate 85. It took the remainder of the day for Parker to make it to Mobile.

Moncrief had been correct. Parker's wife had been from Mobile. It was a clear sky and cloudless sunset as he crossed over the river on Interstate 65. The smoke-stacks of the paper mill upriver let out a white, whispery plume that traveled straight up into the air for several hundred feet and then, as the wind caught it, started to spread in an easterly direction.

He drove the next several miles as the highway started to come into the outskirts of Mobile. He knew where he was going. His destination was on this side of the city.

Parker pulled off the exit, cut back to the east under the interstate bridge, and started to slow down.

The streets were now empty and the sun was quickly setting. The parking lot lights were starting to come on. He could see the burned-out shell of the school entrance wrapped in the yellow tape used by the investigators.

There was no specific reason William Parker needed to be in Mobile. He, too, like his wife, had spent much time in the city. He had an aunt who never had a child and Parker would spend his summers with her in Mobile. They would go, religiously, on Thursdays to Wintzell's Oyster House, where he would sit, as a teenager, and read the signs on the walls, one after the other. The restaurant's owner had made his mark by covering the walls with little, pithy signs that gave homespun humor to a subject. It was a seafood version of Cracker Barrel with a unique charm.

I think I will hit Wintzell's a little later.

The parking lot was covered with piles of trash. All of the investigators had gone and all of the media had disappeared. A short squall must have passed through earlier in the day as the ground had puddles, the trash looked like damp humps of paper and discarded food containers, and—with the humidity—steam was rising from the black asphalt.

"I just needed to see this," he said aloud.

His truck stood parked on the busy two lanes, up next to the curb. He rolled down the window. The sight made him angry. All bombings were bad, the death of children was shameful, but this struck a chord.

He was only there for a moment.

WOOOP.

A siren went off just behind his truck. At the same moment, a blue circulating light pierced the darkness.

CHAPTER NINE

Bertok Genret sat at the airport in Salalah looking at one of his cell phones. Oman was a quiet port in the storm of the Middle East. The land was home to frankincense. It was a collected sap that drained out of trees that were hundreds of years old. It was used well before Christ walked the earth.

Salalah was a port city to the far western end of Oman. The Romans had passed through the city several thousand years ago.

I'll get my wife a bag of frankincense. It would be an unusual gift of his travels.

No, he thought.

This was a mistake he had made before, not often, but before. This week he had told his wife that he was in New York at a trade convention. He made a point of always going through his bags at the airport in Switzerland upon arrival making sure that no items remained that might reveal his lie.

The frankincense trees had endured much. They could be found inland where the desert took over. A day that exceeded a hundred and thirty degrees was not unusual for the high desert of Oman. The shoreline, however, was very valuable property in a quiet world. Countless numbers of beaches existed, sometimes with not a person in sight, or with just a single clay-and-mud home overlooking the ocean.

The ruler of Oman had the love of his people and, despite a lack of great oil deposits, he had managed its finances well. Oman and its leader balanced themselves on the precarious fence of the Middle East. He was one of the few who could talk to both Iran—his neighbor across the Gulf—and America, without losing either. Iran knew he was a valuable outlet that allowed conversations to occur when the United States or Britain could not. Likewise, the American fleet had often used the waters off Oman as a safe haven.

Genret knew that if he kept moving and bothered no one, Oman would let him pass.

I wonder if the Romans had a gun dealer? The thought passed through his mind as he stared out the window at the green grass and palm trees that formed the shape of the drive into the airport. Away from its shorelines, Oman was brown and brutally dry, a bleak pile of sand and rocks. But where money and the ruler allowed, vast green landscaping had been installed. Water meant vegetation, and green was an oasis. The airport was a simple building only serviced by one airline but it was surrounded by a green, well-trimmed garden.

I need to make a mental note.

He would solidify the deal with Abo Musa Mombasa. Musa, a Pakistani by birth, had the title of head of Al Shabaab's security. Faud was the general. It was up to Musa to handle the details.

Al Shabaab, or "the Youth," as translated, was strategically significant more for their location than anything else. The Horn of Africa required ships coming from the Suez Canal to pass close to shore. Many of the ships made the mistake of following the route south past the coast of Somalia. Al Shabaab's reach extended out into the shipping lanes.

It was the militant arm of the Islamic Courts Union. It was not known to be rich, and the five thousand troops fought just about all of their neighbors. They were committed to waging war against the enemies of Islam. They fought the Ethiopians and Kenya. They fought other clans within Somalia. It was a hodge-podge of jihadists who had traveled from around the world to come, fight, and die for Allah and to be accepted as martyrs.

But other jihadists had suddenly appeared in Syria and Iraq. They were the new flavor of the month. ISIS had the new money, robbing the banks of Iraq as it traveled across the country. It was pulling both money and attention away from Al Shabaab.

Opportunity may be knocking. Genret pulled out the silk handkerchief and rubbed his hands in it. *We all look at the endgame.*

Genret knew that there was a life expectancy in his line of work. If he exceeded the imaginary lifeline, his death would be due to a bullet either from a police officer or a customer. The objective was to get in and get out before that happened.

Ten thousand Leafs would be the final ride. It would allow him to get out and perhaps open a small hotel outside Geneva. There were some who made it. His mentor lived in Austria in a villa and traveled to Paris nearly every month.

The good life.

It would be easy to get the container to Oman and from Oman to Yemen. That would just be a matter of bribes and cash. He knew a man in customs who often looked the other way. The problem would be getting the container broken down into parts and crossing the Gulf of Aden in a small fishing boat.

But the reward.

He never considered the consequences. A weapon that threatened the power of an aircraft carrier could change the strategic game. The fleet would have to be more dispersed, stay farther away, and thus be slower to react when needed. Piracy could double as the result of just a sighting of such a weapon.

And the weapon was made to move. Al Shabaab would build look-alikes, constantly changing their locations and hiding the real one.

It was perfect for an army that was close to the sea and at the mouth of the natural waterway that forced ships to concentrate in one area. The Suez Canal pulled in the merchant ships and the ships pulled in the American Navy.

I need the gold.

A substantial down payment had to be made and Al Shabaab was not known to have the deepest coffers. But such a weapon would distract the American Navy and cause it to pull back from the Persian Gulf. Iran had to be a player in this scheme. Tehran was famous for building reversed-engineered weapons with the help of North Korea and China.

A weapon such as this would pull the world's attention away from Iran.

"Iran will provide the weapon and Al Shabaab the money," he mumbled to himself as he looked at his cell.

He paused as he considered the thought.

I should have asked for more gold.

But how would Al Shabaab get the money?

CHAPTER TEN

"Will it work?"

"Yes, I think so."

The two technicians at the FBI lab were taking the small remaining chip from the cell phone found at the church bomb site and pulling the data from it. They had the records as well. The bomber was recognized within a day and his Verizon account had been pulled. It was clear whom he was talking with up until the moment of the explosion.

"How far away do you think he has gotten?"

"If I would have to guess, I would say maybe Detroit or Minneapolis. The Mexican border would be too much of a risk. His beard would stand out. Unless he cut it."

Minneapolis was an area to watch. It had become a fertile recruiting ground for American jihadists.

"Not likely that he will stay in the U.S." The chief agent looked at the telephone records as he spoke. "We've had him on our list for some time."

Omar had been tracked ever since he'd shown up at the mosque near the University of South Alabama and had become more vocal about the needs of his faith.

The FBI had followed him on several trips to Syria and watched as his comments went from following his father's faith to demanding more from America. His dissatisfaction had become more vocal. Somewhere along the way in his Internet comments he'd become more bent on violence as a cure for his hate of the American culture.

"A bad scenario." The agent kept looking at the sheet. "He is an American, thinks like one, and is smart."

"Correct."

"Very dangerous." The older agent looked up. "Perhaps another attack in the U.S.?"

"Not impossible."

"Didn't he spend some winters in Toronto with the Somalis?"

"Yes, sir. I think he married one."

"Let's let immigration know that the Canadian border is likely."

"Airlines?"

"No, not to Canada. He isn't stupid."

Smith thought a moment.

"The last message? Where was it placed to?"

"New Hampshire."

"Hell, he's gone."

It had been nearly two days since the blast.

"My guess is Africa."

Omar loosened up his tie as he left the airport in Cairo. It was important to buy proper Islamic clothes.

America makes me sick. I can now leave it behind forever.

Omar had progressively become more and more upset over the conflict of customs. With a Southern Catholic for a mother and a Muslim for a father, he was torn by faiths until he'd grown secure in his belief in Islam. *Islam is my anchor.* Omar thought of how the mosque had helped him grow in his faith, but to only a certain point.

"I could be here going to Madinah." It was the university that he had aspired to attend. But an American was too suspect. He would not be admitted no matter what pleas he made.

At the airport in Cairo, Omar stopped for prayers, removing his shoes and washing before turning towards the East and Mecca. The Western clothes still caused him to receive odd glances. However, his vest and tie allowed him to only trim his beard before he passed through customs in Canada. Nevertheless, he was "randomly" picked at every gateway for an additional security check. They would ask him in Arabic where he was from. And Omar would act stupid, pretending not to understand what was being said.

"Excuse me, I don't understand," he would say in English.

"Where are you from?" they asked in English on the second try.

"Toronto," he replied. During the winter he'd acquired a passport that he had saved for this specific trip.

"Where are you going?"

"Meet my wife in Cairo. She's returned home to have our baby." He was telling the truth. She was pregnant and they both agreed to return to North Africa for the birth of the child. His wife was to follow in two days. If she missed the window of opportunity, she would be placed in a jail for months, if not years. He warned her of the risks, but she refused to be so quick in leaving her family. She was young and stupid. She only knew the requirements of her faith and that was to obey her husband.

"You must go!" he had told her. He repeated it to her father; however, he was a stupid man as well.

But I followed the faith. Omar had remained a virgin until he took his wife. He never shared a bed with another—especially not a Westerner.

I could have, he thought as he left the prayer room and put his shoes back on. *I was popular.*

There was a girl in eighth grade who thought he was cute. He was elected the class president in junior high school. And always got straight "A's" until his trip to Syria. It was as if a light had been turned on. Upon his return, he spoke out, and as he spoke out more, he was thought of as being odd.

They are all so stupid.

Omar took the bus to the market, where he bought sandals and a change of clothes. He threw the Western dress into a trash pile near a bus stop. An old man looked at him and then went over to the pile and pulled everything out. Omar moved quickly, knowing that the old man would make a comment to another.

Cairo was safe to a point. Here he could find a neighborhood of friends, fellow Westerners, and possibly others from Somalia.

There have to be more who want to go to jihad and make Hijrah, he said to himself as he looked for a telephone store with booths for calling. Once he found one, Omar gave the clerk some money and took the back phone booth near the wall. He knew the number to call. "Hello," Omar said. He recognized Musa's voice on the other end.

"Yes."

"I am beyond." It meant that he was out of both the United States and Canada.

"Allah be praised."

"Please tell all!"

"Call the other number when you get to the next spot."

"Yes, I will." Omar felt strangely comfortable in the Islamic clothes he was now wearing. It was as if he had returned to his true family.

Omar knew that Musa was walking towards Faud as they finished speaking. It would be on the Internet later that day that two American soldiers of Al Shabaab had planned the bombing in Mobile. One had become a martyr.

Much of the Middle Eastern world would be asking where Mobile was. It didn't matter as much as the reply.

"It is the United States!"

"*Allahu akbar!*" Came back the cry.

Omar was far from safe. His journey had several more dangerous legs but he was much closer to his new army of believers.

Omar knew that Faud would be pleased. The American, or *al-Amriiki*, as Omar was known, would be posted on the Internet bragging of his deeds and beliefs. It would raise money. And Faud was good at raising money for Al Shabaab. The word was that he had raised some monies recently from several dedicated followers in Saudi Arabia. The money was for a special project that would tilt the balance of power in the region. And it would scare Israel to death.

Omar would be the next step in achieving that goal.

CHAPTER ELEVEN

"Got an ID?"

The police officer held the flashlight directly in William Parker's eyes. He had a big barrel neck and bulky shoulders that stretched the uniform as tight as a drum.

Parker held his hand up over his eyes. He could see more of the officer. The man was bigger than the frame of the window of Parker's truck. He looked like a bear standing on its paws.

"Yes." William Parker reached for his wallet.

"Easy there."

"Sure." Parker held up his left hand so that the officer could see all of his slow movements. He pulled out a wallet that held nothing more than his license. The money was kept underneath the console.

The officer held up the license with one hand while shining the light on both Parker and the faded picture. It was a poor reproduction.

"Mr. Berks?"

"Yes, Officer."

"Not a good place to be, especially at night."

"I understand."

"We have had a bad time here recently."

"Yeah."

"Get out of the truck."

William looked surprised. He stepped out of the truck and turned to the hood. He heard the click of a holster and felt the Glock pushed into his ribs.

"Can I help?"

Even with the officer's size, Parker could have taken him down in a moment. But this wasn't the fight he was interested in now.

"You are under arrest."

Parker looked forward as the officer held the pistol to his back while placing handcuffs on his wrists. He cooperated. Something else was going on with this particular officer.

"You are interfering with a criminal investigation."

Parker couldn't help but give him a look that said the charge was lame.

"Get into the back."

The policeman shoved Parker into the back of the cruiser. It was like stuffing a large man into a box. His knees were up to his chest as he turned to get an angle across the seat. The cage was slanted in towards back-seat passengers, giving most of them a feeling of claustrophobia.

The policeman slammed the door shut, shoving the handle into Parker's side. Parker grimaced as he shifted himself again. His eyes followed the officer as he crossed in front of the cruiser's lights while talking on his radio. Parker couldn't hear what was being said. He could, however, get a better view of the man. He had a naturally large and bulky frame. His hair was cut short. In fact, it was down to the skin on the sides, like a drill instructor's high and tight. It was the haircut of a man who didn't care for conversation.

William scanned the front of the cruiser as the officer opened the door.

"Ten-four. I'm bringing him in now. We need that tow truck for his vehicle."

Now, in the close space of the car, William detected the smell of Aqua Velva. He noticed the man's hands as well. The nails were closely trimmed but the hands were large. It would have taken an extra, extra large pair of gloves to fit over this man's hands.

Every meal a plate of food. William envisioned a high school football lineman. He was the type who piled up a plate and then asked for seconds. Age would not be kind.

"If you let me make a call on your cell phone I can probably get this cleared up." William hadn't been in the back of a patrol car since the bar fight at the Navy Yard as a young Force Recon lieutenant. A SEAL had jumped his captain and all hell had broken loose.

The cruiser had a cup holder on its front console, and in the cup holder was a dark, beaten-up cell phone.

The man looked through his rearview mirror, staring through the cage like a bear ready to attack. There was silence for a moment. He acted as if the question had never been asked.

They drove to the station in complete silence. Only the squad car's radio interrupted the quiet. At the station, the jailer searched Parker.

"Damn, look at this dude."

The fellow jailer and the arresting officer stared at the scar on Parker's shoulder.

"Where did you get that?"

Parker didn't say anything. He didn't want to aggravate the situation further. As they finished, another officer came into the booking room.

"We got a winner!" He held up the wad of cash that

Parker had kept in the console. They were like a bunch of teenagers in the locker room after a win on the football field.

"One call?" Parker asked.

"Sure, time to call your momma." The jailer laughed. "That's your bondsman."

"Thanks."

They didn't understand who it was standing there. He dialed the number. Parker hoped he had the number right. Since he'd stopped carrying a cell phone, he hadn't called Gunny in awhile.

"Gunny." Parker noticed the jailer raise his head when the word was mentioned. "I've been arrested in Mobile."

The conversation was brief.

"Okay, let's go to the holding cell."

Parker felt the arresting officer stare at him the entire time. It was as if rage was being barely contained. The bear's eyes followed his every move.

"Open it up." The watch officer pointed to the holding cell. He was just as displeased as the arresting officer but for a much different reason. His anger was not directed at Parker.

"I am sorry, sir." The lieutenant held out his hand in an apology.

The two other jailers looked on in shock as they sat behind their desks while all of this was going on.

"We have had a very bad week," the lieutenant said sheepishly.

"I understand," said Parker.

"Where is all of his stuff?"

One of the jailers held up a brown paper bag.

"Is the money in there as well?"

"No, sir."

"Get it." The jailer went to a safe behind the desk, swung the door open, and pulled out a plastic bag marked with a red strip. "Evidence" was printed on the strip. The lieutenant ripped it open and handed the stack of fifties to Parker.

"You need to count it?"

"No."

"Fellows, we need to delete this entire arrest."

Just as he said that, the arresting officer came back in the room. He stood in the rear with his back leaning against the wall. He didn't say anything. He simply stared at Parker as Parker put everything back into his pockets.

"The arrest photo?" the senior jailer asked the question that the others in the room were thinking.

"Yes, everything. It all needs to be pulled. Nothing can remain in the computer."

"Why, boss?"

"National security."

They all knew now where the scars came from. The two jailers were embarrassed and meekly bowed their heads.

The room got silent.

CHAPTER TWELVE

The convoy of white Land Rovers bounced across the path through the desert heading east. The vehicles tossed and turned like small dinghies in a violent storm. Some seemed, at times, to come close to flipping over. The roads of east Africa could barely be called roads. They were more like paths occasionally passing through outcrops of sandy rocks. Each of the trucks was marked with the logo of the MSF. Doctors Without Borders had another encampment somewhere farther southwest, near Dolo. But this encampment was far more remote.

The rains had started to come to east Africa, and with the rains, the danger of roads becoming torrents of water. When the ruts dried out, the mud and potholes full of water remained for several days. With the water came the mosquitoes. Sleep required a net or skin so toughened by a life in this wilderness that it was difficult for the insects to penetrate their prey's skin. In all likelihood, many would get malaria and there was not enough medicine for all.

Karen Stewart tried to concentrate on the vehicle in front of her. It seemed to make the vertigo less painful if she watched the vehicle ahead. They were a fleet of ships at sea. She held on to her backpack in her lap. She was in a rear seat with the security guard sitting directly in front of her in the passenger seat. He held his AK-47 out of the window. It had a rope as a sling. He had big white teeth in contrast to his dark face and a smile that helped put her at ease, but she had never been this close to a weapon before.

As they passed through a village, the children and women would stare at the run of vehicles. Sometimes the children would hop onto the running boards and ride until they either got bored and jumped to the ground or were shaken off by a particularly bad bump in the road.

Karen didn't feel well. She knew it was a mistake but she drank some of the camel milk that the women carried on the top of their heads in large plastic jugs. It was intended to be a special treat. She could tell from their eyes as they pulled a jug down and offered to pour the warm liquid out into a steel cup. It tasted oddly sweet and did not sit well.

The malaria pills didn't help either. Her stubbornness did not let the thought of turning back enter her mind. "I warned you!" Dr. Pierre DuBose shook his head at her. He was sitting in the seat next to her. A veteran of this part of Africa, this was his third tour with MSF and he had learned from his many mistakes.

"Okay." She tried to lean her head against the truck's brace but every time she did, another thump would knock her about.

"It will be better when we get to Ferfer." He was in his mid-thirties, a surgeon from Paris, and on his last tour. This was not his first tour to the eastern village next to the Shebelle River. The mud huts that formed the small circle on the rise next to the river had been in the same location for well over a thousand years.

"The Shebelle has a cruel heart." DuBose spoke above the noise of the truck as everything not tied down rattled. Occasionally, they had to stop when they noticed that something had fallen off onto the side of the road.

"Really?"

"It is only a cut in the rocks and the sand. When the rain starts it becomes a viper." DuBose had a flair for the dramatic. "It will spread like a plague."

"Beyond its banks?"

"Yes, it has swallowed up many children who got too close."

"Oh." She wiped her face with the once-blue-and-orange blouse. It now had a tint of red from the constant dust that clung to everything. The rivers turned red and the water that they drank, even after filtering, had a red tint.

"How far to the border?" She knew that the Somali frontier was close.

"Probably a hundred meters or so. They don't have borders out here unless they want to."

The neighboring countries knew more by tribes or villages what was and what was not Somalia. It was not like the United States and Mexico.

"When will we see patients?"

DuBose let out a big laugh.

"Yes, you are a rookie!" There would be no shortage of patients. The children had scars on their faces from smallpox and other diseases that they had survived. Some would limp in from the west of Somalia with poorly bandaged wounds from random fighting they had innocently stepped into. Many sought the refuge of the remote village of Ferfer simply because it was far from anything that should matter.

The MSF camp was on a flat area amid a round of rocks that overlooked the valley and the riverbed. The village of Ferfer was just beyond. When the doctors opened up for business, the line of patients wandered up the hillside to the gathering of white tents. She had her wish granted. There was plenty to do. She had no shortage of patients in the encampment.

After unloading the vehicles, Dr. Stewart fell asleep in her new tent for several hours. As the sun began to set, the chill of the desert set in and with it she awoke in near darkness. She leaned forward in her bunk and got a face full of net as her mind recognized where she was. It was a hard sleep. Her face was wet. She felt her pillow and it was also wet. The days of travel and riding in seats that didn't recline had taken their toll. Stewart pulled the net back, turned to put her feet on the ground, and then felt for her boots. She had already learned to hit her boots together to make sure there were no scorpions that had climbed into the warmth of the boots. Like all the insect and animal life on this continent, the scorpions had a bite that was far worse than just being painful. She had brought a small LED flashlight with her, and with it she dug through her backpack until she found a Polartec jacket. As she left the tent, a cold still night air struck her. She pulled a scarf over her head for both warmth and as respect for this new world. She had learned already that a woman must wear a scarf or covering at all times.

It was the evening prayer. Stewart stopped as the song of words echoed off the rocks. She could hear the call from the village below. Stewart climbed onto a flat rock that let her look out over the valley and beyond.

She smelled smoke from the other side of the MSF encampment. There were a dozen white rectangular tents all with the markings of Médecins Sans Frontières. Below each sign there was another: a red machine gun in a circle with a line through it. It was meant to signal they were an unarmed encampment. The tents were not in any particular line or row.

I will remember where everything is. More important, she noted the latrine, which was outside the tent and behind one large rock.

She followed the smoke to a small campfire where the guard and Dr. DuBose were sitting. They were speaking in the guard's native tongue.

"Hello!" She pulled up a campstool near the fire.

"There is our rookie!"

DuBose was comfortable in this setting.

"Hello, Pierre."

"Please call me Peter. I did my residency at Presbyterian in New York."

"Yes, okay."

They had traveled for two days together in an odd combination of small airplanes and Land Rovers but hadn't had the chance to really talk.

"Shaata wants you to meet someone. Do you feel up to it?"

"Sure, I guess so."

"We will go meet the village leader."

She followed the guide and DuBose down a path to the outskirts of the village where one clay-and-mud structure stood apart from the rest. To the side of the entrance a curtain was drawn over the opening. The guide called out some words and a young villager pulled the curtain aside.

An old man with a large curved nose, a scarred face, and little hair waved his hand to signal they were allowed to enter.

"*Al-salamu alaykum*."
The greeting was returned.
"*Wa alaykum s-salam*."
She saw a group of women in the back of the room, sitting in the darkness. On that nervous edge of not wanting to offend another culture, Stewart pulled her scarf tighter to her face with only her eyes and nose poking through.

"Don't worry." Peter pointed to a spot near the fire where she was to sit down. "He knows you are a Westerner."

It was, however, slightly odd that her spot was just behind the inner circle where the men sat cross-legged.

The village leader began to talk and as he did, Peter started to interpret what he was saying. She looked into the old man's eyes and watched as he waved the smoke from the fire on occasion. Soon she forgot that Peter was the translator and listened as the old man's words were quickly interpreted.

"Have you been to our world before?"
"No, this is my first time to Ferfer and to Africa."
The old man smiled.

"Good, let me tell you about my people." The old man lived in a mud-and-clay hut in the center of the village. He enjoyed the chance to tell a stranger the story of his people. His smile, lit by the flicker of the fire, showed a pride that continued the story for thousands of years.

"We were not always so poor. We were once a people of the sea. Great traders."

Stewart twisted her legs so as to be more comfortable.

"Have you heard of our trades with the Roman Empire?"

"No." She knew that Rome touched everything in this part of the world. Its power was absolute and its arm extended across the civilized world.

"Rome would come to our ports. For a thousand years they would trade with us for the spices that came from India. We brought them over in our little boats."

She had known from the stories of the pirates that they would go well beyond the horizon in small boats to take on the giant ships. A boat in the Gulf of Aden was, however, far from the coast of India. India required a crossing of thousands of miles or the following of the coastline for months. The journey would have taken a year to complete.

"India was the home to colorful cloths and spices."

Peter leaned back on his hands as he continued to interpret the man's words. Occasionally, he would stop and use his hands to try and grasp what the old man was saying. And then he would resume the interpretation.

"India held the spices but their men were poor sailors."

It sounded like cultural pride, but she continued to listen.

"We would sail to India and buy their spices with gold from the Romans. To this date, the Roman coins have been found in India . . . but Rome was never there."

"Really?"

"Yes. But when cinnamon was brought back from

India my people told the Romans that it came from the interior of our land. The Romans thought that the cinnamon came from places like this village. They would send out patrols, but they never found anything." He laughed at the mental image of a Roman patrol centuries ago walking into the village of Ferfer going from house to house. He pointed to the four walls.

"A Roman came into this house when your Christ walked this earth."

Stewart listened intently.

"But there was no cinnamon. The Romans never solved the mystery. Not one soul here spoke the truth. Everyone kept his or her lips sealed. The cinnamon had come from across the sea."

"You mean Somalia sold the cinnamon as their own but none actually came from here?" Stewart asked the question.

"Yes, that is right. No one knew for centuries."

"Wow." She thought of the scale of the lie.

"Never underestimate a people's determination." DuBose inserted his own comment. "Well, tomorrow you get to see some sick ones. Are you ready to hit the rack?"

The story had caused her to forget how tired she was.

"Yes, please. Thank him."

"Don't leave our village," said the old man. It was a warning. Not so much to scare her as to protect her.

"No, I won't."

"We are a land of lions and baboons." He continued to talk.

"He is right, you know," DuBose added. "Besides the war, there are other dangers. The ants can cover you in your sleep in a moment. You will see some die just from the ants here."

"They told me of some of this."

"We are not just dirt and desert." The old man spoke the words as he waved his hand. "We are also danger."

CHAPTER THIRTEEN

"He was a member of that church." The senior FBI agent was sitting in the operation center that had been set up in Atlanta's regional office.

"Omar was?" The chief of operations was at the end of the table being briefed in a meeting that included a PowerPoint presentation on the subject. "He killed people he had been to church with?"

"Yes, sir."

"How did he go from being a perfect student to being a killer?"

"How do any of them do what they do?"

The question of the American jihadist was broader than just this one target. There were many such men and more seemed to be showing up each day.

"He had a tie to Islam from his father. An uncle was in prison in Syria for more than a decade. We know he traveled there on several occasions and spent time with the uncle."

"But one person converting an American to be a killer?" It was as if the chief thought that birth in America automatically meant unlimited loyalty to the United States.

"He was always on the fringes. First, he started to attend a mosque in Mobile and then he returned to Syria. We understand that he tried to leave Syria to head to Yemen when he was in high school."

"So where is he now?"

"Our guess is that he is in North Africa and probably heading to Somalia or Yemen."

"Sir, we just got this in." Another, younger agent brought in several copies of a printout of a Web page. "This is Musa. He is with security for Al Shabaab. They are taking credit for the bombing in Mobile."

"So Omar has tagged in with Musa and Al Shabaab?"

"It seems so."

"How many does that make now from America?"

"As of 2012, we've tracked at least forty," Smith read from a report.

"Why?"

"They see this civil war in Somalia as the holy war. The jihadist believes he will be a martyr if he dies for the cause. It's an express ticket to heaven."

"Where do they get their money from?"

"Much comes from the Saudis, Iran, some sources in Libya and Egypt. Oh, and Al Shabaab is famous for killing thousands of elephants for the ivory. They don't mind killing the rangers as well."

"Damn. Okay, we need to put him on the Most Wanted list. Very high up. And see if there are any other possibilities of recruits connected to him."

"Toronto is the place to watch. It is a community up there." Agent Smith was summarizing what everyone else thought. "We need to coordinate with Mounties' intelligence."

Omar was in Cairo but they were correct in their guess that he was on the move. He would not be there for long.

CHAPTER FOURTEEN

"Fartuun!"

Omar greeted his pregnant wife at the airport in Cairo with a smile and brief hug. Although it had been only a few days since he last saw her, she already seemed more pregnant than he had remembered.

The wife wanted a baby and a quiet world. But she was a true Muslim and followed her husband's orders to come to Egypt.

"Hello, Husband."

"I have a room for us with friends."

They took several buses to a neighborhood where others from Somalia lived. It was a small community that protected each other from the prying eyes of Egypt's police. He was in a Muslim world, but still was far from being safe. Egypt's military considered any outsider to be an instigator and a threat.

One evening after prayers they took a walk in the market. A café had a television in the corner. It was tuned in to CNN International. In a glance, he recognized a familiar face. He stopped. The television showed a picture from his high school yearbook of both Eddie and himself. He started to laugh.

"Daphne High School!" He could see himself walking the hallways in his Islamic clothes.

"Daphne." He said the word aloud as he looked around at the much different world he was in.

The other students had worried about football and deer hunting, whereas Omar had worried about the fate of his religion.

"Allah knows all."

Omar stood there and stared at the television even though he could not hear what was being said.

"My mother," he spoke to himself.

"What is it?" his wife asked.

"Oh, nothing. I must understand that Allah, blessed be the great one, requires much of us."

Omar thought back to his trips to Syria and the stories of his uncle. His uncle had spent time in the prisons because of his beliefs.

"You know, when my uncle was in prison the guards used to beat one prisoner a day."

She looked up to her husband as he spoke. They continued to walk through the market heading back towards their apartment.

"When one prisoner was too sick to survive a beating, my uncle would volunteer to be beaten." Omar had this crystal perfect vision of what was required of him as a Muslim. The West, with its drugs and barely clad women, had no direction. Omar had become convinced that a sacrifice had to be made and that he was the one to make such a sacrifice.

"They will remember me in Mobile."

"Yes."

She knew nothing of Mobile. He could have used the name of any town in America—Dallas or Chicago or Seattle. But to him, being known in Mobile meant much. He didn't care if he was branded a killer so much as he wanted to be known as a true believer. It was what the mosque thought of their two martyrs that counted. It was what Allah thought that mattered.

"With time, they will understand that being committed to something such as the path of Allah is far more important than anything they will ever accomplish in their lives."

Death was simply a side note.

"I will get you situated with the other wives."

He knew that she had a grandmother still living in Mogadishu and an aunt who lived in Kismayo. It was important to have names when he went through customs. He had to have a purpose for his journey.

"Do you want to go to your homeland?" he asked. She was born in Somalia, as was her father, her father's father, and so on for generations.

She had an immediate answer. "No!"

He knew that her world had been a simple one. She never lived in an apartment or a house with her own bedroom. His world in Mobile would have shocked her. He was middle class with a father who had a good job as a manager for the electric company and a mother who worked at a day care. A small bedroom just for him in their neighborhood of one-car-garage houses was a concept she couldn't understand, just like traveling to Somalia was not a part of her world. Her community did not stretch beyond her Somali neighborhood in Toronto. She had spent her entire life in a six-story apartment slum that contained only Somalis. No one in the building except her and one other neighbor spoke English. But her building was a comfortable world.

It was there in the market that he decided that she needed to return to Canada. The child would be born in that world, as was her wish. Her wishes disrespected him. Under the rule of his new world she would be whipped. In Egypt, it would not happen. If need be, Omar would take another wife in Somalia. But for now, he needed her name and connection to Somalia to complete his jihad.

"I must leave tomorrow."

She had been expecting this.

CHAPTER FIFTEEN

"The director would like to see you." The secretary's message was taped to his chair when he got back from the lab.

"Damn." Paul Stewart guessed the call was coming; however, he did not like receiving it. The CDC had its world of politics and its world of scientists. It was no exception to organizations of its size.

He was happy in his lab worrying about the progression of certain diseases, the reawakening of smallpox and other puzzles needing to be figured out. Politics was not his game and the loss of his wife had made him less tolerant of small talk and egos.

He put on his lab coat and crossed over to the administration office and the director's inner sanctum.

"We are in trouble," the director said.

Paul nodded his head.

"I am on the short list to be gone."

Stewart had never had issues with this particular director. Misplacing the vials was a stupid mistake, but with time the odds of making a mistake were against them. There were too many vials and too many experiments that were put on trays or carts or on the move. It was like America's nuclear missile program. They both played with danger and sometime in the next several hundreds of years the odds would play out.

"What can I do to help?"

"They want a well-respected scientist to be the point man on a reworking of our system."

Dr. Stewart knew that it meant being on the surface. To find Paul Stewart before this at the CDC would have taken an inside job of espionage. He didn't appear to the public and, more important, to Congress. There was no upside with this new position.

But Stewart was the logical choice. He was a leader in his field and was considered the top mind in the study of meningitis in the world.

He also was famed for being a thorn in the side of the administration for years regarding the lapses he found in the labs.

"May I think about it?"

"Of course. Increase in pay and you will probably be sitting in this chair a year or two from now."

Stewart wondered how long he could stall the process.

When he returned to his office there was another note taped to his chair.

"What now?" He looked at the calendar. He wasn't sure if it was a Monday or just seemed like one.

The note asked him to call his assistant. The young PhD had been recruited from Columbia. It was a job that Stewart had hoped his daughter would have applied for. But she wanted no part of working for her father no matter how much it would have placed her on the cutting edge.

"What's up?"

"You remember that strain of Neisseria meningitidis that was documented some time ago in Afghanistan?"

Dr. Chang asked. "It was the one like the hypervirulent strain we found in China some time ago."

"Yes." He knew the specifics far more than he could even hint at. The one in Afghanistan was more aggressive than the one in China. It shared traits with the Ebola virus. It destroyed red blood cells and sent the victim into a state of septic shock in a matter of hours. In the Anhui province of China it had wiped out people like a tidal wave.

The one from Afghanistan was quicker and deadlier. A mountain cave had been found with virtually no survivors from a specific strain of the bacteria. He knew the strain earmarks. It matched the vial frozen in the refrigerator on the fifth floor of the very building they were in.

And Stewart also remembered the survivor. The lab had a sample that predated the Afghanistan breakout. It was the creator of the strain of Neisseria meningitidis that killed in Afghanistan. And now its sister had appeared.

"We had a slide come in from Yemen that looks similar."

"Yemen?"

"Yes, sir, I will send it to you as an attachment."

"Thanks."

Stewart looked up his directory of the CDC on his computer. There was one person in particular that he was searching for. Enrico Hernandez was a part of the security service at the health organization. Stewart also wanted to see a blood sample from the survivor of that outbreak. Only Hernandez knew how to find William Parker.

CHAPTER SIXTEEN

Just as William Parker pulled back to his farmhouse, he heard a rumble in the distance. It was pitch black outside. The farmhouse had no light left on and he was miles from the road. The day had been long with the trip back from Mobile taking several hours. He had accomplished what he wanted and needed to do. The arrest was a diversion, but Parker had to see for himself what had happened at the school.

He turned off the lights to his truck and started to pull the tarp over the cab when he looked to the north.

The lodge was on a hill just above the Chattahoochee River and several miles south of Fort Benning. The base had grown larger with the addition of the Armor School, tanks, armored personnel carriers, and several military schools meant to teach Army officers at every level how to fight.

His farmhouse was also in line with the main runway at Lawson Field. Runways were numbered by the direction of the compass, and a runway's number was perfectly in line with that particular point. Runway 26 would be aligned with 260 degrees on the compass. An airplane or helicopter, particularly in darkness or rain, had to depend upon the alignment as it approached for landing.

The noise was not from an airplane landing.

He stood in the total darkness as he watched movement just above the tree line to the north. The noise indicated some object was heading south.

In combat, aircraft would not show their running lights. A rumble would be heard, without someone on the ground able to tell its direction, and then suddenly an object would appear.

William Parker observed, however, both movement and lights. A pair of lights was on two approaching aircraft with two reds on the right and two whites on the left. They were on the tips of the wings. Two C-17 cargo jets came in low, just above his tree line, causing the ground to rumble. He felt the wave of noise as it bounced off the wall of his house.

The aircraft were on a mission heading south. He looked back as they passed him by and headed directly towards the farm and its operation center.

Parker suddenly realized how much he missed it all.

CHAPTER SEVENTEEN

Bertok Genret watched as the flatbed container truck passed his Rover, then stopped just inside Yemen's border. The truck had made it across the country of Oman arriving on a short-haul bulk freighter that had crossed over from Iran. The first third of the trailer was stuffed with prayer rugs of a thousand different colors. They had the smell of an old mill although each was made in a mud or stone hut in the mountains of Iran.

"I will make a little profit on the side," Genret thought as he patted the container while the driver took a break to go behind a rock. They would drop the load and then take the rugs back into Oman. Eventually they would sell in London or America or Canada.

Genret looked at his watch.

It would be dark soon.

They would reach the small fishing village on the far coast of Yemen just after midnight. A fishing boat rigged to serve as the "mother" boat for several skiffs had its hull emptied for some special cargo. Genret had done this run several times. The missile was contained in several crates marked as coming from Iran. A freighter steaming directly to a port in Somalia had shipped a harmless-looking truck carriage. The carriage would transport the missile to the launch site. It would take a very close inspection to realize that the carriage was a weapons transport.

Because Genret was a transport officer on this trip, he didn't worry about the fee. It would be collected later.

Switzerland had changed somewhat with the increase in terrorism; however, there were still ways fees could be paid that allowed bankers to look the other way. Not everything could be paid in gold coins, and sometimes coins needed to be exchanged for currency. A friendly banker helped that process. His biggest fear was that Faud would have someone rob him once he received his gold. But it would only recycle the money, and Faud would lose a dependable dealer. Far worse, the other dealers would get word that Faud was not to be trusted.

The truck pulled into the village on the Yemen coast just past one in the morning. Genret parked his Rover on the other side of town and walked a mile to a road crossing. There, the truck picked him up and took him down to the rocky beach.

"This will be a bitch," he thought, as the truck backed up the beach as far as it could.

"Clouds, perfect." He looked up at the dark sky. Yemen had a constant patrol of Predators and satellites over its land. They were mostly concentrated on the capital and to the north.

"Let's move."

His workers pulled the rugs out, placing them on a large, flat rock near the shoreline. Then three men climbed in and slid the first crate out of the truck and onto the backs of several others. They carried the crate to a small fishing boat and then rowed out to the mother ship. There, they used a hoist to pull the crate onto the deck. Each would be paid more than they could make fishing in a month. Each suspected what they were carrying were boxes of RPGs going across the Gulf.

Just before dawn, the mother ship would pull out of the harbor with the other fishing dinghies tied in line to its back. They would pass the big freighters coming in and going out of the Suez Canal, making sure not to get too close to any one ship. The captain would move in a slow and deliberate manner, and when on the other side of the sea highway, he would disperse the smaller fishing boats. They would catch a load of fish and then, as darkness neared, head into the shelter of the harbor in Somalia.

Al Shebaab's territory didn't extend that far north; however, moneys were paid for a pass on this one occasion. Musa would meet the boat as it started to carry the load, crate by crate, to the shoreline of Somalia.

It was a pitch-black night with a cloudy overcast. The new moon provided no light. The trucks moved south with little notice.

"Attention on deck!"

Everyone stood as the admiral entered the conference room of the U.S. Naval Central Command's operations center.

"Carry on."

He looked at the single door, and with his glance a guard shut it. Another guard was on the outside to make sure that no one casually walked into the admiral's talk.

"We have heard for some time of the Dong Feng."

The missile was well known to everyone in the room and those who served on Navy ships. The carriers particularly knew of the technology behind it.

"We are not sure that they have yet gained the capability of catching up with a fast-moving target."

The admiral was talking of the intelligence reports that it might take another ten years to perfect the missile. The weapon was such a game changer, however, that the Navy had started to institute plans, particularly in the Pacific, to disperse the forces in case of attack.

"We know that Iran is reverse engineering the missile with the help of the Chinese, and they have tested one. And you know of the *Zumwalt*."

There were whispers among the officers and senior enlisted as a photo of the ship appeared on the admiral's PowerPoint. DDG-1000 was a completely different form of a ship. She was a ghost ship. She had been built from the keel up to be a stealth destroyer. The ship seemed to have been pulled from the pages of a Jules Verne novel. There were no sharp edges or visible railings. She appeared to be wrapped in a gray thin material that changed her shape entirely. Her tumblehome hull had an inverted, tapered bow that pointed aft, causing her to slice through the water like a ghost. She was made for silence. She stood out for the ability of not being seen.

"The *Zumwalt* is heading our way. She will stay out of the Persian Gulf but will do her sea trials to the south, near the Gulf of Aden."

A ship of such size could not be kept a secret. As she passed any other vessel or merchant ship, the crews would be pulled up on deck to see the strange new sight.

"With ISIS fighting to our north, others may wish to

take advantage of our attention being distracted. We will need to keep an eye on everything, particularly as North Africa remains unstable and our friends continue to try and link up with each other."

NavCent did have a full plate. And events were leading it towards deeper waters.

CHAPTER EIGHTEEN

The old man stood outside the medical tent with a small, bony boy standing next to him. The child was leaning on the old man like a grandchild might lean on his grandfather. Karen Stewart was cleaning a deep cut on the foot of a woman when she noticed the two waiting to be seen. She was amazed at the people she had already met in the short time that she had been there.

Karen would put a stitch or two in the foot. DuBose had told her that no numbing injection was required.

"Save that for the more serious injuries."

What do you mean "more serious"? She looked at the cut. It was from a piece of metal, which was rare in this part of the world. The woman had limped and walked for miles to get to the clinic and was being seen only because her husband had come with her. He was a suspicious man and stood outside the tent as Karen treated the wound.

The woman did not budge at all as the needle of the suture entered her leathered skin.

Just like a pit bull dog. Karen remembered from camp as a teenager once that a dog had wandered into the row of cabins. It was also cut deeply. All of the girls screamed as it lay down under a planked step to the cabin.

The dog's owner showed up and apologized for the dog. He was trying to calm the counselor with promises that the dog would never come this way again. It was wounded after cutting through a barbed-wire fence that caught him in just the wrong way.

While the counselor kept the others calm in their cabin, Karen snuck outside the cabin entrance and watched the owner. He pulled the dog out by its collar. It was a pit bull dog. He lifted it up and placed it on the top step. The man pulled out a small kit, threaded a string in a needle, and started to sew up the wound. The dog lay there without flinching. It was impervious to pain.

DuBose was on the other end of the tent helping a woman with a difficult birth. She had been bleeding for some time. It was not likely that DuBose would save either the woman or her child. Her screams penetrated the entire medical camp. Bleeding was the one thing that a patient's will could not stop.

"Mataa, can you see what the old man needs?"

She had one assistant who helped with the patient load. It had already become clear to her that they could work from dawn to dusk and never catch up.

"Peter, do you need some help?"

"No, it is Allah's will." Peter wasn't being sarcastic. He had already taught her how the people who lived in this valley thought. Karen had cried for a day when the first child was lost. And Peter pulled her aside.

"Ask the mother what she thinks tomorrow."

"What?"

"No, really, it is a part of your education."

Karen sat down next to the mother, who was laughing and smiling the next day as she played with a young daughter near her cot.

"I am so sorry," Karen said with tears in her eyes.

The woman had a strange look on her face as she talked to two others who were sitting on the ground nearby. Her reaction to Karen's tears mystified Karen.

Mataa interpreted some of the woman's words.

"She says that 'it is.' "

"Nothing more?" Karen asked.

"Nothing else need be said." Mataa said.

Acceptance was a mandate to survival. Another child would be born and another child would die.

It was the eyes that Karen could not forget.

She taped the wound on the foot of the woman in front of her.

"Mataa, tell her to keep it clean."

"Ya, lady doc." Mataa had started to call her that.

It didn't really matter. The woman would not keep it clean but her body had built up such a resistance to every possible type of infection that the tape would wear off, the wound would heal, and life would go on.

Karen walked out to the old man and the boy.

"*Al-salamu alaykum*." She pulled the scarf around her head. It was taking some time for her to remember to do so, but every time she forgot, the looks were a quick reminder.

"*Wa alaykum s-salam*." The old man pushed the boy forward towards the doctor.

"Oh, my. Hello."

He had brown eyes that followed her with the occasional blink. His head was on a slight tilt, as if he was protecting his neck. She felt his head and it was burning up with fever. She tried to move his head and the child whimpered. Other doctors may not have known what to suspect. Karen was, however, the daughter of the number-one expert in the world on this disease.

"Mataa?" she called for the helper. "Please ask how long the child has been sick."

"He says two days. He doesn't sound very sure."

"Why not?"

"The child is from another village just to the east."

"Okay."

"Should I give this child a cot?"

"Yes, but not in the tent. Take one out of the last tent and put it there, between the rocks." It was the best that could be done for an isolation ward.

"So, what do you think it is?"

Karen was perched on top of the highest rock with the satellite phone. Peter was standing nearby. She wanted to cry when she heard her father's voice.

"Meningitis. No doubt." Karen plugged her finger into her ear so as to hear his voice clearly. "Which strain, I don't know."

"Can't be a surprise. You're in the middle of the meningitis belt." Paul Stewart used his clinical voice when he talked of medical cases.

"We have put him on the strongest antibiotic we have, but we don't have vancomycin."

"I understand. Just make him comfortable."

It was clear that the child might not survive. He could be in admissions at an emergency room in a major medical facility and still not make it to sundown.

"Yes." She didn't like what was being said, but she knew the truth well before she'd made the call.

"Can you get me a sample of his blood?"

She knew he was right. It may help others to know what strain was involved.

"We have a satellite link. I think we can send a picture to you."

They had a remote location link and a generator that could be powered up when needed. She would have a picture of the slide to him before the end of work the next day in Atlanta.

"Thanks."

"Is everything going well?" It was the father's voice that was now kicking in.

"Yes, I am learning so much."

"Well, you will be finished before you know it."

"I know. Dr. DuBose has been a great help."

"Love you. Bye."

The link cut off.

"Mataa, ask the old man how we get to the boy's village."

The nurse hesitated. "I don't know."

"We need to see if we can stop the spread of this disease before it goes farther."

Stewart had been fully inoculated to include the meningitis vaccination. It may have not been the right one, but her risk of getting sick was fairly low. However, the disease could spread quickly. Neisseria meningitidis could infect an entire village within hours. Others would get sick, and death could soon follow. And it was a horrible death.

Mataa spoke to the old man. He shook his head as they talked. Finally, he seemed to agree. He, himself, would take the doctor to the village.

Paul Stewart stayed late and then came in early, still waiting for the slide to come across the Internet. The director had called him several times and left messages that Stewart ignored. He still wasn't ready to give them a response on the other job.

Finally, he opened his email and found the one from his daughter. The slide was attached to the email but was of poor quality. He tried to enlarge it as best as he could.

"Damn!" One enlargement said what he needed to know. It was the same strain as the one from Yemen. The cells were linked together in the purple tint like chains, angry chains, with spikes on the sides. It was also identical to the strain in Afghanistan. He called his assistant.

"Where is Hernandez?"

"The one with security?"

"I need to see his friend."

CHAPTER NINETEEN

Omar took the flight the next day from Cairo to Dubai. Every ticket had to be bought as a round-trip. A one-way would cause suspicion that could keep him in place for days or, even worse, cause him to be turned back to Cairo. In Dubai, he took a bus to the market and nearby he found the Daallo Airlines office.

There he bought a round-trip ticket to Mogadishu, never intending to use the return leg.

The airplane was Russian, old and hot. With his broken Arabic, Omar realized that the flight wasn't going to Mogadishu. Rather, it was flying to Djibouti.

The airplane landed at the Djibouti airfield and taxied past lines of gray military aircraft. Most had the markings of the U.S. Air Force. He had stepped into the beehive.

What have I done?

He was already feeling ill from the heat and smell of the aircraft and its passengers. Every look from an airline clerk caused his heart to jump.

What now? He still had the Toronto Blue Jays hat on and he pulled it down around his eyes. The baseball hat actually helped him fit in with the crowd of passengers, as many of the younger ones wore a mishmash of American clothes and hats. He looked like a cross between an L.A. rapper and a young Muslim. As he moved farther into the Arab world the Canadian passport did cause more scrutiny.

"I need to just keep moving," he thought as he walked down the steps from the aircraft. Another plane was parked next to his and as he entered the room that served as a terminal, Omar realized that the signage for the other aircraft was to Mogadishu.

He watched the mix of civilian aircraft still carrying people from one war-torn country to another. At the same time, the other side of the runway was an encampment of aircraft heavy with bombs. New container buildings stretched from one corner of the runway to another. He stopped for a minute on the tarmac looking at a hangar on the opposite end of the military complex. He pulled his baseball hat down so as to block out the glare.

A small gray airplane was sitting in front of the hangar.

He looked again.

"So that is what one looks like." He spoke the words underneath his breath as he stared at a Reaper drone, parked and ready for takeoff. He could make out cigar-shaped green objects under the wings. The bombs were either heading south to Somalia or east to Yemen.

Soon, some will be meant for me.

Omar was excited about joining the fight. This was the war that his uncle fought. And now Omar was becoming a soldier for Allah.

Some day, the Banu Najjar will be speaking of me.

In Mobile, they would say his name with shock and shame. But in the villages of the Banu Najjar he would be a hero.

I loved history. Omar rarely got less than an "A" in any class, but history was easy. He had read everything he could on Patrick Henry.

He was getting closer by the minute to the battle-field.

Although he was the only white man on board the airplane, he tried to strike up a conversation with his seatmate. He needed to blend in, and another person friendly to him would help.

"I am going to visit my wife's grandmother."

The woman was pleasant but not yet engaged.

"I just came from Cairo."

This struck a chord with her and soon he realized that they both knew friends from his milk delivery days in Toronto. It was a pattern that he'd learned to capitalize on. He would keep talking and dropping names until one struck.

The airplane creaked and bumped as it left Djibouti. It was worn out and barely able to keep in the air. The seats were all filled as passengers carried with them every possession in the world. Plastic bags served as suitcases and were held in passengers' laps. When the airplane hit an air pocket, he watched the bags fly up until passengers grabbed them and pulled them down. He too held on to his one plastic bag that held the few things he had brought.

After some time, the airplane landed in the city of Hargeysa.

I will never make this, he said to himself. He knew it only took one border guard to stop his trip to Mogadishu.

The airplane leaks fuel, he thought as he looked out at two men who were part of the ground crew. They were staring at the bottom of the wing with a look of amazement.

Several of the passengers remained on the airplane. He followed their lead and stayed in his seat. Only two others boarded the aircraft. The door was closed and it taxied out to the runway.

As the aircraft took off, the left engine sputtered.

"Allah."

It was the first time he felt real fear. The aircraft dropped several hundred feet, and then the engine started to settle down. He could feel the airplane start to rise again and gain altitude.

It was dark when they finally arrived in Mogadishu.

Once off the plane, he could see a beaten and worn airfield. The hangars had doors that were on a tilt, and a broken aircraft, its engine in parts on the ground, sat next to one of them.

I am here!

The journey to his jihad had been completed.

And in America, his name was on every evening news story and his photograph was spread to the airports and immigration checkpoints. Omar had beaten the system. He had escaped.

"I need a computer." Omar had spent the night in a house on the edge of the city. He was received by Musa as a hero and introduced to all of the brothers in the neighborhood.

"Yes, that is a good idea." Musa sat cross-legged, patting his stomach after they had finished the meal brought by the women. "Faud wants you to write. Abu Zubeyr wants you to write! We have discussed this and want you to write to the world. Your jihad will be an inspiration!"

Omar smiled. He had only heard of Faud's boss.

Mukhtar Abu Zubeyr, or Godane, as he was called, was the leader of Al Shabaab.

"You will help us raise money and recruits!"

"I can." He had been forming some ideas in his mind for several months. He would tell the world of the importance of his beliefs. He would become the Patrick Henry of his tribe. He would be quoted and seen on CNN. He would reach out to others wandering and in need of direction like he was years ago. "I know we will have other American jihadists."

"We will get you a computer tomorrow. It is important while the bombing is fresh on the world's mind that they know of your actions and see it came from a fellow soldier.

"And you need something else."

Musa signaled with his hand and another man went around the corner of the room and returned. He was carrying an AK-47 machine gun.

"This is for you."

Omar beamed as he felt the oily piece of metal. He stroked the wooden stock.

"We need a picture." Omar said the words like a tourist who had no comprehension of what he was holding, or the consequence of this new life.

He dropped the magazine clip on the floor. It was empty. He showed it to Musa.

"We will get you some bullets soon. First, you must go into training!"

"I know how to shoot."

"You do?"

"Yes." He had killed a squirrel when in high school, well before he became more devoted as a follower. In fact, Omar had shot at a deer once and missed.

"But have you been shot at?" Musa was a hardened soldier who had served his time at the front lines.

"No." Omar said it meekly.

"You will learn how to stay calm when that Ethiopian helicopter is firing at you. When you hear the first rounds over your head or see a brother fall, you will know the true meaning of the fight."

"I will not run." It wasn't the first time that Omar would not know what awaited him. He would be either a coward or a warrior.

"Yes, of course," Musa agreed.

CHAPTER TWENTY

"You are crazy." Peter DuBose listened to Karen Stewart's argument that the village needed help; that otherwise an epidemic of meningitis would spread across both Somalia and Ethiopia.

"We need to see what's going on." Karen Stewart had dumped everything out of her backpack and was picking out the most important items she needed. First, she was filling it up with several bottles of water. And then she was packing the bottles of antibiotics that they had.

"If you are right, and it is meningitis, those pills will not do much good."

"You are right." She hesitated. "But they may help stop it for the children not yet sick."

Karen started toward the tent opening.

"Wait, let me talk to Mataa and figure out what is going on here."

Stewart put her pack down on the end of the cot. She opened up a bottle of water and leaned against the tent pole. She watched as DuBose, the old man, and Mataa held a confab just outside. DuBose was waving his hands. He often spoke with his hands as much as with words. The old man pointed to the east. Mataa was shaking his head as the conversation continued.

Finally, DuBose turned back to the tent.

"Okay, he says the village is on the road to Beledweyne. We can follow the river. But if we have to cross the Shebelle, I told him that we are turning back. I will not let you go on any other condition."

"Okay." She knew that the river could be both deadly and unpredictable.

"Plus, he says it can't be more than a couple of miles."

"We can get there and see how things look."

"Do you have masks and gloves? We aren't going into this mess without some protection."

Stewart had forgotten to pack those things.

"I will get them from the supply tent."

"We aren't going to be gone for very long."

"I understand." She knew that he was ultimately in charge of the encampment. He had veto power over any decision she made.

The four followed the road past the village and headed east into the desert. The road from Ferfer was just north of the river and paralleled the Shebelle for the entire hike. At least on the map it was supposed to parallel the riverbed.

It was a sunny day and they moved quickly. A white man and a white woman looked odd as they followed the two from the village of Ferfer. They left their guard back at the encampment on the theory that his one weapon would do little good if they ran into anything dangerous. They trusted the village leader and his instinct.

"We need to get there quickly and get out." DuBose was insistent.

"This will only be an assessment so that we can call in and advise them of the situation."

"Yes." She didn't argue.

After less than two hours, they crossed over a rise and came down to the small village of mud huts. Two goats stood guard as they approached. There was no other movement.

"Do you have the masks?"

"Yes." She swung her backpack off, placing it on top of a rock just off the road, opened the pack, and pulled out several gloves and masks. The old man particularly looked odd as she showed him how to place the mask over his mouth and nose. At first, he laughed, resisted, and then finally put the mask on. He refused the gloves and after some effort she gave up. He had been exposed to the boy for some time by now. His body had weathered years of exposures to micro creatures of all kinds. His face was pockmarked with his survival of smallpox or other diseases, and he had slept his entire life without a net. His risk was low.

As they entered the first hut she became covered with flies. The dead were in fetal positions in the corners of the huts. The children were still in the grasp of their mothers' arms, and one child had been suckling her mother's breast as both died.

They moved from hut to hut, finding more dead.

After leaving the last hut, they moved back to the west and the rock that she had used as a table for her backpack. She pulled off the mask, took out a bottle of water, and washed her hands. She then poured the water over DuBose's hands, Mataa's hands, and, with his great reluctance, the old man's hands. He stared at her as if the Westerner didn't appreciate the value of clear water. His water had been tainted with the red dust.

"They can't even be buried." DuBose looked back towards the village as he spoke.

"The contamination will probably not be a problem." Stewart rationalized that death stopped the spread of coughing, sneezing, and the disease.

"The scavengers will clean this out by sunup." DuBose pulled off the gloves and tossed them into the desert. "We need to get back."

As they crossed the rise heading back to the east, the old man stopped. Stewart was looking down at her boots and barely thinking of anything other than putting one foot in front of the other. She looked up to see her three companions standing perfectly still.

A pickup truck was in the middle of the road. Several men with black keffiyehs wrapped around their heads, wearing loose, green military fatigues and holding AK-47 machine guns, were standing in front of the truck pointing their weapons at the four hikers.

Karen Stewart had been introduced to Al Shabaab.

CHAPTER TWENTY-ONE

The following morning the tarp was removed again from the truck behind the lodge. William Parker pulled out the key from underneath the brush guard, started the engine, and turned on the radio. He pulled the truck around to the river side of the farmhouse so as to lessen the static, and scanned until he heard an AM newscast.

". . . a YouTube video has been released by the Al Qaeda–affiliated terrorist group in Somalia that calls itself Al Shabaab . . ." Parker turned up the sound to listen to the report. "An American by the name of Omar Fazul appears on the video claiming credit for the school bombing in Mobile, Alabama. He has been listed by the FBI as a person of interest." Parker looked at the time on the truck's dashboard.

He decided to take another trip. His wallet with the Phillip Berks license was inside the house.

I don't need another call to the Gunny. The trip to Mobile and the arrest had been more action than both he and Gunny had seen for some time.

The cabin was painfully silent. He walked up the knotted, lacquered pine stairs that she once jumped two steps at a time. He hadn't slept in the master bedroom for over a year now. He didn't care if he ever slept in there again. The door remained closed.

Damn roof may have fallen in.

Parker stopped at the door for a moment. He put his hand on the wood. His thought that the roof could have fallen in wasn't without merit. An old woman had owned and lived on the property before he bought it.

On his first visit to the cabin, Parker had called out her name several times before he noticed movement. He'd known her cousin, and this common link allowed a conversation to ensue. The cousin had been a Marine who had been killed in the Beirut bombing. Parker had met the young Marine years ago and told her that he remembered him. Parker had attended the funeral as an escort officer. He was a young captain at the time and, being from the same town, was assigned the duty. It was a responsibility that was far more difficult than any combat tour.

She'd invited him into the main room. There they talked of her cousin and the history of her land. She had twisted hands gnarled by years of untreated arthritis.

As he sat there, he looked around the main room to see the door to the kitchen and another to her bedroom open. The third door was closed.

After some conversation, she brought up the fact that she had thought of selling her land.

"It can be done." He had known of the property for a long time. Once, years ago, he had hunted on the ridgeline that intersected with the river. No one knew that the clearing on top of the hill had a view for miles in all directions.

"You want something to drink?" she asked.

"Yes, I would like that."

He sat down on a bench that she had on the front porch. She returned with a plastic cup full of ice and sweet tea.

"Here you go."

"Thank you."

They returned to conversation about the land.

"But I need to stay here."

"What if you sell me the land and you live in this cabin as long as you want?"

"Yeah, but I got to be buried here, too. My family is here." A small clearing was near the cabin with nothing more than large granite rocks marking the several generations that preceded her. They were lined up in a rough row with weeds as high as the rocks. In the midst of the weeds, each marker was surrounded by a tangle of roses. Antique roses that went back decades, they were considered nearly indestructible. They marked her family's place on the land. It was her tribe.

"Sure, absolutely."

They concluded the conversation and, at the end, she gave him a quick walk around the house without opening the last door. Parker pointed to it.

"I don't want to pry, but the last door?"

"Oh, nothing." She pushed the door open with her shoulder. Some time ago the roof had fallen in. It was easier to just shut the door, she'd said.

"Yeah," he thought now, as he passed the master bedroom. "It can be easier to just shut the door."

Parker now used the last bedroom at the end of the hall. It had a window looking out to the front of the farmhouse and another to the side. It was as close as any room came to being an outpost. From this upstairs room he could hear and see anyone who approached. He grabbed the fake license and left the cabin.

He pulled the truck out of the gravel road from his

farm and headed north. In less than two hours, he took the exit near where the SunTrust Bank branch was that he so often used. This time he didn't stop at the bank but continued on to the next stop.

He pulled into a parking lot near a brown and yellow brick one-story building and parked the truck. Parker passed under the entrance sign. He had been there enough times before that the woman recognized him but didn't specifically recall his name. But he had a confident smile that he knew she always reacted to.

"Hello."

"Yes, sir. Good to see you. Can I help?"

"Your computer room?"

"We just added some new Macs. They're upstairs in the old place."

Parker hadn't been back to the library in nearly a year. It was a safe place, far from his farm, where he could research the world with virtually no backwash. He pulled up the Internet to immediately see the news stories on the bombing from Mobile. He was curious about the bomber.

The room was empty, so he pulled up Omar's first YouTube video and watched the man with a beard and checkered black-and-white turban talk with glee of how the bombing had occurred. Every sentence had tagged onto it his request for blessings of Allah. The video told of Eddie, who was assured of seeing the face of Allah.

Parker pulled up Somalia and studied Al Shabaab. It was a gang that thought of itself as a tribe. The country was a mass of feuding tribes such as the Harti and Mareexaan, among many others. Parker looked carefully at the background of Omar's video.

"His first mistake." The background showed a building

and palm trees. Intelligence would scan every detail and soon figure out exactly where the video was taken.

There were also banana trees lined up in a manner that suggested they had all been planted. The growth of the trees suggested a certain time period. The crumbled wall was another clue.

My guess is that this was near a river.

He would be correct. And with a river, the possible locations would be reduced again. He could cross-check Al Shabaab with its strongholds. There would be few that would be on a river. The process of elimination had begun.

"God, this place should be red with blood." The Land of Punt went back over 11,000 years. Cave paintings had been dated as far back as 9,000 years before Christ. It had a continuous history of bloodshed for power. Brothers killing brothers for the throne.

The Marines will never be finished with war, he thought as he went through the news stories for hours. He read of a MSOT raid into the Kenyan village of Wajir, near its border with Somalia. The Special Operations Team had flown through the night, hit the target, and pulled out without casualties. They recovered over a hundred pounds of plastic explosives.

Parker continued to read without stopping. Marines were in Gabon and Uganda. The continent was on fire.

"Excuse me, but we have to close."

Parker looked up to see the librarian standing at the doorway to the computer room.

"Oh, I am sorry." He glanced at the row of windows on the other side of the room to see that it was dark outside.

"Do you need to finish up anything?"

He remembered her from the first time he had wandered into the branch of the Fulton County Library after his first visit to the bank just down the street. She showed a kind heart. He remembered the photograph of her daughter on her desk just behind the counter. It was a college graduation picture.

Parker always scanned for details. It had saved his life in an operation more than once. He realized now that the use of the same library had been a mistake. He had become conscious of the trail he left, like every human being leaves a trail, like Omar left a trail, and how someone searching would ask her of the stranger who used the library. She would take the person to the computer and, with that, they would know what was in William Parker's mind.

"No, thanks."

She would only see him once again.

CHAPTER TWENTY-TWO

"**W**ake up!"

Omar felt the kick of a sandal. He was curled up on a rug in the corner of the house in Mogadishu. He slept with his AK-47 pulled into his chest. It still didn't have any ammunition. The gun barrel was warm from being held close to his body. He slept in the same green fatigues that Musa had given to him. He had become used to living in his checkered black-and-white turban.

"Why are you here, *Amriiki*?"

The room was crowded with nearly a dozen fellow soldiers. Only the American had the magazine with no bullets.

"To come to jihad." Omar stretched his arms as they all started to move about. "It is the will of Allah."

"The *Amriiki* is like that!" The little man laughed as he spoke to his comrades. "He has no people."

It seemed that what drove the fighters was a battle of clans as much as a cause.

"Do you have people?" the man asked.

"Yes, I am Syrian. I am of the Banu Najjaad. It was a tribe of people now in Syria," Omar answered.

"I have heard of them." It was clear that the little man was lying.

"I am the son of Salim, who was son of Mustafaa. . . ." He began to rattle off his lineage. It was full of half-truths but it did not matter. Omar's point was to impress. As the old men wore long beards, the lineage spoke of the fighter.

"And *al-Amriiki*?" the elf of a man asked.

"Yes, and *al-Kanadi*, and *al-Somali*," Omar boasted.

They all laughed when they heard the last list. He was American, and Canadian, and Somali.

"Yes, your people are fighters."

"They are."

"Maybe it is true then. You have come to our land to do jihad."

"I will see the face of Allah."

The other soldier, no older than Omar, had a look of amazement on his face.

He was a member of the "Army of the Youth." Al Shabaab was a mixture of Somalis and Afghans and foreign fighters. It fought for the establishment of Sharia law, waging war against the enemies of Islam. Sometimes their enemies were defined as members of another clan within Somalia.

"You are the one who killed the Americans in Mobile?"

"Yes." Omar was proud of his credentials.

"Where is Mobile?"

"In the South."

"How far to New York?" the other soldier asked.

"Maybe a thousand miles?"

"Let us go!" Another soldier came into the room. He carried his rifle strapped over his shoulder and had the swagger of having served in combat. He was their new drill instructor. "You are all stupid. You will run when the first helicopter comes down."

"Sleep is not needed," he barked at them. Omar soon learned that he was right. Sleep was a luxury not provided in Somalia. He had his plastic bag, which he stuffed with his few clothes, and also inside was another, smaller, green bag full of corn. It would serve as his pillow. He learned quickly to sleep in the corners of rooms, to sleep while sitting up in the front seat of a truck, or while rocking back and forth in the bed of a truck. Sleep and food were to become luxuries.

They crowded outside through a tight hallway to an awaiting pickup truck. Musa stopped him as he came through the front door and pulled him aside.

"I have something for you." Musa handed him two round cardboard-like containers. Each had some weight to it. "Look at them."

Omar tore the tape off to find a brand-new Russian hand grenade within the tube. He pulled the tape off the other and another grenade came out.

"And this is also for you." Musa dropped a dozen bright, brass rounds of ammunition for the AK-47 into Omar's cupped hands.

Omar recalled receiving a .22 caliber rifle one Christmas from his mother's father. His father became outraged later when he found out that gifts had been given on the Christian holiday. His grandfather didn't care.

"I will keep this at my house for you to use." He showed Omar the closet where the rifle was kept. He put a box of bullets on the shelf just high enough that it would take an intentional effort on the grandson's part to get to them. "Any time you want to use it, just let me know." Omar loved his grandfather although the two were poles apart. His grandfather loved Pabst Blue Ribbon and his Camel "smokes" as he called them. Often, he would tell the boy to go and get his pack. He eventually died of lung cancer.

Omar beamed at both gifts. He felt the weight of the hand grenades as he put one into each of the pockets of his green jacket. He stuck the bullets into his right pocket as well as on top of one of the grenades.

"Faud is very pleased with you. Your broadcasts have been a success."

"Allah be praised."

"But you must learn how to be a fighter!"

Omar was ready to learn the trade.

"I will not see you for some time. We will get you to a computer once in a while to send other videos. But they must see you are truly on your jihad!"

The truck was fully loaded. Omar had to feel for an open spot in the bed near the cab. They all sat on crates with their legs hung over the sides. They moved in the darkness without lights so as to get outside the city without being spotted. He could tell that they were moving both south and inland. A sign said AFGOOYE.

The driver drove as fast as he could until they came to a rough part of the road. Omar soon fell back to sleep with his neck braced up against the back glass of the cab. Once, his head slammed against the glass, causing his ear to ring. He looked up to see several soldiers standing beside the road behind a burned-out shell of a truck. He could hear them chatter at each other, both the truck driver and the leader of the guard post, and realized from the broken words that they were seeking payment to pass. The driver laughed at the head guard and then drove on. The tollbooth was for those less armed than the well-gunned truck.

The road required the truck to often swing hard to

the left or right to pass craters left by the American bombers. In the darkness, Omar heard a buzzing noise above and in the distance.

"What is that?"

Another soldier sitting next to him spoke some English.

"Predator."

The aircraft that he had seen only a short time before in Djibouti was now on the hunt for him.

The truck traveled across the countryside at its slow pace until midday. It would wander off the road, and as it did, the truck would brush by the trees and growth that choked off the narrow route. The men on one side or the other would let out moans when the truck went too far off the road. Many did not have pants or shoes. Most wore sandals and long, olive-colored cotton shorts, and the thorns would tear up their legs.

There was no water to be had. A dark cloud passed by and as it did rain started to fall. Omar took one of his plastic bags and cupped it over his hands trying to catch the droplets. After a while, enough water accumulated in the plastic bag that he drank a mouthful.

They often ran into large pools of water and mud that covered the entire width of the road. Some were so deep that the men all got out, with the red-tinted water up to their waists, and pushed the truck forward. One time the pool consumed so much of the roadway that they all got out, pulled two axes from the cab, and cut a path through the brush, thorns, and trees so as to bypass the water. Another time, the river was so flooded that they dragged logs from a mile away and lashed them to the sides of the truck to better help it float across. Transportation was a constant battle.

The journey took them through the backcountry and then towards the ocean. Finally, at a house near the coastal town of Baraawe, the truck came to a stop. They were close enough to the ocean that if they were all silent, they could hear the waves in the background.

Praised be Allah. Omar had had little to drink and eat. He felt his jacket to make sure that the hand grenades were still there. The bullets were also in his pocket.

A tall Somali came out from the house.

"I am your trainer." The man looked as if he were not inclined to be a friend. "Your fellow soldiers are inside. Go find yourself a place."

Omar went into the main room only to find it filled with men leaning up against all of the walls. He passed to another room.

"Allah be praised." Omar saw in the corner an empty space, and next to the space was another white man. "I know you from Toronto!"

"Yes, brother!"

They hugged and patted each other on the back. The man was the son of one of his customers on the milk route. He was originally from Minneapolis. They always had given him a small tip when the Canadian weather was at its worst.

"So, I have heard of you." The fellow American sat down, moving his bag to make space for Omar.

"Tell me all." Omar put his sack up against the wall.

"My father says you are famous. You have become the face of Al Shabaab."

"It is the path that Allah has directed me to. So how is your family?"

"Do you recall the young man that lived in the hallway with us?"

"Yes. The skinny one with the scar on his face."

"He has become martyred."

"Oh?" Omar had heard the phrase more and more often as he had traveled with his fellow soldiers to Baraawe.

"He blew up a jeep full of Americans. They were near the border with Ethiopia."

"What?"

"They were military advisors. CIA."

When in doubt, any American killed was a member of the CIA.

"He will see the face of Allah." Omar slid his jacket pockets to the side so as to not sit on the grenades. "I am so thirsty."

"Don't complain. No complaints to the tall one. Our trainer is far worse to those who complain. He will tell you to steal a boat and go back to the West."

Omar put the rifle on his lap. He pulled the magazine out and for the first time had the chance to load the magazine.

"You have bullets?"

"Yes."

"Here, give me half of them and I will let you have half of my milk." The fellow American pulled out a plastic jug.

"Milk?"

"Fresh from the market!"

Omar gave him five rounds and drank the warm camel's milk from the jug. It had an oily taste to it as if the jug had been used before to carry something else. He didn't care. It hurt him to stop drinking at just half of the jug.

"What are those women doing?" Omar watched as half a dozen women, both girls and older women, climbed the stairway of the building. It was made of thick clay walls, with large openings for doors and windows, and had a central stairway to a second floor. From the second floor, a third stairway went to a partially covered roof.

"If the Americans see women, the Predators will not strike."

"Really?" Omar was learning the lessons of war.

"If it is an MSF camp, they will leave it alone." The man took the jug back and drank from it. "So, we put up flags and sometimes tents."

"MSF."

"Doctors Without Borders. A cover for the CIA." The American didn't know what he was talking about. MSF tried to stay as far away from governments as possible. But for Al Shabaab it didn't matter. If the soldiers believed it was a CIA plot, then it was a CIA plot.

"Tomorrow we go back to the beach."

"The beach?" Omar didn't understand.

"The trainer loves to run us through the beach."

"Through?"

"Yes, you will see."

The American from Minneapolis was right.

The trainer was sadistic. He had a thin stick, like a whip, which he used to slap the new ones. Often he would hit them across the face, causing welts to rise. The theory was universal. Boot camp would be so miserable that combat would seem to be a vacation. He wanted to see who would run when the first shot was fired. And if they ran, it was better to remove them now.

"Dig."

He pointed his stick to a soft sandy part of the beach. The recruits were lined up in a row and each dug, with his hands, a hole the shape of a burial plot. The sand burned Omar as he dug and dug.

"Now get in."

Each climbed into his hole lying down on his back.

The trainer then walked from hole to hole, putting his sandaled foot on each trainee's stomach. If the recruit let out a yelp, he struck him across the face with his stick. Later, he brought them into an alley where he had broken bottles into fine shards of glass.

"Now, do push-ups!"

Their hands bled and they cried out in pain.

"No complaints!"

"This is stupid," Omar mumbled. He knew better than to speak so that the words could be heard.

The day was brutal. At noon, they were allowed to drink water from a twenty-liter jug. It had a red tint to it. Omar swallowed the water in large gulps without caring about the color. The water, like the American's camel milk, had the taste and feel of oil residue. It seemed that the jugs had also been used for cooking oil. The water was far from clean. Omar quickly became sick and had to be carried by two of the recruits back to the house.

He dragged himself outside to the thorny bushes nearby and shook while everything passed through him. While huddled on the ground in the fetal position, Omar thought of the winters back in Toronto. It was such an opposite world.

The next day, the local commander visited the encampment. He was seen shaking his fist at the trainer. Two others with him found Omar huddled in the corner. They gave him bottled water to drink and bananas.

"You are to go to Jilib tonight." The commander smiled as he spoke. His words were in broken English. "We need more YouTubes."

Omar swallowed the last of the banana as he drank from the bottle of water.

His stomach was fragile but he would survive. He was ready for combat.

"You are the face of Al Shabaab. Godane thinks well of you."

The truck left after midnight. It took all of the night to pass through the potholed roads filled with puddles of dirty red water. Near dawn, they crossed open flatlands dotted with cattle.

Jilib stood on the banks of the Jubba River. Mango trees, and the more recent rains, caused the city to look both green and very tropical. Omar looked at his surroundings from the truck bed with his back braced by his plastic sack. He felt the clip in the rifle and knew that the weapon was now capable of firing. They had taught him at the training encampment how to shoot in short bursts while always taking aim.

They reached a building near the riverbank. The courtyard was lined with banana trees and papaya. He heard a noise in the top of the banana tree and saw a monkey jump from one branch to another.

If I could only show Fartuun!

Omar realized that much time had passed since he last talked to her. He wasn't worried about his wife so much as the upcoming birth of the child. His possible new son could change much.

I must get a phone.

The same commander from Baraawe was standing at the gate to the house. It seemed that he had returned by another vehicle sooner than Omar's truck.

"*Al-salamu alaykum!*"

"*Wa alaykum s-salam!*"

"We have a computer. It has been some time since your last video and Faud thinks it important that you send another message to the world."

"Gladly." Omar would talk of the training and the

dedication of his fellow warriors. "I will call Americans to the fight."

"Yes, and it will cause money to come to our war." It was clear that the leadership of Al Shabaab understood, from Faud to the commanders, that the *Amriiki* had become their poster child. He had become the international face of their army.

"May I call my wife?"

"Yes, of course. We will get you a phone."

Omar thought for a moment. NSA would certainly be listening in, but did it really matter? He would never see his mother again in Mobile nor his family in Toronto. He had little chance of seeing his wife again. By now, he knew that the FBI had been to everyplace he had ever lived, several times. Only in Somalia had they not caught up with him.

"How was training?"

"We need better food and more ammunition. I have yet to fire my rifle."

Omar felt comfortable making the complaints with his new status as the face of the army.

"Yes, of course, immediately."

Omar had made his first mistake in Somalia.

The commander kept his word.

Later that evening a guard showed up with a cell phone. Omar tried to use it from the house near the river but could not keep the signal. He walked up to the roof and tried again to call his wife in Egypt, but the signal continued to bounce out. Omar saw an abandoned, three-story shell of what must have once been a rich man's mansion farther down the riverbank, just to the west of the house he was in. The abandoned mansion had probably been built by an Englishman who grew sugarcane when the area was under the British Empire's control. It was a long walk, but not impossible, and it had been so long since he had heard her voice.

Omar put his rifle over his shoulder and checked for his two hand grenades in each of his pockets, as if that provided additional security. He walked out of the compound and headed up the street towards the tall house.

After some walking he arrived at the mansion. He entered and, climbing what was left of the staircase, Omar reached the top floor, went out on the roof, and tried his call again. The phone rang and he heard her voice.

The conversation did not go well.

"Hello, my wife!"

He encouraged her to come to Somalia and support the fight. Her refusal to come was a disrespect, and violated Sharia law; however, it was still good to hear a voice he recognized.

"I have been through some training and am ready for battle."

He tried to persuade her by telling her of her grandmother in Mogadishu.

"The people are so friendly. They truly care about you."

He told her of the monkeys and the beauty of Jilib. He told her of how green and tropical southern Somalia was and the bravery of his fellow jihadists. It was to no avail.

She told him that she was returning to Canada.

"My child needs to be born in Toronto." She told him that she wanted a divorce.

Omar was alone on the roof. He finally gave up. If Allah meant that he would never see his child, so be it. He wanted to call Mobile but decided that it could only cause more trouble. There could be no doubt that his parents' telephone was on the closely monitored list. He didn't care about what they heard from him, other than possibly the tracking of the signal to Jilib, but it did matter that the FBI would bother his mother.

Omar did miss his mother. He thought of her and began to cry. He would have a child that she would never see. And it was likely that he would never see her again as well.

Finally, as he wiped his face with his sleeve, he started to head towards the stairway down from the roof.

"Allah has sent me on this journey. I must continue and be strong."

Omar looked out over the houses, trying to get his bearings. He saw the river and the street that paralleled the river. He followed the line of houses and saw what he thought was where the commander's house was.

Then it caught his eye.

A block away from the commander's house there was another, larger building with openings on the sides like an airplane hangar. It had light brown tarps, similar in color to the surrounding buildings, that hung across the opening. It could only be seen from the vantage point of the roof of the abandoned building, and only by someone searching, like Omar was. It took an intentional look on Omar's part to notice the hangar-shaped building at all.

"Odd." He spoke the word as he stepped towards the edge of the roof.

The sun was starting to set so Omar stopped looking at the odd building and concentrated more on his feet, as bombing had damaged the stairs and he had to move more like a goat than a human. He was out of breath when he reached the bottom.

Omar stopped at the side road that led to the odd building. From the alleyway it was impossible to tell more about the structure.

"I wonder," he said to himself as he decided to take a side trip. The building could not have been more than a block from where he was staying. Plus, he was an armed warrior. Omar turned up the alley and walked less than a few yards.

"Who are you?"

Two guards came out of a side street. Both put their rifles directly in his face.

One of the guards pulled back the slide and chambered a round.

"I am Omar. I am with the commander."

The two guards looked far different from the other soldiers he had served with. One of them swung the butt of his rifle, connecting with the side of Omar's head. The blow knocked Omar to the ground. He started to get up but the other guard slammed his rifle into the center of his back. He tried to suck in air as the red dust clung to his face. He could feel the rifle barrel jammed into the back of his head.

"I am Omar. I am the *Amriiki*."

It was a dangerous thing to have said.

His face was buried in the dirt for what seemed an eternity. Finally, he saw the boots of a soldier. He had only known the commander as one who wore boots.

"You are very lucky."

He pulled Omar up from the dirt, forcing him to his knees.

"You should not wander off. There are lions in our country. They are known to even walk in the streets of Jilib." Omar knew the commander was telling the truth. He had already heard the stories of men who had gone into the bush at night to use the latrine and had never returned. There were children from Jilib who disappeared on cloudy nights.

"Why did you go down that alley?"

"I got lost. I was using the old house on the river to make the call." He pointed to the shell of the mansion near the river. Omar's life was saved by the lie. He was important, but the other building held something far more important to Faud.

CHAPTER TWENTY-THREE

The old man struggled in his run back to his village of Ferfer. His legs were rubbery and he stopped often to catch his breath. He was running away from where the sun sat in the sky, and trying to get word back before dark. As he approached the village, two women with their children looked up and stared at him crossing the rutted road that led up past the riverbed. They were carrying large plastic jugs balanced on top of their heads as they walked back from the river with water.

"Oh, ya!" He mumbled the words. "Oh, ya!"

The women stopped and soon the villagers started to gather around as he caught his breath while leaning against a wall. He started up again and moved towards the MSF encampment. The guard that had watch over the station saw him run up the hill alone and knew that there had been trouble.

The old man told of the capture of the two young doctors and Mataa. He jumbled his words.

"They let me go. They shot at me as I was running."

The old man's life was spared by bad aim.

"We must go to the army station." The guard pointed

to the other side of Ferfer. Just beyond the center of the town, the Ethiopian Army had a small outpost of soldiers. "We will get word out."

The director at MSF called the World Health Organization's operation center. They had the difficult job of relaying the news on to Atlanta.

"Dr. Stewart?"

"Yes."

"We have a serious problem."

The call had awakened Paul Stewart in his home in Buckhead, a suburb of Atlanta. Once his daughter had told him of the decision to go to Africa, Stewart had moved the telephone from the kitchen to the night table next to his bed.

"Is it the Neisseria meningitidis?" It was the first time in his life that he hoped a deadly disease was the reason for the call.

"What?" It seemed that the WHO had not gotten word of the illness of the child near Ferfer. "We have a report of a meningitis outbreak in Yemen. Is that what you are talking about?"

"No." He paused. "Why were you calling?"

"Two doctors from an MSF team were captured today by some soldiers near Ferfer, on the border of Somalia. We understand that one of them may be your daughter."

"Yes." He felt a wave of fear and nausea. It was a call he had thought of as his worst nightmare. He couldn't get any other words out.

CHAPTER TWENTY-FOUR

"Do we trust him?"

Abo Musa Mombasa had asked the important question. He was in charge of internal security. Faud, however, outranked Musa.

"Godane doesn't." Faud looked into space. "But Godane doesn't always understand how we get our money."

Faud had called together a meeting of several of the leaders of Al Shabaab.

"Godane doesn't trust any of us, does he?" It was a dangerous comment that could only come from one of the few people who maintained the link between Al Shabaab and Al Qaeda.

Al Shabaab had kept control over southern and central Somalia, but at a price. Most of Faud's friends from the earlier wars were now martyrs.

A meeting of the leadership was rare, since their gathering together increased the risk of a Predator strike. No cell phones were used to set it up. Spies were known to be everywhere.

"He has been the reason why we have already gotten substantial money from both Egypt and Saudi Arabia." Muhammad Al Faud studied the faces of each of the men in the room. "You know what that money has meant. We have received the gift from our brothers in Iran that can change everything. Our boats can be more courageous in reaching out to the ships that pass our land. And with the capture of more freighters, it will mean even more money."

"Yes, brother." Musa did not say the "but" that was in his head

"We need to get him into combat quickly." Musa came up with the idea. "If he braves a helicopter attack or some machine gun fire, we will know what he is made of."

"But if he is killed, we lose someone who has shaken the West seriously."

Faud pondered the thought. "And other wars are pulling away our Western brothers from us."

Faud was playing a chess game in his mind. Omar was like an RPG. It had great value until it was shot. Likewise, word that Omar had complained about the lack of food and ammunition was heard, and remembered.

"It is settled. He will join the fight in Garbaharey." Faud had fought in the battle of Gedo in the west, near the Kenyan and Ethiopian borders. It was a damaged city where the only thing constant was killing.

Omar was excited, like a child at Christmas, with the news that he was going to war.

"I will fight like no other!" he said to Faud. "You will see."

The truck left immediately. He had more room than before; however, as the truck moved out of town and towards the northwest, it soon picked up some other soldiers heading towards the front. These fighters all had the same green uniforms with sandals, but now he was seeing the men outfitted with brown vests that carried magazines of ammunition.

"A vest?"

"I have an extra one." The driver was a happy sort who shared everything. He tossed a brown vest to Omar.

He looked at it. Two of the pockets had magazines in them. The rifle clips were empty. The fourth pocket was torn. It had a dark brown tint to the canvas.

He felt the cloth. It was stiff. And then he pulled his hand back.

"Blood!"

The war was coming closer by the minute.

At a crossroad just north of Jilib the pickup truck stopped at another sentry post. Like the others, it was basically a stack of blocks behind the burned-out shell of a car. He could see the tops of the heads wrapped in the black headbands that were the uniform of his fellow troops, along with the guns they carried. In the beginning, the guns were unnerving. Now, however, he had become used to them; it was like passing dangerous animals in the zoo.

Just behind the guards he could see another group of soldiers with the same black headbands. One was taller than the rest.

"Hello!"

Omar heard the familiar voice of his friend from Minneapolis and Toronto.

"Brother."

The guards stared at the two white men hugging each other.

"Come, sit next to me." Omar had his plastic bag stuffed in the corner, and the two huddled together while others jammed into the truck bed. "We will ride together to war!"

"We have ammunition!" the driver yelled out to everyone as he came back to the truck from the guard post.

Omar watched as one of the soldiers put two large green cans into the bed of the truck.

"And this!" The driver held up a rocket-propelled grenade launcher.

"Let me see it." Omar felt the weight of the weapon as he lifted it up in the air. The nose was top heavy with the weight of the grenade. "How does it work?"

"Easy. Aim and squeeze." The driver pointed to the trigger.

Omar waved the weapon around, acting as if he was shooting at an imaginary target.

"Have you been to the front?" the driver asked as he lifted the nose of the RPG so Omar wouldn't be aiming it at the others.

"No."

"If you hear a helicopter you must run into the bush."

It would not be the last time that Omar would hear of the helicopters used by the Kenyans and Ethiopians in war.

CHAPTER TWENTY-FIVE

I must survive.

The stubbornness she had inherited from her father gave Karen a chance.

The captors held their guns to their chests yelling as if they were more frightened than the prisoners. There were four of them with the little white pickup truck. It had one tire that was the wrong size, causing the truck to be on a slant. One of the guards pointed for them to sit down. She tried to not make eye contact and pulled her scarf further over her head and face. Her knees hurt as she held her hands above her head.

"Stay easy," Peter whispered to her.

The guard heard him say something and went over and struck him with the butt of the rifle. Peter rubbed the blood from his cheek but continued to look down.

It soon became clear who the leader was. He seemed to be barely in his twenties, skinny, with bony knees that stood out with his ragged, torn shorts. He would yell at the others and move his hands in a frantic shake.

Finally, they pushed the old man aside and told him to go. It seemed a decision of necessity. She would learn later that the little food they had meant that an extra person was a burden that could not be fed. The burden needed to be dismissed if it was little threat and shot if it was more. Because of a small silver cross Mataa wore on a necklace, the guards realized he was a Christian. One of the guards pulled out a machete and was ready to use it when they squabbled for some time and he put it down.

Karen watched the old man trying to move as fast as he could despite his age and tired legs. As he reached the top of the hill, the youngest one fired his AK-47 with what seemed to be a well-aimed shot. Without meaning to, she screamed, causing the others to turn towards her. She could see the bullet kick up some dirt near the rock by the old man. He never looked back. He only ran faster and then finally disappeared. Her scream had saved him from a second shot.

As the old man disappeared over the horizon she thought about how much she wanted to run and catch up to him.

If both Peter and I ran in two different directions one of us would have a chance.

But she hesitated and Mataa shook like a leaf.

The young one ran over to her yelling, shaking his fist, and then raised his rifle up ready to strike. But the leader intervened, putting his arm between the young one and Karen. She barely spoke the language but got the sense that the leader was more concerned for his newfound goods than feeling any sympathy for the captives.

A third man, with a pockmarked face, drove the truck and turned it around while the three prisoners knelt by the rutted road. Both she and Peter remained still.

The driver yelled as the smaller wheel got stuck in a rut, and the two guards came over and pushed. The leader kept watch over the captives. The truck rocked back and forth and then jerked out of the furrow. It turned towards the village of the dead.

"They are dead. A disease." She struggled to speak. It was hard to both breathe and say anything.

"You say nothing." The leader spoke English. He turned to the young one, who pulled a length of cord from the cab of the truck. He tied the hands of Karen and Peter, on separate ropes, to the back tailgate. Mataa's hands he wrapped tightly with the cord, but left him free from the tailgate. It was as if they cared little whether Mataa made the journey. In fact, it seemed that they hoped Mataa would run and be shot. They then sat on the back end as the truck started to move towards the east. It meant that they would all pass through the village of the dead.

"See, lady." The leader pointed to the huts. The village was silent. "They won't follow."

He was right.

The old man would bring news of the capture of the two Western doctors. He would also tell Ferfer of the village of death. The Ethiopians would hesitate to follow the trail.

They continued on well past midnight, heading south and then east. She overheard them talking. They were determined to avoid the larger town of Beledweyne. They were set on keeping on the move; their bounty, like two sacks of gold, in tow.

Finally, sometime after midnight, they stopped at a grove of trees near the Shebelle River. She could see that the road went straight into the water, as if it had been used in the dry months without restriction. Now, the crossing took more of a plan.

Karen could tell, after listening to the conversations between the men, that the leader was called Xasan. He had yellowed fingernails, which were broken, and dirt was jammed underneath.

"We are thirsty," Peter bravely spoke up.

"There is a river." Xasan pointed to the water. It ran red like all of the mud puddles they had passed.

The guards let them go down to the water's edge.

"Don't drink," Peter whispered. "Don't drink." He repeated the whisper.

She cupped the cool water and poured it over face.

"God, I want to drink." Her self-control gave her the only chance to survive.

As they stood on the river's edge, Xasan suddenly stopped. He pointed to the shore just a few yards from Karen. He silently waved his arm for her to move towards him. The moon's light glimmered on the surface with one beacon of light extending in a straight line like a flashlight. She saw something move across the river's surface.

"Mamba." Xasan pointed to the snake as it moved back into the reeds next to the water's edge.

Oh, God. She tried to control her breathing again. The land was as terrifying as these people. Hunger and thirst and death.

The young guard seemed the most frightened.

He moved around the road looking back and forth with his rifle pointed into the darkness. He constantly pulled it up to his shoulder ready to fire. He yelled out a warning in his language, as if the shouting would scare off the mamba.

The snake had reason to be feared. Karen recalled the briefing she had been given before coming to Ferfer.

"Avoid the mamba! It will run from you if you let it. But if you corner it, it will come after you and you cannot avoid its strike!" the instructor had told her.

"But how do we treat someone if they come to the refugee camp with a mamba bite?" she naively asked.

"Don't worry. He will never make it to the camp." The instructor was right. The victim would be dead before the snake released its bite. The venom was considered to be the most deadly in the world.

They fear mambas but not Neisseria meningitidis? She thought of how strange the dichotomy. With a mamba at least one had a chance. Given an escape route, the snake would run. There was no such option with the meningitis.

Xasan yelled at him again. And then things became quiet again.

They all lay down at the base of a tree with Xasan and the young one on the other side of their prisoners. The driver had the luxury of sleeping in the cab of the truck, which was parked under the branches. The fourth guard had broken his leg sometime in the past. It was deformed and he dragged it as he walked. He slept in the bed of the truck.

It seemed that the captors were all of the same family or at least of the same clan. They all had large, curved noses that seemed to reflect a common inheritance.

"You not tied up." Xasan untied both of them as Karen and Peter huddled together next to each other. "Nowhere to go." He left Mataa tied up.

The two understood. It seemed that all of the bushes were full of thorns and any escape would be, without a weapon, as deadly as staying with their captors. Mataa stood the best chance at escape but they seemed to care little about him.

"My backpack."

One of the guards had tossed it into the back of the truck.

"It has a net. Can we have the net?" She had remembered to always carry a net with her in the bottom of the sack.

"You afraid of sick?"

"Yes." She didn't hesitate. "We are doctors."

"You are doctors?" Xasan asked.

"Yes, we don't come here to fight."

"Where were you when my son died of malaria?"

"I am sorry. If I could, I would have helped."

He didn't seem to care.

"Here, here is your backpack."

She lay down next to the tree and Peter. She reached deep inside the backpack and felt for the mosquito net.

"We will have to share," she whispered.

Fortunately, both she and Peter wore boots. They huddled close together as they wrapped as much of their upper bodies as they could with the net. Her scarf also helped protect her from the constant buzzing that came from being so close to the water's edge. She waited for all to quiet down. She nudged Peter and handed him a bottle of water she found in her pack.

"You first." He pushed it back.

She drank from the warm water, trying to stop at the halfway point. It seemed more brutal to stop without emptying it than to not drink from it at all.

Karen handed the half-filled bottle back to him. He finished the bottle in what seemed to be one gulp.

"Here, save this."

She put the empty bottle back into the backpack. Only a day before, a plastic bottle meant nothing. Now, anything had to be saved as it might have some other use later.

"I also have this." She had half a pack of chewing gum; she had forgotten it was at the bottom. They split the four pieces and ate one each. She chewed on it until finally the exhaustion and fear took over. She wadded up the backpack and used it as a rough pillow. She took her scarf off and balled it up into as tight a wad as she could manage, and then she buried her face into the center and started to sob in as muffled a cry as she could manage. The silk became wet and she immediately thought how its dampness might attract more mosquitoes. The buzz was a continuous hum circling around her head. The smell of the plastic gloves from the visit to the sick village still lingered on her fingers. It brought back her thoughts of that horror as well.

"We will make it," Peter whispered to her. "Don't let anything else get into your brain."

If only she could believe it to be true.

CHAPTER TWENTY-SIX

Several thousands of miles away, and some many hours later, Skip Nease held his watch up close to his eyes. He pushed the button causing the green glare to illuminate the dial.

Zero three zero one. They are late.

He pulled his hat down so the brim would be just above his eyes. Nease lifted the night vision goggles and scanned the horizon. A farm building's fluorescent light some ten miles away gave off a glare that lit up the goggles. He turned them away from the light and scanned down into the mud village below the monitor's bench. Nothing was moving in the complete darkness.

Nease looked to his left along the bench where his other monitors sat, as they also were scanning the simulated village. On the far end, one monitor had a poncholike blanket over his head that also covered his laptop.

"Good. Can't see him," Nease whispered to himself.

"Boss?" His friend leaned over to him.

"Nothing."

They continued to wait in the darkness. It was a perfect night to simulate what they wanted to do. The moon was hidden behind a total cover of clouds from a front that had been moving in all day. Nease had confirmed the weather was a "go" to Camp Lejeune midafternoon.

The last monitor on the far end wore a headset that was tied to a radio. There should have been no traffic. In the airspace of Georgia the aircraft had to report in, unlike during combat, until they made their final turn to the target.

Nease continued to wait, growing more uncomfortable as he did so.

My damn back! He had made too many jumps fully loaded with combat gear. The drop of over an extra hundred pounds of water, food and, most important, ammunition, was only a problem over the last ten feet. He was one of the few who could claim a combat drop that came only once in Iraq and Afghanistan. Helicopter drops and fast ropes were common, but the parachute drop was rare. However, it had come at a price to his body.

Damn foot. His right foot had started to go numb whenever he sat on a hard surface for too long. He stood up for a moment. Standing always helped, and soon the leg and foot came back to life.

The others looked at him but didn't say anything. They knew he could be grumpy.

Nease sat back down and lifted the NVGs again to his eyes.

They have come a long way. He had bought these at a local gun store and was impressed. They lit up the darkness with a clear glow that helped him make out each of the T-20 targets behind the walls.

If we had these back in the day. He remembered the ones in Panama that were classified as top-secret gear, twice as bulky, with batteries that lasted for two or three nights at best.

A dull "whoop" caused the forest to become silent. It was followed by another sound that echoed the first. He scanned the night horizon for any signs of movement but saw nothing.

Nease sat up in the chair and as he did, his head rose above the embankment. His face felt the slightest of breezes from across the village. He waited a moment. It became silent again.

They have pulled it off. He had to admit that he was impressed by the MV-22's ability to stay quiet. As an Army Ranger, he wasn't a fan of the tilt-rotor aircraft that the Marines had been using. It had speed, but he preferred the quiet Blackhawks that he had been trained on for years. The Blackhawks didn't have the range or the speed of the Ospreys but they were not fragile. The helicopters could take multiple rounds of green tracers and keep on moving. It was an oddity of war that Soviet ammunition had a different color for their tracer rounds than American ammunition. They always knew who the bad guys were.

Nease waited and felt the tension grow. It was a dangerous silence. It was the type of silence he enjoyed.

The next sound was the silent thump of a round from an M4 rifle. He knew the quiet noise of each and every particular weapon that both the Marines and Rangers used. He turned his NVGs to the left and saw the train of men stepping through each doorway and the slight flicker of a spark as the round hit the target. It was, to Nease, a work of beauty. The Marines moved, shot, and moved again. These were live rounds and each bullet meant something. The village was made for live rounds.

It was the distance that caused the Marine Special Operations Command to want to visit the farm. It required the Ospreys to leave New River in North Carolina and make the run, with refueling, across South Carolina and most of Georgia. It was as close as they could come to simulating the hit on an embassy or a village in mid-Africa from a base like Djibouti.

Nease had hoped to see the aircraft and meet Mar-SOC Team 8132, but he knew better. They would be back in North Carolina before first light. It was important that the operation came as close as possible to the real thing. No one lingered to discuss what happened. His monitor would download the target-hit value and send it on to the MarSOC team back at Lejeune.

"In and out," he said to himself. The mission went as planned. "In and out."

"It went well." The Marine lieutenant colonel was bent over speaking to the young officer sitting in the sling seat of the MV-22.

"Yes, sir." He had his M4 pointed to the floor, or deck, of the aircraft. He had to pull up his earphone to hear what was said.

"Less than ten minutes."

Ten minutes or less had been the goal. The mission was to make the raid and cover the village from one end to the next. The officer had a printout of the satellite shot that had been distributed to the Marines on both teams and both aircraft. He gave a thumbs-up to his boss.

The flight back to Lejeune was in near total darkness. The huge engines that powered the MV-22 were as long as a small car. It was intimidating to stand near the propeller of one. It gave a sense of the force required for a machine to both land like a helicopter and then fly through the air at more than 300 knots. The aircraft was an imposing improvement on technology as long as everything stayed in balance. The cabin was small, and with each Marine fully equipped with his weapon, vest loaded with extra magazines, helmet and radio gear, it was a squeeze. The Marines of Team 8132 made it particularly tight as every one of them, with the exception of the captain, had been linebackers for their high school and college teams.

Captain Abo Tola weighed about as much as the gear he carried; however, he could run each of his fellow soldiers into the ground. His three-mile physical fitness time set records at every Marine base he had been stationed on. If the course was flat, he would turn in something with a twelve in it—such as his best time of 12:58. For three miles, Tola ran four-minute miles.

He had inherited the right to be fast. Captain Tola was born in Ethiopia. His parents applied for citizenship and moved, when he was twelve, from Addis Ababa to Washington, DC. He moved from a small capital to a big one.

"You still running?" the Lieutenant Colonel pulled up a seat next to the Captain.

"Yes, sir." Tola was quiet. He didn't talk much about his track scholarship to the University of Michigan nor how he acquired his citizenship through his years of service with the Marines.

"University of Michigan?"

"Yes, sir. I went there on a track scholarship." He always said less rather than more. In fact, he was a record-breaker in the 800 meters at Michigan. He would scorch the track with times in the 1:40s. "I remember the first time we saw snow. We arrived at the airport in the dead of winter. My mother thought it was sugar!"

The two laughed at the thought of the two cultures crossing. His life now, however, was to defend America, and he was very good at it.

Tola looked straight ahead for a moment at the Marine across from him on the aircraft. The aircraft dropped suddenly as it hit an air pocket. The loose gear lifted up, was suspended for a second, and then fell back down.

"I am told my grandparents were from the Kara tribe," Tola said to the Lieutenant Colonel. He had a very cheerful way about himself, like the Kara tribe was known to be. They were modest people from the village of Kara. More specifically, he was from the village of Labuoko. Tola appreciated that his mother carried him to Addis Ababa where she got a job as a housecleaner for the American embassy. His father worked in a small bank, first as the man who cleaned, and then later, after trust was established, he became a teller.

Tola could remember his people running everywhere. When they got lazy they walked everywhere.

"My tribe is Boston Irish." His boss laughed at his own joke.

It was true, however, that this American world had tribes but that they just didn't call themselves as such.

"Red Sox?"

"Hell, yes."

Tola was a member of a special generation of new Marines. Like all of the services, Tola's language skills and familiarity with the African culture of Ethiopia had become a valuable asset. The Marines' Special-Purpose Air-Ground Task Force had teams in at least half a dozen African nations teaching their government forces modern warfare.

"Where was your last rotation?"

"I was on 14.1." Tola had led a team of Marines to

Takoradi, Ghana, as a part of a training cycle for that country's defense force. The teams and task forces were designated by an odd numbering system, such as Team 8132 and Task Force 14.1. The Marines knew what it meant.

The two sat in the aircraft in the dark feeling the vibration of the engines that came through the structure. Tola looked around in amazement at the rows of wires and boxes that covered the inside wall. The Osprey was a flying computer. The green and yellow glow from the flight deck was the only illumination to be seen.

"Are your men ready for Saturday?"

"Yes, sir." The deployment back to Morón would be his fifth. He was in high demand in Spain, where the Marines African Force was based. The command was called the Special-Purpose Marine Air-Ground Task Force Crisis Response. It was a long name that covered much of the shield painted on the sign in front of the command headquarters in Morón. It meant that they had the responsibility to be the "911" for any action across the continent.

It meant that Tola had the chance to return to his native Ethiopia and its border with Somalia. He would actually return, however, with another runner and Marine who he had yet to meet.

CHAPTER TWENTY-SEVEN

Omar was in a deep sleep in the back of the truck when he first met war. The vehicle slammed to a sudden stop as he looked up to see each of the men scrambling off the truck and into the brush.

"Come on, you fools."

The driver pointed to the sky.

"A helicopter!"

Omar felt the excitement as he grabbed his rifle and plastic bag. No one let go of anything that they wanted to keep in this army.

He slid off the truck onto a sandy road and then followed another soldier to the bush. The thorns snagged his clothes as he pushed by heading for a tree grove on a rise above the road. He kept following the other fighter as he heard in the background a combination of noises from the smaller Kalashnikov 7.62 rounds, the larger 30-millimeter chain gun, and the thud of an explosion. The man stopped in front of him, turned, kneeled down, and fired his AK towards the sky.

I'm not stupid. It is too open here. Omar ran past him trying to avoid the swing of the rifle. He reached the tree, got behind the small trunk like a little boy, and aimed his rifle back towards the others. As he did, he saw movement in the sky above and to his right. A camouflaged gunship was puffing out a trail of smoke. It had a circle on its side of red, black, and white. He aimed his weapon at the moving shape and fired.

Shit! His word of thought went back to Mobile and not the Muslim self of Somalia. He had learned the first lesson of war. Omar had failed to pull the slide back and chamber a round.

It may have been to his good fortune, as the gunship seemed only to have seen his friend in the bush. The whap-whap of 30-millimeter bullets tore up the dirt. Omar saw his friend picked up off the ground and thrown around like a child's doll. He came back to the earth as a limp and loose object.

Omar chambered the round and waited next to the tree. Soon it got deathly quiet. The gunship had moved on.

He stayed motionless for some time but after a short while his knees suddenly felt on fire. He jumped up with his rifle and as he did a round went off. Red ants had covered his legs. He threw the rifle on the ground and jumped around as he slapped his legs to knock the ants off him.

"Allah!" Omar's mind returned to his new life and his new language.

The ants burned. They ruined the high and fear that had accompanied his first brush with both combat and death.

As he walked up to the limp body, Omar saw how the helicopter's rounds of ammunition had plowed a path through the scrub bushes. There were broken limbs everywhere. He saw the shape of the man in the brush lying in a pool of blood that had puddled in the dirt.

"Hey, man," Omar said to him, not expecting a reply. A 30-millimeter round had caught him directly in his torso. The man was nearly severed in half. Omar thought he heard a moan but it was only the man's lungs letting out the last bit of air.

The truck had also caught a rocket to the cab. It was burning in a raging torrent. The men all collected together near the side of the road and watched the fire.

"Where is everyone?" The driver was collecting a head count.

"The one with me from Kismaayo is dead. Praise Allah, he is a martyr. He is looking at the face of Allah as we speak." Omar issued the warrant. No one else was hurt. They all talked in excited voices.

I am so thirsty. Omar thought of the last of the water jugs that was in the truck. As he started to realize just how close death had come, he went from humble to cocky.

"I shot at the Ethiopian!" he said with glee. They all checked his barrel and confirmed that it smelled of burnt graphite and nitro. The gunpowder was on the slide. "I think I hit him."

"It will be Allah's will if they crash. We will take a dull knife to his neck," the driver yelled. "We need to be ready. The front cannot be far now."

They decided that it was necessary to bury their fellow warrior. The truck was still burning and they determined that the dead one needed to be carried to a distance farther than the two trees.

"Not the tree. Ants!" Omar let out a breath as he spoke. The ant bites still burned. He pulled up his pants and rubbed sand onto his skin. The sandpaper-like rub knocked off all the ants but they still had done a good job biting him.

"Were they red or black?" the Minneapolis friend asked.

"Red."

"Oh, they are the worst," the driver spoke up. "We need to bury him in the sun, not under the trees, because the ants will not come out into the sun."

They went to a spot that was halfway between the two trees and started to dig. They used their hands and the butts of their rifles to dig into the dirt. When they got down a foot or two, they carefully moved the body into the hole.

"It is important that we do it this way." The driver had a specific idea of how to bury the body. They laid him in the shallow ditch and said prayers to Allah. Then they carefully collected piles of sticks that they laid over the man. The sticks were covered with what small rocks they could find.

"Are we finished?" Omar asked.

"No, my friend. We need to gather thorns."

The helicopter's 30-millimeter rounds had provided several piles of broken branches. They gathered up a pile and stacked it tightly on the grave. It was a natural barbed wire meant to keep out the predators.

"This will keep the lions and baboons away."

The men again moved to the west but this time with much more care. The RPG survived, so the one with the weapon was assigned to walk behind the others. If shots were fired at them, they didn't want to waste the round on just one single attacker.

"We will stay in groups of two but fifty meters apart."

Omar was gaining respect for the driver. He had a good understanding of combat.

Omar thought of how thirsty he was. There were puddles of water in the potholes. A desperate man had difficulty walking through the puddles, feeling the warm water on his sandaled feet, but not stopping to scoop up a handful of liquid to drink.

They walked for several miles keeping off the main road and expecting anything to appear at any time. They cut through the brush, and the thorns tore at Omar's side. He didn't mind, as the thorns were far less of a fear than an ambush or another helicopter.

As it neared sunset, the driver, who was in the lead, stopped the men with a hand signal. They all knelt down with their rifles raised. They waited, and as they did, Omar could hear the sound of a truck nearby. He felt the hot wooden stock of his rifle.

This time I am ready. He knew that there was a round chambered.

There was movement to the front and then there were voices.

"It is our men!" the driver yelled back. They had caught up to another patrol. The men gathered around a bigger truck that was embedded in mud in the water-logged road.

"Brothers, we need your help," the leader of the group welcomed them as they approached. The few in the other patrol had been pushing the truck, trying to rock it out of the ditch.

"Do you have water?" Omar asked.

The other man looked at him like the strange, white ungrateful sight he was to a Somali fighter. Finally, after staring at Omar and the driver and determining that Omar was legitimate, the leader spoke.

"We do." He pointed to the base of a nearby tree where a tarp covered several boxes. Omar, the driver, and the others pulled back the tarp to see bottled water and cans of food.

"Allah is great!" they all yelled out as they broke open the bottles and began drinking.

"This was left by the retreating Ethiopian cowards," the leader of the second group bragged. "We shot at them and they ran like the cowards they are."

They drank from the water but the leader would not let them open up the cans of biscuits and other food items until the truck had been moved.

"Get in here and help."

"We must do prayers." Omar looked at the setting sun and each turned to prayer. They took a little water from one shared bottle and symbolically washed before praying.

Once prayers had been completed they returned to the task.

"Come, *Amriiki*. Help!"

Omar looked at the mud-covered men and hesitated. Finally, he stepped into the muck and sank nearly up to his knees. The mud felt good on the ant bites. They pushed until darkness and finally freed the truck.

"Tomorrow we chase down the dogs," the driver spoke as they all huddled on the bed of the truck tucked together like sardines with their rifles on their sides.

"Tomorrow." Omar pulled his plastic sack up to the corner of the truck and laid on it. He could hear the sound of helicopters in the distance.

Tomorrow, I kill someone.

CHAPTER TWENTY-EIGHT

The director of the CDC entered his outer office to see Paul Stewart sitting there.

"We need to talk." Stewart hadn't had any sleep since the telephone call.

"I know."

They walked into the inner office and Stewart closed the door behind them.

"There are two problems."

"I learned about your daughter. You know that I will do anything that I can to help." The report had spread across the CDC as fast as a stream of gas being lit by a match. And it was just as hot. A member of the family was caught in crossfire.

"Yes, thank you. Did you see the WHO report?"

"No."

"We have a breakout of meningitis near where Karen was. She was actually investigating it when she was captured." Stewart looked at his hands as he spoke.

"It is the meningitis belt." It was well known by all the infectious disease experts in the world that meningitis thrived in an area that crossed Africa near the equator. It was famed for devastating Mecca several years ago when thousands had made the journey of the Hajj only to die from a raging infection. "Why is this unusual?" the director asked.

"This is a Neisseria meningitidis. We have the bug in the lab."

"In our lab?"

"Yes."

"Oh, shit." The bug being kept in the lab meant that an aggressive reporter could connect the dots whether they should or not. After the scandal of the loose smallpox vials, this would be a body blow. A leak from the CDC would show that the Neisseria meningitidis bacteria was of a new serogroup C meningococcal disease. It was the same hypervirulent strain that appeared in the mountains of Pakistan and that was frozen in the lab on the top floor of the CDC. The problem was that the frozen sample in the CDC predated the outbreak in Pakistan.

"WHO is activating an FMT." Stewart had followed the traffic all night. The World Health Organization was forming a team.

"Like the Ebola outbreak?"

Ebola had struck West Africa as quickly as a mamba snake struck its target. The disease multiplied exponentially by the hour when it broke out.

"Where is this again?"

"Next to the border of Ethiopia and Somalia."

"An exploding pandemic in the middle of a war zone?"

"Yes. Fortunately, it is in a low-population area. But a man reported that Karen and a French doctor with the MSF camp were seized after they had visited a village where an outbreak occurred."

"How many sick were there?"

"None. They were all dead."

"Oh, God." The director sat back in his chair. Stewart could see that he was trying to use his scientific mind to analyze the options. "What of your daughter and the Neisseria?"

"She got all of the shots, but I don't know her odds. It's a lottery ticket." Stewart took his glasses off and rubbed his face with his hand. "With this beast, you could contract it in an emergency room at Emory and be deathly sick in a matter of minutes."

"And the Ethiopians?"

"The minister of health is starting to get things rolling. They are mobilizing their medical teams and the FMS is turning into a major encampment at a place called Ferfer."

"And the military?"

"The Ethiopians are moving their troops into the area."

"What are your thoughts about Karen?"

"I don't know. I really don't know." Stewart sat slumped into the chair. He did have one thought but he wasn't ready to play all of his cards.

"How bad is this bug?"

"There was a breakout in Afghanistan some time ago."

"And?"

"There was one survivor."

"Really?" The director leaned forward in his chair. He was thinking of the antiserum.

Stewart was thinking of something else.

"I may need the help of DOD and the CIA."

"For this, we can do that. For this, we can do just about anything."

"Thank you." Paul Stewart didn't care about being the director of scientific security anymore. He didn't care about his chance of being the director of the CDC. His résumé was finished. All he wanted to do was find Enrico Hernandez of the security section.

CHAPTER TWENTY-NINE

During the night Karen was woken up by a grunting sound that came from deep in the dark. She started to fall asleep when she heard the same grunting sound from the other side of the truck. It was as if the grunts were surrounding their little camp.

Xasan and the other guards stirred when they heard the noise. She could tell that they were on edge. Their voices went from whispers to loud babbling.

The captors pulled down broken branches from the tree they were under and some dried brush and gathered them in a pile between the tree trunk and the truck.

Xasan had a lighter. They poured some gas from a can kept in the truck bed and started a fire. The wood crackled as it began to burn. The smoke rose up to the first limbs of the tree and then was pushed back into them.

Karen pulled her legs up as she looked through the net over her face. Peter did not stir. She watched as the driver came out of the cab and helped. Xasan took a stick from the fire and walked around the circumference of the tree at the edge of the darkness.

"Hey, you!" The guard kicked Peter in his boot.

"Oui?" Peter mumbled as he started to wake up from his sleep.

"Where is your other one?"

Peter and Karen looked to the other side of the tree trunk. Mataa was missing. Peter smiled for a moment.

"I don't know," Peter said in a reassured voice.

"Don't be so cocky, *Amriiki*." Xasan pointed the burning stick at Peter's face.

It didn't matter that Peter was not an American. The comment was a rub in other ways. Doctors Without Borders considered their neutrality very important. Karen knew that the survival of several refugee camps depended upon neutrality.

"What do you mean?" Karen asked.

"Look at the ground." Xasan waved the torch at the spot where the third prisoner had been lying. The ground was dark with a circle that looked black against the sandy dirt. The blood followed a path into the darkness.

"Oh, shit!" Peter gasped.

"What is it?" Karen didn't understand.

"A pride of lions. Did you hear grunting?"

"I'm not sure what I heard. I thought I heard lions roaring but that seemed impossible."

"A lion dragged Mataa away."

Daylight came as a relief to both the captors and the captives.

Karen could feel Peter's body shiver as they fell back asleep under the tree. His body heat passed out through his clothing. He started to mumble in French. She squeezed his arm.

"How are you doing?" She was taking on the role of being the strong one.

"Okay." He looked pale. Peter kept rubbing his leg just above his boot. Finally, he pulled his pants leg up.

"Oh."

His leg was white with red splotches dotting the skin from where the mosquitoes had got him.

"I must have rolled over in the night." His pants had pulled up in his sleep and exposed the skin. The leg had been below the net.

"Come on, *Amriikis*!" Xasan seemed ready to leave the river. It carried with it certain dangers. "We must cross."

The strength of the river's flow had not lessened during the night. Its edge ran into the weeds, making it far more frightening. The water would be near the floor of the cab and they all kept looking for the slightest unusual movement. A mamba still roamed the area.

Xasan pointed and yelled like a foreman on the docks. No one was to be spared. He pointed to Karen and Peter to help push on one side while the other guard would push on the driver's side. The old man would stay behind the wheel. Xasan rode in the bed, just behind the cab with his AK rifle held up. His job was to scan for the mamba.

Karen felt every movement of the water as the truck plunged into the river. The vehicle moved quickly, making it seem that the crossing would be swift and safe. And then she heard the wheel spin out.

"Push! Push!" Xasan yelled as he jumped up and down in the bed trying to help dislodge the truck from the riverbed. It didn't budge and then a log came towards them with the current. Karen and Peter were on the down side; she looked up, yelled, and braced herself over the edge of the bed. She felt Peter do the same.

The log swung into the truck with a loud thud while the driver continued to hit the gas. The engine stuttered, and then roared, and as it did, the truck suddenly pulled forward out of the riverbed and on to the rutted road.

"Oh, my God," she gasped. The hunger, the lack of sleep, and the exhaustion caused her to simply hang there on the side of the truck bed.

"Allah! Praise be." Xasan waved his rifle in the air.

"Where is the other one?" Peter asked. The man with the broken leg was missing. "Did he go under?"

"He was where the log hit."

The guards looked up and down the riverbank for a short while, seeing nothing but the torrent of water passing by. For one short moment they yelled out when they saw a movement in the water. It was the same place where the night before they had seen the mamba.

"He is seeing the face of Allah, praise be," Xasan finally declared.

The truck continued to move to the south and east following the rutted road that ran parallel with the riverbank. The noon sun broke through the clouds and when it did, the temperature rose rapidly. Karen could feel her skin being fried by being so close to the equator. She used her scarf to cover up as much as possible. The men made both her and Peter walk behind the truck. Ropes were not necessary anymore.

Peter started to wobble when he walked. Despite the blazing sun, he looked like he was cold.

"How are you doing?" she whispered. Xasan didn't like their talking.

"Just got this headache. I will kill them both for an aspirin."

"They know we are missing. I left the gum wrapper at the riverbank on top of a rock. I put another, smaller rock on top of it. They should see it." Karen was offering him hope.

By midafternoon, they could hear voices and the sound of cattle. They all got excited, even Xasan.

The village was no more than a half dozen huts but more important for Xasan, two Toyota trucks were parked below the protection of the trees. They both had antiaircraft machine guns mounted in their beds. The barrels of the guns extended almost beyond the front windshield.

"Brothers!"

They were fellow Al Shabaab fighters and all from the same clan.

"Xasan!" The leader hugged his cousin. "You look thirsty and hungry."

"We could eat!"

"We have food and water. And cans of tuna!"

"I am famished!" Xasan grabbed the plastic liter jug and started to drink.

"Who are these?" The other man was unusually tall for a Somali and not as dark-skinned as his cousin. He had jet black short curly hair with black bushy eyebrows that extended to the point where the two almost touched each other.

"We have captured some *Amriiki*! They will be worth much in ransom."

"We must get the news to others. There is word that there is an *Amriiki* who is a fellow warrior just south of here. He will be able to tell us more about our prisoners. We need to feed them and keep them in good health like the goatherd takes care of his flock before going to the market!" The tall one had a better sense of the need to ensure that his prisoners survived.

"They should eat." Xasan had not considered the thought until now. He told the driver to get a can of tuna for each of them, and a jug of water to share.

The prisoners had value. How much was the question.

CHAPTER THIRTY

"Dr. Stewart?"

A man was standing at the door to Paul Stewart's office. He wore a loose blue polo shirt and khakis; clipped to his collar was a CDC temporary pass. His appearance alone was unusual, in that a temporary pass visitor was supposed to have an escort at all times.

"Yes," Paul Stewart looked up from his computer screen and pushed up his glasses on his nose.

"Enrico Hernandez." The man stood there with his arms folded. "I understand you were looking for me?"

"Oh, yes." Stewart had been calling security repeatedly. "Thank you for coming." It wasn't a thank-you of courtesy. It was a sincere thank-you. "Please come in and close the door."

The man in front of Stewart was solid, with a bit of a mid-thirties paunch. He wore black, well-shined shoes like a past Marine would and had short black curly hair.

"So, this is about Colonel Parker?"

"Yes, yes it is."

"What's up?"

"We have an outbreak of a disease in Africa and he can help."

"Okay, so why me?"

"No one knows where he is."

"I guess not." The comment was made in a matter-of-fact way.

"We need his help. *I* need his help. His blood might be what is necessary to save lives. How do we get him here?"

"Not easy." Hernandez hesitated. "Not since his wife died."

"Oh, I didn't know about that."

"Sad situation. He lost his parents on the Pan Am flight over Scotland."

"Lockerbie?"

"Yes, sir." Hernandez didn't look comfortable talking about William Parker.

"I am not sure I ever knew that." Stewart rolled his head back. "And his wife?"

Hernandez hesitated again. "I guess it was on the news."

It wasn't as if the story was a great secret that could not be found out. Still Hernandez hesitated.

"Look, my daughter was kidnapped by the rebels in Somalia. The disease that Parker beat in Afghanistan has popped up in the same area. She is a doctor with a refugee organization and was investigating the outbreak when they captured her. I'm desperate."

"Oh, I am sorry." Hernandez had a daughter as well. "Okay, it was a real tragedy. We never thought the man would get married but he finally did, to a lady named Clark. They were into the running thing in a big way and did the Hawaiian race together. One of those crazy nuts went off the deep end and drove his car into the crowd. Mowed down several. It just missed him."

"Oh, God."

"Yes, sir. The worst of it is that Parker beat the man

to a pulp before the cops got there. It took the Gunny a lot of the national security pull to get that all off the record. Cops didn't mind, but it was bad."

"Gunny?"

"Yes, sir, Gunny Moncrief is the only one who can get to him."

"I really need Parker's help." Stewart's voice was broken.

"I got laid off from the security staff here. The cuts in staff got me. I'm just hanging around until I get a new job." Hernandez started to stand up. "Let me have your number and I will have Gunny get in touch with you."

"Thank you."

"You said it was your daughter?"

"Yes. My only daughter."

"I will get right on this."

"This isn't that easy." Kevin Moncrief was standing outside his truck with Enrico Hernandez at his side. William Parker's farmhouse was as still as water on a pond. There were no sounds and nothing moved other than a breeze out of the west. It was just after high noon. It hadn't taken long for Hernandez to call Gunny and for them to link up.

"He doesn't have a phone." Moncrief was repeating what he thought Hernandez knew. "No computer, nothing."

"It's Stewart's daughter."

"Yeah."

They met at the Atlanta airport so they could take one truck. It was important that they took Moncrief's truck, just in case on the ride up to the lodge on the property Parker saw something familiar.

"But he isn't expecting me for another two weeks."

They waited for a while. Moncrief pulled a weed from the overgrown grass and started to chew on its end. It was a change of pace from his cigars.

The cabin looked like it had been closed for the winter months. The shutters were all sealed and a kudzu vine had started to wind itself around one of the posts that was at the entrance.

"Can't stand it," Moncrief said out loud. He walked over to the post and started to pull the kudzu vine off of it.

"It won't help unless you get it out of the ground," Hernandez commented while standing at the truck. "It's like the stuff we had at the CDC. It grows in hours, not days."

Moncrief gave him a look that only a gunnery sergeant could give to a staff sergeant.

"Okay." Hernandez came over and started to pull the kudzu out of the ground.

"Don't know if he's out there or . . ." Moncrief stopped and pointed to the woods.

"Do you think he would mind if we tried the door?" Hernandez asked after putting a handful of kudzu into the truck. "I got the impression that the doc wanted to talk to him soon."

"You think another hour or two makes the difference?"

Hernandez didn't say anything.

"Okay, let's try the door, but it may be booby-trapped." Moncrief smiled. "You first."

The door swung open without a problem. They walked into the lodge. There were no lights on and it was still . . . Moncrief walked into the kitchen and felt the stove.

"Nothing in the fridge." Hernandez was looking inside. "It's cold but no light."

"Yeah, he's good."

"What?"

"He knows what is in the refrigerator, but if he opened it at night, the light would spotlight anything in the room."

"Oh."

They walked around the large open room with the stone fireplace at the end. It was surrounded by glass doors that looked out on a stone porch and a grassy, flat piece of land cleared of all trees, and beyond, to a slope down to the river. In the distance Moncrief could see the stacks of a paper mill and the streak of white smoke that twisted into the air with the air current.

"Leave him a note?" Hernandez looked for something to write with.

"Well, we . . ." Moncrief's cell rang, interrupting him mid-sentence.

"Hell, Gunny, should we answer it?'

Moncrief's cell phone continued to ring. It showed the caller.

"Fulton County Library."

"Hey," said Moncrief into the phone.

"What do you need, Gunny?" The voice was Parker's.

Moncrief looked around the room. He had stopped wondering how to outguess William Parker before this.

"We need to see you."

"Good, I have something to show you."

"He said what?" Hernandez asked as they drove back north.

"Said he had something to show us."

"Did he say what it was about?"

"Something to do with Mobile."

CHAPTER THIRTY-ONE

Ferfer changed overnight.

The report of the disease to the World Health Organization caused a call to go out as it had when Ebola struck West Africa the year before. In a matter of hours, helicopters started arriving and landing on a small open piece of ground behind the Ethiopian military outpost on the other side of the valley from where the Doctors Without Borders refugee encampment stood.

Two MV-22s came in low over the valley, banked hard over in a turn, and then started to transition one by one for a landing. The aircraft had MARINE marked in a darker gray on the rear of its fuselage. Two similarly marked Cobra gunships stayed on top, circling like wasps waiting to sting.

The MV-22 Ospreys were marked with the squadron numbers of VMM-166. They were followed by the Super-Cobra attack helicopters from HMLA-269. The Super-Cobra was a two-man gunrunner that protected its bigger brother with both a 20-millimeter belly-mounted Gatling cannon and several missiles. It didn't have the speed of the Osprey but when they met up and got into the action it provided extra protection.

The open landing zone already had more than a dozen Russian-built transport helicopters parked in a line on the east side of the landing zone. A red smoke grenade on the far end of the open patch showed the drift of the wind, and the Ospreys turned into it. The first aircraft started to transition from forward flight to its helicopter mode. As the blades spun, a cloud of dust started to churn up. Small rocks and the red sand circled in what looked like two rising tornados for each engine on the aircraft.

The Osprey kept its engines running as teams of brown-camouflaged men fully decked out with special-fitted helmets, ear sets, goggles, vests, and HK rifles jumped out of the aircraft following a straight line past the propeller wash and then ran in different directions. The instant the last boot hit the ground, the Osprey's engines increased in volume and it slowly lifted off the ground. A moment later the second Osprey followed suit, moving into the landing zone, dropping off its cargo, and then pulling up into the sky. A team of fourteen operators spread out in a circle.

"Captain?"

Marine Captain Abo Tola looked up to see an Ethiopian soldier with the markings of a major standing there with his hand out.

"Yes, sir," said Tola.

"Welcome."

"Yes, sir. We are here to save some space for our logistics team."

Tola knew the uniform of the Ethiopian officer. This major served with NDF, or National Defense Force. His unit was a secret unit of fighters considered to be one of the toughest in the world. They were notorious for brutal hundred-mile hikes across the desert, surviving on only that which they could carry or find from the land. They wore berets. They fought and trained with the neighboring Kenyan Special Forces who were considered just as fierce and just as secret a unit. And they shared a hatred for Al Shabaab.

"I have heard of your unit." Tola tried to pay him a compliment. "Linda Nchi?"

"Those crazies from Al Shabaab have been a pain for some time."

Operation Linda Nchi was the code name in Swahili for the joint mission of Kenya, the Somali military, and Ethiopia against Al Shabaab in 2011. It was all started by Al Shabaab's kidnapping of two health workers from the Doctors Without Borders refugee camp in Dadaab. Ethiopia officially made no comment to the world as to its involvement with the operation; however, Al Shabaab was on everyone's list.

"I am afraid they aren't going away as we had hoped." Tola had seen intelligence reports that Al Shabaab was tattered and filled with infighting; however, there was another intelligence rumor out there as well: the group was in the market for a "carrier killer" missile. "What are your thoughts on our encampment?"

Tola knew that the major would let the Marine have the call, within limits. No field commander was going to sacrifice the decisions he had to make to protect his men no matter what protocol might ask of him.

"Your call."

"The bluff about half a click to the east there would fit our follow-along."

"Yes, that would be good."

Tola's staff sergeant was standing just behind the two and within hearing distance. He, like Tola, was ready for battle. He carried a Heckler & Koch M-416 rifle fitted with a suppressor. In his shoulder holster he had a special operator's 1911 .45 caliber automatic. He was fully armed for combat. Like Tola, he had pulled off his goggles and replaced them with his wraparound eye-wear. The glasses were ESS CDI eye pros that could take a blow to the face. His eyes would be far more protected than the rest of his body. He looked like the Terminator. And he was as close a product to the Terminator as America could train and produce.

"Staff, on that bluff, as we talked."

"Yes, sir." Tola saw him go to his radio and direct the others towards the bluff.

"Come in to my tent and I can give you a lay down." The major pointed to a desert drab tent with two guards standing out front.

Inside, a satellite photograph of the area had been blown up and laminated.

"The MSF refugee encampment is here." It had already grown from what Tola had seen in the last satellite update. "The World Health Organization has brought in its on-site team and our health workers have set up an encampment here." He pointed to the health workers as all being to the other side of Ferfer.

"Should there be some protection on that side?"

If the border was truly followed, the military forward operating base was between Somalia and Ferfer as well as the health camps. But Tola knew that the border mattered little to a terrorist force.

"We have rapid reaction teams but the MSF is not happy about us even being here."

Tola shook his head. Doctors Without Borders was notorious for risking lives to keep its declared neutrality. They would watch the sick be chased away from camps in other African countries so that they would not be accused of taking sides. However, there were two trump cards here. First, like Ebola, the Neisseria meningitidis was able to spread quickly. And second, two of their staff had been kidnapped. It called for a bending of rules.

"The WHO wants protection. They have seen about a dozen deaths already. They are trying to do inoculations to as many as they can reach."

The two were interrupted by the sounds of heavy helicopters passing overhead.

"It is our SOCSS coming in."

"What?"

"Our logistics coming in to set up our base of operations."

The aircraft flew past the Ethiopian post and Tola knew they were heading to the bluff.

"Good." He glanced at his watch. SPMAGTF Crisis Response–Africa would be on the ground, self-protected and fully up for operations well by nightfall. This special-purpose Marine air-ground task force was unique and tailored specifically for this mission.

"We would like to start doing some patrolling just to know what's on the deck."

"Of course."

Tola wanted a sense of the battlefield. He didn't care about the border.

"We have a unit from the CDC joining us on our FOB."

"Yes, I have heard such."

The Ethiopian major didn't say what Tola guessed he would have said if given the chance. Ethiopia flew Russian helicopters for a reason. They wanted to maintain their independence even if it meant varying from the West on some equipment. The Russian financing didn't hurt either. But the Marines were here as guests. They had a reason to be in play with the American doctor being one of the kidnap victims, but still they remained guests. Tola anticipated this.

"We will keep you informed on all we do as much as we possibly can."

Again, Tola would let the major know all that could be safely shared. If there was some piece of intelligence that needed to remain with the Marine force so as to ensure it was protected, Tola would make certain that such was the case. Otherwise, he would keep the Ethiopian major informed.

"And you are Ethiopian, my American brother?"

"Yes, my mother was from the village of Labuka. We are Kara."

"I am Kara!"

The two smiled and shook hands again, this time grasping each other's arms up to the elbows.

"We are in a common fight," Tola said as he squeezed the major's arm.

"Al Shabaab must be stopped. This American terrorist that they have is a disease no different than the meningitidis." The major raised the subject of the man from Mobile.

"Yes. But first we need to recover Dr. Stewart."

If she is still alive.

CHAPTER THIRTY-TWO

The child had a high fever all night. She kept crying and holding her neck. The whole family had become sick earlier that afternoon.

The sky was a crystal clear blue over the mansion and his corner of the lake. He had bought the stone house and the land for his wife when she told him she was pregnant with their first child.

The villa had large glass doors that swung out onto a porch that extended the full length of the structure on both the back and front. Slate covered the roof. The trim was a copper metal that had turned a grass-colored green with time. They were on a secluded drive that wound up to the top of a small hill. It had been purchased for millions of Swiss francs.

The summers were perfect. The days rarely got hot and leaned more towards chilly on occasion. The evenings were always cool, particularly when a breeze came across the lake. They were known for their parties during the summer. She wore gowns from Paris and designer shoes from Milan. She was known for her collection of shoes that ran in the hundreds of pairs.

He did have neighbors. Some were small farmers

with large black-and-white cows raised for their milk. The cows would wander across the hillsides and even come on to his estate. The two girls loved them. A person could hear the cows' bells, strung around their necks, from some distance. A cow was sometimes found and then gently channeled back to where it came from; the girls would throw small stones at the cow and occasionally get a moo out of it. The farmers were not pleased but they would put up with the stranger.

Everyone in the village suspected where the money came from.

He rarely drove his convertible Rolls-Royce, but his wife would take the girls to town and school every day in a black Range Rover.

The villa came with a butler who would drive him and his wife on occasion as well. He was an old Swiss who was born in the valley and tended to the villa. He'd worked for the last owner and would continue with the next. Genret had not planned for there to be a next owner. Genret had the money to keep the villa in his family for generations beyond the life of the butler.

"Bart, we must get a doctor," his wife begged.

"I am afraid that we are all sick." Genret stood there in a robe and pajamas looking particularly odd, as he also wore a pair of sunglasses. "I cannot stand the light and I have a pounding headache."

The headache had become so severe that he'd even resorted to the bottle of narcotic pills he kept hidden in the back of the closet. Genret had paid enough for his security team that he felt comfortable that both his gold and his bottle of narcotics would be left alone. However, he knew that he had only survived this long because he always kept on alert. There was no safe place for a man who dealt in weapons sold to the likes of Al Shabaab or others.

* * *

Genret's security director brought back a doctor from the nearby town.

He pulled the Rolls up to the villa's front door. Normally, Genret would be waiting outside but the bright sunlight prevented his going past the drawn curtains.

"Let me show you," the security director said.

"Who is sick?" the doctor asked.

"They all have been ill for the last day or so. The children seem worse. One of the daughters is very bad."

"And what are the complaints?"

"High fevers, and they scream if they are not in complete darkness. When the sun came up they all cried."

"Can they move?"

"I don't know."

"Okay, wait here."

Bertok Genret thought that unusual.

"Should I not show you where to go?"

"No, I know this villa. I have been here before. The Countess who lived here before was ill."

Genret stood by the car while he waited for some word. After a brief moment, the doctor came out running. He was generally a calm man who rarely got excited.

"We must get help."

"What is wrong?" Genret was stunned.

"Are you the only one who has been exposed to them over the last forty-eight hours?"

"He came back from a trip late Thursday, and no one else has been here besides the family and me."

"The military will want to isolate the villa."

Genret looked out over the lake.

"Will they be okay?"

"No."

* * *

The World Health Organization's headquarters was just beyond the valley in the city of Geneva. Word got to them later that day that another case caused by the Neisseria meningitidis bacteria had been registered. The lab slides didn't take long. Everyone in the village had been started on an inoculation program. And the WHO began giving shots to each of its physicians, scientists, and employees. A Swiss team was leaving for Somalia when they received the news that their family members at home were in as much risk as they were.

Genret and his children died that night. The wife survived but had to have both feet amputated. The price of gunrunning was high.

CHAPTER THIRTY-THREE

"Do you know where you are going?" Hernandez sat in the front fidgeting with Gunny Moncrief's radio. "He doesn't have a cell phone."

"Yes. Leave the radio alone." Moncrief enjoyed listening to his baseball on a channel with Sirius. It was a close one between the Braves and Philadelphia.

The truck headed back north, and after passing Interstate Beltway 285 that circled the city, he pulled onto the exit to Hartsfield-Jackson Atlanta International Airport.

"Are we stopping?"

"No. Just listen to the game." Moncrief had forgotten what a pain Hernandez could be. He drove the truck around the loop, passing through a tunnel near the terminals. It was the meeting spot. They slowed down and as they did, Moncrief looked up in his rearview mirror. A black truck suddenly appeared just behind them.

"Okay, let's go." He headed south to the beltway and then turned onto the west side of Interstate 285. They traveled north, again, until the highway intersected with Interstate 20. They traveled on I-20 west for more than a dozen miles. The black truck stayed in his rear-view.

The exit off I-20 had the usual Waffle House and a new Walmart, but the road soon turned into woods and the occasional small fields of grass and stumps of trees. They drove for another thirty minutes until they crossed a bridge over a river. Just beyond the bridge, Moncrief took a turn to the left onto a dirt and gravel road.

Several hundred yards in, a gate spanned the road with several signs that said No TRESPASSING and WARNING—DOG.

"Damn, Gunny, I haven't been here for years." Hernandez looked around the woods. "I didn't know you had a dog."

"Don't." Moncrief was looking in his rearview mirror to make sure that the truck had also made the turn. "Need one, though. Best burglar alarm system in the world. Here, go unlock the gate."

He handed Hernandez a key on a chain containing an eagle, globe, and anchor.

The two trucks pulled up to a small shack no bigger than a one-car garage. The house was tucked underneath some tall pines and in the shade it was nearly impossible to see. A small skiff was on a trailer bed parked next to the house. The Boston Whaler could not have been more than thirteen feet in length.

A flatbed trailer was parked on the other side of the house and next to it was a van that was marked MONCRIEF PAINTING COMPANY. Less than fifty yards on the back side of the cabin, the river they had just passed over cut through the property. The sound of running water filled the forest.

"Come on." Moncrief turned off his truck.

* * *

"I need to see your computer." William Parker swung the door closed to his truck.

"Hey, boss." Hernandez held out his hand.

"Hernandez, how's your daughter?"

"Growing like a weed."

"Gunny, sorry to bug you."

"No problem."

"Let me show you something."

Despite his isolation, Moncrief had one telephone line running to the cabin. It was used for his sole source of business besides his Marine Corps retirement. Moncrief's paint company had a Web site that got him just enough business. Not too much and not too little. He didn't want to do more.

"Sure."

They walked into the cabin, which was divided into a bedroom and small living room with a large lounge chair in front of a television and two open doors. One room had a small bed with the blanket stretched as tight as a drum, and the other room had a small kitchen. It was as close as you could possibly get to being a BEQ; the Bachelors Enlisted Quarters room of old—not one of the revised enlisted barracks of more recent times.

"It's over here."

A small desk was in the corner with an old computer and printer.

"Need to upgrade."

Both Parker and Hernandez looked at each other and smiled.

Moncrief sat down at the table and started up the computer.

"Go to Google and search for Omar and Al Shabaab under YouTube."

It didn't take a minute for several choices to show up. Omar had been busy even in combat. The videos showed a white-faced, bearded man who seemed overly theatrical. He moved his hands as he spoke. There was a burned-out, armored personnel carrier in the background.

"Any idea as to where this is from?" Moncrief asked.

"Yes, I think it is south of Luuq in western Somalia." Parker sounded authoritative as if he had studied the footage for some time. "There was a battle there a few days ago and that is a Kenyan APC. It is still smoldering from the round it took."

A wisp of smoke rose from the wreckage.

"Look at his hands." Parker pointed to the screen over Moncrief's shoulder. "See how he uses his finger one way and then another?"

Omar gestured, then pointed with his index finger, and then gestured again. Then he waved his hand with his thumb out and his index finger up.

"So what do you think?"

"When you got me out of jail didn't you talk to the operations group from the FBI?"

"Yes."

"Did they have someone from TFOS?" Parker knew who they needed to talk to.

"Probably. If they didn't, I am sure that they would know how to get in touch with that section." TFOS was the Bureau's Terrorist Financing Operations Section. They had the job of tracking the money that fed the terrorists. Gunny Moncrief had kept the telephone number on his desk.

"He is telling somebody in the United States something. The letters he formed are D and L."

"D and L?"

"I think what he is really doing is activating another cell." Parker looked at the screen closely.

"But they have a million guys looking at this video." Moncrief was thinking of the scrutiny Omar's videos had gotten.

"Sure, but he doesn't care about the thousands of techs at DOD or the FBI who are looking at it. He only cares about one out of the millions who are looking at it. The Internet has become our own worst enemy." Parker was right. The Internet had given Al Shabaab and every other terrorist group in the world a free and unlimited ride. Instant communications around the world were always available. A terrorist cell from Toronto or Minnesota could be on standby to respond immediately.

"So what's the TFO section have to do with all of this?" Hernandez asked.

"You can't trace the people who are watching it, but you can trace the source of money. The money can tell you who is really vested in this guy." Parker continued to study the screen as he spoke. "Even the most basic terrorist operation needs money, whether for gas or fertilizer or the odd purchase of a pipe at Home Depot. And the more money, the more serious they are."

"Shit." Moncrief let it out like a breath of bad air. "What's the scenario?"

"Who knows?" Parker kept watching the video. "He obviously needed to send another signal to both the world and his bosses. Faud and Godane are known to be temperamental. They will keep him as long as he proves he's useful."

Moncrief had heard the names before. Godane was the CEO and Faud the CFO of Al Shabaab.

"They will always want weapons. And the more they can afford, the more dangerous they become." Parker continued to study the face of the man. "Their pirates steal any ship that comes within a hundred miles of the coast. And if Al Shabaab had something to shoot at

American jets or destroyers to help its pirates steal the ships, Al Shabaab would be in the market to buy."

"We didn't tell you why we were at your cabin." Moncrief pushed his chair back from the table. "Dr. Stewart needs your help."

"Yeah, he wants to talk to you real bad." Hernandez had been squatting down as they spoke but stood up when the subject was raised. "Really bad."

Parker kept studying the video. The picture was frozen on the one frame of Omar staring into the camera. The barrel of his AK-47 rested against his shoulder. He wore a smirk of a smile as if he was getting his revenge on America. "What's going on?"

Moncrief went back to Google and searched for the World Health Organization's Web site. It had one category of health alerts. He clicked on "News" and an emergency alert appeared on the screen warning that anyone traveling to or from either Yemen or Somalia needed to be aware of an outbreak of meningitis.

"Meningitis is all over that part of the world. It's called the belt." Parker wasn't immediately impressed.

"Not this one." From his years with security at the CDC, Hernandez did have some sense that this strand was something very different. "They are acting like this is a bad bug."

"Yeah, Colonel." Moncrief rarely mentioned rank. It was a trump card that he used only when he needed to get Parker's attention in a special way. "And you are the only one that they know for sure who has survived it."

"So, they need me to come in and give them some blood?" Parker didn't see the complication. Donating a tube or two of blood wasn't that difficult a process.

"Stewart wants to talk to you today. He has been sitting by his telephone at his CDC office since daylight."

"Okay." Parker sensed something more to the story.

"There were two doctors taken by Al Shabaab from an MSF encampment. Wasn't one of them an American with the name of Stewart?"

"Yes, sir." Hernandez spoke again. "Stewart lost his wife not too long ago."

Moncrief stared at Hernandez with a frown that could have frozen him in his place.

"I mean . . ."

"No, don't apologize." Parker kept looking at the screen. "You don't need to apologize." There was a silence in the room for what seemed to be several minutes.

"I don't want to meet him at the CDC. There are too many cameras."

"He will meet you anywhere."

"You need to call the FBI—and not from a cell."

"I know a temp store at Walmart where we can buy one with a few minutes on it. You can stay in the truck." Moncrief paused. "I will call the folks I talked to about Mobile. One of them was a wounded Marine who got a job with the FBI after Afghanistan."

"Okay, let's get the word to them that he is using this video to activate another cell and then we can go see Dr. Stewart."

CHAPTER THIRTY-FOUR

The rain started during the night. Karen Stewart huddled underneath the small truck with Peter by her side. They shared a piece of plastic that kept them somewhat protected from the dirt below, but the smell of grease and fuel was only inches from their faces. At least the truck had been parked on a mound so that the water ran away from it and the spot where they were twisted together. The ground under the truck was also crammed with several other fighters. Only the driver slept in the cab. He had a beard that was long and had gray streaks through it. The beard gave him seniority.

"I am thirsty, so thirsty," she whispered in the middle of the night.

"Yes." Peter's voice was weak.

Despite the close quarters under the truck they were still able to have the net pulled over their faces and arms. But it gave no protection to their legs, and the buzz of mosquitoes continued through the night like a dentist's drill. She looked down at her legs to see her khaki-colored, pocketed pants covered with black as if someone had spurted her with black ink. There were mosquitoes covering her from the net down to her boots.

"I must drink."

It was a danger, but Karen pulled out from underneath the truck and opened her mouth to the sky. But the rain had stopped. She continued on, and in the darkness felt around the bed of the truck until her hand touched a bucket half tilted over. It was upright enough that it had captured some of the rainwater. She drank the cupful of water not caring about the oily taste.

"Where are you going?"

As a reminder of her captivity, she felt Xasan's hand on her boot.

"I am going to the bathroom."

"Okay, don't go too far. Remember the lions. The baboons are worse." He chuckled but she knew what he said was true.

She wandered out into the darkness barely able to see beyond her hand. Finally, she stopped a short distance away between two thorn bushes. She got down on her soaked knees and began to throw up. It was a dangerous loss of fluid. She sobbed and sobbed but was determined that Xasan not hear it.

"I don't care if I die here. He isn't going to know."

She had steeled herself to fight for survival.

At daylight, Xasan ordered them to gather some wood. It was wet on the outside, but when they peeled away the bark, the inside was dry enough to burn. He had them pile it up near the front of the truck and then he poured some gas on it. He had a lighter that was, as Karen learned quickly, as valuable as a Kalashnikov.

The fire started to crackle in the early morning

light. The other men had a metal pot and they filled it with the red water from the river. Soon the pot began to boil and after much time they poured some of the steaming water out into the bucket.

"You!" Xasan pointed to Karen. It was a reminder of her place in the hierarchy of this world. She understood and took on the task. She washed out the bucket with some of the hot water, first cleaning her hands and then rubbing the inside as best as she could. She carefully took the bucket to the water's edge and held it in the current, without wasting a drop or exposing it to the contaminated water, until it cooled. Before she walked back, she turned her back to the others and drank. She filled herself with as much as she could stomach. And then, while the other men were boiling something else in the metal pot, she pulled Peter's arm. He was sitting in the mud and water, out from underneath the truck and up against the wheel.

"Quickly, drink."

"What?" He started to say something out loud but she put her hand over his mouth to silence him. She looked into his eyes.

"Drink!"

He guzzled the water. She stopped him twice and he gasped for air and then drank again.

"Hey, *Amriiki*!"

She pulled the bucket up from Peter and walked back to the campfire.

"Don't do that again!" Xasan warned.

"Okay," she said, and then thought for a moment. Her dead body was of no value. Her body alive was of great value, at least in their minds. She had some leverage.

"We must eat or we will both die." She could not believe that she had the boldness to speak.

Xasan came across and raised the butt of his rifle.

And then he hesitated. It seemed that he too realized the value of the prisoner.

"Okay, we are making some soor."

It was a strange word to her. She soon learned, after being given the plate that the other men had shared and emptied, that it was a gritslike meal. It was warm and tasteless, but it was the first food she had eaten since they'd been kidnapped. She took her plate to Peter and helped him slurp the warm meal down. It covered the sides of his mouth and she watched as he used his fingers to gather up every grain and eat it.

As the sun started to rise, she saw the men suddenly look up. They grabbed her and pulled her to the base of a tree just beyond the truck. The river had risen during the night and as it did, the huts that were closest to the water's edge flooded. The back wheels of the truck were now under the red rising water, but it wasn't the water that had spooked the men.

The old man jumped into the cab, started it up, and drove underneath another tree. The other men pulled their larger truck down the road, finally running it into the bush, and cover. Just as it came to a stop, a green-and-black camouflage helicopter came across the tree line. Karen looked up to see a red, black, and white circle on its fuselage.

"Ethiopians!" Xasan cried out as he knelt down under the tree.

Karen wanted to scream out and run. She thought about it for a moment but then realized that Peter would never make it. And in the crossfire of bullets, she would have little chance of survival as well. In a split second, she considered her options and decided that her best chance at staying alive remained with Xasan.

"God." She looked at the trail of the last helicopter as it headed down the river. She held out her hand as if she could reach up and touch it.

"Allah," Xasan said. He looked up at the helicopter and pointed his rifle at it.

It didn't seem possible that the two names—God and Allah—could have been for the same power.

"We must move." Xasan seemed to have a plan. The road now looked more like a small river with a bank to it but at least the road cut through the bush. "We will meet not far from here."

Karen thought that as she and Peter got deeper into Somalia and Al Shabaab their chances for escape or rescue lessened. But with more soldiers, they had a better chance of not starving to death and perhaps getting some medicine.

"Peter, how are you doing?"

He smiled. "Do you want the good news or the bad?" He said it with that slight French accent.

"I think I know what you are going to say." Karen smiled back. "You don't have the meningitis."

"Yes, Doctor, good diagnosis. I would be dead by now if I did." He bleakly smiled. "But I do have the first stages of malaria."

"Malaria you can survive." Karen was determined to keep her patient alive. "Somebody will keep looking for us!"

CHAPTER THIRTY-FIVE

"**O**mar!"

The commander called out his name.

"Omar!"

"Yes." He had been sleeping in the corner of an abandoned hut near the small town of Diinsoor with the six others in the squad. As he had learned in combat, sleep was as rare as the ammunition and RPGs his men needed. And it was "his" men. The six members had voted the *Amriiki* to be the new squad leader. They had another one at the beginning of the last firefight, but his name was Hiiraale and he always put them in front of him.

Hiiraale is gone, Omar thought to himself as he got up from the hard floor. Omar was proud of his responsibility.

Soccer in eighth grade was the last time I was voted to lead anything. He remembered that the Titans in his home in Alabama had voted him to be captain for a game. This was different. This was leading men in combat. This was far more a matter of trust than anything on a soccer field.

Hiiraale would never have been the squad leader if

Omar had been from Somalia. Hiiraale's face was covered with freckles that could be seen through his colored skin.

Omar grabbed his plastic corn bag. He never left his bag behind.

And Hiiraale is balding! Omar laughed to himself.

Hiiraale was a sight to see.

More important, Hiiraale could not lead. The squad had chosen Omar to be their new leader. He stood up for his men even when it was stupid to do so. He dangerously spoke out to the commander that the men needed better supplies. The commander already knew that. He didn't need to be told again.

More dangerously, Omar said the tactics being used were stupid. The Ethiopians and Kenyans would send out patrols and then pull back. Their main force stayed near their borders. The patrols caused Al Shabaab to chase after them. The men would get excited, fire at shadows, and then run forward.

"Hold up, men!" Omar would yell. It didn't do any good to stop them. They would chase, wildly firing their weapons, and then, when out of ammunition, would run back to anyone they could find. Many were shot in the back as they ran away. Once, the men ran past him when Omar held his ground. He saw the enemy soldier running directly for him. Like his grandfather had taught him, Omar aimed and squeezed the trigger. The bullet struck the man in the center of the chest. It was no harder than shooting the squirrel in his grandfather's tree.

The squad saw this and stopped running. They turned and fought. Then the enemy started to run. His squad all screamed at the top of their voices praise for Allah. After they killed several, Omar ordered his men to stop the chase.

"Let them come to you!"

Soon thereafter, he was chosen to be the new squad leader.

"This is stupid," he had told the commander after the firefight.

But they were moving forward, which the leaders thought good. It was like an American company that bought and expanded no matter what. Bankruptcy would come soon.

It was well into the next battle when the commander realized the error. At first, the enemy's artillery fired random shells that burst in an erratic and unpredictable way. Once a round landed close in and hit one of the other squad leaders near Omar's position. It caught the man squarely on. It was the misfortune of war as he was instantly turned into a red mist. Parts of his body were found on top of the thorn bushes. There was nothing to bury.

Omar ordered his squad to stop and wait for the enemy. But the others kept running ahead.

The other squad leader's death didn't slow down the other squads from running blindly to the front. They yelled "Allah," and continued to move forward. And then they reached the envelope of the artillery fire. The enemy had set determined targets and when the attackers stepped into the range of the cannons, artillery shells began falling like rain. Omar could hear the whomp of a round as it came out of the artillery barrel followed closely by another whomp, and another.

Omar's squad was spared the artillery but Al Shabaab had lost the battle.

They were in full retreat as the artillery broke their back. The Ethiopian infantry followed thereafter, firing well-aimed shots from behind trees. Only Omar's squad stood waiting for them. They killed more that day than any in the battles of the past. Omar and his men mowed down the approaching soldiers in a reverse of their tactics. But it caused Omar to brag.

"I told them it was stupid. This is not the way to fight. We must set our traps. We must wait and ambush," Omar complained to anyone who would listen.

His complaints were noted by all.

"Omar, we have news." The commander sat on a bucket as he spoke. "You have a special mission."

"Oh?" Omar suspected the leader of much by now; word had gotten around that the commander was unhappy with both Omar's success and his criticisms of the command. "But my squad needs me." He didn't want to leave behind the only men he ever knew who had trusted him with their lives.

"Are you here for the needs of Allah or your own self-satisfaction?"

The question was a loaded one. There was only one answer.

"Allah's will is all."

"Good."

The unit was heading back to the east, towards Jilib. It was a place that he relished. Often, given his hunger, he dreamed at night of the bananas he had picked from the trees in Jilib.

"You will go back to Jilib tonight. The word is that there are two *Amriikis* that have been captured to the north. Godane wants you to go to them and make a video for all to see."

"Where are they?"

"We think they are near the Shebelle."

"So be it." This news put everything in a different

light. Omar knew that his men would understand. The need for his service elsewhere was greater.

"And you are to be congratulated."

"Oh?" Omar put his rifle over his shoulder as he listened.

"Money is coming in from America through the Kenyan border. Your videos from combat have been heard. Four new recruits came last night. All from your Minneapolis."

"Praise His name." Omar knew he could be of value if only Godane and Faud would understand what he could do to help the jihad. "And any other news from America?"

"No, should there be?"

"Yes, there will be great news again soon!"

The trip was not as easy as Omar had thought it might be. The road to Jilib had only become more of a massive mudhole than before. Where it was dry, the bumps gave him headaches. And then, where it was wet, they all got out and pushed. The muck had only increased as trucks regularly carried the wounded back from the battle.

"Oh, please," he said to the driver. "Try not to hit every pothole!"

The driver gave him a cold look. Omar was in the front passenger seat, which was meant for the oldest and highest-ranked one in the party. There were, however, several in the truck that were older, had lived through more battles, and were not *Amriikia*. But it was important that he stay in the cab as it was not good to see a white man with the wounded. His fame did not precede him on the journey. Some would not understand. Omar kept his turban wrapped around his face so as not to attract more attention.

They traveled through the night without using any lights, as the helicopters were like the lions. Both seemed to feed on the dead. They were hated green-and-black predators that caused everyone to run for cover except for the wounded, who could not move but only moan as they lay there as targets for the machine guns.

One truck, a bigger one than the others, was crammed full of wounded men. When a helicopter caught sight of it, Omar ran to the base of a tree and watched as the gunship's guns and rockets tore the limping vehicle and its passengers to shreds.

"They will see the face of Allah. They are martyrs, all," he screamed out to the others, who looked at the strange white man in amazement.

There was no food on the journey. Once, they were stopped by a woman who balanced two large 20-liter plastic jugs of milk. They raised enough money among themselves to buy the jugs full of camel's milk.

Omar poured some out into a cup he had in his bag and drank. He then refilled the cup and passed it around the circle of men. The jug was also passed around. He expected it to return to him and then be passed around again until it had all been portioned out in a fair manner.

"Where is it?"

The men were directly in front of him, yet both his cup and the jug were missing.

"Who has it?"

Omar never saw either the jug or the cup again.

At the morning light, they saw the buildings of Jilib in the distance. The pace of the truck quickened as they realized food and safety were in sight. Near the edge of the city, Omar got off the truck, grabbed his rifle and plastic bag, and walked down the street that paralleled the river. It would take him back to the villa where he had stayed with the commander just before they left for the battle to the west.

The house with the courtyard and banana trees was still a headquarters for Al Shabaab and its army.

"I am Omar. I have come here with orders to report to the regional commander."

The guard looked at him strangely as they all did when they first saw a white man dressed as a fighter. Some raised their rifles, not sure of what they were seeing.

"Wait!"

The guard yelled out for his squad leader, who came out to inspect the sight. He went back inside and soon the regional commander himself came out to greet their brother.

"*Al-Amriiki*!" he yelled as he grabbed Omar. "You must come in and eat!"

They brought him into the large room and a woman carried in a cup of warm tea and bananas. The tea had the slightest taste of sugar. Omar sipped it and his hand shook as the power of the sweetness overcame his senses. It had been weeks since he had tasted sugar such as this.

"Oh, praise this."

The regional commander entered the room and sat down with his legs folded. He placed his rifle across his legs.

"Let me tell you the plan. The road along the coast is not safe. The TFG has attacked several of our places, including Baraawe." He was clarifying the fact that no road or route was clearly within the hands of Al Shabaab. "You will go tonight to the beach where a boat will take you up the coast to Marka."

"I know Marka. We passed through it. It is just south of Mogadishu."

Omar remembered the ride from his arrival in the country at Mogadishu to join the army in the south.

"From Marka you will head inland, where you will cross to Tayeeglow." The names were strange to him but the man drew a map in the dirt on the floor. It was a loop from Jilib in the south, via a boat to the north, and then inland to the west. The journey was in the shape of a horseshoe.

"Where are the Americans?"

"We think they are crossing inland from the She-belle River to the village of Tayeeglow. You will have a guide who will take you to Tayeeglow and from there you will go northwest. You will find them and make videos for the world to see."

It was dangerous; however, no more so than the time Omar had spent in combat. He was now a veteran with the confidence he sought when he first came to the country. He was on a jihad. It was his voyage to see the face of Allah if such was required.

"Do you need anything?"

When he left his squad he gave his two grenades to the new leader.

"Yes, some hand grenades?"

"Of course." He was given two more Russian grenades still in their containers.

Omar had not been on a boat since he rode the Mo-bile Bay with his grandfather years ago. He had forgotten what it was to be seasick.

His thoughts quickly evaporated as the small boat with its outboard engine headed north in the dark along the blackened coast. Only in the distance could he see any lights, and they appeared at random as in any war-torn country.

The boat owner had pointed to the bottom of the boat. He pulled a fishy tarp over himself. It was hot, and the boat rocked.

"You must stay down. White man will not be good."

Omar didn't know that the TFG and others constantly patrolled the waters. The man at the engine showed a face of fear. Again, they traveled through the night. Wars require nights. Darkness provides safety.

Finally, after hours of bumping up and down, the boatman tugged on the tarp. They headed in towards the shoreline and a point of sand that stuck out from the shore. The boat pulled up into the sheltered surf and as Omar climbed over the edge a man appeared out of the darkness.

"*Amriiki?*"

"Yes." Omar shook the hand of the other man. He could feel the bony cage of the other's arm as if his skin had been stretched over a skeleton.

"Come, we must move."

Omar followed the man to the sand dunes that lined the shore, crossing between two dunes and onto a dirt road. Suddenly the man stopped and signaled him to lie down. He looked like the deer that Omar remembered seeing as a child with his grandfather as the man's head swiveled left and right, sensing both sight and sound.

Suddenly, rounds of green tracers went off in the distance. Other green tracers being fired in the opposite direction followed them. The two paths of bullets crisscrossed.

Every fifth bullet. He thought of his training. Four bullets unseen followed a green tracer round. Each one of those five could kill. After the shooting, they pulled into a ravine and a hole between two rocks and waited the day out.

"Not good to be killed by our friends."

Omar held his Kalashnikov on his lap and felt for the hand grenades in each of his pockets.

"No, not good."

"We have received over one hundred thousand dollars since he started making his broadcasts." Faud motioned with his hands to the others while they met in a house on the far northern side of Kismaayo. The abandoned villa was near the beach and had two roads that departed from it in two different directions.

"Where is this money coming from?" Mukhtar Abu Zubeyr asked the question. He was also known as Ahmed Abdi Godane and led the meeting as he also led Al Shabaab.

"Much from Eritrea, but most is from America by our couriers that cross from Kenya." Faud depended upon a trusted system in which certain carriers would pack the money in from Kenya by crossing through the nights. It was originally carried out of the United States in small bundles hidden on passengers. Everyone on the journey of money could be trusted. Not a penny was ever missing. The remainder of the world would consider such a thing as not likely to ever happen, for the risks of being accused of stealing were too great. Under the law of Al Shabaab, a thief's hands were both cut off. As a result, none of the couriers took such a risk.

The couriers were famous within the Somali community. A select few had done it for decades with more reliability than an automatic teller machine.

"But where in America?"

"We know that some of it is from women in Virginia. They started sending money after the *Amriiki*'s broadcasts."

Godane's facial expression indicated he was not pleased.

Faud knew that he didn't like the American. Word had quickly gotten around of his constant complaints about the food, the ammunition, and the strategy being applied. It was the strategy criticism that cut deep. The men understood the hardships and even took pride in doing more with less food and less ammunition. They ran over an Ethiopian unit and then scavenged the site for food, boots, magazines, and anything they could carry. But men being chewed up by the enemy's artillery because of the ordered attack was not to be the subject of criticism.

"There may be more." Faud held his hand up.

"You mean money? We need more for a second missile. Much more. Especially since our Swiss contact has died," Godane said with disgust.

Faud knew that an Iranian-promised second and third missile still depended upon money for the go-betweens. And now that process had to start again from the beginning.

"I talked to the American and he promised something else. He would not tell me what it was." Faud didn't like secrets.

"What of the word that we have two for ransom?" Godane asked.

"We do have two who are in the wilderness. Omar has been sent to meet them. A videotape of one jihadist American with another captive American will be of great value."

"And he is away from the troops for now." Godane

smiled. "We don't need our *Amriiki* telling all how much wrong we are doing."

"We will soon have a new Islamic state and it will control the Horn of Africa. The courts will have to listen to all that you direct." Faud was speaking of the Islamic Courts Union that was intended to oversee all, including its militant wing, Al Shabaab.

"An Islamic state that controls the Horn of Africa. Our people had that power several thousand years ago. And now, today, every ship that hopes to use the Suez will pass through our gates. Allah be praised."

CHAPTER THIRTY-SIX

"**H**ow much do you have this month?" The woman in her mid-thirties, short, stout, and covered in the Muslim tradition, walked with a waddle as she moved quickly through the mall just outside Richmond.

"Here." The woman by her side, who looked like her sister in size, shape, and appearance, quickly handed her a brown paper bag. She looked around as she did it. The first one slipped the paper sack into a beach bag she had slung over her shoulder.

"It will go out tonight." She was meeting the boy from Kenya who was booked on a flight out from Dulles to Kuwait City that very night. He would hide the money in a false-front bag with some pepper and frankincense. The two items would cause any dogs on the trip to move past the bag. He would take a flight from Kuwait City to Kenya only a few hours later. And then he would head out by motorcycle to a crossing near El Beru Hagia. It was another village on the south-western border of Kenya with Somalia. He would avoid the town and cross by a path nearby to waiting Al Shabaab fighters. It would all take less than two days.

"I have saved some for the other."

They both knew who and what she was talking about. He needed money for a cheap van he must buy, and gas to head north of Richmond. Time remained of the essence.

"I will drop half of this off for him and then meet him before he leaves for Africa." She nodded good-bye and they left in separate directions.

The drop-off for the first delivery was relatively simple. She carried a FedEx overnight box with her. The money was bulky as it was a collection, ten to twenty dollars at a time, from the fellow members at the mosque. She stuck the wads of bills, nearly a thousand, in the box and then sealed it. The drop-off was a FedEx box in an office park just north of the beltway on the Charlottesville side of Richmond. By the time she made it to the box, the area was dark and quiet. It was what she had hoped for.

She drove up to the steel FedEx drop box and pulled down the handle. She wedged the box into the drawer, pulling up the handle so that it closed on the box. As planned, the box did not move. She then drove away.

When her small old Toyota pulled off into the darkness another car's lights came on. A worn-out Honda drove out from the rear of a physician's office, cut across the parking lot, and pulled into the left lane. The Honda stopped at the FedEx box and the driver pulled out the package.

The man behind the wheel looked to be no more than in his early twenties. He was clean shaven and had a close haircut. He looked very different from the jihadist he was. He was from Minneapolis and was more determined than ever to see the face of Allah.

"Omar has taught me well."

He had met the *Amriiki* in Toronto the summer before. He listened as Omar had taken long walks with him and told him of the importance of his faith. Like Omar, he was a virgin, determined not to be with a woman until he was married. He, like Omar, had learned to hate the language of the television, of the music videos, and of America. Omar had told him that only the true faith could give his life meaning.

He had watched every broadcast that came over the network. After Mobile, Omar had become a celebrity in the community. He went to the mosque and talked with the others. As soon as he went to prayers, they said "Have you seen the new one from Omar?"

"No, I must." He never revealed that one would be more important than the rest. He would go to a friend's house, pull up the Internet, and watch as Omar told of the battles he had been in. Omar showed the scars on his knuckles from training with the glass and a wound he claimed he had received in combat. The messages encouraged the brothers to come to Somalia and join the fight against the Americans and Zionist Jews. The video begged for money.

The others would talk about how they were going to join the fight as well. They would be jihadists and become martyrs. He kept his mouth shut.

"You must not say anything to anyone," Omar had told him. "It is your fate from Allah that you will do more than many here in the United States."

It was particularly difficult for him to keep his silence. He hugged his mother the last time he saw her, squeezing her tightly.

And then the message came.

Omar gestured, then pointed with his index finger, and then gestured again. Then he waved his hand with his thumb out and his index finger up. It activated his cell.

He pulled onto the interstate heading for an exit off the highway just north of Dumfries, Virginia. He had an address written down on a piece of paper. The FedEx box covered a butcher's knife.

It was important that he arrive no later than ten o'clock in the morning. It had all been planned out for several months. He and Omar had worked through every detail.

He had worn a John Deere camouflage hat and a Redskins sweatshirt that was one size too large when he went to the gun show in Richmond several months before. He'd had on blue jeans, well worn, and a pair of Converse sneakers.

He called himself Bobby. It sounded like the perfect name. His false license also said Bobby, although his given first name was Shirwa. He knew that a police officer would be more suspicious of a license bearing the name Shirwa, so he used the alias instead.

Bobby went through the show looking for the one gun booth that was selling ammunition by the crate. He talked to the owner and stayed there for more than an hour.

"What is it about this Class III?" Bobby asked. He already knew the answer. A Class III collector could purchase and own the same guns that a military unit could own.

"Sorry kid, but no chance." The storeowner had a wad of snuff in his cheek and a plastic bottle that he would spit into. "Do you know what it takes to get a Class III?"

Bobby already had some idea. It required background checks that he would never have passed in a million years. The sheriff and multiple agencies ran the checks and rechecks. It was bulletproof for someone such as himself. But Class III allowed a gun collector to own virtually any weapon from silencers to large-caliber sniper rifles.

"I know. Maybe someday."

"Here, this is John. He has a Class III," the owner introduced the two.

"Wow, what an honor." Bobby shook the gray and balding man's large, full-fisted hand. "It is a big deal."

Bobby only cared about one weapon.

The knock on the door came at three in the morning. The woman from the mall heard it in her sleep, hesitated, and then knew who it was. She looked through the curtains to see three black Yukons with blue lights flashing.

"FBI."

She didn't remember much in the fog of the moment other than a dog being brought into her house, drawers being emptied, and a woman agent showing her a badge.

"I am with the TFOS."

"What?"

"The Bureau's Terrorist Financing Operations Section. TFOS."

It appeared that the FBI had had her on their watch list for some time. Despite her dealing in cash as much as possible and with small bills, the deposits and withdrawals varied and seemed to be timed to a certain time of the month. From the money activity, it didn't take long to link her up to the terrorists.

"We just missed a drop," another agent told the woman standing in front of her.

"Check the airports for any flights to Kuwait City." The agent had a sense of the plan used. They would catch up to the courier and count the cash. They had a source who told them what amount of money to expect. At Dulles they would see that the money was short.

CHAPTER THIRTY-SEVEN

Doctor Paul Stewart looked exhausted. He wore baggy pants with no crease, a checkered shirt with several pens in the pocket, glasses, and brown lace-up shoes with thick spongy soles meant to make long days on his feet a little less painful. The hair pushed back from his receding hairline remained uncombed. He also wore his white lab coat, which should have been left at the CDC, but after decades of living in it, the coat had become a part of him. He forgot to take it off and it was good that he hadn't, as the large pocket was where he kept his Tums. He would pull out a roll and peel one off all too regularly.

"Hello, Doctor Stewart."

"Oh, hello." Stewart had been told to go to a small park located between the CDC and the Emory campus. The park had a trail and was one of the few places in the area that did not have cameras. The day was both hot and humid. Stewart wasn't good at this game, but he understood that Parker entering the CDC would only raise alarms that were not needed at this point.

Moncrief and Hernandez stood behind them on the path.

"Let's take a walk." Parker pointed down the trail.

Stewart had little time.

"Colonel." It was the only form of address he ever knew for the man. He didn't even know his last name until just recently. "I need your help."

"What do you want of me?"

"There is a CDC team setting up in eastern Ethiopia near the Somali border. They and a bunch of others are trying to fight what you had."

"Had? The same bacteria? The meningitidis?"

"Yes." He paused. "But not just any meningitidis. This form of Neisseria is very bad. The bug was locked up and frozen until we brought it out with you. Somehow the infection that you survived has awoken again in Somalia."

The bug once in Pakistan had infected Parker. On a prior mission, his chewing a piece of gum with the bacteria implanted in it was all that was needed to initiate their attack. The gum was coated with the organism and Parker knew it. The bacterium was what caused meningitis. It unlocked an infection that spread through the mucosal membranes of the nose, throat, and lungs, going from there into the blood and into meninges that surround the brain. For the lucky few, death followed quickly. Spreading the bacteria had all been planned and William Parker had a part in that plan. It was directed at one particular terrorist group that Parker had been embedded with in the tribal area of western Pakistan. It was not supposed to spread beyond that one valley.

"So what do you suggest?"

"Aren't you O positive?"

"Yes."

"We have no time." Stewart looked down at his feet

on the pine straw and gravel trail. He reached for another Tums.

"I still am unclear as to our course of action."

"You mean why not just take some blood here?"

"You have the best lab in the world within a quarter mile of where we are standing." Parker looked up the path as he spoke. It led to the street, which passed directly in front of the CDC complex.

"I need you to consider going to Ethiopia. I need you to go with me."

Parker looked at the doctor.

"My daughter is a prisoner of Al Shabaab and she is in the middle of all of this." Stewart hesitated. "I am not sure if she is even still alive."

William Parker had had his own share of death. "I am sorry." Parker folded his arms and stood there for a minute.

The heat and humidity were causing the doctor to sweat. He wiped his forehead with his sleeve again and again. He was turning red and the sweat stain was coming through the plaid shirt.

"Take your lab coat off, Doc."

"What?"

"You are going to stroke out on me." Parker pointed to the shade. "Let's go over there."

Parker looked at his two teammates while they stood there in the shade.

"So you want me to go to Ethiopia?"

"Yes."

"And?"

"It will allow us more time to create a stronger response."

"We will be right there when they find your daughter."

"Exactly. There would be no time to develop an antiserum. The only thing that might work in the short run is a transfusion." Stewart continued to sweat.

"From another O postive?" Parker was trying to consider all the possibilities.

"She is vaccinated with the antiserums that we have, but this disease is different. It is like Ebola. Some will react and survive. Others will not. A blood transfusion from someone who has survived this particular beast can build antibodies that can carry over to another. It is a long shot but until we get a vaccination that works, it is our only long shot."

"I need to think about this." Parker always had an operations plan. He didn't just jump. Even the best of plans went out the window when the first shot was fired.

That might have been from Patton. Or Marshall?

"We don't have much time. A military airplane leaves from Dobbins tomorrow morning at six a.m."

"How are you going to get country clearance?"

Military aircraft going into countries at war was generally not as simple an idea as one might think.

"This is as bad as Ebola. The Ethiopians are happy to receive the help. They know that Ebola has killed thousands and it doesn't seem to be stopping anytime soon."

"Yes."

"They will clear anyone who can be of help. Several have died in Yemen, a family died in Switzerland, and the last report from my daughter was that they found a village which had been turned into a ghost town.

"So we know that the virus has been on at least one international flight. The Swiss was a gun merchant that was known for selling weapons to Al Shabaab. It may be spreading like Ebola."

Ebola had a sister that was traveling across mid-Africa and Yemen, and into Europe.

"I understand."

"A base has been set up with the Marines near Ferfer. Your going might help some of them not get sick." Stewart was clearly playing all of the cards in his hand.

Parker stared at him.

"Moncrief and I will see you tomorrow at Dobbins." Parker set forth his terms. He would not be going without Moncrief.

"Moncrief?"

"Yes, the one you and Hernandez got to find me." Parker pointed to Moncrief leaning against a pine tree with a short cigar in the corner of his mouth. "He doesn't know it yet, but he is going, too."

Paul Stewart was soaked from his sweat when he got back to the CDC. He parked his car in the garage and went straight to the director's office. The director was in an unbroken chain of meetings for the remainder of the day.

"I need to see him."

"Doctor Stewart, if anyone could get in, it would be you. But . . ."

"I need to see him now." Stewart stood in front of her looking like he was going to have a heart attack at any moment.

"I will get fired for this." The secretary had been there for several administrations. It wasn't likely that she was in any more trouble than the clerk who had left the vial of smallpox on the wrong tray.

The director came out of the conference room. Through the open door, Stewart could see half a dozen people around the table and most were from the public affairs department.

"Yes, Paul?"

"I need to head up the team to Ferfer." By now, the town didn't need any introduction.

"I don't know. It is a combat zone. You can do better work here."

"Our response time will be critical. The extra hours of being on the ground can make the difference."

"You know so much. What if they find out who you are? What if they find out who your daughter is?" The director looked directly into Paul's eyes. "It may make things more dangerous for Karen."

"This Neisseria bug can do more damage than a bullet."

The director hesitated.

"Okay, go. I will tell everyone in that room that you are going so that there is a chance we can contain this for at least a period of time. They are all of our P.R. people and they will put a lid on it."

"Thank you."

"Don't get sick, don't die, and bring your damn daughter back." The director turned back to the door. "You look like a walking cardiac event ready to happen."

Paul wiped his forehead with his sleeve.

He didn't know that I was planning to go anyway. Stewart had come close to not asking. Around the same time his coworkers at the CDC would be seeing his dark office the next morning, he would have let the pilot report that another passenger was on the aircraft.

"Don't die?" he mumbled to himself as he walked past the secretary.

"What?"

"Oh, nothing. I just got my orders."

CHAPTER THIRTY-EIGHT

The forward operating base at Ferfer was meant to stay as small as possible; however, with the concern for both security and the disease, it had tripled in size since Captain Tola first arrived.

"I am not sure that we can defend this base given its current size," he reported to the major as the last Mar-SOC team arrived. Several fourteen-man teams made up the battalion. The logistics support almost doubled the size of the footprint of the base. Teams of Special Operations Combat Service Specialists, or SOCSS, provided the food and water and all-terrain vehicles that were needed if the unit had to reach out anywhere else. Ammo came in by the pallet loads. They all were high-speed warriors born for this kind of situation.

"Go ahead."

"We can protect the CDC encampment. The docs are starting to arrive." He pointed over his shoulder to some white tents that stuck out from the generally brown camouflage coverings of the Marines' gear. The tents were all sealed with plastic sides, like large air bubbles. "But the MSF doesn't want our help. Hell, sir, they don't even want the Ethiopians' help."

"I have heard that."

"CDC has to have air-conditioning for the portable lab, and the other medical encampments have the same need. So you could walk here in the dark from Mogadishu by following the sound." Tola and his MarSOC team hated noise. "This will all attract attention."

"Is everyone up on shots?"

"Yes, sir, everyone was given a booster before they stepped on the bird at Djibouti."

"Everybody has a team buddy. Everybody needs to know what to look out for with this disease."

"Yes, sir, all the teams have been briefed."

"How about the Ethiopian special ops?"

"I'm impressed. They don't say much but they have been patrolling on all flanks. I think they even stopped one or two Al Shabaab patrols." Tola was impressed by the modified AK-47s they carried. There are more Kalashnikovs in the world than there are teenage boys, but most are knockoffs from villages in Pakistan. The Ethiopians were carrying the Bulgarian-modified ones handmade in a Russian factory. "And they know the local wildlife. Some of this stuff is as bad as Australia."

The captain knew what he was talking about. He had done one float to the new Marine outpost on the northern coast of Australia. Darwin was the new Marine Corps connection to that region. The float was a tour of duty and Darwin was known for the fact that everything that moved on the ground had a chance of killing you before a call could be put out for a medic. Darwin had taught the captain to respect both the wildlife and the people who had lived there all of their lives.

"What is the plan?"

"We are waiting for the last of the CDC team to get

in. WHO is on the other side being protected by the Ethiopians, and the MSF is nearby. We have talked to the man who was with the doctors last. He has given us an idea of where they were and what the bad guys look like. We have issued a warning order to my team to go on a patrol tonight that follows the doctors' route as we last know it."

"Near that village?"

"Yes, sir, they are calling it the Village of Death."

"Is the old man going with you?"

"Not even thinking about it. He is spooked pretty good."

"Okay."

"We are on our own but we have a MQ-9 Reaper on top and air cover as well. Two Hornets are on station and they are being joined by two F-35s. The Ethiopians have some Russian-made gunships with which we are trying to coordinate fire." It wasn't a good day for an Ethiopian gunship to take a shot at a MarSOC patrol. Both the aircraft and the patrol stood to lose.

"F-35s?"

"Yes, sir. The new bird."

The F-35 Joint Strike Fighter for the Marines was in the pipeline to replace the AV-8B Harrier. It was a flying computer. The airplane was virtually invisible, very fast, and could land in a parking lot. It would never be seen by Al Shabaab. Two of them would sit on top and, in the integration with the MarSOC team, the air strike would drop an iron hammer on Al Shabaab. The Marines on the ground were linked with the fighter in the sky. The Marines in the air and on the ground were a new generation of iPad warriors. The jet could find targets with its sensors that could never have been seen otherwise, and the iPad Marine on the ground could know where any attack was coming from in an instant. The MarSOC team on the ground had a new set of eyes that could see through anything.

"We have a name for this operation."

"Yes, sir."

"Operation Shebelle."

Captain Tola's patrol didn't leave the compound until well after midnight. They took the long way around the encampment and Ferfer, cutting into Somalia well north of the one road that led to the east and the village of dead bodies. As they crossed the border, Tola held up his hand and made the motion to pull back on the M4 receivers. A round was loaded in each of the chambers. The rifles were the best that Special Operations and the Marine Corps stocked. They were Heckler & Koch semiautomatic M416s with Trijicon M150 RCO sights. The German-made weapon was accurate, dependable, and deadly. It was buried in a pit for several days, dug out, loaded with a magazine, and still put ten rounds in the center of a delta target at one hundred meters. The delta was in the shape of a man. The kill zone was the imaginary spinal column, from the head down to the center of the chest. Each man carried six magazines of thirty rounds and five clips for their M45 MEUSOC pistols.

The sidearm was unique.

Marine Colonel Robert Young had designed the pistol. He took the M1911 originally built by John Browning and created a new monster. It had the drop power of the .45 caliber slug, which was like getting hit in the chest with a sledgehammer and could last over eighty thousand rounds before the Precision Weapons Section at

Quantico even thought of pulling it off the line. Each member of the team carried one.

The team crossed over the other side of the valley and then headed south until they came to the road. They then turned and followed it to the east. Tola's night vision goggles gave him a perfectly clear view of the land, the bush, the trees, and his men as they moved along slowly.

A drizzle of rain kept the night dark.

The NVGs caused the lead operator to stop on more than one occasion as he and the others saw the glow of eyes. As they got closer, it gave them the sense that they were walking through a zoo without bars.

"Shit, sir, that's a lion!"

Tola's staff sergeant had been on several tours but he was like a child seeing his first wild animal.

"Yes, and they will move."

The creatures seemed to sense that the strange shapes and smells were something more deadly than another predator. The spent graphite from the gunpowder, even though each weapon had been cleaned a thousand times, still gave off a pungent odor. They still needed to think up a way to disguise the smell.

The huts in the village stood like tombstones marking graves. They were just shapes in the dark that made no sound whatsoever. The scavengers had picked apart the bodies some time ago and the only thing Tola could see with his NVGs and Trijicon on his M416 was what looked like rags and cans and some plastic jugs tossed around.

They stayed upwind from the huts and moved around to the east where the road started up again. The old man had told them that he had last seen the men with their captives heading east on that road.

Tola and all of his men had been trained as scouts,

able to pick up a trail even days after it had been left. The rain had made it easier, as puddles had filled up the tracks but left a definable path of potholes.

"A small truck. Probably a Toyota." Tola bent down and felt the track with his hand.

"Yes, sir," the staff sergeant whispered to him over the communications system.

"And one wheel off." The staff sergeant had picked up that a wrong-sized wheel had been used on the back right side of the vehicle.

"We now know who to track." The unique imprint made it easy. They could separate this one truck's tracks from any others.

The trail turned to the south and the river. Slowly, they worked their way down to the crossing point.

At the tree, Tola felt the cold wet embers of the fire underneath the branches.

"Sir, got something."

Tola turned to his staff sergeant who was standing by a round smooth boulder near the edge of the river. He had something in his hand.

"Evergreen?"

"Yes." Tola looked at the empty gum wrapper underneath the smaller rock.

"Well, she was alive up to this point." The staff sergeant held it up like a piece of evidence that needed to be saved.

Just then a thump went off behind them. "What the hell?"

It was the sniper. Every team had at least one trained long-range shot who was equipped with another weapon. He came out of the dark dragging something.

"Sorry, sir." He had a sheepish grin on his face. "The damn thing came after me."

The mamba stretched more than six feet long. It was

dead. A bullet had exploded the first foot where the head should have been.

"Don't go anywhere near that head." Tola knew what he was talking about. Even the smallest piece of a fang could scratch, possibly penetrating the gloves that they all wore. And with a scratch, a Marine would be lost.

"They crossed the river here. This is enough for one night. The air cover might get confused if we go farther."

The worry of a random Ethiopian gunship taking aim on them put limits on what they could do. Tola worried about friendly fire as much as Al Shabaab. In fact, Al Shabaab didn't have any aircraft. They had given up the sky.

"You got to get rid of that freaking snake. Others might come through here and know we were here."

"Yes, sir."

The Marine pulled it into the water and let it float away. There would be scavengers that would enjoy the meat. The winner had finally met its match.

"Well, she was alive this far. Hope she can give it a few more days."

Tola looked across the river. He had an idea of what needed to be done, but knew that his boss would not like it.

The patrol returned to the compound as the first rays of light started illuminating trees and tents and vehicles.

"Sir, we got a problem."

Tola waited at the gate while the last man came in. His staff sergeant was standing next to him.

"What's that?"

"Two of our guys are reporting headaches."

CHAPTER THIRTY-NINE

Moncrief used his retired Marine identification card to get both Parker and himself on Dobbins Air Force base. The guard checked the passenger's driver's license and made no comment to the "Phillip Berks" sitting in the front seat. The guard did give Parker a bit of a stare, though, as Gunny had a high and tight haircut and his passenger was just the opposite. The passenger had his hair pulled back with a camouflage baseball cap and both men had on desert-brown camouflage utilities that were made by someone other than the U.S. military.

The brown camouflage utilities had been given to them some time ago by a French Foreign Legion major whom Moncrief had served with in Kuwait. Moncrief had exchanged a Marine KA-BAR combat knife for two sets of the clothes in different sizes. His uniform bulged a little at the waist whereas Parker's didn't. They wanted to try to blend in.

"These uniforms will keep them guessing." Moncrief smiled as they headed towards base operations. "Oh, by the way, boss, thank you for making me a part of this."

"You sure?"

"Oh, yeah. You know we were meant for this shit."

Parker smiled. They pulled up to base operations to see a guard at the side gate with his M4 being held tightly to his chest. He was at the ready.

"Airman?" Moncrief rolled down the window.

"Yes, sir."

"CDC."

"Got it, sir. You can pull up to the aircraft and unload."

The tail of the C-17 cargo jet stood above the back ramp like a three-story building. The white lights of the cargo bay illuminated several sealed pallets inside. A final pallet was being loaded when Moncrief pulled the truck up. They stopped and pulled their backpacks and large bags from the bed of the truck.

"I've never made one of these runs without a weapon," Moncrief said as they handed their bags to a cargo master. Parker held on to his backpack.

"I still haven't." It was clear that some kind of weapon was in the backpack.

"Thank you."

Parker turned around to see Dr. Paul Stewart standing there. He still looked exhausted but at least he had changed to another checkered shirt and khaki pants.

"Hey, gentlemen." An airman in a flight suit with earphones around his neck and a cable that extended into the cargo hole came up and extended his gloved hand. "I am the chief. Just let me know if there is anything you need. We will be rolling in just a few."

Moncrief ran his truck back to the parking lot and locked it.

I wonder if I will see this truck again, he thought as he patted it on the rear bumper. He walked past the airman and tossed the key to the guard. "Hey, give this to the op's chief."

"But, sir."

"If he needs to move it, tell him it's got a full tank of gas. Likewise, if it is still here in a week, he can have it."

"Oh." The guard stood in disbelief.

The auxiliary power unit had provided a constant buzz while they were there, but as Parker and Moncrief walked on board the engines started to wind up. A warm kerosene breeze engulfed them as they walked onto the ramp.

"It will be about ten hours straight into Djibouti," the airman said as he pointed to the front of the pallets. "We set up some cots to make it a little more comfortable for you and we've got plenty of box lunches."

A dozen other staffers from the CDC were there and already belted into their seats. The aircraft was made for changes of use so the seats were on roll-in platforms. The cargo hold had no shortage of room. The staffers looked on in disbelief when they saw Dr. Paul Stewart buckle up. No senior scientist or head of his department had ever made a trip such as this.

At 0600, the aircraft rolled forward and was on the active runway in less than a minute. The engines sped up and the plane moved forward until the nose lifted up and started a steep climb over the city of Atlanta. It reached ten thousand feet and then started to climb again, only to turn on a forty-five-degree bank and point itself to the northeast.

The aircraft flew through the day and well into the night as it crossed the North Atlantic, the boot of Italy, and then followed the Nile to its source. The sky was clear until they started south over the Suez.

"What's the weather look like over central Africa?" Parker stood just to the rear of the pilot and looked out through the Plexiglas windows. He could see the twisting trail of lights that followed the villages that were linked up by the Nile. To the west was a vast wasteland of the darkness of the Sahara. He saw small flickers of light in rows that were the ships coming up to and leaving the Suez Canal. The cloud cover was broken in front of them but to the south a solid line of storms extended from as far as he could see to both the left and the right. Soon they would enter the storm.

"It's the beginning of the rainy season."

"IFR landing?" Parker was asking if the final leg would be controlled by instruments and an air traffic controller looking at a radar screen somewhere.

"Yes, sir. We will get some IFR time."

The aircraft entered a thick mass of clouds as it started its descent over the Gulf of Aden and a turn back towards Djibouti. The airplane pitched back and forth as it descended through more than ten thousand feet of rainstorms. Finally, it broke through the ceiling just beyond the runway. It landed only a few short minutes after starting the downhill run. The C-17 did not linger while on the ground. Anything below ten thousand feet was within striking distance of a sniper shot or a ground-launched missile. Danger lurked everywhere. The airplane came to a rest and then kept its jet engines at a high spin while it quickly taxied to the far end of the base.

"We have orders to get you three out of here and then unload the cargo," the airman hollered at them over the roar of the engines. "They have some folks waiting for you."

The three used the door instead of the ramp to exit the aircraft.

A half dozen Marines in full combat gear and with their weapons held across their chests in the ready met them as they stepped onto the tarmac. One of the men had a pistol in a shoulder holster.

"Gentlemen." He saluted. Warm air was pushing at them from all sides.

"We have your ride waiting for you."

The Marine pointed to two MV-22 Ospreys that were sitting at the side ramp with their engines running and the blades in the tilt-rotor liftoff mode.

"Follow me in a line, one after the other!" The Marine led them across the runway to the side tarmac and into the rear of the Osprey. It had a dull yellow light on, and Parker could see several combat-ready Marines on the side seats with the barrels of their weapons pointing down to the deck. Each had a different type of helmet than Parker or Moncrief were used to. It was like a motorcyclist's skullcap helmet shaped to the head with space for earphones. They all had wrap-around clear-lens glasses and night vision goggles attached to the helmets.

Stewart was given a flight helmet, as they all were, and his head looked small within the shell.

"You all right?" Parker asked as they sat down next to each other.

"Yes," Stewart shouted.

The aircraft began to vibrate as the blades spun up to a different pitch and then Parker could feel the lift push him down into the seat.

Damn, where is my bag? He used his hands to feel below the seat until he felt the backpack's strap. He pulled the pack onto his lap and felt for the zipper. Parker didn't like the idea of going into the wilderness without his weapon. A fully loaded HK P-30 .40 caliber automatic was in the pack with two magazines carrying fifteen rounds each. It was the easiest customs that he had ever cleared.

"What's the flight time?" Parker asked the aircraft chief, who was sitting next to him with his shoulder holster on and the butt of a MEUSOC .45 automatic sticking out. He had on a sandy brown flight suit and a vest with additional clips of ammunition in the pockets.

"Two and a half hours."

"Thanks." Parker gave a thumbs-up. At that same moment, the blades rotated to a forward position and the aircraft's speed pulled them sideways in their seats.

It quickly spun up to over 300 knots as it headed farther into Africa.

"I have heard of you," the chief yelled back to Parker. "Welcome aboard, sir."

Secrecy was a relative thing.

The Ospreys pulled up to level flight somewhere over Ethiopia. Parker unbuckled his belt and leaned forward in the space between the cargo hold and the flight deck. He looked up in the darkness to see a shape much bigger hovering above them. He held on to the bulkhead as he watched the Osprey pull in behind a four-engine turboprop C-130J refueler. The Super Herk held steady at a slightly higher altitude. The basket for the fuel pipeline had an iridescent glow to it. The Osprey bounced up and down until it settled into the zone of clean air behind and center to the four engines of the Hercules. The pilots of the Osprey looked like surgeons working on a heart transplant. As any aircraft, an Osprey pilot needed to know how to refuel in all kinds of weather. The machine was made to be faster than anything that came before, with a tilt-rotor and helicopter capability. It had changed the concept of modern flight. It could go longer and move faster but it would also get thirsty. The C130-J gave it unlimited range, easily allowing it to go from Spain to Djibouti, the same distance as Anchorage to Miami. In what seemed like minutes, the aircraft slid backwards and away from the refueler.

Soon after the Osprey had refueled, the two started to descend. Breaking through a steady cloud cover that hovered over the valley, they followed each other, trailing a certain distance, with Parker's bird as the lead.

Parker looked out to see a twisting dirt-red river and several lit encampments. Each seemed to be separate from the others. A few lights lit the village of Ferfer. There looked to be a few thousand people in rows of structures that followed the main streets.

The aircraft turned toward glow markers that signaled the landing zone. As it made the descent of the final hundred feet, the Osprey again shifted from one type of flight to another. The aircraft became a helicopter and started to settle slowly as its wheels sunk into the dirt. Despite a gentle rain, dust and small rocks were thrown about everywhere.

"Let's go." The Marine in charge signaled the men to depart the aircraft without hesitation. It was clear that the Osprey meant to stay on the ground for as short a time as possible.

Parker followed the line of men heading to a tent.

Dr. Stewart is totally out of his element, Parker thought as he followed the man to the edge of the landing zone and the first tent. Another man, not in military camouflage but in a blue scrub suit, was standing at the entrance to the tent as well. He was covering his eyes with his sleeve.

Stewart looked exhausted. Moncrief looked ready to roll.

"God, we are back!" Moncrief said to Parker as the quiet resumed for a minute between Osprey landings.

"Yeah." Parker turned to watch the second aircraft hover and then land. Other Marines and two women dressed in loose-fitting cargo dress followed them out to the other side of the landing zone. The bird had barely touched down when its nose started to rise.

"I need a weapon." Moncrief's first words would have been Parker's if he didn't already have something in his backpack.

"I am sure that they can come up with something."

The two followed Dr. Stewart, who was led into the tent by his fellow CDC doctor.

"Welcome to Africa." Captain Tola extended his hand in the dim light of the tent. There was a makeshift table in the center of the room with a blowup of a satellite picture of the valley for miles in all directions. Marines sat on the sides in front of computer screens. Parker noticed that virtually all of the screens had images on them with a bold red TOP SECRET banner on the top.

"You are Colonel William Parker?" Tola held out his hand.

"Parker does fine." He didn't want the command to think that they had to entertain someone of high rank. He was basically there as a medical guinea pig ready to be poked and tested. And it appeared that his alias had not lasted long. He was no longer being referred to as Phillip Berks.

Why did I do this? he wondered as he stood there amid a tent full of warriors with much to do. They were running combat patrols every night while he and

Moncrief would look out over the land with a pair of NVGs. It was worse than being suited up for a football game and never coming off the bench.

"He is the hope for all of us." Paul Stewart said aloud. It would not take long for all of the camp to know why two civilians with no connection to the CDC or WHO, or even Doctors Without Borders, were there. "What is the report?"

"The death count is at thirty. We are treating at least sixty more who we suspect are infected. Almost all right now are in the MSF encampment. WHO has issued a GAR and we are trying to stop any movement out of the area." The GAR was the Global Alert and Response that first got word to Stewart. "It is still early but this has all the signs of an outbreak on the same scale as Ebola in Guinea. It is moving exponentially. Ebola went from sixty to six hundred to six thousand in a matter of weeks," said the CDC doctor

"What the hell have we gotten into?" Moncrief mumbled the words next to Parker.

"I have two Marines who are sick," Tola inserted the comment. "And we cannot take them out of here. We can't take anyone who gets sick out of here."

The disease needed to be contained as much as possible.

"I have another question." Paul Stewart looked ready to collapse.

"Doctor, we believe she is alive," Tola said. "I took a patrol out last night and we found a wrapper from a piece of chewing gum. It was clearly a signal that she wanted us to find."

CHAPTER FORTY

As Omar and his guide headed west they ran into more and more fighters of Al Shabaab heading away from the sound of the artillery shells. The thud of the impact caused the ground to vibrate. At night he would see the flash of yellow explode in the distance, especially when they reached a higher point of land. During the early morning hours a cloud of smoke would follow the explosion. One shell out of ten caused a black trail to rise up into the sky, meaning that a vehicle had been hit. The black clouds would last for some time as the fuel burned off.

"We need to head more north." The guide pointed towards the distance. Somalia seemed to go on forever.

"We need food," Omar complained.

"Yes."

"Do you know where we can get some?"

"No."

The conversation was always short. They did stop for prayers, getting on their knees and pointing to the northeast. And in the middle of the day, the two would stop and seek cover under a tree.

Chocolate. Omar became obsessed with the thought

of the Baskin-Robbins that was down the street from where he went to college. *A chocolate milkshake with dark chocolate ice cream.*

In the evenings, they often ran into a patrol. Each time they heard a noise, they stopped and lay on the ground behind a rock. They would start to call out so that the patrol would not be surprised. Once the two connected, the man with Omar would hug a member of the patrol and talk in a fast rattle of Swahili. It seemed the man had cousins across all of Al Shabaab.

Sometimes the patrol had some biscuits and stopped to start a fire.

"Must eat and move," a member of the patrol would say. They would build a fire between several rocks, bring out a metal pot and another plastic liter jug of water, and put it to a boil. A man then took out a bag of rice and poured it into the pot. They shared one metal plate with each one having a corner of the plate for his portion.

Omar would talk religion as his guide relayed his words on to the others.

"We must obey what Allah says." Omar was strict in his interpretation.

They listened to the white man with a look of bewilderment on their faces. The men lived in a dark world where a television was a foreign object. Its images, always images, of an unimaginable world. It was when Omar and his guide met the second patrol on the road to Baydhabo that they learned more of the two prisoners.

"Yes, we have heard of two white people. A man and a woman."

"Where?"

"North of here." The man pointed off across a long stretch of sand, rocks, bush, and a scattering of trees.

"Allah be praised." Omar pulled out a map and un-
folded it.

The man could not read.

"What village were they near?" he asked his guide.

"He doesn't know."

Omar became frustrated. He swung his AK-47 from
one shoulder to the other.

"Was it by water?"

Again the question was changed into a string of
words that climbed and sunk with a variety of sounds.

"Near the Shebelle."

"The river?"

"Yes."

"But it is a long river." Omar needed more details.

"Tayeeglow."

"Tayeeglow?" Omar looked at the map. There was a
town thirty kilometers to their northeast with the name
of Tayeeglow. "But it is not on the Shebelle."

"Yes, but it is on the way to the Shebelle."

Omar and his guide stopped to sleep below two trees
that night.

"We sleep in the tree." The guide pointed to two
large branches that extended out from the trunk.

A quiet had descended as they continued to head
north and east. It seemed the fighting was off to the
west.

"Why in the tree?" Omar asked. The risk of lions
and baboons was constant but they could make a small
fire and the smoke and flames would keep the predators at bay.

"See." The guide pointed to the ground. A line of
large black ants led to a battlefield where one army of
ants was waging war with another. A stream of red ones

was moving in the opposite direction. Omar had already learned that the small red ones were more dangerous.

"I had a friend once." Omar's mind went back to Mobile. "He had a boat and the gas can exploded." The ants had a path that they followed as willed by Allah just as Omar's friend's life was willed by Allah.

The boy was given use of a duckboat that they used to travel the back nooks of the bay. It was meant for shallow water and had a flat bottom. They snuck cans of Budweiser from the ice cooler that was on his father's truck and stole packs of Marlboro cigarettes.

Omar was not with his friend the time that the cigarette dropped into the bottom of the boat where the fuel had leaked. He did visit him at the burn unit in Mobile. The friend died soon thereafter. It was another brick in the wall of why he had a special path. If Allah had wanted it, Omar would have been on that boat that day.

"We will sleep in the tree." Omar agreed with the guide's advice. "It is Allah's wishes."

"No ants in the tree."

"Yes. No ants, brother."

Omar used his long black turban to tie himself to the tree trunk. He hung his rifle from a nearby branch. He would drift away for a few minutes thinking of his wife and child and then start to roll off the branch. It seemed that whenever he started to roll he let out a noise that woke him up.

By early morning he could barely keep his eyes open. The dim light was like a dose of morphine. He fell asleep sitting erect. And then the hot sun started to penetrate through the small leaves of the tree.

Finally Omar awoke, rubbed the back of his neck with his hand, and felt the sweat from a short deep sleep. He swung his legs across the branch.

"Our prayers." He mumbled the words. There was no answer.

"Hey," he called out again as he looked around the trunk of the tree. There was complete silence. It was then that he realized that the guide was gone.

Omar climbed down and headed northeast. He was learning to survive. Soon he would achieve what he wanted. Along the way he would become the most wanted man in the free world and he would not even know it. Someone else would help him reach his goal.

CHAPTER FORTY-ONE

"Colonel Parker, Dr. Stewart needs you." The nurse had on a white plastic bio suit with the hood pulled down around her neck.

"Yes." Parker had been taking advantage of the opportunity to sleep. *I may need this later on.* He had a gut instinct that a reserve would be needed. Once he had that extra sleep, Parker could go for days on adrenaline alone.

"What time is it?" He pulled on his camouflage jacket as he looked at the tactical watch he wore. It showed 3:00.

"Three a.m.?"

"Yes, sir. He needs you now."

Parker followed her across the compound to the CDC tents. A strip of yellow plastic marked the "do not cross" area and encircled three tents that were interlinked and sealed. Plastic tunnels led from one tent to another and to another. Generators ran continuously, one for each tent. He followed her to the regular canvas tent on the far end that was lit with two lightbulbs strung on a wire. In the dim light he saw a metal sink with pink plastic bottles and water that would run when she flipped a switch.

"Scrub!" She barked the order like a trauma nurse who was used to handling gunshot wounds at an emergency room. Her voice and manners indicated that the woman, who stood barely to his chest, was a pit bull dog when it came to taking care of the patient.

"How did you get here?" he asked as he took off the jacket and scrubbed from his elbows down to his hands. The water was warm. It had been brought in by the 24/7 run of Sea Stallion helicopters supporting the base.

"Got tired of the boring life of an emergency room."

"Too boring? An emergency room?"

"Here, put this suit on."

She is unaware that I am the only one here who doesn't need this suit.

He suited up and went through a zipped and sealed first chamber to find Paul Stewart looking at a computer screen blowup of the virus. It had a loop to it like a twisted donut but with small spikes on the ends similar to the bristles of a new beard.

"Hey."

"The nurse called me Parker."

"I am sorry. They are all good and they all have TS's." The top-secret clearance cost the CDC, via the FBI, more than $100,000 per background check. At the CDC, only one out of five made the cut unless they were well published and had unique knowledge necessary to the organization. Those few scientists who had the knowledge unique to a disease but not the ability to get a top-secret clearance were allowed in, but were constantly on the watch list. They never had the access that the few others with top-secret clearances did.

"What's up?"

"We have two Marines that are sick."

"I heard."

"One is from California."

Parker was waiting for a pitch. The doctor hadn't gotten him up in the middle of the night to socialize.

"You've got blood typing of the Marine?"

The lab technicians had taken blood samples, DNA swabs and even chest X-rays.

"Yes, we do; yes, we do." Stewart was hesitating.

"And?"

"I would like to do a transfusion. You and the Marine share the same blood type."

"O positive?" Parker knew his type. It was a part of combat that he had written it with markers on the top of his boot and taped it on the side of his pants. If a medic got you transported in time from something bad, he and other combat veterans knew that it was important to not lose a minute on the typing of blood. The final lace of his boot had strung into it a metal dog tag that had been printed with "O positive."

"Exactly."

"So the transfusion might give him a chance?"

"I think so. It might buy us some time. His friend was not O positive."

It was clear what had happened to the other Marine during the night.

"Dr. Stewart? You didn't bring me to Africa just to do blood typing or transfusions, did you?"

Stewart looked embarrassed.

"You had one transfusion in mind. A last-ditch effort if the others didn't work."

Stewart turned back to the computer screen. He didn't have a poker face.

CHAPTER FORTY-TWO

The van sped north on Interstate 95 leaving the Richmond area behind after Wassef picked up the FedEx box of money. Well north of the city, he took an exit where there was only a Chevron gas station on a side country road. After passing the gas station, the road twisted to the right and into the darkness. He traveled on it for several minutes not seeing anything, not even a farmhouse. He drove another five miles or so until he came to a dirt road that intersected with the highway. It was obviously rarely used, as the branches of nearby trees pushed out from the sides, giving it the appearance of a path more than a road. Wassef turned the lights off and pulled the van onto the road, drove a hundred yards, slowly backed it up under a tree, and turned the wheel. When finished, it was below the branch of an oak that was nearly as wide as the door to the van and pointed out towards the county highway.

Allah, prepare me for this journey. Wassef sat in the still silence and dark. He had a sheet of paper that had his scrawl on it. He could not read it in the darkness without a flashlight and he would not turn one on. He knew what was written on the paper, which was all that counted.

The country road remained silent and dark. There had been no rain in days so the road was dusty and dry. He could feel the dust as he sat in the van not moving. He could smell the van, and the oil, and gas. He remained still. A car door could be heard. A light was seen. He continued to sit there in the dark.

A car's lights followed the road in the distance. It originated in the opposite direction from where he had come. He watched as the lights moved and turned with the curves of the road. He sat up like a cat that had suddenly seen a mouse. The car moved down the road and off into the distance. It never slowed down nor seemed to care about what was off to the sides in the darkness. It confirmed that he had not been followed.

Probably a carpenter going to work, Wassef thought as he sat there. He could feel the smooth cool steering wheel under his hand. *The man probably drives the eighty miles or so into Washington each and every day. He lives in a single-wide trailer on land he rents, and drives the miles so he can live in the forest at night. He probably hates the city.*

The thought randomly went through his mind as he sat there in the darkness.

As it neared first light, he realized that for a moment he had fallen asleep.

Allah, forgive me. He had promised himself not to fall asleep. He wiggled to the back of the van, quietly, without opening the door or making a sound. Wassef had a bucket and bottle of water, which he used to wash himself. And then he pulled out his prayer rug and turned it towards the east in the small space he had in the van. It was to be his last prayer. He took his time and slowly whispered the words.

As he climbed back into the driver's seat, he looked at the FedEx box next to him, lifted it, and saw the kitchen knife under it. He had followed orders well. There were to be no other weapons, as the purchase of weapons left a trail. The knife was all that he needed.

He pulled the van out onto the paved road and headed back towards the gas station. As he passed it, he made a point of turning the left blinker on and heading south. If there were eyes at the station, it was important that they saw a van heading south and not north. He rode the next few miles to the south, took the exit, and pulled into a BP station. The van was nearly empty of gas but he only put $42 of gas into it. He paid with a twenty, two tens, and two one-dollar bills. Everything was planned so as to reveal little to suspecting eyes. He bought two Red Bulls and a bag of Lay's Potato Chips.

"Breakfast?" the clerk asked as he paid for it all with another well-used ten-dollar bill.

"Yeah, the breakfast of champions."

She laughed.

"See you later." She smiled.

She will be on CNN tonight. He opened a Red Bull and sipped it as he walked out to the van. This time, he pulled out of the station and turned to the north.

"It just doesn't feel right." The senior agent of the TFOS team in Richmond had more than a decade of experience. She watched the video feed from the holding cell at the jail. The two women in their burqas with the niqabs pulled back sat in silence with their hands folded. They were too content.

"Have we checked all of their contacts?"

"Yes. All that we know." The other agent had been up all night. "They didn't have a lot of money."

"What was the final count?"

"About two thousand dollars."

"But they have been a regular channel for some time?" She knew the answer but was going over the points both in her head and out loud.

"Yes, we picked up the trail several months ago. We got the okay and started monitoring their calls. A lot to Kenya."

"That made it easy." It took out a lot of the guess-work when the calls were being made to central Africa. The red flag went up the pole.

"You know how much funding was needed for Oklahoma City?" The bombing of the courthouse was a classic plan and execution. "Just over four thousand bucks."

"Really?"

"Yes. The terror money trail doesn't have to be very wide nor very long." She sensed what they found was just the tip of an iceberg.

"And they have said nothing to each other since?" She gazed at the monitor while she spoke.

"Not a word."

"They look too content. It is as if they know the other shoe is going to drop."

"Yes."

"Something is going on." The senior agent knew that an alert too early could send someone underground. The only thing worse would be an alert too late. "I am going to call Washington. We are too close to too many things to just let this sit."

CHAPTER FORTY-THREE

Karen Stewart started to laugh.

It was an uncontrollable and painful laugh as she looked at herself in the side mirror of the truck. She saw a red-dotted face with dirt outlining the edge of her nose. Her teeth were yellowed and she was burned from the equator's sun. It was a stranger in the glass. A horribly ugly stranger.

But what made her laugh was the hollowed look around the eyes. She had lost so much body weight that the person she was staring at was the petite teenager that she always hoped she would return to one day. Her belt had been pulled up to the first notch, and still the pants sagged. She laughed as she thought of how her dresses would fit over her new frame.

God, will I ever get home? She didn't want the thought to enter her mind. They were back down now to Xasan and the old man, who was the driver. They had followed the river south to the point where another road cut to the southwest. She had never paid attention to the sun, but as survival called for it, she was observing everything in her power. They were headed away from the riverbed and into the country.

"Peter?" He had become so ill that they had let him ride in the bed of the truck when the road was passable. It wasn't a favor so much as Xasan got tired of lifting the dead weight back into the truck. Every time they made him walk with the jab of the rifle he would shuffle a hundred yards and then collapse.

But if the truck ran into a mud hole, all, including Xasan, had to get out and push. They would go a mile and then get stuck again. It was an endless loop. For some time they had not seen another human. She sensed, however, that they were heading towards a war.

"Peter?"

"Yes, my lady?" He had become delirious over time.

"How are you doing?"

"Fine, a little hot, but fine."

The rain, the mud, and his fever soaked him through.

"We will stop." Xasan held up his rifle. It was the first time that Karen thought he wasn't sure where he was going. There was some confusion on his face as he argued with the old man. Finally, the driver got out of the cab and they walked down the road as if to compare thoughts about the direction in which they were headed. They turned and started to walk back. At the truck, the old man swung the door open and began to climb back in when he suddenly stopped. He grabbed his chest, his eyes rolled up into his head, and he fell back into the mud.

"What did you do?" Xasan screamed as he pointed his rifle towards Karen.

She ignored his yelling and knelt down next to the body. Doctor Stewart felt for a pulse on his neck. She could feel the whiskers of his gray beard as she pressed her fingers into the place where there should have been a pulse.

Without thinking, she started pushing on his chest. His body sank down in the mud until it hit the hard surface below. She continued to push, repeatedly, pushing and pushing with one hand over the other. She kept pushing without feeling the hunger or exhaustion of the days in captivity.

"Come on," she muttered out loud.

Out of the corner of her eye, she saw Xasan put his rifle over his shoulder and stare at the process.

And she continued to press, pushing as hard as she could.

Suddenly, the old man's eyes opened up and he started to cough. He pushed her arms aside as if he could not understand why this stranger was beating on his chest.

Xasan sunk to the ground. He started to cry.

"Allah?" He said the word almost as if it were a plea to understand what had happened.

The old man had survived a heart attack.

Karen fell back on her rear end.

"He needs some aspirin." She said it as if there was a nearby pharmacy that could provide a bottle. Xasan got off his knees, walked around the truck, opened the door on the passenger side, reached into the glove compartment, and took out an old bottle of Bayer aspirin.

"What?"

She wanted to scream.

Xasan gave her the bottle. She opened it and gave the old man two white tablets. She then stood up and took the bottle to the back of the truck, lifted Peter's head, and gave him two tablets.

"We need some water," she said.

Xasan went back to the cab and pulled out a two-liter plastic bottle and handed it to her. She gave Peter a drink and then gave the old man a drink as he was about to sit up.

Xasan pointed to the old man and said something in Swahili.

Peter lifted up his head as if the aspirin had had an immediate effect.

"He says that man is his father."

Karen stood up in the confusion of the moment. She had saved the life of someone who would have shot her without hesitation the day before.

"I want to go home."

No one heard her.

CHAPTER FORTY-FOUR

"Captain Tola?" The commanding officer of the SPMAGTF-Crisis Response on the ground signaled to him to come over to the operations tent. Tola was readying for another night's patrol when the C.O. gave him the signal to talk.

"Yes, sir."

"I need to speak with you a minute. Let's go over to the one."

Tola followed the C.O. to a bunker on the far end of the compound. A Marine guarded a small structure made of sandbag walls with a tin roof covered by more sandbags. The guard stood next to the entrance with a locked and loaded M416. A line of tape encircled the structure with warning signs that said DO NOT CROSS. DEADLY FORCE AUTHORIZED.

A sign painted on a square of plywood and hanging over the entrance read COMMANDING OFFICER. Below the words there was a shield, which spelled it all out— SPECIAL-PURPOSE MARINE AIR-GROUND TASK FORCE— CRISIS RESPONSE. The Marine unit on the ground was a MAC, or Maritime Airborne Company made up of MARSOC critical skills operators. The unit was custom-designed and built for this mission. It had at its core a company of Marines or CLT that had been formed out of the 2nd Marine Special Operations Battalion.

Tola liked the lieutenant colonel. They had done two combat tours together and it was clear that his boss was on the fast track even at this early stage in his Marine career. However, the winds of the reduction in force were starting to blow. Word had passed through the commands and then the media. The armed services were to be hit by a hurricane force. One in every three Marines was being laid off and returned to a different world. Only a few would survive the assault that was coming. The major, despite being very good, and decorated with two silver stars, had a fifty-fifty chance of staying on.

And yet the dangers were not going away. Al Shabaab, Al Qaeda, and ISIS were raising the battle flag across several thousands of miles. The fundamentalists in the Philippines and the western Pacific didn't even make page ten with their occasional car bomb. Gaza was on a mutual path with Israel that assured only more bloodshed. But despite all this, the military was being hit with crushing blows of force reduction. The Army was going down by a third or more. The Marine Corps, Navy, and Air Force were following the same path.

"We have some word. Some significant word." He looked at his watch and then the two went into the bunker. In the center was a portable computer on a table with several stools in front of it. The computer was cleared for "Top Secret." The Marine guarding the bunker from the outside carried two hand grenades. One was an M67 fragmentation grenade and the other had phosphorus explosive material that would burn at a thousand degrees when ignited. The computer and the satellite dish it was connected to would not survive. It mattered little, as the encryption was incredibly complex, but they would take no chance. Everything would be destroyed before it had the opportunity to land in someone else's hands.

"We have a videoconference in five minutes." The major pointed to one of the stools for Tola. Another Marine was in the tent. He was a communications lance corporal. "Are we linked up?"

"Yes, sir."

"The satellite has a fifteen-minute window." The major and Tola pulled up the two stools.

A screen showed the logo of central command.

Suddenly, a conference room appeared with an admiral sitting at the end of the table, flanked by another officer.

"Do we have everyone?" the admiral asked. "Is everybody up on the satellite?"

A split screen showed another admiral who announced he was NavCent, and a third admiral who was commander of the task force somewhere at sea in the Gulf of Aden.

"I am going to let my J-3 bring us up to date with the limited time we have," said the first admiral.

A Navy captain in a gray-blue-dotted camouflage uniform started to speak. Stitched into his uniform was the black-threaded insignia of a Navy SEAL.

"Intelligence reported the DF-21 possessed by Al Shabaab was in a building in the city of Jilib." The captain inserted video from a Reaper nighttime intelligence film. "We believe they only have one of these."

He played another video taken by a similar nighttime surveillance aircraft. It showed two helicopters move in and stop near the building; then small black figures seemed to pour out onto the ground.

"SEAL Team Six sent in a team. It was a trap. The missile had been moved."

A bright flash appeared on the screen where the building once stood.

It was clear that the team had been sent in to destroy the missile but, even more important, to confirm both its existence and its destruction.

"Intelligence assets both up top and on the ground are trying to obtain more information."

The captain became somber.

"We lost three SEALs last night."

Tola looked at his hand and then his watch. He knew that as they were engaged in the conference call, they were being watched. The broadcast went both ways. In a SCIF in Bahrain, the split screen showed the several commands across the theater. He knew that as long as the "carrier killer" was in Al Shabaab's hands, the U.S. fleet would stand farther off the shores of Somalia. And with the carrier farther off at sea, the capabilities of the Hornets and F-35s would be stretched even more. There might be gaps in the air cap, and with them there might be gaps in response times.

Faud had moved the afternoon before the attack. He and his command had traveled south to the outskirts of the coastal city of Kismaayo.

"We move our chess piece." The details of the attack had been reported to him. "Each time, when we move it, we need to prepare the last place for a trap."

"Praised be Allah. There were several martyrs from last night, but the Americans suffered as well."

"Yes, blessed are the names of those who are martyred."

Faud paused a moment.

"We must keep our carrier killer on the move. We must keep them guessing. More time and more money will lead to us obtaining a second and a third device." Faud said the obvious. "The Romans had over a thousand years here and they never knew that cinnamon came from India and not Somalia."

The people could keep a secret. The missile could be moved in a matter of minutes. It was the shape that was the concern. The missile had to be broken apart and reassembled on each and every move. The Predator would identify one long shape or one long truck. And so they waited for a rainstorm on each move. The winds gave them a chance that the Predator would not be on station. And they also waited for a certain window where the satellite was likely to be off its location. Al Shabaab knew how to work the system.

"What of the hostages?" Godane asked the question.

"The *Amriiki* was sent to find them. We have already told the infidels that we want five million apiece. The money will be raised every time they make an attack on us." Faud did not tell him that they were not sure where the captives were, nor where Omar was.

"They are gathering forces at Ferfer. We need to consider an offensive." Godane looked at a map and pointed with his hand as he spoke.

"The disease?" Faud asked.

"Diseases are Allah's will," Godane did not hesitate to say in response.

CHAPTER FORTY-FIVE

The driver in the Honda Civic took the Quantico exit from Interstate 95, and as the car came down to the light, a police car, sirens blaring, pulled in behind. Wassef turned on his blinker and pulled to the side of the highway. As he did this, his hand felt the handle of the knife and moved it to the space between the passenger seat and console. He had learned the lesson from one of the tapes to roll down the driver's window and put both hands in sight.

Wassef knew that the gesture would make the Virginia state trooper feel more comfortable and that was the point. He smiled.

"Hello, Officer."

"Good morning."

Wassef knew that his clean face and short haircut would also help to disarm the officer's suspicions.

"I am sorry, is there a problem?"

"Yes, you have a taillight out."

"Oh, I will . . ." He started to open the door.

"No, don't get out. The traffic here is too busy. We have all these Marines going to work on the base."

"Yes, sir."

"Got your license and registration?"

"Sure." He pulled out his Virginia license with the name Wassef Hamri from Richmond, and the car's registration.

"Okay, where are you going?"

"I am in school at William and Mary, and going to visit my aunt and uncle in D.C." Wassef had done nothing wrong. His record was flawless, although he had never stepped foot on the William and Mary campus. He kept his face composed.

"Okay. Get that light fixed. No ticket."

"Yes, sir. Thank you."

He waited, took his time putting the license back into his wallet, and let the officer's car pull out ahead of him. The trooper moved into the left lane, did a three-sixty, and took the entrance back onto the interstate.

Wassef smiled.

It is not as hard as I thought.

He drove the mile up the highway to the Enterprise rental location, and went in with both his license and a wallet full of money.

"I reserved a van." Again, it was a part of the plan that the vehicle needed to be reserved. If he had walked in without a reservation, wanting a van, it would raise questions. The license had him as being just over twenty-five.

Shit, if that officer had thought about it! The clerk looked at the license and then handed it back to Wassef. His license was legitimate but his being in college at twenty-five was a stretch.

"We have your reservation in order. You have the only van that we carry."

The young girl was perky for the start of a new day.

She was particularly short with only part of her face visible just above the computer terminal.

"Thank you." He added the "thank you" and "sir" whenever possible. It was another tactic that made people take less notice of him. In fact, he was dressed in a white-collared shirt, khakis, a brown belt, and matching brown loafers, and he did it all so as to attract less attention.

Amazing how terrorists can look so different. Wassef had wandered onto an online search of past terrorists one night. He looked at the photographs and thought of how his picture would soon be added to the lot. He would look different from the others. *Perhaps they will use me as a guide for "how to look if you don't want to get stopped."*

"I will leave my Honda here on the lot if that is okay?"

"Certainly, please park it in the back. We have a lot of people pulling in and out. It will be safer there," she said pleasantly.

"Absolutely." He smiled.

"And since you are paying with cash we need to have an extra deposit."

He frowned. And yet it was all part of the orchestrated plan. He would reluctantly pay the money. Wassef pulled out his wallet and gave her $300 in used twenties.

"Here are the keys!"

Wassef moved his Honda to the back of the lot, pulled out the FedEx box, and bent over so as to slowly slip the knife under the box. He knew that he was on a security camera and that the tape would later be pulled. He closed the door and locked the car with the key.

The van was white, which was perfect. It was so similar to a delivery van that the witnesses would hardly take notice. There was nothing that he had done so far that stood out.

Wassef adjusted the seat, turned the mirrors, and reached into his back left pocket, where he had folded a printout from Google Earth of the street address to which he was heading. He looked at his watch and realized that all was in place and he was on time.

The Koran calls for punishment for the disbelievers. He repeated the thought in his mind over and over. The Koran was calling him to do something that he had never done before.

Wassef's van passed the entranceway to the Windview neighborhood at eight in the morning. It was important for him to be there at eight. He followed through the maze of streets, and passed signs that said DEAD END, where the cul-de-sacs held only a few homes.

The houses looked similar in shape and color. It was a neighborhood of consistency. Each yard had been cut, trimmed, and cleaned. And it was trash day. Gray plastic trash bins, all of the same size and make, were lined up on the curbs.

Trash day. Wassef didn't like the idea. It was the first wrinkle in a perfect plan. It meant that he had to have the luck of Allah with him.

The Google map led him to the third cul-de-sac on the right. He had traveled the route several times on Google Earth. His tracking of the locations on the Internet would leave a trail for the FBI to pick up. But Wassef didn't need more than an hour. If the two women who provided his support were not at their house, the women had to keep their mouths shut long enough for it all to work. They never knew the entire plan but they did have an idea as to where he lived. An FBI HRT team would be at his apartment soon enough.

The Bureau's HRT, or the Hostage Rescue Team, did much more than just rescue people. It was a special team of operators trained in tactical operations. It had all of the toys and any type of transportation required. If Wassef hadn't heard the faint sound of the blades of a helicopter by now, his mission was a "go."

The last house on the right of the cul-de-sac had roses in the front yard. They were the difficult type that required constant attention. The hybrids were red and white and the leaves were large petals of green. Wassef's mother, Matta, had roses even in the cold where they lived. The flowers were dormant for the winter but came back in the late spring. The cold helped. The months of subfreezing weather pulled the plant back into its roots. It gave the plant the chance to "reboot." The bugs and diseases had less time to do their damage.

Matta would like their roses. He thought of how much effort had been spent on these flowers. He thought of how it made the home different.

Wassef pulled the white van into the driveway. His heart started to beat quickly. If the plan failed, it was a harmless enough visit, although certainly odd. The police would arrest him, link him to the two women, and he would get a few years in prison. He would be on the news as an American jihadist. He smiled.

Wassef rang the doorbell and heard movement inside.

The corner of the porch had a Home Depot–type

camera, made for night and day; however, it looked cheaply made and probably did not feed into anything more sophisticated than the man's recorder. He heard the fumbling of the locks.

I hope it is him. Wassef feared that it would be a wife and not the man he had met at the gun show. He had prepared himself for the man. *If it is him, it is easy.*

"Hello?" The man had on a white T-shirt, loose pants, and brown leather moccasin slippers. His tone was a question. It was likely that he had a revolver close at hand and a pickup truck in the garage that was covered with stickers such as NRA and hate for gun control.

"Yes, sir!"

"Oh, the boy from the gun show."

Wassef held up the FedEx box with his left hand. Fortunately, there was no screen door. The man swung the stained-glass door to the inside.

"Yes, sir, good to see you again."

"What on earth are you doing around here?" The question proved that the man was still unaware of what was about to happen.

"I found that my aunt lived just down the street and I remembered you. This was on your front porch." Wassef started to hand him the FedEx package. It would not have been unusual. The man probably received parts and gun gear by FedEx all the time. Wassef knew that he was retired from the power company and probably did little except work on his guns.

As the man reached for the box with his dominant hand, Wassef pushed the box towards his chest and thrust the blade of the butcher knife into the center of his chest just below the sternum. He felt the resistance of the muscle as he pushed the blade all the way to the handle. He could feel his hand shaking as the knife struck deep.

The man gasped for air and reached out with his hands, grabbing his assailant by the shirt. Wassef continued to push at the blade. The man started to fall backwards but his hands held on to Wassef's shirt, pulling them both to the ground.

As the two started to fall together, Wassef felt the hilt of the knife push into his own chest. He was face-to-face with his victim, the man's gray eyes staring directly into his. Wassef felt the last warm breath pass over his face and smelled the sour breath of coffee that had been swallowed a short time before.

The two came to rest on the floor. Wassef had to pull himself out of the man's grip and then he rolled over onto the floor.

Odd. He thought. The white shirt was stained with only a little red blood, as if there was just a small cut below.

Wassef's heart started to race. His fate had now been sealed. He stood up. Walking to the door, he peeked out and saw no activity on the street. He closed the front door behind him. He reached into the man's right pocket until he found a chain full of keys.

"It will be easy," he whispered to himself. Wassef could not hear anyone else in the house. As Wassef moved past the man, he was struck by how the dead man looked, his two hands frozen in an imaginary grip, and his gray eyes looking at someone who wasn't there. Wassef moved quickly down the hallway to the back and quietly swung the door closed to the room.

Wassef sensed that when he saw his objective he would know it. He passed by the kitchen with the white

Mr. Coffee pot on the counter next to a green coffee cup. He turned from the kitchen to the hallway that led to the garage.

Not in the garage. He knew that it would not be outside the burglary alarm system. What he didn't know was whether it had its own system. The second door on the right in the hallway had three brass keyholes. They were all lined up from top to bottom above the knob. He started to search through the keychain, matching the make with the type of key. Time was no problem. The house remained quiet. There wasn't even a television on in the great room.

She must still be asleep.

After three tries, the first key fit. He twisted it and felt it unlock. He did it again, going through several keys until another unlocked. Finally, he tried the third lock and it opened as well. He put his hand on the metal knob. The door was also metal and it was in a frame that was metal. He turned the knob but it didn't budge.

Another key? He looked at the knob to see a fourth key slot. Again, he went through the keychain looking for one that seemed to fit. None came close. He tried the door again and it didn't budge. His hands started to sweat.

I can break it open. Even with a metal door, if it came down to just one lock it was possible, but the noise would reduce his time before someone came. He leaned back against the hallway wall and considered the problem.

Possible! Wassef thought. He slid his hand over the lip above the door and felt a fourth key.

"Allah is great."

He turned the key and felt the door open.

If there is a separate alarm I will have less than thirty seconds.

He stopped, let go of the knob, and then went into the laundry room across the hallway. In the dryer, Wassef found several sheets and pillowcases. He pulled out a sheet and wadded it up in a ball.

The knob turned open, and as it did, he felt for a light switch. The room was the size of a typical closet but what was in it was not typical. The walls had racks of weapons, including Thompson submachine guns and Barrett .50 caliber rifles. Another shelf had pistols and another one had an open wooden box that was split into little slots. Each slot held a hand grenade.

The room smelled of gun-cleaning fluid and there were rectangular cans marked "gunpowder."

Wassef was looking for only one thing. He found it in the corner behind the shelves. The man had bragged that he might have known who had one.

Wassef moved quickly, pulling it out and wrapping it in the sheet. He then turned back to the weapons closet and carefully took out a grenade, pulled the pin, and then slid the grenade back into the wooden crate. He did it again a dozen times.

One bottle of gun-cleaning fluid was on the shelf next to the pistols. He squirted the liquid in a stream around the wooden shelf and crate and then made a trail out to the corner of the door. Then Wassef turned off the light. He left the door slightly ajar and went back to the kitchen. One drawer was near several bottles of liquid that made up a makeshift bar. He opened the door to find a match, gathered up his load, and started out. Wassef lit the carpet near the streak of gun fluid and then turned the hallway light out.

He looked back at the closed front door as he pulled out of the driveway.

The blue sheet covered the weapon, which was just behind his driver's seat. Wassef tried to move slowly, not speeding, leaving the quiet neighborhood behind.

He was on the interstate in just a few minutes. There were no sirens. They would come later.

CHAPTER FORTY-SIX

"**W**here did they come from?" A new face assigned by Doctors Without Borders stepped out of his tent in the MSF compound. He had been pulled in from Paris as soon as the word had gotten out that they had lost two of their own. MSF—like the World Health Organization, the CDC, and the Ethiopian Minister of Health—had to constantly work hard to fight the disease at its front line.

"You wouldn't think there are that many who live here." A nurse from the south of France was smoking a cigarette as she stood outside their tent.

A line of tired and thin people stood at the entrance point. Helpers moved around in white suits, with blue gloves and boots. Each helper and nurse wore a face mask. It was an odd sight: people in Bedouin wraps, black turbans, and sandals on their feet; or children in bare feet—all standing there. They did not all look sick, but they all looked frightened. Word of the village of death had started to cross the borders.

"What's the count?" the doctor asked in French.

"We lost well over a hundred in the last two days.

We have a problem with the bodies." The logistics of death were mounting up.

"Is anything helping?"

"It seems that those who have been inoculated with the general meningitis vaccine are holding their own. Some get sick, but when we can keep their fluids up they seem to be making it." She took a pull from her cigarette. It had the bitter smell that only French tobacco has.

"You know that those things will kill you." He was a young thoracic surgeon who was regarded as a pain in the ass as much as a good surgeon. Chest surgery wasn't needed here; however, his dedication was.

"We are surrounded by stacks of bodies that are dead from this deadly disease. I will enjoy my cigarette."

"And now this report that we have to worry about being attacked." The doctor turned back into his tent before changing into the infectious-disease suit. "The military has brought the war to our front door while we are trying to save these lives."

He looked out to the rise of land on the other side of the valley and several helicopters circling the armed camps beyond Ferfer. And then he looked back at the line of the sick, wondering which ones were here for a shot. And which ones simply went back over the hill to pick up their AK-47 again.

"The world is mad."

The noise of a vehicle caused him to turn back towards Ferfer. It was climbing the road up to their compound. The doctor could see a young Ethiopian solider behind the steering wheel and another one beside him. The passenger had gold-rank insignia on his shoulder boards that flickered in the bright light of the rising sun.

"Now what?" A young German surgeon had, by seniority, become the director of the MSF encampment and, as a result, had the job of speaking with the visitor.

The nurse watched as she continued to smoke, her arms folded.

"Hey, you." The Ethiopian officer walked up to the edge of the tents. The medical staff had strung white-and-red tape around the line of tents and posted signs yards apart. The top sign had the large red letters MSF and the words MÉDECINS SANS FRONTIÈRES below. The other sign was more significant. It had an AK-47 in a red circle with a line across it. The camp was meant to be unarmed.

The officer stopped short of the tape.

"Here goes." The doctor went to the line and stopped. He knew that the people beyond were watching. He would not cross the line, and he would not allow the Ethiopian colonel to cross it either.

"Doctor, thank you for helping my people."

"We are here to help." He was right. They provided medical care to the poor in over seventy countries. But only once in MSF's history had it asked for military help. Its neutrality had come at a great price. In the south, Sudan raiders struck an MSF clinic, killing hundreds. The lack of medical care there, as a result, caused thousands to die. Because of incidents like this, MSF continued its attempts to maintain neutrality.

"You need protection. We detect movement." The colonel pointed to the line of the sick. "You know that some of the people who want to kill you are standing in that line right now and looking at us." He never took his hand off his pistol in the holster on his belt.

"We are unarmed and remain so."

"You think this piece of tape and these plastic signs will stop a bullet?"

"Is there anything else, Colonel?"

"No."

"I have to go on shift." The doctor turned back to the nurse. "Give me one of those cigarettes."

"I thought you didn't smoke."

"Boss, something's up." Moncrief looked like the cat with the mouse's tail sticking out of his mouth. With Gunny, however, the tail was a chewed-up stump of cigar.

"You know if you go out of the wire you will have to ditch the cigar." Parker gave it back to the Gunny in spades. "They will smell your Cuban coming from a click away."

"How did you know that it was Cuban?"

"I know you." Parker's guess was close to the point.

"I talked to the Ethiopian colonel. He wants to meet you."

"Let's go." Parker followed Moncrief past the sand-bagged bunkers that had been thrown up at the entrance to the Marine compound. The road led down the hill to a similarly bunkered entrance at the Ethiopian base. Moncrief waved his hand and a guard stood up and motioned for them to come forward.

The Ethiopian camp was just as organized as the Marine camp. Tents that looked more like ones used by the Bedouin were lined up with their sides rolled up during the heat of the day. As Parker passed the tents, he noticed that they were all empty. He walked up to a tall, thin man with dark black skin who was wearing a beret and a camouflage uniform with gold-rank insignia on the shoulders.

"Colonel, this is Marine Colonel William Parker." Moncrief never used such a formal statement except when there was a purpose for doing so. The two shook hands.

"I know why you are here." The colonel squatted down.

"Oh, really?" Parker and Moncrief squatted down as well. It seemed the accepted way to talk to each other in a country that had few chairs in the desert.

"You have survived this disease."

"Yes."

"You are blessed."

"Yes."

"But will you survive the attack?"

Parker hesitated.

"What can we do to help?"

"Would you like to go on one of our patrols to-night?" The colonel wanted Parker and Moncrief to see how they fought their battles.

"We are not armed." Moncrief was speaking to one of the Ethiopians. It was nearing midnight. Parker was looking on. He was armed with his Heckler & Koch automatic pistol in his shoulder holster but it would only help in a close-quarters situation. The Ethiopian was the senior enlisted and spoke perfect English. He had a sister who lived in Denver.

"No problem." He turned to another of lesser rank and gave an order. In a short moment, two young soldiers came out of a tent. Again an order was issued; the two soldiers turned and shortly came back with what looked like two brand-new Kalashnikovs.

"Are they new?" Parker asked.

The senior enlisted officer took one, turned it over, and looked at the serial number.

"Six years old." The weapons were in immaculate

condition. "When a recruit is accepted and is allowed to join our battalion, he is given his beret and his weapon. Both are for life. He must sleep with his rifle, clean it, and care for it." He handed the automatic to Parker. "Take care of it."

There was little known of the Ethiopian Battalion 50th. They were feared and were fearless. It was the secret battalion that even the CIA knew little about. One was in training for years to be admitted, and it was a grueling, relentless physical and mental challenge.

"What about *them*?" Parker was talking about the two who volunteered to give up their rifles to the Marines.

"They get to stay at home tonight. For them, it will be a bad night. We don't like missing the action."

"I understand." Parker pulled the rifle to his shoulder. He looked through the sight to a light on the far end of the camp. He felt the wood stock in his left hand.

"What is it sighted to?"

"A hundred meters center of aim. If you shoot farther, you must raise the aim point a notch for every fifty meters."

"Ammunition?"

"It has a fully loaded magazine. That should be enough."

The patrol gathered together at the Ethiopian front gate. They all bounced up and down several times in what looked like some kind of dance but it served a practical purpose.

"No noise?" Moncrief asked Parker. He wanted to know if Parker heard anything jingling as he hopped up and down. If so, he had a roll of black electrical tape to keep it still. They and the patrol were totally silent.

It wasn't until they had gone more than a mile and crossed the valley that they got the news. Parker was in the center of the patrol. Moncrief was near the front.

One, then another, stopped to raise a hand. It was barely visible in the low light. Parker knelt down with one knee on the rocky ground. He heard the slight sound of movement and then saw Moncrief approach.

"What's up?" Parker whispered.

"They didn't just come out here tonight to do a random patrol."

"What?"

"They saw some movement last night. And they suspect that a splinter group is going to attack MSF tonight."

"What is their plan?"

"They are going to set up an 'L' and catch the Al Shabaab fighters on their way back. Lock and load."

Damn, Parker thought. Tola and the others would not be happy that he was out on a patrol, getting ready to enter into a firefight.

"Don't worry. They want you to just stay back and see how we fight."

As if one can stay back in a combat patrol. It is the "stay back" part that usually gets you in trouble.

Parker slowly, quietly, pulled back on the bolt and chambered a round. He felt for the safety and put his thumb on it. He could feel the grooved safety flip switch and thought of which way it needed to be turned if he wanted to fire.

The patrol continued in the dark, following the wall of the valley on the other side of Ferfer. The medical clinics and stations were on the far side of the valley and were lit up like circus shows. He watched the people, particularly in the MSF encampment, moving around as if there was nothing to fear from the darkness. He could see the line of people still in the dark, waiting to be treated. It seemed that the line had only gotten longer as the day progressed. The people were squatting or lying down on blankets, waiting their turn.

They cut through the bush for most of another hour until they came to a high spot that paralleled a ravine. The line of soldiers stopped and the senior man slowly came back, pointing out a spot for each man to take. Parker could see through the low light that five of the men had been turned on the far end so as to face up the ravine. If the enemy pulled back into the ravine after the attack they would be walking into a plowed field.

And then they waited.

Eventually he heard well into the distance the sound of a gunship. It seemed very far away, as if it were on another mission.

They waited in the dark and silence for what seemed to be hours. Suddenly, the moon broke out between the clouds and, when it did, for only a short moment, Parker thought he saw movement.

Pop, pop, pop, pop!

Bullets started to fly across from where they were and he saw people scrambling at the MSF station. Some were ducking behind rocks. Some looked like rag dolls that were picked up and thrown about in a lifeless flop. Still, the patrol held its fire. They were too far away. Another round of shots was fired and then Parker saw movement in front of him, as if the Al Shabaab patrol was going in for the kill.

At that same moment, the helicopter noise suddenly got louder. It appeared without notice, breaking through the cloud cover. The yellow flashes of the Ethiopians' helicopter's guns streaked down to earth like a Roman candle spurting out flame.

The helicopter's fire was between the MSF camp and their patrol.

They are knocking them back, Parker thought. The attackers will retreat and their retreat will take them to a place of supposed safety. Their meeting point would be in the ravine. They were running directly into a trap.

The bush suddenly got quiet. The helicopter pulled off. Moans and screams could be heard across the valley from the encampment, but in front of Parker it was silent. He waited. He looked to his side to see another soldier, tense, with his weapon on his shoulder.

Then Parker thought he saw movement again.

Again, the moon broke through the cloud cover for a moment. It was the worst possible thing that could happen to the attackers. With a glance, Parker looked from left to right and counted five men going down into the ravine. For an eternity, the Ethiopians held their fire.

And then the rounds went off.

A red flare was popped somewhere to his left. In the red light, Parker could see the fighters below firing blindly into the dark, while the Ethiopians struck their targets. He saw an object fly up into the air to his left and then heard the rumble of a hand grenade. Shots continued to be fired.

Suddenly, out of the darkness, a figure ran straight at the Ethiopian soldier to Parker's left. The Ethiopian soldier fired one shot, but it missed, flying just above the attacker as he raced toward them, up the side of the ravine. And then the Ethiopian's gun misfired. He frantically pulled the slide back but in that nanosecond the jihadist would be on top of him.

Parker stood up, aimed, and squeezed. He never heard the sound, but felt the rifle kick back into his shoulder. It was well aimed, striking the man in the right shoulder. Parker knew by the way the attacker was holding his weapon that the right shoulder was his dominant side. Parker didn't want to kill him.

He twisted around in the dark and fell to his knees.

They had a wounded prisoner.

* * *

Captain Tola was not happy.

"You did what?"

Moncrief looked sheepish as he stood in the group that had gathered in a dimly lit tent in the Ethiopian compound. Their captive, who was visibly shaking, sat handcuffed to a metal chair. A white bloodstained bandage was wrapped across his shoulder.

"As a gag," he mumbled. "Allah."

Tola looked at Moncrief skeptically.

"You shot him?" Tola asked Moncrief.

"Yes, I did." Moncrief was providing the cover story.

Parker stood in the dark in the back of the tent. It would not have helped the situation for Tola to know that Parker was on the patrol, or that he'd fired the clean shot.

"We have ourselves a prisoner." The Ethiopian senior sergeant looked displeased as well. The 50th gave what it took. The few members of his unit who had ever been captured by Al Shabaab had been pulled in front of a camera and had their heads cut off, slowly. Al Shabaab would cut them from behind so that the pain lasted longer. They made a point of not cutting the artery until the last stroke. The sergeant was happy to handle this prisoner in the same way.

"Whose prisoner is he?" Tola asked.

It became a debate. The man who fired the shot had the right of possession.

If Moncrief claimed him, the man would go into Marine custody. He would be interrogated and sent to Djibouti. Ultimately, it was a far better circumstance than if the Ethiopian 50th kept him.

"What does he know?" Parker asked.

The Ethiopian questioned the prisoner. The man mumbled something that suggested that he would never tell.

"They killed more than twenty men and women who were waiting for medical care, and blew away six kids at the MSF camp." Tola was not pleased with the slaughter, nor the fact that MSF had resisted allowing a protective guard. It didn't matter to the world-news feeds that MSF had refused help. It only mattered that the media reported the MSF clinic was near to both Marines and local military posts.

"Ask him again," Parker interjected. "Tell him that if he is truthful, the Americans will take him as a prisoner. If he is not, the Ethiopians will keep him."

The translation was made and the man looked up with large brown eyes as if a puppy had been whipped for a mistake. They waited in silence as the man thought through his choice.

"The Americans will make Israel sound like a better place to go," the Ethiopian sergeant added.

The man started talking. He kept going, taking only short stops to gather his breath. The sergeant tried to interpret the run of words as quickly as he could.

Parker only caught one word.

"Mo-bi-lee."

"What did he say?" Parker raised his hand to stop the flow.

"He said the *Amriiki* that killed in Mo-beel was nearby."

"Mobile?"

"Yes, Mo-beel."

CHAPTER FORTY-SEVEN

Wassef drove the van along the interstate, north towards Washington. He stayed in the center lane of traffic, letting the faster, more deliberate drivers pass him without notice. He followed a tractor trailer that had WALMART printed on its side. Soon, another truck came in behind him. Because the rig was as large as the Walmart truck, the driver could see that the white van was not the vehicle slowing traffic down. Wassef reached behind the seat for the sheet and felt the object below it.

The radio reported a fire south of Dumfries.

They will bring the engines when the smoke alarm starts. He knew that the man with the armory room would have the best alarm system possible.

It would be tied into a police station that would know that a Class III collector lived there. The call would go out to both the Dumfries Police Department and the fire station. The whole police force would know his name and address. In the entire city, there were only a few names that would register so quickly with the call. One of those names might be the U.S.

senator's home; the other might be a federal district court judge. This address was just as important.

They will try to enter but his body will block the door. Wassef kept running it through his mind.

And then the first grenade will fall to the floor. He had the scenario correct. *The first blast will stay within the room but will stun the firemen. They will then withdraw from the house. The second blast will cause the neighbors, all standing outside looking at the blaze, to run for their lives. The police and firemen will retreat from the scene. There will be no other option.*

The tractor-trailer started to slow down as it passed the first sign for the Pentagon exit. Omar had told him what to do.

The FBI's Hostage Rescue Team would be getting the alert by now. The Bureau was not stupid. They would enter the containment room and start to pound the two women with questions. The questions would be neither calm nor cool, and with the excitement, the women would know what had happened.

Not much longer. He held on to the steering wheel. He'd picked out a soft target, which was a military term to describe a target that was unguarded. But the target also had to be capable of making the front page. It required something that would make a statement to the world. He had the perfect soft target. Omar's second cell would prove that the *Amriiki* could do more to attract the world's attention to the jihad. Wassef would see the face of Allah. His name would be said with joy by millions across the seas.

The HRT would not find the video he'd made until much later. In it, he spoke of Omar and the inspiration that Omar had given to others to join the fight. He had emailed a copy to several other jihadists in both Toronto and Minneapolis. And he emailed one to an ad-

dress never used before in Kismaayo. It would circle
the globe by nightfall.

The van passed the Pentagon mall and Wassef took
the exit to the George Washington Parkway. The law
enforcement agencies would be getting the email alert
in the next fifteen minutes but he didn't need that
much time. The White House would go to lockdown,
as well as the Capitol. The president would be taken
belowground. It did not matter.

Wassef turned on his right blinker and moved across
the lanes of traffic to the exit. He merged onto the
Parkway and then took the highway to the south. As he
did, the rumble of a Boeing 757 landing at Reagan
came over his head. It was a Delta flight with a red,
blue, and white coloring.

The van traveled for only a few miles and then took
the exit to Reagan. Wassef followed the loop around,
passing the terminal, and then he started to head back
up the Parkway to the north.

I will not have much time. He began saying his
prayers. His hands started to shake and he felt the sweat
on his palms.

"United 762, you are cleared for full stop, Runway
15, wind 320 at 5 knots. Tower is 119.1."

"Thank you." The copilot for the Chicago-based
Boeing 737 hit the mike button. He repeated the information. "Cleared for landing, Runway 15, wind at 320
at 5 knots. 119.1. Have a nice day."

"Yes, sir, it is a nice day," the controller commented
on the perfect blue sky over Ronald Reagan Washington National.

The runway followed the compass heading of one
hundred and fifty degrees, with the wind blowing in

nearly the opposite direction, blowing straight into the nose of the aircraft at a bare five knots.

"We might be able to taxi off at Lima." The chief pilot swung the aircraft down the landing corridor at Washington. The runway's altitude was just fifteen feet above ground level. The conditions were perfect for an easy landing. The air would flow over the wings in a perfect application of Bernoulli's principle of flight. As the air curved over the wing, the molecules on top would speed up, causing the aircraft to actually be sucked up, away from the ground.

"I will bet you lunch if you make Lima." The copilot had trained in the Navy, as had the chief. They were used to putting the aircraft down hard. It wasn't so much hard as it was making a firm planting of the machine on the earth. In the Navy, they both had tail hooks. United Flight 762 was not equipped with such. But with the wind in their face, the airplane could settle fast, and if the pilot hit it exactly on the white paint of the number 15, the aircraft had an outside chance of slowing down quickly enough to stop in front of the crossover before the turn to the taxiway. The first and closest taxiway was Lima, or the "L" taxiway.

The flight had been uneventful. They pulled back from Chicago's O'Hare with fifty-six passengers, including a Congresswoman and more than a dozen lobbyists. A retired Marine major general sat in the last seat in first class. It was the early bird out of Chicago.

"Airspeed is on." The copilot read out the numbers.

"Flaps are full."

"Check."

The chief pilot loved Reagan. It took a special skill to turn the aircraft through the many turns required from passing over the radio tower at American University to a path that followed the Potomac. No aircraft could venture too far afield after September 11th. He felt like he was in his Piper Cub making the turns that made flying a joy.

"Landing Checklist complete."

"Yep." The copilot looked out over the Pentagon as the airplane continued to slow and drop from the sky.

"Looks like a busy day." The pilot was concentrating on aiming his aircraft just short of the number 15, expecting it to drift slightly in the final seconds before the wheels touched down.

"Yep, we got a few."

Planes were lined up on the taxiway waiting for the landing craft to hit the ground, clear the active runway and let the planes on the ground move on to their take-off.

"What the hell?" The copilot saw a white van suddenly pull directly off the George Washington Parkway and onto the grassy knoll that was just beyond the water inlet at the end of Runway 15. He stared for a second as the van stopped and the door slid open.

"Oh, shit!" He grabbed the control stick from the pilot and pushed the nose down. He had been trained in combat and on landings at sea in rough winds. He pulled back on the power and pulled up on the landing gear. It was an extreme measure.

"What the hell?" the chief pilot started to resist.

"We got big trouble and need to get it down now."

The airplane had no time to spin up the engines, or gain altitude, or bank to any direction. It had to shoot the runway and hope that some of the aircraft made it down now.

"Hold on!" the copilot yelled. "Honey, tell the kids that I love them. I will always remember the night we first met at the Academy." The flight recorder would be studied for years to come.

He didn't have a chance to glance back at the van. If he had, it would not have helped. The trail of smoke from the rocket-propelled grenade to the plane's tail section was only a matter of yards. A strong-armed pitcher with a ninety-mile-an-hour fastball could have easily hit an aircraft landing at Reagan from the grassy hill just short of the runway.

The burst shook the airplane, tearing through the back fuselage and ripping the vertical stabilizer from the aircraft. The copilot's action saved most of the passengers on the front end. The aircraft slammed into the tarmac, skidding forward until coming to a stop. Reagan was closed down for two days.

The security officer at Reagan had been making his loop when he saw the white van suddenly slow down, jump the curb on the Parkway and cut across the grass, just missing two trees. He reacted instantly.

"Terrorist attack at end of Runway 15. White van. All assistance is requested." He had served ten years with the Marine Corps Reserve and had been called up for Operation Enduring Freedom. His unit had provided security for more than one logistics convoy. He knew trouble when he saw it.

The officer put on his blue light and siren. His Yukon hit the curb and bounced up in the air.

"Come on."

The suspension held the truck stable as it careened onto the grass. The white van stopped and the officer watched in slow motion something that he was never able to erase from his memory. A man slid open the door to the van, picked up an RPG, and pointed at the aircraft that was just passing overhead. He stepped clear of the van so that the back blast did not blow into the vehicle. The streak from the grenade followed the aircraft, hitting it at the tail.

The officer stopped the truck, jumped out with his Glock and aimed the white dot of the front sight on the center of the man's chest.

"STOP!" he screamed as if his voice mattered with the explosion occurring just to his right.

The man turned and aimed the weapon at the officer. It didn't matter that the round was spent. The officer did not process the information. He reacted. He felt the automatic jerk as three rounds left the barrel. Three small red spots appeared on the man's shirt at the center of his chest. He fell to his knees.

Fox News interrupted its broadcast with a far-too-familiar broadcast bulletin

"We have just learned that there has been a terrorist attack on an aircraft landing at Reagan National Airport. The aircraft, a United flight from Chicago, burst into flames as it struck the runway. Miraculously, there are reported survivors."

From Fox and CNN it went international, and was soon reported by Al Jazeera. The report was translated into Arabic and broadcast to Kismaayo.

"*Allahu akbar!*" Faud jumped up and screamed.

He kept yelling as he heard the news. The *Amriiki* had been right. He had other cells.

CHAPTER FORTY-EIGHT

"Hey ho!" Omar yelled at the top of his lungs. He had seen movement on the other side of the road that he had been following for most of the day. He stooped down behind a large boulder waving his Kalashnikov in the air above the rock. He knew that they were neither Kenyan nor Ethiopian, as he saw one who was in an olive-drab uniform with a black turban. It was the uniform of Al Shabaab.

He waited for a response. There was none.

Omar stayed hunched down with his shoulder against the rock. It had been facing the morning sun and the heat passed through his clothes into his shoulder. He looked around the side of the rock and saw a figure kneeling behind a bush.

"Tarriq, is that you?" Omar yelled out. Tarriq had been with Omar in the training camp. He was the one veteran in the group who had fought in the battle of Raam Caddey several weeks before. A scouting party of Ethiopians had crossed paths with a scouting party of the mujaahidiin. Both parties fired at each other with bursts of ammunition and hand grenades. Several rocket-propelled grenades were fired and, as Tarriq reported, several Ethiopians were slaughtered. A few of the mujaahidiin became martyrs.

"Omar?"

"Tarriq, yes it is Omar." He stayed below the rock until the identification process was complete. "How do I know that you are Tarriq, my friend?"

"You complained about digging a hole in the sand at the beach."

"Yes, Tarriq, yes, my friend." Omar stood up to see his friend just on the other side of the boulder.

"*Al-salamu alaykum.*" Tarriq came up to hug his brother.

"*Wa alaykum s-salam.*" Omar held his hand over his heart. "Do you have something to drink?"

"It is just like Omar to complain!"

Omar thought it a joke.

"I have traveled all day."

"And why are you alone? Have you lost your mind?" Tarriq was older. He was actually born in Great Britain, somewhere outside London. The two had become friends because of the common link of being jihadists from other lands.

"I had one with me but he deserted."

"A dog."

Tarriq was not alone. He had three others with him who were from Baraawe on the coast. They had gotten lost and separated from their unit. Omar explained that he was heading to the northwest to find the two captives.

"Allah is great." Tarriq was encouraged by the news. "*Amriiki?*"

"Yes."

"It would be better if they were Europeans." Tarriq sounded like he had some experience with the prisoner and kidnapping business.

"Why do you say so?" Omar had slung the rifle over his shoulder. They started to head northeast to the village of Tayeeglow. One of the men had fought a battle there several months ago.

"Europeans, especially the French, will pay millions for the hostages. The *Amriiki* will take forever and pay nothing." Tarriq did have the correct information. "This is the road to Tayeeglow!"

The rutted road forked to the left and right and Tarriq indicated that they should take the right path. Rain clouds were starting to form again in the sky.

Soon they came to a burned-out wreck of a large flatbed truck. The rain started to come down. They all huddled underneath the vehicle and waited. Soon the water started to run through the red dirt in streams.

Nightfall came, and with it, the mosquitoes. Omar pulled out his plastic bag and from it took a net that he wrapped around his head and arms. He laid the plastic bag out in the rain cupped in a way so as to gather water. Soon he was able to stick his face in the plastic-contained puddle and drink.

"We ate roots and drank our own urine when we went into Kenya last year." Tarriq's friend looked much older. He carried a Dragunov sniper rifle that he had picked up off the battlefield somewhere. Omar studied the weapon and thought of how many Kenyans it must have killed.

Omar listened to the talk of battles as the rain continued to pour down. They often mentioned the helicopter gunships and how they would appear out of nowhere without warning. He tucked his head against the inside of the tire rim with his Kalashnikov across his lap.

Chocolate milkshakes. And ice cream bars. He

could taste the ice cream as it dripped down the sides of his mouth.

Omar's stomach hurt from hunger but soon his heavy eyes outweighed the growl from his empty stomach. He awoke in the middle of the dark to the loud, vibrating sounds of the four men snoring. Omar stuck his head out in the soft drizzle of rain so as to breathe in air that wasn't saturated with the smell of burned-out diesel and lubricant.

I wonder if Wassef got the message? He had sent the sign from his last video recording to awaken one of the cells. It was difficult to get to a computer on the front. But when they neared a town or a city, he was able to use a cell phone to make a video. He had kept the phone that he borrowed in Jilib to call his wife.

In the pitch-black, cold and wet underbelly of the truck, he opened his plastic corn bag, dug down to a rag, and felt for the phone. Omar pulled it out, turned it on, and saw a voice message. The buzz of the phone didn't bother the sleeping men.

We would all be dead if the Ethiopians showed up right now. He covered the phone with the rag so that the light was barely visible. And it was there, in the wet mud and dirt, that he learned of the second cell's success.

"*Allahu akbar!*" He hit his head on the undercarriage of the truck. The others started to wake from the noise only to see him in the rain dancing and holding his hands up in the air.

"More Americans have died!" he cried out in joy.

CHAPTER FORTY-NINE

"**W**ake up!" Xasan nudged Karen's boot with the butt of his Kalashnikov. It was a nudge and not a kick. He had changed since the near-death of his father. She could smell smoke and hear something crackling. It was a good scent that reminded her of home in Atlanta when her mother cooked a turkey for Christmas lunch. It was the only time during the entire year when her father would turn off his pager and cell phone for a few hours.

I am losing it. She tried to turn over from the cold side exposed to the damp to the warm side on the ground.

"*Amriiki,*" Xasan whispered.

He had never whispered before. Xasan's use of a reasonable voice woke her up more than his screaming. "*Amriiki,* don't you want to eat?"

Her kidneys had started to hurt during the night. She was now living with constant dull back pain in the flanks of her lower back.

"What?" She turned over again to see a small fire at the edge of the overhang of a tree. It was early morning light and the clouds seemed lower than she had seen them in the past. She focused her eyes and saw something on a spit overhanging the fire. It was a small animal of some sort on a wooden pole above the flames. One end of the pole was stuck in the dirt on one side of the pit while the other was balanced on a large, twenty-liter plastic jug from the truck. Xasan went back to the pole and turned it, waited, and turned it again. With each turn, what little grease there was caused the fire to flame up and crackle.

"What is it?" She pulled herself off the ground and stood next to the fire. The warmth helped dry out her damp and muddy clothes.

"I found my little friend." Xasan smiled his toothy smile. He pointed to the edge of the darkness where there was a pile of skin and fur. From the shape of the skull she could determine that it was either a small goat or dog. It didn't matter.

Karen went back to the truck to see the old man in the cab asleep but almost sitting straight up. A tarp covered the bed of the truck. She lifted it up to see the shape of Peter in the fetal position. His pants were stained. The smell was overwhelming.

"Peter?" There was no noise. He remained motionless.

"Peter? We have some food."

She saw a movement.

"Karen?"

"Yes."

"I am not sure I am going to make it."

"Peter!" She pulled the tarp off the bed of the truck, revealing his crumpled-up shape. She climbed in and lifted his head, and as she did, she felt his cold and clammy skin and the bristles of his unshaved face.

"Do you have the aspirin?"

"Somewhere." He had been allowed to keep the bottle. The old man had felt better and therefore it was assumed that no further medication would be needed.

Karen had saved one life and now shifted her priorities towards keeping Peter alive. She felt his pants pockets and found the shape of a bottle in one.

"Here, swallow this. I don't have any water right now but try to swallow it or chew it." She slipped a pill into the corner of his mouth.

Soon he seemed to feel better.

They ate the rubbery meat, chewing on a piece for what seemed like hours. It didn't matter. This was the first protein they had had for some time. It had no salt or pepper, but the burnt meat certainly had flavor.

"Soon we will see men and get rice," Xasan said as he gorged himself on the goat. He sucked on the bones while they sat around the fire until they heard a sound in the darkness.

He pulled back on the slide of his Kalashnikov, forgetting that he already had one round in the chamber. A flash of brass popped up from his rifle when the prior round was ejected into the air.

At the same time, he kicked dirt over the fire. It smoldered and then smoked. Eventually, with his continuous kicking of the dirt, it went out.

"Who is there?" Xasan had taken a position behind the hood of the small truck. His father stayed in the cab with his rifle raised as well.

Karen had crawled into the bed of the truck huddling next to Peter with the tarp pulled up. She kept her head down, listening for any sound.

"Who is there?" Xasan repeated the question in Swahili.

"Hello, brother!" a reply came back.

"I do not know you!" Xasan was ready to shoot. His reply was frantic as if they were a moment away from the crack of automatic rifle fire.

"It is Tarriq of the mujaahidiin," the voice came out of the darkness.

"I have heard of a Tarriq. Show yourself!"

After some time, a small man came out of the darkness with his rifle raised over his head.

"Fires can be dangerous. It will pull in a helicopter."

"Yes, Tarriq." Xasan paused. He saw the man look at the last of the goat entrails near the bush. "We have bones and you might cook what is left."

"A fire can be good for some things." Tarriq pointed to the remaining organs of the goat as two other men came out of the darkness. The fire would soon be re-built.

Another man came in from the bush. The strangers all waved to Tarriq as if they knew him well.

Tarriq asked the last man out of the bush something in Swahili. The stranger replied. Karen heard the accent of an American. She pulled the tarp away and looked over the edge of the truck.

"Where are the doctors?" the American voice asked.

The commander pointed in Karen's direction.

The man came over to the edge of the truck.

He was white and skinny and had a straggly beard.

"I am Omar." He spoke the words in unaccented English.

She didn't say anything.

"You are the Americans?"

"I am an American and he is French." She shook as she spoke.

He gave her a twisted smile as if he were a thief who had opened a woman's purse after stealing it, and then discovered that she had just come from the automatic teller machine. It was an evil smile that she would not forget.

CHAPTER FIFTY

The mother tug had left Kismaayo just after midnight. It had three small wooden fishing skiffs strung behind it in one continuous chain. It took a course east-northeast. The men were armed with Kalashnikovs, PKs, F1s, and RPGs. They were heading out to sea for a day or two of fishing. If the radar showed nothing, they would scatter the skiffs and catch what they could and bring it back to the market. If the radar showed a big fish, they would catch a container ship.

The waters were dangerous. Kenya's navy was known to patrol the shoreline, and farther out, the U.S. Navy or United Kingdom were on the prowl.

"It is hard to see." The tug's master held the metal wheel tightly in his grasp. He watched a small radar screen just above and to the left of the wheel. It was not as old as the tug, which was held together by wire and tape and luck. The diesel engine kept a constant vibration going that passed through the boat.

One rod is not right. The tug master knew the engine like a mother knows the cry of a baby. It had the slightest click that indicated a piece of metal buried deep inside the old diesel was nearing failure.

One trip, and then. . . . They were always one trip away from failure. But the capture of a "big fish" would mean a new engine. It would give life to everyone, and his take would be the largest. Or, so to say, his would be the largest after Faud's. The tax collector always came first.

"The rain is setting in." The ship's master looked out the window. He held the wheel as the old tug continued to roll up and down in the increasingly rough seas.

"It is impossible." The master was getting frustrated with the situation. The weather seemed to cover most of the gulf. It would take hours of holding on to the wheel and looking at the compass to get anywhere. The seas and the winds were against them. It barely mattered if he looked outside through the film-covered glass, as all he saw were waves. There would be no other ship or object this close to shore, or on his course, other than perhaps another fishing tug from Kismaayo, although they had seen no other boat pull out from the dock that day.

"What are the men doing?"

"They are all sick."

The master smiled at the young pups that always wanted to go. He knew that they dreamed of riches if a big one were caught, and some fish to sell if not. He thought of them under a tarp, in the back, behind the protection of the wheelhouse and huddled together like sardines. They would be grouped together as close as fish in a can.

"Should I wake the men up?"

"No, they are probably sick and not asleep."

A beep from the radar pulled the master's eyes down from the gray and black that surrounded the boat. A running light on top of the steering house flickered and reflected back from the wall of fog that they were driving into.

"Another fisherman?" the master asked out loud as he saw the smallest of blips on the screen. It had been acting up lately. He hit the side of it with the palm of his hand, as if that would shake the tubes inside and restore their connection. Sometimes it worked.

"It must be."

"It doesn't look bigger than our boat."

The blip was small and close.

And then it disappeared.

"Allah protects us," he mumbled under his breath. He pulled back on the throttle and, with it, the engine's rumble came down a notch.

And then the blip appeared again, this time as only a flicker. If the object was any real distance away, the radar would not have registered anything.

"Another tug would be nice." He always liked running into a brother on the sea. They would pull alongside and exchange word of where the dangers were.

And again it disappeared.

He pulled back on the throttle again, and as he did the rumble reduced further. The master could hear the men stirring in the back as if the engine's reduction in revolutions was a wake-up call for them to prepare for their skiffs.

"Hold the wheel," the master told his son. "I will be back. Keep its heading, but stay slow." He didn't want to run over a brother's tugboat because his defective radar hadn't given him a good signal. He pulled apart some of his turban and wrapped it around his face so that only his eyes would feel the rain and salt water. As he opened the door and walked towards the bow, the yellow light flickered on the wheelhouse above.

The engine of his boat could barely be heard.

He stopped at the edge of the steering house, turned around, and spoke through the open door.

"Stop the engine."

His son obeyed the order and there was silence.

"Anything on the radar?"

"A flicker. It is there and then it is gone."

The master turned to the bow.

Suddenly a wall of gray appeared out of the rain with its bow slicing through the water at just ten degrees off the tug's bow. It displaced the water with its tonnage and the wake lifted the tug up off the water's surface.

"Allaaah!" the master screamed as the odd-shaped object passed by on their port side. The man grabbed on to the door of the wheelhouse to hold on tight as the tug came to a nearly forty-five-degree list. He saw, in the corner of his eye, several of the men on the tail of the boat fly off into the water. In that second, he knew that each would die.

He continued to hold on. The gray ship had no windows nor any light. It was shaped like a manmade sea monster with no sharp edges, or form, or glass.

And then the tail of the ship passed by the tug. The engines were churning up the water with the force of ten or twenty knots. The wake threw the tug up and over to a list on the opposite side. With the sudden change in displacement of tons of water, the tug swung over hard, and with the swing he heard the screams of several more men as they flew off the tug from the other side.

And as suddenly as it appeared, the gray ship disappeared into the rain.

* * *

"We have the man you wanted to see." The guard was standing at the door to the room where Faud was sitting on a carpet with his legs folded underneath him.

"He is here?" Faud looked up from his portable computer. It was one of many that he had, and used. He would switch them on hourly and would often keep them in a truck over a hundred meters from wherever he was staying. It was a precaution he had learned to live with, and one that had kept him alive. Cell phones and computers were switched out. Web addresses were changed daily, if not more often.

"Yes, we brought him directly from the dock."

Faud was still in the house on the far northwestern side of Kissmaayo. They were preparing to move again as soon as the Kenyans began pressing an attack to the west and neared the city.

"Bring him in."

The man was an African whose people were from the south of Somalia. His dark skin was the result of Mother Nature after centuries of evolution for the people who lived near the equator. The skin reacted to the harshness of the blinding sun, making his people much darker than most. His years at sea only made the skin dryer and more wrinkled.

"*Al-salamu alaykum*." Faud stood up to hug his brother.

"*Wa alaykum s-salam*," the tugboat owner replied as they greeted each other with a pat on their chests and then a hug.

"You brought in the Danish ship several years ago."

The tugboat captain smiled.

"And you were the one who got the yacht."

Several foolish Americans had tried to cross near the Horn of Africa in a private yacht. The tug had pulled it into port but it was a disaster, as the Americans had resisted. The young and foolish gunmen with the captain sprayed the cabin with automatic machine-gun fire. The teak wood was shredded and pools of blood were everywhere. The bodies were thrown over the side for the sharks. But there was no bounty. Later, an insurance company from the Virgin Islands negotiated a deal to buy the yacht back for pennies on the dollar. The tug captain was embarrassed by the circumstance when he was told how much the living brought, versus the dead.

"Yes, brother." The tug owner let his eyes fall to the ground.

Faud realized he had said something that he hadn't intended to.

"Have tea with me." He pointed to a place on the rug and the two sat down. "I have asked some brothers to join us."

Several other soldiers dressed in the olive drab of their uniforms joined them but sat back from the two.

"So, what did you see?" Faud asked.

"It appeared out of the rain."

"Did you have radar?"

"Yes, but it is old, and only a blip showed up for a second. Several of our men were martyred when the wake almost flipped us over."

"Blessed are our brothers who are seeing the face of Allah. Allah be praised."

Faud held out both hands palms up as if making a blessing on their souls.

"How did it look?"

"Unlike anything I have ever seen before."

Faud turned to the portable computer, struck some buttons, and did a Google search, while a woman dressed in a burqa brought in several cups of tea. Her hands were covered in black gloves and no skin was shown whatsoever. It was only her eyes looking through the slit above the niqab that showed any sign of a human being. All of the men looked past her, as it was a sin to look at her. It was the law.

"Is this what you saw?" Faud pointed to an image on the screen.

"Yes, that is it."

"And sound?"

"Nothing, until it was just upon us."

"Yes, I have heard of this."

Faud looked at the picture of the *Zumwalt*. The DDG-1000 was the stealth ship that they feared. It made no port calls and stayed at sea. His intelligence reported seeing the ship as far away as the Pascagoula shipyard in Mississippi.

"I remember who first told me about this." He spoke to his lieutenants. "He lived less than fifty miles from the American shipyards and sent us photographs some time ago."

The ship was built just outside the city of Mobile.

"We need to move it again." Faud didn't say what. The tug master had no idea what he was talking about. The others in the room did. The DF-21 had to be moved again.

"Where is Tarriq? Have we heard from him?"

"Yes. He found our lost brother and they are with the captives near Tayeeglow."

"And they are an *Amriiki* and a French one?"

The one lieutenant nodded his head in the affirmative.

"One is a doctor from Paris with the MSF. The other is also with the MSF. She has complained of back pain and he has malaria," the junior officer reported.

Faud held up his hand. They stopped talking.

"Is the chai good?" he asked the tug master.

"Yes. I have not had sugar in so long."

Faud smiled as he sipped the tea. He waited till the man finished his tea and left. And then Faud called the rest of his men back into the room.

"The MSF and the French will pay well for the one from Paris. The *Amriiki*, I don't know. But they must both be alive." Faud hesitated as he looked out from the arch and towards the sea.

"And Omar." He considered his options. "He does not know that Tarriq was ordered to find him?'

"No."

"If he has more cells, as he says he does, there may be value there as well. The money has poured in after the Reagan attack."

Faud paused again.

"If only more had died." Only the few in the very back of the aircraft were killed as they were flung onto the runway by the force of the blast. The pilots were being praised as heroes for dropping the airplane down so quickly on the runway. The attack had triggered a well-trained Reagan fire crew to be on the runway before the aircraft had even come to a complete stop. As a result, a fire had been avoided.

"We need more missiles and more money. Keep Omar alive."

CHAPTER FIFTY-ONE

"**I** am Buckley Warren."

"And that is not your real name." William Parker said what everyone standing there thought. It was a group combined of the MarSOC major, Captain Tola, Moncrief, and Parker.

"No, it is not, Mr. Parker." The slender redhead wore a black baseball cap, a long, curly beard, and a khaki tactical shirt with pocketed tactical pants. "And you know that."

Moncrief slid in between Parker and the new arrival. He didn't want any blood, especially since it wouldn't be Parker's. The two had a long history, even if it wasn't with Buckley Warren and Parker. It was a history between the CIA and Parker.

"Something about you knowing my name and me not knowing yours is a problem." Parker stared at him.

"Not for me." Warren was a wiseass, to boot.

"Okay, we are on the same team," the major intervened. There was a mutual distrust for new arrivals. It seemed that, at this point, "more people" were not so much a help as a hindrance.

"What do you have to add, Mr. Warren?" Moncrief asked.

"Faud is the money man for Al Shabaab. With Omar's rise in popularity they have raised a large amount of money and new recruits. They use the hawala system to run the cash." Warren sounded like a former Air Force computer technician who had been recruited for the Agency. He rattled off the facts like he was rattling off the capabilities of a new piece of computer gear. "Hawala is a system of trust where legitimate money is transferred on an honor code. We just caught two in Virginia who were running money through Kenya."

"So Omar is a problem on several fronts?" Tola asked.

"Several. He also is the poster child for recruits who are coming in from the United States, Britain, Australia, Sweden, and especially Canada," Warren continued. "They come here, learn the trade, and then get a jet out of Frankfurt to New York with their legitimate, original United States passport."

"It's very hard to stop them."

"And our tracking of his cell phones tells us he has at least one more cell to activate."

"Omar?" Parker clarified.

"Yes, sir." Warren paused.

"Some records of Al Qaeda just surfaced in western Africa. The French made a raid on a village where the Al Qaeda cell left quickly and didn't burn anything."

Parker continued to listen.

"It had payroll, recruitment instructions, and money to pay and convert the locals. Faud handled most of it. He runs it like a bank with expense sheets and reimbursement vouchers. It is amazing. They are going to spread this system across central Africa. It is a franchise of terror."

"Neisseria, Ebola, and Al Qaeda. What next?" Moncrief asked.

"And like your medical diseases, this man-made organism learns from its mistakes. They figured out that the imposing of Sharia law came down too hard on the locals in Afghanistan. The cutting off of a common thief's hands isn't too bad, but when you start stoning the village elder's granddaughter for being caught with the local sheepherder, you start to lose the public." Warren paused and looked around to see if anyone else was within hearing distance.

"It is the homeland that we have here. Omar is a threat to America." Warren was outlining the priorities of the mission. "Your disease problem is tragic but Omar's recruitment of money and soldiers that come back to hurt America must be stopped at all costs."

Warren crossed his arms as if to separate himself from loyalty to anything other than the mission given to him.

"Your point?" Parker asked.

"My point, Colonel," Warren used the title to rely upon the man's reputation for following orders, "is that we have an MQ-9 sitting up top with a Hellfire missile and if it looks like Omar can't be gotten any other way, we will take him down."

Parker stared right back at him.

"I am here to tell you," Warren added, "that the MSF is getting ready to offer two million francs to get their French doctor out of here. It leaves your gal out there with no one thinking of paying that type of money."

The major and Tola shook their heads.

"And our intercepts tell us that she is very sick."

CHAPTER FIFTY-TWO

"So, you are from Atlanta?" Omar said.

Karen Stewart's back was killing her. It had gotten so bad that she had reached into Peter's pocket and pulled out the bottle of aspirin. More than half of the tablets were gone.

At least our heart patient hasn't asked for more. She unscrewed the cap and took out two tablets that she chewed on. The continuing lack of water didn't help, but the bitter aspirin would ease her pain. She made a point of taking no more than two per day as her pain was shared with Peter's.

"I was raised there."

"Pace Academy." Omar sat across from her with his legs folded.

She couldn't fold her legs anymore due to the back pain and instead was lying on her side.

"Yes. How did you know?"

"There is nothing secret on the Internet."

An American voice. It was odd how the voice sounded so comforting after the time spent with Xasan and even Peter. Peter spoke English with his French accent, almost singing the words, while Xasan's pitch was choppy and made sounds like a telegraph.

"And you?"

"I am from Mobile."

"Are you?" Somewhere in all the confusion of the last several days she remembered hearing of a church bombing in Mobile. It had struck her as odd that an attack had occurred in the Deep South. "That's where that terrorist attack recently occurred, isn't it?"

"Yes. Have you heard about Reagan?"

"The president?"

Omar laughed. He was not above bragging.

"No, the attack at Reagan National Airport in Washington. It just happened yesterday."

"Why?" She asked the question as a scientist trying to understand why some diseases pick out children and not the old, who have lived a full life. It was the voice of the kidnapped trying to understand why someone would torment another.

"You are like the others. Allah has told us to not do drugs. Allah has told us to not fornicate. Allah has told us to not obey parents that do not obey His word." Omar looked up at the sky. "Your whole Western lifestyle makes me sick. If I wear a beard with my turban, you look at me strangely. If I stop to pray, you send me to the back of the cafeteria and make fun of me. Your world is too different and has no meaning."

"You mean our world of freedom?" she spoke in a voice of amazement.

CHAPTER FIFTY-THREE

"I have some good news." Paul Stewart was in the makeshift dining facility sitting across the table from Parker and Moncrief. He was in the white surgical suit that was commonly seen on the CDC side of the encampment. The DFAC, or makeshift cafeteria, was in the middle of the two encampments. Although Marine security extended around both camps, there was a dividing point. The only shared area was the DFAC.

Everyone took care to not cross over the middle ground, and even the DFAC was divided, with white suits sitting on one side of a partition. At the entrances on both sides were large metal sinks with bottles of soap. And in the middle there were plastic sheets that went from the ceiling to the floor with splits in the middle and wash sinks on both sides of the split. Signs everywhere reminded one to wash. Paper plates and plastic utensils were used and then destroyed.

"You have news?" Moncrief looked up.

"Yes, it is about your sick Marine."

"Oh?" Parker asked, trying not to look Paul Stewart directly in his eyes. They had just come from the meeting with the CIA. Neither Moncrief nor Parker liked the idea of a Reaper strike.

"The Marine with your blood is doing better," Stewart said to Parker.

"We have another survivor of the meningitis?" Parker asked.

"Yes." The doctor had a white Styrofoam cup full of black coffee. He sat down at the table and sipped it. "His temperature has dropped and he can handle light in the room. He is also starting to eat."

"Good." Parker asked, "What now?"

"We try to pull a common factor out of your blood sample and his." Stewart played with the coffee cup in his hand as he spoke. "It is what will lead to an antiserum that will stop this thing."

"The International Red Cross has set up a camp south of here at Dolo Bay. We are trying to stop the spread of this disease now. It seems that even those vaccinated with our other, older vaccines are not getting sick."

"Dolo Bay?"

"Yes."

"It's near the Kenyan border." Kenya had been waging war with Al Shabaab for well over a decade. Parker knew that if the Ethiopian Army was capable, it would protect the IRC clinic and help slow the surge of the disease. The two armies joining the fight against both Al Shabaab and the disease gave the locals a chance.

"Yes. We may be able to contain it on this side. Mogadishu is another question. They have over a million and a half people in the city with no clean water. There will be thousands at risk."

Djibouti would help as well as the other nations trying to hold on to parts of Mogadishu. Like a fire through the savannah, it would take time and death for the flames of the disease to die out.

"The one benefit of war is that it hurts the exportation of the disease. There are few flights out of Mogadishu, unlike Cairo or Dubai." It was a matter of statistics to Dr. Stewart.

"So I am not as indispensable as you once thought?" Parker smiled.

"No, you can go home." Stewart issued the edict having no idea of everything else that was going on. "We have another donor. The Marine is O positive and has survived."

"I like that." Moncrief couldn't seem to help himself. "We can be in Djibouti on the next Osprey."

I never thought of Djibouti as a place I'd want to escape to. Parker shook his head and then gave Moncrief a look. It did tell Parker what he'd wanted to hear: he had his freedom back. Since healing the disease did not rely upon him solely, he was now free to chase someone he had wanted to find for some time.

"Doc, have you seen the video?" Parker knew that he couldn't hold the truth back. The father needed to know what was going on.

"No."

"She's fine."

"Really? Can I see it?"

"We got a guy here from the Agency. Let's go see him." Parker stood up. It was important that he learn what both the father and the doctor thought.

They used the same secret communications bunker, or SCIF, as it was called, that the satellite feed came in to the day before. Stewart, Parker, Moncrief, Tola, Warren and the MarSOC major crowded into the SCIF's small space.

Stewart was given the main seat.

"This was posted on the Internet just a few hours ago." Warren pulled up the screen through a feed directly from Langley. It showed the close-up of a man sitting in front of the trunk of a small tree. He was holding his Kalashnikov in his hand like a small flag, with the butt on the ground. He had a peculiar smile.

The man spoke: "Al-salamu alaykum." He paused for effect.

"Greetings from the war to create a true Islamic state. Our jihadists have responded from around the world. They have all taken the tests from Allah and understand that to obey Allah is the only way. We have two friends here that want to go home."

The cell phone panned to both Karen and Peter, who were sitting on the ground next to Omar. Karen was covered with a turban wrap that showed her face from the forehead to just below her nose. She didn't look directly into the cell phone. Peter was white, with sunken cheeks, and swayed as if he was trying to hold on to his balance.

The man in the video continued: "Our representative has suggested the ransom we require for their chance to go home to their families. Monies from the MSF and Dr. Stewart will allow them to go home today. We look forward to your response soon."

Paul Stewart trembled. He was mentioned by name. It meant that they knew they held a hostage who was the daughter of a leading scientist in the field of infectious diseases.

"Why did I let her go?" He looked down for a moment.

"Doctor, what is her condition?" Parker needed to know.

How much time did they have?

"He is in the early stages of malaria." The scientist

and physician took over. "My guess is that she has a urinary tract infection that may lead to kidney issues."

"So they have some time?" Tola asked.

"No." Stewart looked at the frozen screen. "As she becomes weaker, she will be more at risk for the meningitis bacteria. He may as well. They both may have hours and, at best, a few days. If they only had some antibiotics, it could buy some time."

Parker looked at Moncrief and then towards Tola.

"Well, gentlemen, it has been a pleasure serving with you." Tola extended his hand as they stood in front of the tent. The others had gone their separate ways. "You two are out of here. I can tell our JTAC guy to get you two seats on the next bird." The Joint Terminal Air Controller ran the coordination of men on the ground and aircraft in support.

"Yeah." Parker stood there in thought. Then he asked. "Skipper, how is this going to end?"

The Marine captain hesitated.

"Oh, we will get him, yes sir, whether it is today or tomorrow or next week."

"But what about her?"

"I don't know, sir. We will keep sending out patrols, but I get the sense that with every minute she is getting farther away. And if she gets deep into the bowels of Al Shabaab, extracting her will be a problem."

"Okay, thanks." Parker didn't say more. He shook hands with Tola, and he and Moncrief headed back towards their tent.

"You know, it is like painting half of a house." Gunny Moncrief sat on the end of the bunk putting his clothes into his tactical bag. "Hard to do."

Parker packed his own gear and listened as Moncrief continued to rattle on. He pulled out his HK automatic and dropped the clip. He pulled back on the action, making sure that the chamber was empty. The pistol's barrel extended half an inch farther than the slide. The barrel over the last half inch was threaded like a pipe that could be screwed into a joint or coupler.

"She seemed nice," Parker heard Moncrief say.

"You never met her."

"Well, her father is a good man. He saved your life once."

"He had to."

"He did." Moncrief pushed on.

"It would help to have another doctor back here." Parker said.

"They have plenty."

"He's the son of a bitch that blew up those kids in Mobile."

Parker put the clip back in the pistol, pulled back on the action, and let a round go into the chamber. He reached back into his bag and pulled out a round black tube and began to screw the suppressor onto the end of the barrel.

"Okay, got it." He stood up. "There is only one way to do this. Let's go talk to Tola and see if he is as crazy as you are."

CHAPTER FIFTY-FOUR

The sensitive message communications bunker or SCIF, on board the U.S.S. *Theodore Roosevelt* didn't look anything like the one in the field. It had large flat-screen displays on the end wall with a row of manned workstations around the three other walls. A large chair was in the center. The SCIF was a smaller version of the control center at NASA but contained the same intensity as a rocket launch. It had a buzz going on just like the much smaller field SCIF at Ferfer. It was crammed with both the watch serving at one in the morning, and everyone else who had a pass to get in. And just like the SCIF in the field, this one had an armed guard at the portal. No papers were allowed in and no papers were allowed out.

"Burn bags" were at every desk for the few documents that were printed and used. The bags would be carried by armed escort, even on the *Roosevelt* where a noncombatant wasn't within a hundred miles, to the shredder and burner.

The admiral came through the hatch. It was his ship and his SCIF. He had both the command and responsibilities for the "Big Stick," or "TR," as the Navy had nicknamed his ship. She had some age on her but an overhaul had bought another decade. She hauled more than ninety attack fighters, fixed-winged aircraft, and helicopters. He wasn't going to put her in harm's way.

"Attention on deck!"

The sailors all started to stand at attention, but before the first one was able to rise, the admiral spoke.

"Carry on!" He took his seat in the big chair in the center.

"What do we have, Jenny?"

She was the duty officer of the day. Or, in this case, of the night.

"The *Zumwalt* has picked up some movement with its own dispatched drone just to the northeast of Kismaayo." The destroyer carried its own unmanned aerial drone that could be launched and recovered from the ship. It gave her another set of eyes.

The admiral knew that Jenny wouldn't have had his aide knock on his hatch at midnight for the movement of a company or battalion of troops of Al Shabaab. They had no air force and were no threat to either the ships of Carrier Group 12 or the *Roosevelt*.

There was one exception.

"Show me."

She punched some keys on her computer and a thermo-night image appeared on the screen.

"They would know that the satellite was out of position at this time," she added to the informal intelligence brief that she was giving. "And they probably have been tracking the MQ-9 traffic out of Djibouti and know that it was in a handover mode."

"Was it?" the admiral asked.

"Yes, sir. Sorry."

"No need. You're doing a great job."

The MQ-9 Reapers had to cover a lot of space near

the Horn of Africa. The activities in Yemen, Ethiopia, Kenya, and Somalia alone covered thousands of square miles. There was a lot of water from the Gulf of Aden down the coast to the Indian Ocean. It was an illusion for one to think that the unmanned aircraft covered the entire planet at one time. And Faud was not stupid. It only took a man with a cell phone living near the end of the runway in Djibouti to hear the buzz of one Reaper taking off.

"In fact, sir, the Air Force reported just yesterday that one of their birds was lost on takeoff from Camp Lemonnier. The MQ-9 crashed short of the runway."

Lemonnier was created by the French Foreign Legion, and then the Djibouti Armed Forces took control until the United States moved in. It was in poor shape when, after September 11th, America wanted a location near the Gulf. Now, it was CLUville—or rows of containerized living units. It was also home to CJTF-Horn of Africa. Reapers had been based out of the airstrip until several crashed into the local neighborhoods. They were now scheduled to be moved to a place where neighborhoods didn't exist.

"I thought they had moved everything."

"Not yet. They are still in the process of moving the Reapers to Oman."

"So, what do you think?"

"I think we got something, sir. They look like they are getting ready to move their missile because they think we can't track them."

"What has Al Shabaab been up to otherwise?"

"Another suicide bomber hit a Djibouti unit in Mogadishu last night, killing six."

"Djibouti still has a presence in the city?"

"Yes, sir, they are helping the AMISOM, as peacekeepers." The African Union Mission to Somalia was trying to help hold together the fragile union of several governments against Al Shabaab.

"The bomber?"

"Yes, sir?"

"Where was he from?"

She was surprised by the question.

"Norway."

"Omar is having his effect. We have Americans in northern Iraq with ISIS, Brits and Swedes in Yemen, and Omar in Somalia. His videos are impacting recruitment. How is the humanitarian effort going on the meningitidis?"

"The Ethiopian minister of health and MSF still do not need our help, other than what has been given. MSF and the WHO are on the ground with a small unit from the CDC. The International Red Cross is now set up in Kenya."

"Doesn't need our help? How many were killed by the attack on the MSF clinic?"

"The MSF refused protection from both the Ethiopian army and our Marine unit on the ground."

The admiral shook his head.

"Okay, so what's the bottom line?"

"We think they are moving the DF-21. There has been some truck movement with trucks of the size that it would take to move the components of the missile."

"If we use the SEALs, it may be another trap. If we destroy it, then we could have a team go in afterwards to do a battle damage assessment to see if we got it." The admiral wasn't going to make that mistake again.

"Let's set a mission for our Joint Strike Fighters. They can keep a low profile and be ready." He was speaking of the F-35 squadron that had just joined the fleet. The aircraft was the new stealth. The Lightning was a flying computer that took technology forward another decade, although it wasn't a cheap date. The cost per flight hour ran in the thousands of dollars and it was slow in development. But the intelligence from the Lightning was remarkable. It delivered encrypted video directly to the men on the ground. Its sensors saw through buildings and could follow the enemy anywhere. It was the father of a new expression. The Marines in the air and on the ground were a new generation of iPad warriors. The jet could find targets with its sensors that could never have been seen otherwise, and the iPad Marine on the ground could know where any attack was coming from in an instant. The MarSOC team on the ground had a new set of eyes that could see through anything.

"Let's watch Faud for his next move." The admiral gave his order.

"But if it launches?"

The room was silent. There were nearly five thousand sailors on board the *Roosevelt*.

CHAPTER FIFTY-FIVE

"**C**an it be done?" Parker and Moncrief were talking to Tola away from everyone else.

"With most Marines, no, sir." Tola didn't hesitate. "With most special operators, no."

The question was whether a light, fast-moving Marine could track and find the kidnapped hostages.

"Can you do it?" Parker asked.

"Yes, sir." Tola's answer was narrowing down the problem. He wasn't worried about himself; he could move at a pace over miles and miles that even his other Marines could not keep up with. He wasn't convinced that Parker could as well. The suggestion was that the two find Peter and Karen Stewart and Omar.

"Your best time in the three-mile is easily under fifteen minutes?"

"Yes, sir." It was well under fifteen minutes. His one-mile time was under four minutes. He ran just behind Alan Webb at the University of Michigan with times for the 1,500 meters below 3:35.

Parker was older but not too much less capable. His record for the 800 meter at his college still stood with a time of 1:50. One still had his speed and one had endurance. While Parker was slower, he had learned to last longer. His endurance made up for the speed he had lost.

Both were fast compared to any others and both had running in their blood.

"A MarSOC team with all of the gear, no matter how ready they are, cannot move over land fast. And tracking their movement by Osprey would only be a guess." Parker's plan made sense.

"So, a two-man mission. I come because of my ability to uplink with a follow-along MarSOC team, and you in case she needs help fast," Tola outlined the suggested scenario. A field blood transfusion was not out of the question.

"Pure Apache war party," Moncrief put in. "Cochise didn't have all of this gear, didn't wear Kevlar, and could move a hundred miles in a day following his enemy." Moncrief knew all the stories of Cochise and his battles with the Kit Carsons of the West.

The dilemma was that the MarSOC team was too well equipped. A man carried well over fifty pounds even before he decided how much ammunition to bring or how many hand grenades. Radios and water and even a limited amount of food added up. So mobility over distance was made up for by the use of the Osprey. But the MV-22 could be heard. It lost the element of surprise that could only be accomplished by two silent fighters on the warpath.

"The more we talk about this the more time is lost." Parker looked at his watch. Stewart was moving away from Ferfer and not towards it.

"You know this place." Parker was making his bid to get the captain's help.

"What about my major?"

"Why don't we let Dr. Stewart take care of that," Moncrief suggested.

"She is sick and is getting sicker by the minute. We know the trail, but don't know where they are," Parker said.

"Okay, I am in."

"Here is where we found the gum wrapper." Tola pointed with his Kalashnikov to the rock near the She-belle River. His weapon and Parker's had been borrowed from the Ethiopians along with the added feature of a Russian-made suppressor. He wore the olive drab uniform of the mujaahidiin, along with a black turban. Parker was outfitted with the same. Underneath, they carried Camelbaks.

The Ethiopians had scavenged the uniforms from the raid the night before. Other than one different article of clothing, the two looked like fellow mujaahidiin fighters. It was their intent to buy just a second from the enemy.

But a closer look would cause a problem. They were traveling fast in a run-jog-run pace across the land. It wasn't a hard trail to follow, as the truck's one lopsided tire left a clear footprint. Water from the rain caused the tracks to puddle but the smaller tire left a very visible trace.

However, the run—and the thorns—caused them to make one concession. Both Parker and Tola were wearing the new, lighter XPRT tactical combat boots that were more like a pair of Nikes than the issued combat boots. MarSOC had access to the high-speed shoes and a trade-around got Parker a pair. They were black and it would take a hard look to realize that they were different, but they were also not sandals like most of the enemy wore.

"Let's cross here." Parker pointed to where the road disappeared into the swirling water. He spoke in little more than a whisper. When they got closer to their target, they would go to the tactical-operations hand signals. Until then, they made no more sound than an Apache war party.

"Sure." Tola pulled a tablet computer out from underneath his cotton uniform. He held it and the AK-47 up as they crossed the fast-moving red water.

On the other side they stopped for a moment to drink from the Camelbaks.

"What's the tablet show?"

"It has a direct feed from an F-35 on top." Tola showed the screen to Parker. "It picks up a lot, encrypts it, and beams it down. We can see where we are, where our backup MarSOC is, and anything with a heartbeat within ten miles."

"As long as it keeps Warren off our back."

Warren had been very specific. The Agency would go along with Parker's efforts to save the two doctors, but if it came down to Omar or the doctors, all they would see would be a flash of light. He suggested that the Hellfire decision was made even easier because the Agency was not going to risk Al Shabaab catching Tola and Parker as well as the others. The tablet served as a homing device should it come to the F-35 doing more than just surveillance.

"Let's go."

Tola led the way. They exchanged the lead position, moving at a pace that sometimes broke into a run.

They would run for five miles and then stop. The stops were not very long.

Once Parker was in the lead and held his hand up.

He signaled Tola, who was not far behind, to come up ahead. He pointed to the bush directly in front of him, where there was movement.

Tola shook his head.

They waited as a lioness crossed the road with two cubs following behind her.

"We must wait," Tola whispered.

They had to give her plenty of room. The two men were not game to her, but they could have been a threat to her young. Tola checked his tablet.

"We are already twenty miles ahead of the MarSOC team." He pointed to some small red triangles on the pad. "At this rate we are beyond their help."

"We knew that."

A second team had been boarded on two Ospreys that were to follow in trace. The aircraft were to stay as far away and as high as possible. They were to be on call.

"How about the Ethiopian raid?"

The ENDF was directed to attack the outskirts of Beledweyne to the north. The National Defense Force had brought in some Chinese-made, Type 88 howitzers that were laying fire down on the best of the Harakat Shabaab al-Mujaahidiin. The effort was meant to keep Al Shabaab distracted.

"They are laying into them at this time."

The battle would last for several hours and then the Ethiopians would withdraw. It was the withdrawal that was the hard part. The Ethiopian commander didn't like the idea of pulling away from Al Shabaab if ENDF was, in fact, winning. But it was important that they not be considered a continuing threat. They didn't want Al Shabaab to move more towards the Ethiopians if they thought ENDF was winning and advancing. It was meant to be a diversion, period.

The rain began again. They paused under a grove of acacia trees while large droplets fell through the skinny, palmlike leaves above. There was a small clear opening directly under the acacia where there was no savannah grass. It was only mud, dirt and—always—trails of ants. They squatted down, keeping away from the ant trails.

"What is the longest run you have made?" Tola asked quietly. They ate a PowerBar while waiting for the torrent to subside.

"A 50K." Parker had pushed himself before. "Just after my wife was killed, I had to burn off some hate. It helped."

It was the first time in a long time that he'd said what was really on his mind.

CHAPTER FIFTY-SIX

"He has meningitis." Karen Stewart tried to rotate Tarriq's head to the side. His skin was red hot and he kept his eyes closed.

Omar considered the situation as he watched the man curled up next to the fire. The heat caused their cotton uniforms to steam the closer they got to the flames. He tried to clean his rifle with the dry inside of his sleeve so as to keep rust from forming.

"You need to keep your weapon clean and greased even if you must use some of the lube from underneath the truck," he said to the men as he pointed to the nearby truck. He had seen many men killed in his short time in combat due to rifles that jammed at the wrong time.

"I remember Abo from Australia was blown apart by the Kenyans when his Hungarian gun jammed just as he stood up." Omar loved to tell his stories of combat. "May Allah accept him as a martyr!"

"What of Tarriq?" one of his followers asked. They were of the same clan and were cousins in some way.

"He needs antibiotics." Stewart looked back over to the truck as she responded. Peter was still under the tarp, closer to dead than alive. "He has no hope without some medicine."

The disease was the will of Allah. They knew little of being saved by medical care and after watching death walk in and out of their lives with frequency, the rush for antibiotics didn't matter.

"The clinic at MSF has antibiotics," she added.

Omar looked at her like she had lost her mind.

She tried to make him see reason.

"He is highly infectious. You must understand that, Omar."

He continued to clean his rifle.

"What was that?" One of the men held up his hand. There was a soft rumble that seemed to come from some distance away.

"The fire!" Omar jumped up and started to kick dirt and mud onto the burning sticks. Soon, it was dark with only smoke lingering in the thick humid air. The men knew to separate and went out in four different directions. Omar moved away from the truck knowing that the Reaper would strike at the object in the center of the group.

He crawled on the rocky ground, wet with the rain, to an outcrop of rocks several yards away. A blanket of clouds covered the sky; however, they were at a higher altitude than they had been for the last several hours. He listened for the sound again. It hadn't disturbed nature, as the mosquitoes continued to hum around his head.

"I am sure that something is there," he whispered to himself.

He would have been right. The F-35 was more than twenty thousand feet above, but its sensors were relaying a view as if the camera were only a dozen yards away.

* * *

Tola stopped and grabbed Parker's shoulder. He pulled him back to just behind a group of thorny bushes and bent down on one knee to show Parker the rugged iPad. It gave off a subdued green glow.

"There are five of them, and a woman near one that is curled up as if he is sick, and another in the bed of the truck." The signal was being sent from the F-35 back to the base and on to Tola. The first system had been called "Rover," which started the process of integrating all the knowledge of the battlefield into something the man on the ground could easily carry.

"How far?"

"At least twenty miles."

Pop-pop-pop. Three shots rang out, with the bullets cracking just above their heads.

They scrambled in different directions.

The damn screen. Parker realized they had let their guard down to look at the image on the tablet. He waited, like a hunter, for the next sign. He hugged the wet earth, barely breathing. Slowly, he slid his Kalashnikov up to his shoulder. There was no further movement and then, minutes later, he heard a voice to his far left. He waited, and in a few minutes he heard a second voice. They had found Tola.

"*Al-salamu alaykum!*" He heard Tola's voice.

It was important to wait to see how many there were.

"*Wa alaykum s-salam,*" a voice returned the greeting.

Parker slowly raised his head to see three figures in the low light standing near a shape that looked like Tola. They had their rifles pointed at his chest.

Twenty yards. He had only shot the AK-47 several hundred rounds, if that. And he had fired only a magazine or two before leaving the base camp so that he could get the feel of the Bulgarian suppressor. It had little effect on a shot within fifty yards but beyond that it caused the round to drop.

Parker listened to the conversation. He had a natural sense of language and had picked up Swahili quickly. Sometimes they shifted to French, which made it even easier for him

"Who are you?" Tola was being asked.

"I am a brother from Jilib." Tola held his hands up high. He continued to hold the stock of his rifle in his hand.

"Where are you from?"

"I am from Tunisia." Tola was smart. His voice didn't crack or seem the least bit on edge. He sounded like a neighbor talking over the fence to another.

Parker watched as the three men moved in the direction he had hoped for. One fell back slightly after holding the rifle too long. Any rifle held at arm's length is like holding the end of a broom. The broom may be light as you pick it up, but if you hold it by its end for any length of time it will soon weigh a ton.

"Do you know Abo Xafs?"

"Yes, yes I do." And then Tola said something that saved his life. "He is the explosives expert."

Parker figured Tola had studied his intel. Abo Xafs was a bomb builder with Al Shabaab.

They started to put their barrels down, and when they did there was a muffled thump that came out of the darkness.

Parker took each, one at a time. He was a hunter. He knew that the shot had to be a head shot, dropping one in the back of the head, followed by the next one, and finally the one closest to Tola. The order of the shots meant that they had no time to turn around and see what was happening to the others. The bullet had to strike the brain stem so that there would be no time for any reaction on their part. Anything less was unacceptable.

Tola fell back onto a rock.

"Are you okay?" Parker called out as he saw him fall.

"Yes." Tola felt his legs and chest with his free hand. A bullet could do damage and the body did not always sense the pain or injury. "No blood!"

"Are they alone?" Parker asked as he approached the dead men with his rifle pointed back towards where they had come from. Another one hidden in the bush could fire at any moment.

"Yes, they are."

Tola kept his rifle trained on each as he turned them over like scorpions. Each of the men was limp and did not move.

"They were looking for someone named Tarriq."

"Tarriq?" Parker brought down his rifle. He could smell the burnt graphite from the gunpowder. He still felt the edge.

"They said he was with the *Amriiki*."

Parker had not heard all of the conversation.

"Wait one minute." Tola searched the leader and pulled out a Russian hand grenade. It was one of the older F-1s that looked like what the Americans called a pineapple. The Russians called it "the Lemon" due to its size and shape. Tola pulled the pin and placed it under the body just below the arm. If someone tried to retrieve the rifle, it would go off.

If the grenade exploded, Tola and Parker would hear the sound and know that someone was behind them. No Al Shabaab fighter would leave a weapon on the battlefield.

"I am going to pull the MarSOC team off from behind." He pulled out the tablet again but this time knelt down and covered it with his arm. "They are too far behind us to help. With these patrols out looking for our man, there is too much of a chance for trouble."

"I agree." They were now on their own. Parker pulled out the magazine from his Kalashnikov and checked the bullets. He had another fresh magazine under his jacket that he slid into the rifle. A round was still in the chamber.

"We need to move." Tola pointed in the direction of the road. "And move quickly."

CHAPTER FIFTY-SEVEN

"**M**ore of the boat captains are reporting movement." The lieutenant was standing before Faud with his report.

"What type of movement?"

"*Amriiki* fighters overhead. Some of them are the Super Hornets and some are something different."

"Different?"

"Yes, something different."

They did not recognize the signs of the F-35 Lightning IIs.

"The carrier is near." Faud put his rifle in the Toyota truck and started to get in. He paused for a moment.

"What happened to Abo Musa?" Musa was to bring word of another gunrunner who was to meet Faud in Said.

"He was killed in Yemen yesterday by a Reaper strike."

"What? Why didn't anyone tell me?"

The lieutenant looked down at his feet.

"May Allah accept him as a martyr," Faud said the customary blessing.

When will they say that about me? he thought as he climbed into the truck. Little did he know that a Reaper, or F/A-18, was sitting above him at that moment and only needed a confirmed target. Faud would be on the approved list for the remainder of his life.

"What of our weapon?"

"It has been moved to Jamaame." The village was between Jilib and the coast.

It was only a few miles northeast of Kismaayo.

"Tell them to ready it for fire."

"That may expose it."

"The carrier is near. There may be no reason to save it for later."

"Yes, sir."

"And the *Amriiki*?"

"We have not heard from Tarriq. When we last did, he was near Tayeeglow."

"What unit is near Tayeeglow?"

"We have a thousand men in Xudur, which is only twenty kilometers away."

"And the Ethiopians?"

"They were repelled from Beledweyne."

"A great victory for us." Faud closed the door and put his rifle through the open window.

The lieutenant shook his head.

Faud knew the lieutenant. His father was a martyr in the battle of Mogadishu that cost the Americans so much. His brother was killed in Al Shabaab's attack on the Westgate Mall in Nairobi. His brother and others murdered many men, women, and children before they were also shot.

The lieutenant would fight and die like his family before him. It was Allah's will.

"Yes, get the missile ready."

CHAPTER FIFTY-EIGHT

Kevin Moncrief stood outside the operations center of the MarSOC camp. He walked back and forth nervously, and occasionally looked in to see the movements on the tactical screen.

"When are you going to put a team on top?" Moncrief asked the major at one point.

The operations center was wall-to-wall with Marines on portable, field-hardened computers. They were all focused on their computer screens, all armed with M4s next to them.

"We are getting ready to launch. As soon as they let us know they are near their target we will go."

"Save me a seat."

"No way." The major was pleasant but inflexible.

"Listen, I can talk to Warren or go up the chain." Moncrief wasn't one to take a no. "But here is the bottom line."

The major listened with folded arms.

"I know how my guy thinks. I know what he will do. And that can be important to the success of your team."

The major wasn't persuaded.

"Let me think about it."

Moncrief was going to be on one of those Ospreys if he had to tie himself to the landing gear.

"Okay, I will be ready."

He started back across the compound to his tent to suit up when he saw a man standing outside in his white scrubs.

Oh, shit. He wasn't generally good with people—particularly one who had his only child in harm's way.

"Hey, Doc," Moncrief said to Paul Stewart.

"Why are you still here?" Stewart was almost slumped over with exhaustion.

Moncrief was surprised that he cared.

"They are out there and moving well."

"Isn't it just the two of them?"

"No, that's not the plan."

"You are going with them, aren't you?" Stewart asked.

"I am trying to work that out right now."

"With whom?"

"The C.O."

"I will go talk to him."

Stewart moved past Moncrief and headed towards the operations tent.

Kevin Moncrief was going to be on that bird.

CHAPTER FIFTY-NINE

"We have a lead on another cell." An agent was manning a front-row workstation when the classified email came through from the National Security Agency.

The Federal Bureau of Investigation's Strategic Information and Operations Center had kept a special work group focused on Omar since Mobile, and now Reagan. As at other high-speed operations centers, the rows of desks and computer stations faced a wall of digital flat-screened panels. A large panel dominated by several side graphics showed information from around the world.

"What is it?" The SIOC duty officer had a number of people on the list he had to keep informed regarding Omar. He typed in some key words and a photograph of Abo Omar Fazul *al-Amriiki, al-Kanadi, as-Somali*, popped up. It showed his date of birth, making him no more than twenty-five years old, and his place of birth being Mobile, Alabama. It showed a picture of his wife with a last-known location of Cairo. And another photograph showed a small ranch home with a black mailbox on a wooden pole in the front yard. It was a well-cut yard with the bushes trimmed and roses blooming in the front flower beds.

Another photograph showed an older man with the light brown skin of someone born in the Middle East, and a black moustache, in a pose for an Alabama driver's license. He wore a white shirt with the collar edges sticking up slightly, and a striped tie tied in a large knot. Another photograph showed a woman, a schoolteacher, with large-rimmed glasses.

The house could not look more American. The operations chief played with his mouse, amplifying the photograph of the suburban home somewhere across Mobile Bay.

"NSA had him on the list."

Omar was an easy one to track. Despite the media's uproar about NSA's search through millions of Americans' lives, this one passed all the tests for a closer scrutiny. They had every telephone call pulled in from America to Somalia, and from Somalia to America. As a result, a federal court had cleared it so that Omar could be the target of all levels of scrutiny.

Omar had another distinction. He was rapidly moving up the FBI's Most Wanted list. The government had just issued a reward of $5,000,000 for him.

The tracking of telephone calls to the wife in Egypt was also high on the list. They knew that the wife was pregnant with their first child. And they knew that she was trying to leave Egypt. Her loyalty to the cause seemed to be withering. The mother-to-be did not seem to be as committed now that her child was involved.

The resident agent in Cairo had been working with the Egyptian intelligence service on keeping track of Mrs. Omar Dhaahir. Despite the public chaos reported by the media in Egypt, the intelligence service still had a strong grip on what was going on locally. They particularly had no love for the jihadists who were passing through Cairo from around the world to either Somalia or Iraq or Pakistan. The connective tissue to the tumor called Al Qaeda often had a common passing point, and the crossover was Cairo.

"What did they find?"

"We had the emails we pulled from when he was in Toronto." The Bureau could reach deep and well into the past when they had a strong target. "He mentioned 'Papafour five eight zero' more than once."

The email from the NSA showed the transcription of a telephone call made from a cell phone, triangulated to a location on the plateau on the west side of southern Somalia. The location was pictured on a map. The call was to Cairo.

"He is asking his wife to tell the Somali milkman to deliver $45.80 worth of milk and eggs to the Waajib." The junior agent read the transcription out loud while the others in the room listened.

"So?"

"P4580 is an MSDS."

The number was known in the chemical transportation world as a reference to a greenish-yellow, corrosive, oxidizing chemical; a liquefied gas with a horrible, irritating odor. It was an odor that didn't last long to the person inhaling it because they quickly died.

"Which one?"

"Chlorine."

"Hell, the stuff is used everywhere," the watch officer spoke his thoughts aloud. "So it is likely that someone from Toronto is going to come into the United States and be looking for a concentrated source of the stuff?"

"We are talking trucks or maybe a railroad tank car?" The shift agent who took the incoming email turned his chair around as he spoke to the central desk. The entire shift of officers all turned their chairs so as to face the chief officer.

"Probably a tank car in a populated area?" the chief asked the group.

"Yes, sir. You remember South Carolina?"

They all had studied the South Carolina incident. It didn't involve a crime or a terrorist act. It did involve a railroad tank car that ruptured near a small town. Nine died as they were running from a slow-moving, green-yellowish cloud that seeped into the air-conditioning of a nearby factory. One witness said he saw people running, and as the cloud reached them on the far side of the factory they dropped in their tracks, gasping, with their hands to their throats.

"We need to watch the crossover point Omar used when he left the U.S."

"Do you think another would be crazy enough to use the same trail?"

"Perhaps." The chief agent was on duty when the word came across about the attack at Reagan National. He had been on duty when too many calls like that had come across the wire.

"I have another idea. If we are sure it will be chlorine gas, we can stop it at the source."

"How?"

"We stopped every airplane that flew over America in 2001. Why not stop the movement of any large quantities of the stuff?"

"It might work."

It was the big containers that posed the most danger.

A fourteen-thousand-gallon railroad tank car full of chlorine gas could wipe out much of a city. A small tank of gas on the back of a delivery truck was less of a threat. Could they identify and stop every railroad tank car moving the chemical?

CHAPTER SIXTY

Omar returned from his walk. Karen could see him from the chest up moving through the savannah grass just beyond the grove of acacia trees. He could be seen pacing around, waving his free hand, as if someone was disagreeing with everything he was saying.

He walked back to her and the others.

"Tarriq is dead." She greeted him with the news. The body was just behind her, curled up in a fetal position. It was cold and lifeless.

"May he see the face of Allah," Omar gave the edict.

The others were not as sure. They wore the face of fear. One had been complaining of headaches through the night. He would likely be the next victim. Their silent partner was moving through the group one at a time.

"You seem to not care." Stewart stared at Omar.

"It is war. There will be losses."

"But what if the loss is your captives? What will your people on the telephone think?"

She had struck a cord.

"Godane doesn't know what he is doing. We let the Kenyans slaughter us by falling into their traps." Omar didn't care who was listening. "We need more kidnappings and more hostages. We need money for more ammunition and weapons."

Karen pulled herself up into the bed of the truck. The rain had come in torrents and then stopped. The monsoon would attack and then retreat. It had caused puddles of water to form on the tarp and she would cup her hands together to try and capture some of the liquid. She would drink and then try to get more for Peter.

She had given up on ever being dry.

If they could build a fire, there was a chance they would start to dry out. But the men were afraid that the fire would attract the enemy. They would only build one when they thought the lions or baboons were close. She had not seen a baboon but could tell, even with her little understanding of Swahili, that the men were more frightened of the baboons than the lions. It seemed that the lions only came when desperate for food.

"How are you doing?" Peter looked worse than before.

"Okay. Just thinking of my mother's cooking."

"It's not good to think of that."

"You know I have a child?" Peter turned his head to her.

"No."

"Yes, I have a son. He and his mother live in Nice."

"What is his name?"

"Pierre. He's a junior in high school." Peter was opening up in a way she did not like. He was accepting approaching death.

Acceptance is dangerous.

"His mother told me that if I did not leave the MSF, she would leave me. I had dreams."

Karen didn't say anything.

"I had a dream of the child that I did not save. I had a dream of the children that I did not save because I stayed home." Peter held his hands over his chest.

"My mother died last year." Karen meant to change the subject but didn't realize what subject she was changing to until it was too late. The words just came out. "My father lives for his work. He has become helpless without her."

"And you left?"

Peter struck a nerve.

"I didn't know how to help." Karen rubbed her neck with her hand.

"Why are you rubbing your neck?"

"Just a crick from when I fell asleep."

She pulled the tarp back a moment and looked up into the dark clouds. The rain was softer now but still fell on her face.

"I think I heard something."

There was the faint sound of a jet, well above the clouds.

"Another jet," Peter mumbled.

"Do you think they are even looking for us?" she asked.

"We are worth money to these men. Always remember that. And yes, someone is looking for us. I feel it in my bones."

Tarriq's men continued to stare at Omar. They were without a leader and knew enough English to realize that criticism of Godane was not wise. Their faces showed that they were uncertain of this *Amriiki*.

"We will go on and meet up with our brothers. Godane and Faud are sending a battalion of men to meet us and bring us to Jilib." Omar waved the cell phone. It gave him power over them as it was a real form of communication. It made them believe he had orders and a plan.

"Jilib has the bananas." Omar wanted them to think of food. It would give them direction. Omar had taken charge.

Xasan and his father looked like this was a journey they had not planned for.

"Jilib?"

"Yes, have you ever been to Jilib?"

"No." Xasan had never traveled to the coast.

"There is plenty of food to eat in Jilib and there will be money." Omar needed them to all move together to Jilib so he could reach the other fighters.

"Tell us. What is the reward?" Xasan wanted to know.

"You will not get a new tire, my friend. You will get a new truck." Omar sold the idea. "You will get a bag of *Amriiki* money."

"A new truck?" Xasan sounded doubtful. There were no new trucks in Ferfer or Beledweyne.

"You will get paid in *Amriiki* money and can go to Kenya to buy a new truck."

The U.S. dollar had international appeal.

"How much?"

"More than you can dream."

Their group now consisted of Omar, the three followers of Tarriq, Xasan and his father, and the two prisoners.

"We need food and water. And our brothers are less than a day away."

Karen and Peter knew that once they were with the larger mujaahidiin force there would be no escape. But they had no energy to do anything but breathe, and that was hard enough.

"Less than a day." Omar waved the telephone in the air.

The rain came, however, and bought the trackers more time.

CHAPTER SIXTY-ONE

"Amazing." The Marine major looked at the display showing the location of the tablet with Captain Tola. It had moved far from the Shebelle River and deep into the interior of Somalia.

"What does that scale indicate?" Moncrief looked over his shoulder as they talked.

"They have gone nearly a hundred miles."

"Damn." Moncrief knew that the captain would move fast but he didn't know how fast.

"And in this weather." The major was amazed.

The wind had started to blow the flaps of the tents. Rain came in waves and then would stop for a while.

"The team that went to the departure point is on its way back right now." The major pointed to another set of red triangles. They, too, had tablets that kept track of their locations. Their red triangles seemed to be nearly on top of the base's location.

"What is the weather forecast?"

"This is the beginning of a good-sized monsoon. It is going to get much worse over the next twenty-four hours." The major held up a fax showing a map that was covered with lines forming a circle to the west of

Ferfer. The lines near the center of the circle were closer together. It was a wall of weather moving in.

"What will this do to the Ospreys?"

"What do you mean?"

"Can they reach our men?" Moncrief looked into the major's eyes to detect what the true answer would be. He didn't like the idea of leaving his man out in the dark without help. If it meant putting on a pack and heading out now, by himself, Moncrief would do what he knew Parker would do for him if their positions were reversed.

The major smiled.

"You said you wanted to go?"

"Yes, sir, without a doubt."

"Then you are going to find out the hard way."

Moncrief thought he had gotten the answer.

"This is combat. They go, period."

CHAPTER SIXTY-TWO

They were getting close and knew it.

Tola and Parker stopped one more time under two large acacia trees. They squatted down between the trunks of the trees to get out of the wind.

"We need to make sure we are downwind when we get close." Parker held up his hand to feel the wind direction. It was coming from the northwest and Ferfer.

The flight time for the Ospreys will not be long. He wasn't sure if the aircraft could make it through the turbulence that was building above them in the clouds. The aircraft would, however, have what pilots called a "push." It meant that the aircraft would have a tailwind that shoved them across the surface of the earth. If the MV-22s had a speed of three hundred knots, it would be relative to what their ground speed would be. With a push, the aircraft could be doing four hundred or more knots on the ground. The climb up would be brutal and the descent would be like riding in a washing machine on full tilt. And they would have to turn into the wind for the transition because the nose of the tilt-rotor needed the resistance of going against the wave. But they would move fast.

"We could be alone on this." Parker kept his hand in the air as he felt the gusts come and go. It was the increase and decrease of the wind that troubled him the most.

"Sir, I understand that you received the Navy Cross."

Parker didn't think of those times. It was not something that one typically talked about. There was, however, one exception. Two men in the middle of Somalia with no one else who was friendly for nearly a hundred miles could discuss anything.

"It was a long time ago." He didn't say more.

"You didn't like that guy from the Agency?" Tola was hitting all of the hot buttons as he wiped off his wet face with his hand.

"I have learned to not trust the CIA." Parker dropped that subject as well. It took him years to learn that his parents had been lost to terrorism because the CIA didn't act on a suspicious suitcase that had been loaded on Pan Am Flight 103. The file was sealed after the crash at Lockerbie and had been locked away forever in some secret vault at Langley. The Agency thought they were tracking a suitcase of heroin for New York that would be exchanged for money to support the terrorist activities sponsored by Libya. In fact, the Samsonite didn't have heroin in it, and the bomb tracking at the time was in its infant stage.

"What about you? You say you are from Washington?"

"Yes, actually we call it Lincolnville. It is more Alexandria, Virginia, than Washington."

"And you ran track there."

"Yes, and cross-country."

"Do you like doro wot?" Parker asked.

"Yes, you know of doro wot?" Tola wiped his face again with his hand. It was a chicken-and-hard-boiled-egg dish with Ethiopian farmer's cheese. "Don't talk to me of doro wot now." He laughed quietly.

The wind started to subside for a moment.

"We will be close very soon." Despite the rain, the thorn bushes had been broken down from the truck. In one place he could tell the truck had gotten stuck. It looked like a wild-game watering hole with the deep ruts in the center and hundreds of footprints to the sides. A small piece of rag had fallen out of the truck bed leaving its calling card on the edge of a newly made mudhole.

"Yes, it is time to start moving to the east so that we remain downwind." Tola had a good sense of the track. The wind and rain would help as long as they kept the elements hitting their faces.

Parker pulled back the slide on his Kalashnikov to see the bright gold of the round that was partially in the chamber of the weapon. He slowly let the slide move back into place without making any metallic noise. It was the metallic noise that he feared the most. Metal on metal would give away a position more quickly than any other sound. It was not a sound made for nature.

"Let me send them an update." Tola covered the tablet with its plastic holder. He tapped on the keys several times sending an encoded message to the F-35 on station above, which was instantly relayed to the operations center.

Parker listened for sounds during the break in the wind. He thought he heard the hum of something large.

"We have a new friend." Tola showed the message to Parker. It said that the mission warranted extra support. A C-130 gunship was parked overhead as well.

"Why a gunship?" Parker knew that the extra power was a blessing. Its automatically fed artillery guns could rain down fire on any enemy position and rake the ground with hot, burning shrapnel.

"This is why."

Tola showed the tablet to Parker. The F-35's cameras were able to look through the overcast and see what appeared to be ants all moving in the same direction. They were coming from the east. A battalion or more were heading towards their location on the ground. It looked like a convoy of trucks. The image was so clear he could tell the different sizes and shapes of the trucks.

"So we do know that they are close. Very close."

CHAPTER SIXTY-THREE

Faud's truck was running as fast as it could with the driver cutting between the potholes and bomb craters left from more than a decade of war.

"You know we have uranium here," Faud said to his driver.

"Uranium?"

"Yes, what is needed for power plants and energy."

"Don't go too fast or we will lose the banner." Faud was holding on to a flag with the Red Crescent, marking the truck as being an ambulance. It didn't matter that the banner was a lie. He knew that it would cause anything in the sky above to hesitate before shooting at them.

"Yes, brother." The driver was stupid but loyal. He had been with Faud since the beginning.

"I have not been home now for more than ten years." Faud was from Saudi Arabia. "I was actually born in Mecca. My mother was on the hajj when she delivered.

"It was the year of the plague." Faud held out his hand in the wind as the truck turned again and then hit a rut that caused it to fly up into the air.

It was the year that another form of meningitis had

swept through the camps of the visitors to Mecca. Thousands became ill and thousands died. Somehow he was spared. It was meant to be.

They passed through an arch that had been partially blown away. It was on the edge of another small village through which the highway passed. Children with bare feet ran along the side of the truck. It gave them something to do.

Faud lifted his Kalashnikov more to change positions then anything, but when he did, the children stopped and ran away. They knew that curiosity could be overcome by fear and death.

"What is that up ahead?" the driver asked.

On the other end of the village there were three trucks parked across the road. The bed of each of the trucks was packed with armed men. One truck had a large antiaircraft gun mounted in its bed. It was an odd sight, as the truck was too small for the weapon. When it fired the frame would shake and the gunner would hold on for dear life. It could not fire on the move. Faud had seen many of these outfitted trucks as they were, oftentimes, the only thing that could take on the Russian gunships the Kenyans used.

"They must want their toll." Faud had seen plenty of renegades on the roads. They would hold up a passing vehicle for blackmail even if it were a truck loaded with fighters heading to the front. It often amounted to nothing, as the thieves would see that they were outgunned by the trucks they were stopping and would have the good sense to let them pass.

"I will tell them who we are."

They would look at the sign of the Red Cross and think that they had someone who would pay. The thieves would be wrong.

The truck came to a stop. The men had their guns trained on the vehicle.

"*Al-salamu alaykum!*" Faud opened the door and waved the greeting at the center truck. He didn't hear a reply.

Two men came from around the center truck and ran up to him. They grabbed him before he could raise his weapon. The others with Faud looked on in shock. Another, younger man came from behind the first truck with his pistol raised.

"Brother, what is this?"

The lieutenant continued to point the weapon at Faud's chest. He didn't say anything.

An older man came from behind the truck as well.

"Godane!" Faud said his name without thinking.

It was Sheikh Mukhtar Abu Zubeyr himself—leader of Al Shabaab and a member of the Isaaq clan.

"Faud, you knew that the fleet was near?"

"Yes, but we have not . . ."

"Be quiet." Godane held up his finger to his lips. "You moved the missile without telling me."

"It was for its protection." Faud was becoming defiant.

"And you protect this *Amriiki* who speaks poorly of me." Godane was furious.

Tarriq's reports had made it back to Godane.

"Take him away." Godane looked away as if Faud was no longer standing there.

Faud struggled as they pulled him to the side of the road. His rifle fell before he could reach for it. They turned him towards the trucks and he saw the men crowd forward to see what was happening. They didn't bother to tie his hands as they forced him to his knees.

The lieutenant came up. Faud felt the barrel of the Hungarian pistol press against the side of his forehead.

"I am to be a martyr," Faud said.

CHAPTER SIXTY-FOUR

"What's going on?" Moncrief had just returned from his tent where he had reclaimed a set of utilities. The combat uniform was of a United States Marine. He had an M416, a vest loaded with magazines and a MARSOC .45 in his shoulder holster. His question was directed towards Buckley Warren, who was standing at the edge of the compound with a satellite phone next to his ear.

Warren turned away as if Moncrief wasn't standing there.

"What is your name?" Moncrief put a finger on Warren's chest.

Moncrief had figured out that Warren knew that Parker and Tola were nearly on top of the target. It would be a Tomahawk dispatched from the DDG-1000 that would follow the signal to the kill point. The explosive would be set for an aerial burst that would chew up every living thing within a hundred meters.

"I said, what is your name?" Moncrief put his finger on the man's chest again.

The major heard him and joined the two men. Both Moncrief and the major stood there while Warren kept talking on the cell phone, ignoring them both.

Moncrief took out his .45 automatic and pulled back on the slide. It snapped forward like the crack of a metallic whip. He then put the nose of the barrel up against the other side of Warren's head.

"Wait a minute." Warren looked up as if he were looking into the face of a maniac. He was.

"What's going on here, Gunny?" the major asked in an effort to calm the situation.

"Sir, he is going to tell them that they have a track on Omar. He is probably telling them to have a Tomahawk spun up to take everyone down. And I mean everyone."

"Is this true?" the major asked. "I have a Marine out there."

"You have two." Moncrief put his other hand underneath the butt of the pistol to steady the aim. He spread his feet apart and looked down the sight. "Two Marines out there and two innocent hostages."

Warren slowly put down the cell phone.

"I doubt you'd shoot me."

"What would the difference be, given how secret this mission is, whether I shot you or didn't shoot you? Think about it, Warren."

The field operative paused.

"Are they going to claim you, when you were putting in a call to order a missile strike on two hostages? Or will they say this was an accidental discharge of a weapon in combat? Happens all the time." Moncrief kept the barrel pressed against the side of Warren's head. He leaned forward into the man's skull, feeling the pressure of the metal barrel against the scalp.

"Warren, we are witnesses," the major interjected. "No one here can order the Tomahawk strike but you."

"What if he gets away? What if there is a third cell

and a fourth cell? What are you going to do if the next target is Los Angeles or Denver?" Warren made his point. Omar had a cell phone and no matter how quick the NSA and CIA were, the cells could be buried so deep that no one would ever know about them until it was too late.

"I will tell you what," Moncrief said. "If we get this guy and there is a chance he is brought back with a heartbeat, we have a better chance of learning the truth than if you just dust him."

At that moment it started to rain again. The rain came down in a torrent with sheets of water pouring out like a fire hose.

The three men did not move. Moncrief held the pistol to Warren's head without blinking.

"There is a chance that if you don't figure this out quick I may blow your brains out without even intending to do so." Moncrief stood his ground. "This is the land of the mamba. You can die a thousand different deaths out here and no one on that cell phone would even know it."

"Okay, you get a chance. But only one." Warren was playing the odds.

"No, he gets more than a chance," the major interrupted. "If a Tomahawk takes our team down without a reasonable chance at survival you won't have to worry about Langley."

"Now tell them." Moncrief felt the rough grip of the pistol in his hand. It was made that way, so that a person could feel the weapon even through the tactical gloves that most soldiers wore. But Moncrief didn't wear the gloves. He was like Parker in that way. They both wanted to feel the steel, knowing exactly when the round went off and where it was going. He knew that the trigger had been set to very light poundage, and it required more energy to hold off the squeeze than to pull the trigger.

"The size of this slug is similar to a small marble." The major moved backwards and away from the blast.

The rain started to slow down while Warren still hesitated.

"Make up your mind, Mr. Warren. The Ospreys have got to take off in this break." Moncrief didn't really care for the guy. The rain had kept everyone in the tents or on board the aircraft so the only witness was the major, and it was his man out there as well.

Warren finally put the cell phone back to his ear.

"Hello, hold off on that. We have a good chance of getting this guy and finding out what he knows." Only Warren could help make himself look good.

"Hey, Major, we got an extra seat on the Osprey, don't we?"

"Yeah, I think we do."

"You are going to need a helmet." The major handed Moncrief one he was not used to. It was much lighter than the old Kevlar bucket, as he and others liked to call it. It was made of a carbon-fiber combination with some other Kevlar-type materials that were able to stop a small round on a direct hit.

"What do you call this?"

"This is a FAST helmet. It's not like the old brain buckets." This one had the NOD mounted on the top front with some straps that helped hold on the night eyes as well.

"Here you go, Gunny, let me help." The Marine in the seat next to him helped adjust the strap. It had padding on the inside and openings in the sides for the comm gear. They all were on the same communications link.

Warren was strapped in to a seat near the cockpit.

"He doesn't have a helmet?" the Marine next to Moncrief asked as the engines started to spin up.

"No." Moncrief wasn't worried about Warren. He wasn't getting off the bird.

"This should be interesting." The Marine had a smile on his face as if a rookie was getting up to bat.

The Ospreys had used the landing zone for several days now. It was the only flat space near the encampment, and with the several landings, all of the small stones and rocks had been blown aside. However, the ground was still wet and the aircraft's wheels had sunk into the muck from its weight. The turbines spun louder and louder as the aircraft pulled on its sunken feet until finally it released.

Moncrief had an M416 with a suppressor attached to the barrel. He kept it pointed down, as the others did. The aircraft was dimly lit. He felt himself sink into the canvaslike seat and then the Osprey popped up. Moncrief's head slammed back against the frame of the aircraft as he held on to his rifle with as tight a grip as he could muster.

Warren was whipped backwards as well and popped his head against the wall. He looked like he had been knocked out cold.

Couldn't have happened to a better guy, Moncrief thought as the tilt-rotor aircraft continued to rise and sway. As it left the earth, the airplane rocked back and forth, up and down, while the pitch of the engines seemed to struggle with the power of the wind. It continued to climb and then the propellers rotated forward. He felt the gravitational force pull him down into his seat and then release him as the aircraft started to move forward.

The Osprey bounced wildly as it climbed out through the clouds and wind. Moncrief tried to look out the window and saw only a flicker of light on the ground before the aircraft was enclosed in complete darkness. It continued to bounce wildly for several minutes as it climbed out of the weather.

Finally, the ship broke through to some clear airspace.

The plan was that the aircraft would not descend unless and until Tola sent the signal. They waited well to the north, and above the first layer of clouds closest to the ground.

The crew chief came over to the leader of the MarSOC team and yelled something in his ear. He was talking with his hands as well, with one hand looking like a rollercoaster ride.

"It looks like it is going to be rough going down," the Marine next to Moncrief yelled into his ear. "We may not make it in."

CHAPTER SIXTY-FIVE

It was near midnight when several men and women gathered in the conference room at the headquarters of Médecins Sans Frontières. They represented both the leadership of the organization and doctors who practiced medicine from around the world. It looked like a meeting of the United Nations.

"We have two doctors in their hands. The report is that he has malaria that is progressing, and she may have the beginnings of kidney failure." The international president was chairing the meeting. She had served time in the field, as they all had. And they all knew the risks involved. Nevertheless, despite their effort to remain neutral, terrorists did not hesitate to pull them into the storm.

There was one way out.

"Our donors have agreed to fund the release of the doctors. They are offering two million dollars for each of them." She passed around a list of donors with their contributions. Both Ebola and the meningitis had strained their budget and the sources of help.

"It makes it difficult that she is an American," one of the doctors spoke up from the back of the room.

"She is the daughter of Paul Stewart. He has worked to stop disease around the world. In fact, he has been instrumental in helping us with Ebola," the president replied.

"We have over four thousand field staff fighting Ebola. And now we have another thousand fighting the Neisseria meningitidis, with clinics on the Ethiopian and Kenyan borders," the same voice called from the back. "What do we do about the clinic at Ferfer?"

"Good question," the president responded. "Right now, we have our representative in Said trying to get word to Godane that we're willing to negotiate for a release of the doctors. His reputation is that he will deal; however, the hostages are very sick and time is running out. We can't lose more doctors. We need to move the clinic in Ferfer back farther into the interior of Ethiopia."

It wasn't clear whether Godane would learn of the offer before one or both of the kidnapped doctors became too ill for it to matter.

The circle of trusted followers that surrounded Godane was getting smaller.

"So what is the status of the *Amriiki*?" Godane asked his new head of security and intelligence. He had replaced Abo Musa Mombasa, who had become a martyr in Yemen while making a deal for more arms. Godane was referring to the approaching American fleet.

"Our fishing fleet reports aircraft flying low only fifty miles from the coast."

"And the *Amriiki*? What of him and the doctors?"

"We have sent reinforcements to find them. The rains have slowed their passage but they should reach them by tonight."

"Good."

"We think the Americans know where the DF is located."

"Can it be moved?"

"Only with the risk that its location can be confirmed."

Godane considered his options.

"We will move to the hostages. And when we have them in hand, they will serve both as a source of money and as a source of security. Then we will see if the missile serves us well." Godane would personally take charge of both Omar and the hostages.

Godane knew that ISIS had been drawing away both support and money from their cause. Omar had helped bring attention back to this war, but he had too much of an ego to be tolerated much longer.

The sinking of an American aircraft carrier would be such a shift of power that Godane's name would be burned forever in the minds of the true believers.

"Before the missile is put at greater risk, we must use it." He gave his order. It would be a matter of timing. Without the protection of holding the hostages as shields, he knew that the risk was incurring an all-out retaliation by the Americans on him and his army. He needed to reach the hostages and ready the weapon for its use.

"May Allah be praised!"

CHAPTER SIXTY-SIX

"We must bury Tarriq now." It was one of his fighters who spoke the words to Omar.

"Do it." Omar didn't seem to want to be bothered. "Let the doctors dig the hole."

The fighter had known Tarriq all his life. They were of the same clan. It bothered him that Omar didn't seem to care.

"We will help." Xasan and his father both started towards the edge of an acacia tree where the grass was not too high and there were no thorn bushes. Another of Tarriq's fighters had become sick as well. It seemed that one minute he was healthy and joking and the next minute he was curled up on the ground in the mud clutching his head. The progression of the disease caused fear in them all.

Karen watched as they started to dig. She had no energy left and a pounding headache made her feel both nauseous and dizzy.

They started to dig as the rain subsided. One of the men had built a fire underneath the tree and it smoldered more than burned. The wood was wet even when they pulled off the bark of the branches to what was once the dry core.

The old man stopped, stood up, looked up into the sky as if he had seen something, and then collapsed like a sack of potatoes being dropped to the ground.

"Ah-yaa!" Xasan yelled. He ran to the bed of the truck and pulled on Karen to come help.

She tried to get up and started to fall as her head pounded inside her skull.

"I need a fire to see," she mumbled the words. "Bring him to the fire."

Xasan pled with the others to stop while he pulled his father by the shoulders closer to the fire pit. He placed his father up near the trunk of the tree with his head supported by the base. The man's eyes had rolled to the back of his head.

The fire started to crackle as Karen pulled herself over to his body. She felt for a pulse but the body was still. It had already begun to cool.

She laid him flat and put both of her hands on his chest and pushed with what little strength she could muster. She pushed again and again. Her ears were ringing.

"Xasan, come here." She pulled his hands together and placed them over the old man's chest. And then she put her hands on top of his.

"Push, like this."

He didn't understand the words she was saying, but he did understand what she was doing. He pushed, first lightly, and then as she pushed down on his hands harder, he began to push harder.

Karen collapsed back onto her side.

"Keep pushing," she told Xasan.

He needs to keep pushing until he is convinced his

father is gone. She knew the man was dead but Xasan didn't.

"Ah-yaa," he cried out with tears streaming down his face.

She felt the cold mud on the side of her face and it felt good.

This is a good place to die, Karen thought as she lay there next to the fire. The heat was warming her face while she barely noticed her back, which was wet and cold.

Omar stood in the shadows.

Xasan kept pushing with his hands until both became numb. He thought he heard a breath and started to yell with joy but then the body remained still and cold.

He finally collapsed next to his father.

"We need to get to the others," Omar finally said. They were down to Xasan and two other fighters who had come with Tarriq and Omar. The third fighter lay in the mud and the rain without moving. He too would be dead by dawn. "They cannot be more than a mile or two away." He looked out into the dark and the road that was now filling up with water.

The smoke of the fire rose up to the branches of the tree and then the wind carried it to the southeast, in the same direction as the road, and directly into the faces of the two hiding in the dark.

CHAPTER SIXTY-SEVEN

Every movement by the fire was being watched.

Parker and Tola slowly crawled up to another acacia tree within distance of an easy pistol shot. They watched the fight for the old man's life and then saw Karen Stewart collapse to the ground.

She is hurting. He could see that she barely had the energy to move.

Her weight is down. Parker knew she was ill and that meant she would not be able to get herself out on her own two feet. And the French physician was nowhere to be seen.

Is he already gone? Parker stayed there in the damp grass, looking for the French doctor, as another torrent of rain fell down. The mujaahidiin's olive cloth stuck to his skin. There were two holes in the center where bullets had struck the prior owner.

Parker continued to watch for movement near the fire.

There is Omar. That was the one thought that Parker had as the rain came down and he lay in the wet grass. Omar could not run from him fast enough.

Parker thought back to his trip to Mobile and the

yellow evidence tape that surrounded the school. He thought of the kindergarten schoolteacher who lost her life protecting her children. And he thought of the children.

Omar moved back and forth in front of the fire with his Kalashnikov over his shoulder. Parker watched his mannerisms and how he moved his hands.

Right-handed. He made a mental note.

And then Parker scanned the others sitting close to the fire. One was trying to save a man on the ground. The others were looking on as if it didn't matter. One of them looked at Omar once. Parker knew that look. Years ago he saw another man stare at him in the same way. It was in the mountains of Pakistan and it was the look of hate. Omar was alone whether he knew it or not.

He and Tola waited, motionless, in the grass. The skill of staying perfectly still was a basic requirement of being a recon Marine. It took a willingness to be comfortable in the environment. He was soaking wet, yet concentrated not on his discomfort but on the target. He controlled his breathing with slow, easy breaths. The rain was a friend just like the dark. If it made Omar uncomfortable to leave the cover of the acacia tree, then it was to Parker's advantage.

Parker felt the presence of Abo Tola near him but did not hear the slightest sound from his right. Tola had been trained well. He was a natural hunter. As Parker learned to hunt in the South, Tola learned on the plains of Africa. It was in the DNA of both of them.

After some time, the camp became still. They all cowered by the fire. Then Parker saw something interesting.

A thin man, slightly taller than the rest, who had been trying to help the other, older man by the tree, came over to Karen Stewart. He bent down, said something, and then helped her up. He walked her over to the back of the small vehicle and then lifted her up as she crawled inside the bed of the truck.

Parker sensed that the man who carried her was the most natural hunter of the group. After he had helped her up and into the truck, he went to the edge of the tree's cover and stopped. He looked out into the dark directly at Parker. He stood there for a minute or two as if he was staring directly at a threat. Finally, he turned back to the fire and sat down by the body on the ground. He put more wood on the fire, as if to ward off danger.

"What is it?" Omar sat up from the fire watching the back of Xasan as he stared into the dark. Xasan didn't move for some time. Omar pulled up his Kalashnikov and felt the cold metal in his hands.

Xasan finally turned back to the fire.

"There are lions out there." Xasan sensed there was death somewhere in the shadows. "I must bury my father soon."

He would wake at first light and dig the hole himself. It would be near the grave for the other man. And they would need a third one soon for the other sick one.

"We will need to cover it well. We will need to stack sticks and mud and then cover it all with piles of thorns." It was the only way to keep the lions out. The lions were very near.

Parker waited for the rain to begin again before moving back. As the water came again in waves, he used the cover of sound to pull slowly away from the truck and trees. He felt Tola follow him. They crawled for more than a hundred yards, making sure that they were well out of sight and sound before moving to the cover of several large thorn bushes.

The bushes were the same ones where they had left some of their gear beneath some savannah grass.

"I am letting the MarSOC team know where we are and what we saw." Tola was covering the tablet with his body as he tapped in the words. They would all home in on the grove of trees and the F-35 above would scan the target area.

"Okay." Parker kept a lookout towards the grove when he heard something. It was far to the east. The rain had stopped again, briefly, and as it did, sounds started to travel through the air again. "I hear a truck."

It was more than a truck. He held his hand up as he strained to listen.

"It is a truck stuck in the mud and its wheels are spinning."

Tola pulled him over to the tablet. He didn't have to say anything.

The sensors from the aircraft well above the clouds and the rain showed a line of trucks not far to the west.

CHAPTER SIXTY-EIGHT

"Sir, we have ground movement." The officer of the day in the *Roosevelt's* SCIF had the report the admiral had been waiting for all night. He had sat in his chair through both the storm and four cups of black Navy coffee.

"What is the monsoon doing?"

"It is building. It is coming out of the east with the point of center almost directly over Ferfer. The report is that the river is three times its size. The Shebelle is washing away villages and displacing hundreds of people, if not thousands." The duty officer showed night sensor video from different camera viewpoints on several different aircraft.

"And the DF?" There were few things that made a sixty-year-old man worry anymore. His two sons had graduated from the Academy and were on ships in the other ocean. His wife played bridge back in Newport News with her friends, and her daily emails showed the usual worries of a Navy wife. And he wasn't sure if his career wasn't one command away from being his last. None of the events of life worried him. But this did. He was not going to be the man who lost the first United States carrier since World War II.

"There is movement."

"We need all aircraft off this ship now," he said it calmly but in a voice that no one questioned. The fueling and taking off of nearly ninety aircraft took frantic energy.

"Turn her into the wind." With its nose heading into the storm, the aircraft would have immediate lift. Every flight would be brutal and if a jet engine faulted, one or two would be lost. A downed aircraft in this weather meant a remote chance that the pilot would be found.

"Sound general quarters." The horn blared through the ship. The admiral relayed his command to the group. "Have all of the group disperse except for the *Zumwalt*."

They had intelligence on the Dong Feng but it was only guesswork. No one was sure how effective a weapon it was. The fear was that if it was half as effective as they thought, it was extremely deadly.

He had a plan.

"We need a strike by a Tomahawk on that missile's last-known and suspected location," he barked the orders.

"Yes, sir."

"We need the *Zumwalt* to bring her course parallel to the *Roosevelt* and stay alongside."

The one hope was that the missile could see the *Roosevelt* and not the *Zumwalt*.

"She will provide both our protection and our defense."

The *Zumwalt* was armed to the teeth. It had more than eighty cells for a variety of Tomahawks, Sea Spar-

rows, and anti-submarine rockets, and it had two automatically fed and computer-directed 155-millimeter
guns on the deck. More important for this situation, it
was equipped with two MK46 30-millimeter GDLS
guns. It could lay up protection.

"As soon as the aircraft are all dispatched, we will
head at full speed to the northeast."

The Dong Feng's sensors would see the *Roosevelt* in
front of it but not the shadow nearby.

The lieutenant carried Godane's cell phone since
Godane never held one on his person at any time. It
was a matter of safety. The conversations were all
tracked and it made his being a target too simple.

Godane heard it ring, which was unusual. Virtually
all of the cell calls were outbound. It wasn't meant to
be used for an incoming call. If more direction were
needed on an issue, he would call back from another
number. He heard the lieutenant talking to the person.
He immediately knew what the conversation involved.
The lieutenant disconnected.

"It is Sana'a." The capital of Yemen was the location
of all go-betweens.

"Yes."

"The French are prepared to pay for both hostages
but they want proof of life."

The MSF had let its corporate donors make the deal
for them. They were more suspicious than the charity.
The donors had been through this before when MSF
executives and even the donors' own corporate executives had been kidnapped in South America. They had
a plan and they hired the best—who required proof that
the two captives were still alive.

"Any word from Tarriq?"

"No, sir."

"What of the American fleet?"

"We are seeing more and more aircraft."

"Even with the monsoon coming?" He had wrapped his head with his turban to protect his face from the gusting wind. Small rocks and stones flew through the air as well as larger chunks of debris from years of destructive warfare. It wasn't uncommon for a child to be hit by a flying piece of tin roof. There were dangers everywhere as a result of the decade of war.

"Yes, the weather seems to be no factor in slowing them down. It appears that they are worried about us."

Godane considered his options.

"When we get close to the hostages we will fire the missile." He wanted some insurance that an air strike wouldn't hit him or his circle of leaders of Al Shabaab. The two doctors gave him that insurance.

"Let's go."

The convoy of trucks pulled out of the city heading north and into the wind. They flew across the potholed road splashing through the deep puddles of water that covered the countryside.

"I need the phone with the number for Al San."

The lieutenant in the back handed him the cell with only one number in its directory. The call went to a cell at a house by the beach just south of Baraawe. A Brit who tried to mine uranium when the British Empire ruled the southern half of Somalia had built it well before the years of war. The house was far from his mine, but he built it with cheap labor and made the walls thick to help cool it during the hot months. A large mason-block wall covered with stucco surrounded the house. The first floor had a long porch that faced the ocean and ran the length of the house. High arches opened the porch to the interior. The main room was a large hallway in the center of the house. It was a large, well-covered house with a thick roof. And just outside the walls that surrounded the old plantation, a vehicle stood with two guards sitting in it. They would not let anyone come close. One was a man named Al San.

It would be Al San's finger, under orders from Godane, that would launch the missile.

Omar held the cell phone tightly during the night. He watched the other men while they stared at him. The rain kept coming and with the rain, he thought it would be better for the army to come to him. His group would not have made it far with the little truck with the bad tire and the four fighters who were left. The truck would go fifty yards or so and then be up to its axle in muck. If they didn't follow the road, the truck would push the thorn bushes aside for a few feet until they jammed underneath the front end. Some of the thorns were like metal shards that were able, if they caught it just right, to puncture a tire.

"I am going to make a call," he lied to the men. He wanted an excuse to climb into the cab of the truck to get out of the rain. He held the phone up to his ear for a minute or two, as if a call was being made, and then laid it down. He had not heard from Faud for some time. Other calls from strange numbers had shown up but he was hesitant to answer.

The rain fell on the windshield. He looked back on the fire and the two bodies lying near the front of the truck.

They will attract lions. The lions will not care about the disease or the heart attack. They only smelled flesh, and they would tear the bodies apart with their massive jaws.

When the sun comes up, we will move. They could not be more than a mile or two away from the other Al Shabaab units. Once with the others, they would have safety in numbers.

I wonder if he got the message. Omar's mind shifted to the third cell. His wife was to make the call and get word to the friend in Toronto, the one who ran the milk delivery to the Somali apartment building. He knew what to do. And he knew how to get into the United States without anyone knowing.

Omar fell asleep.

He shook himself awake and saw that the weather continued to be bad. It was nearly impossible to see first light as the clouds choked out any rays of sun. But for the first time in days, Omar was dry and out of the rain.

He realized that he had been asleep for some time as he felt the warm dampness of his turban's wrap around his neck. He pulled the turban off and shook his greasy, wet hair and ran his fingers through it. He felt the bites from the mosquitoes.

At least the storm had one good effect.

There were no mosquitoes.

He rewrapped the turban and had started to open the door when he saw something move in the dark.

CHAPTER SIXTY-NINE

Parker and Tola knew that time was short.

"I can't get a signal." Tola had played with both the tablet and communications gear that he had. The wind created static as the air molecules moved faster and faster. The static electricity caused the signal to crackle.

"Where is the MarSOC team?" Parker asked. They had heard a truck spinning its wheels to the east, not too far in the distance. "Do we know if they are on the ground?"

"In this weather, they may have turned around," Tola speculated. "And if they are down, it was not a fun ride."

"We can't wait." Parker knew that Stewart was very ill. He had not seen the other doctor but had to assume that they were both under the tarp in the back of the truck.

The plan was simple. They would move in a two-link chain with Parker in the lead. Any shots to the left would be taken by Tola, and Parker would take the ones to the right. It was important to move into the wind and move quickly. Surprise meant that several well-aimed shots would result in a successful mission.

"We need to get them and move out of here. We have to head back to the west and hope that the rain continues." Parker had an idea as to how he could save Stewart's life. He didn't know about the Frenchman.

"Agreed?" he asked Tola.

"Yes. I am ready."

They began to crawl forward until they got to within fifty meters. The closer they were able to get to the camp, the better the probability of successful shots. The Kalashnikovs had suppressors on them so the silence might buy another half second, but one round from a fighter would give the other army a location and a range.

They paused while Parker scanned the campsite again. The friendly one who had helped Karen was asleep against the trunk of the tree next to another body. The other two were huddled up with each other and their rifles. Omar was missing.

Shit. Parker thought to himself.

There was no time to wait.

He felt the bolt of the Kalashnikov to make sure that it was both forward and tight. He pulled the stock up into his shoulder, put the first head in his sight, and felt the trigger on his bare finger. He stopped for one second to look behind and check that Tola was at the ready. And then he squeezed.

A thump caused the first man's head to slap back.

The man asleep against the trunk of the tree looked up in surprise.

Parker squeezed off the second round and the other man's head popped back just as the one at the base of the tree started to reach for his rifle.

Parker and Tola stood up in a low crouch and moved

forward at a quick pace through the savannah grass. They never looked down.

Seeing the two strangers come out of the darkness, the remaining fighter at the base of the tree made the decision of his life. He dropped the rifle and held his hands up high.

Parker scurried into the campsite looking in a circle for the man he most wanted. He went to the bed of the truck and slowly nosed his weapon under the tarp not knowing what to expect.

Two frightened people with large hollow eyes looked back at him.

"I am an American," William Parker said to the two. He repeated it again.

"I am an American here to help."

"Where is he?" Parker hadn't made this journey for just the two hostages. And they were not safe until he found Omar and got them away from the approaching army.

"I don't know." Tola swung around with his back to Parker, keeping his rifle trained on the one who surrendered. "I will check the cab." He turned towards the cab while still keeping an eye on the one with his hands raised.

"We need to get the hostages out of here. We need to get them into the dark."

Parker went to the back of the truck and slowly dropped down the bent tailgate.

"We will get them out of here and then I will come back for Omar."

Tola shook his head in agreement but never fully turned his back to Xasan. He started to turn towards the cab trying to cover two points at the same time.

Parker had the job of getting the hostages out of the fire zone and into the safety of the dark.

"Come with me." Parker helped the two captives slide out of the truck bed. As he did, he could feel their bones through their clothing. They were wet and both were shaking like leaves in a windstorm.

"You will be all right. We just need to get you out of here."

He pulled Karen up like a toddler and he grabbed the Frenchman by the back of his belt. The man weighed little at this point.

They started to move towards the darkness. The truck was to their rear and Tola was to Parker's back left.

A window cranked down. It was a sound that caused Abo Tola to turn his weapon around towards the truck cab.

In that instant something fell out through the window.

"Grenade!"

Tola didn't think. The grenade was to the side of the truck but well within range of both Parker and the hostages. Abo Tola jumped on the grenade and, as he did, he pushed it as deep as he could into the mud. The fuse was smoking. Instantly, there was a horrible "thump" sound.

Tola stayed limp.

Somehow, in the randomness of combat, the man with his hands held high fell to his knees and then collapsed. A fragment of the grenade had struck him in the head. Xasan was dead.

"Shit!" Parker screamed. He dropped the two hostages to the ground and ran towards Abo Tola.

At that moment, the door to the truck opened and he saw in the corner of his eye a figure run into the darkness.

Parker kept his rifle in one hand and felt Tola for a pulse with the other hand. His friend was badly wounded.

"Hold on!" he yelled.

Just as he started to clear Abo Tola's face of the mud to see if he was breathing, he felt a hand on his shoulder.

"I will take over from here, sir."

Parker pulled his rifle to his rear, ready to shoot, when he realized that several shapes had come out of the darkness. One was the MarSOC medic. The others surrounded the campsite. They disappeared into the black, taking up positions that would stop anyone else from coming in.

"Will, are you okay?" Gunnery Sergeant Kevin Moncrief was checking on his friend.

"I need your .45."

Parker took the MEUSOC semiautomatic and quickly moved into the darkness.

He followed the road, knowing that the target was scared and only willing to take the easiest route.

He won't go into the thorn, Parker guessed. He would go where he thought his comrades might be. He would follow the road.

The grenade had sent a signal that everyone heard. It would not be long now before the shit hit the fan.

Parker had only one goal right now. The hostages were being taken to a flat field some several hundred yards away where two MV-22 Ospreys were sitting in the dark. Once they got word of the rescue one bird would start to spin up its turbines. But Parker wasn't here for the flight.

Parker stopped as the wind died down for a moment. He bent down to listen. He heard a man's heavy breathing ahead. He pulled back on the pistol's slide, quietly, making sure that a .45 ACP cartridge was seated in the chamber. The barrel was extended with a suppressor. But it was pitch black and he was blind. He was going on instinct.

However, Omar was running in the dark as well. It was an even playing field.

Parker did have one other advantage. Omar wanted to escape. Parker wanted to kill. And Parker didn't care what happened to himself.

The grove of acacia trees was in a small valley. The road led up from the valley to a plateau that extended for a mile or so. The thorn bushes grew thick on the side of the rise. Parker kept moving. The thorns cut through his cotton shirt and pants. Parker continued forward.

And then he heard a noise. It was a metallic sound and not a sound of nature.

A pop of something metal filled the air. It sounded like a small firecracker.

Parker hit the ground and waited.

The thump of a second grenade shook the ground. It had fallen into the mud and puddles of the wet road. But it wasn't as effective as the first.

Parker attacked in the direction of the sound. His instincts took over. He felt the presence of the man and followed it until he saw the shape of a figure hunched down on the ground.

"I am not armed," Omar cried out as he huddled down like a child. "Help me!" he screamed. "Help me!"

Gunfire started to ring out overhead as the soldiers of Al Shabaab were approaching.

The lights of trucks started to flash in the distance.

The grass broke up the beams like flashlights waving in the air.

"Help me!" Omar screamed again.

Parker ran to Omar, knocked him over with a solid left hook, and pushed his face into the ground.

"It does not bother me that you will die here." Parker remembered Mobile and the pictures of the children. He remembered the schoolteacher's face. He continued to push Omar into the ground.

The lights grew brighter.

And then Parker felt a hand on his shoulder.

"Sir, we need to get down."

The Marine pushed Parker to the ground just like Parker had pushed Omar into the mud.

Parker heard the Marine whisper, "I have him. We are ready for Big Bear, over."

Parker tried to look up as the Marine laid down and covered both of them with his body. Parker could feel the magazines from the soldier's vest push into his back.

I know what is going on, he realized as he lay there with the back of Omar's neck in his hands. And then it struck.

The ground shook as if there had been an earthquake on a plateau of the western Somalia plains. It repeated itself like thunder that rolled in wave after wave. Parker felt the warmth of hot air pass over his body.

The C-130 gunship came through the clouds, never really visible, pounding the earth with its 155-millimeter artillery rounds on a hydraulic system that was a large version of a Gatling gun. The shells tore through the line of vehicles just over the ridge and the few men who survived ran frightened into the night.

One truck that was struck on the far end of the convoy held a cell phone. The shell was a direct hit. The vehicle was vaporized before the order could be put in to launch a missile. Godane was dead.

Parker walked to the MV-22 with his prisoner in hand. The Marine had used a zip tie to bind Omar's hands tightly. They walked past the campfire seeing the dead bodies that remained. Xasan had died of his own fighter's cause—shrapnel from a grenade—and rested next to his father's body. No one would come to bury the dead. The Reapers would do that.

Omar was like a child. He was kept under armed guard, bound to a chair in the aircraft with no hope of escape. More important, they made sure that there was no hope of his jumping from the craft. He had a long trip ahead. They all wanted to make sure that he had a heartbeat to face everything that awaited him.

"How is Abo doing?" Parker asked as soon as he got to the bird.

"The mud helped." The medic was attached to a MarSOC team.

Parker knew that Tola could have been wounded in an emergency room in downtown New York and not have stood a better chance of surviving than he did with this medical team.

"Where is he?"

"Sir, he is on the other bird. One nice thing about all the doctors being here is that they have more medical gear than we have in Djibouti."

Parker looked around the aircraft.

He saw the sunken-down shape of a woman.

"Does she have meningitis?" he asked the medic.

"Yes, sir, I would bet that she does."

"She is O positive. We need to give her a transfusion now."

"I only have plasma with me."

"I understand. We've got the same blood type. Trust me, she needs a transfusion now." Parker pulled up his sleeve, baring his arm to the medic.

The aircraft struggled with the winds as it climbed up, but the front had passed through. It soon reached calm air and the transfusion began.

"Thank you," Karen whispered as she looked up at the stranger's face.

The Navy SEAL team from Carrier Group 12 had preferred to wait until darkness. It didn't like giving up any advantage that it could have over the enemy. But this mission was different. Time was of the essence and there was no idea as to when a cell phone call might have been made.

The location of the missile was another educated guess on the part of intelligence, but again, the consequences were too great for it to hold back the mission.

The Blackhawks circled well to the north, staying as high as possible as they crossed the coastline, and then turned back to the east and south. Finally they dropped like rocks falling from the sky.

The admiral had debated as to whether to put a Tomahawk on the target but, again, he needed confirmation. His intelligence people wanted something else as well. This was the first chance to look at a DF-21 missile up close.

The *Zumwalt* moved close to the shoreline, taking a position that bisected the house containing the missile with the carrier group. The ship stood with its weapons armed in case any other action needed to be taken. It was a blocking force between the carrier killer and the carrier.

The SEAL team later called this one "easy."

The Al Shabaab guards were still waiting for their cell phones to ring with orders. They would not learn until later of the battle that occurred or the martyrdom of hundreds of their fellow fighters. It would be described as the martyr Godane's last stand. The flag of Al Shabaab had been ripped apart by the C-130 air strike.

The SEAL team took out each guard with careful, deliberate head shots.

Several charges of plastic explosives were placed on the rocket, but before it was blown apart, a team member took out its guidance computer. The treasure would be well used.

The Blackhawks flew back to the group with no injuries and no losses.

Paul Stewart held his daughter's hand as they placed her on a gurney and took her into the isolation clinic. They pulled the needle out of Parker's arm as they finished the transfer.

"Thank you." Paul Stewart pulled Parker into his embrace. The grime, the soaking wet, and the smell of days in combat didn't matter. He had his daughter back.

"I have to check on my man." Parker didn't like thank-yous. He went straight to the other clinic to see a man fully bandaged with an I.V. running to his arm. The medics had surrounded the other gurney.

"What's his status?"

The Marine major was standing by as they started to carry Tola back to the landing zone.

"He is alive and stable."

"Good." Parker reached over and squeezed his friend's arm. Abo Tola had received no wounds to his face or his head. The mud had absorbed much of the energy like the other grenade that Omar had thrown. The rains had helped in one unexpected way. They made the grenades less deadly.

"It was an old Russian F1," Parker mumbled to both Tola and himself.

"They stopped making them years ago." Some arms merchant had sold the World War II grenade to Al Shabaab. The man made money but the goods were not the best. It was fortunate for both Parker and Tola that this was the case.

"They have a C-17 standing by at Djibouti," the major said as they carried Tola to the Osprey. "The bird is equipped with a complete emergency room and he will be in Bethesda before noon tomorrow."

"Good." Parker didn't smile but he did feel relieved. "You will have some paperwork to do on him when he gets better."

Abo Tola would become one of the very few that would wear a ribbon blue with stars.

CHAPTER SEVENTY

A second Osprey left the makeshift camp near Ferfer later that same day. The monsoon had been followed by a day of crystal clear weather, as if nature wanted the monsoon to scour away the stains from the battlefield.

"We have a C-17 waiting on us in Djibouti." Moncrief looked like he had a renewal on life.

After food, a hot shower, and warm clothes, Parker only wanted to sleep. The MV-22 didn't take as much time as he remembered. It picked up the trailing Cobra gunships soon after the engines started to spin up.

"Were they out there as well?" Parker pointed to the gunships.

"Yes, they were on the last leg, but we held them back to keep sound to the minimum."

"It must have been a hell of a ride." Parker remembered his rough landings in bad weather and figured this storm was even worse.

"Well, I thought we were going to flip over at one point." Moncrief didn't smile.

They both looked back at the small man chained in the back. He wore an olive-colored flight suit that would soon be exchanged for an orange one. Warren was sitting in the back talking to him but getting no response.

"What's the story on our buddy?" Parker asked, pointing to Warren.

"He had a very bad headache. He tried to hit the medic up for some high-powered stuff. He got two aspirin instead."

Parker laughed. "How's the French doctor?"

"He's got malaria but he is going to be all right. The MSF has sent a confidential letter of appreciation to the president. They weren't crazy about the military intervention, but knew that Karen Stewart was an American citizen, and that it was our call. Plus, they saved about four million dollars that they are now able to put toward both Ebola and the meningitis strain."

"Where are we going now?"

"The C-17 is going to take us directly to Andrews. We will get some catch-up time."

"Actually, we are going somewhere else." Parker unbuckled his seat belt and stood up in the small cargo bay of the MV-22. He went up to the crew chief and spoke into the chief's ear. The chief shook his head and gave him another helmet. Parker put the helmet on and started talking to the pilots. It wasn't that the Osprey was going to change course. It was that the C-17 was going to change destinations.

Just like its arrival, the Osprey came across the heading of the runway at Camp Lemonnier like a typical aircraft flying the strip. It ran the length of the runway and then stopped near the numbers on the far end. The tilt-rotors cycled through a transition and the aircraft slowly put its feet down on the ground. The wheels were muddied, as was the Osprey.

The aircraft taxied to the end of the runway and then to an open spot of tarmac where a much larger aircraft—the C-17—was waiting. The Osprey looked like a child when it pulled up next to the Globemaster. The C-17's engines were running and the deck of the runway was awash with warm air that smelled of kerosene.

The MV-22 spun its engines down and finally came to a stop.

Parker picked up his backpack and followed the prisoner from the airplane, accompanied by Moncrief. A slew of men carrying M4s and wearing bulletproof vests that bore Velcro patches reading FBI surrounded the aircraft. MarSOC Marines accompanied them in full combat gear. As Parker passed the prisoner, he saw one agent putting a bulletproof vest on him while another read out his Miranda rights.

A man with gray hair was standing on the side. He walked up to Parker and Moncrief.

"Sir, I am the chief agent. I understand that you have requested that your prisoner be taken to another destination?"

"Yes, that is right." Parker nodded his head as he pulled the backpack over his shoulder.

"I wanted to tell you that the director thanks you." The agent held out his hand. "And he agrees."

The C-17 climbed out from Djibouti and headed well out over the Gulf of Aden before it started to turn again to the west. Parker noticed that two F-35 Lightnings were on the wings as the big ship crossed over the water and then well above Egypt. The airplane leveled off high above any danger from the ground below.

The flight was heading into the sun as it traveled west. Parker had no idea of the time, and sleep finally overtook him. His body repaired itself by a deep sleep, although it didn't last long. When Parker awoke, he thought of Abo Tola. He was aware that Tola was on an airplane like this one, heading on nearly the same course as it crossed over the Atlantic. But he knew that the captain would be in the care of the surgeons at Walter Reed soon and, with their attention, would soon run again.

"I need to bring Abo some doro wot," Parker said mostly to himself.

It occurred to Parker that his friend would be with his family soon.

"He will be okay," Moncrief said.

"Yeah, I think he will."

"Look at our boy." Moncrief pointed to Omar, who was surrounded by agents all wearing vests and dressed in dark Navy tactical uniforms.

"Yes."

The older agent came up to where Parker and Moncrief had set up camp. The benefit of the C-17 and its cargo-loaded seats was that they both had a bench of seats to themselves.

"Sir, our prisoner doesn't know yet where we are going. Would you like to tell him? By the way, his buddy was caught at the Canadian border. They had another cell planned to hit a railroad car of chlorine gas as it passed through Denver. We had stopped the delivery of every large-quantity load of chlorine gas in the United States, which is how we learned of the impending attack."

Parker was pleased to hear the news.

"I'd be happy to tell him what to expect."

Parker walked up to the handcuffed man sitting coupled to the seat. He didn't make the conversation long. He bent over and whispered into Omar's ear. He could hear Omar breathe in quickly.

The C-17 was on final descent when the crew chief came over to Parker and Moncrief.

As the wheels touched down, Parker noticed all of the agents stand up, with one holding his hand on Omar's shoulder.

"Sir, you might want to see this," the chief said to Parker, gesturing towards the window.

Parker stood up and crossed over to one of the windows in the rear of the aircraft. He looked out to see a line of black Yukons with their blue lights flashing. It wasn't the Yukons themselves that were unexpected; it was the crowd of people on the other side of the fence.

The members of the bombed church were all standing outside the fence to see Omar return to Mobile. The jet came to a stop and the engines spun down. The crowd stood there in complete silence.

"We will use the cargo door." Parker and Moncrief slipped down the steps on the far end of the aircraft. They waited until the prisoner was put in the second Yukon and taken away.

A lone police car was sitting at the end of the tarmac as the others left.

A police officer was standing in front of his unit with his arms crossed.

"Oh, jeez," Parker said to Moncrief. It was the officer who had arrested him at the scene of the bombing.

"Sir, do you two need a ride?" the officer asked.

"To Georgia?" Moncrief said.

"Anywhere." The officer opened his front door. "I have something for you."

"Yeah?" Parker asked.

"This cell phone you asked to borrow that night. This one with the cross. It was my wife's. It doesn't work. Someone found it on the grass a day after the bombing and remembered it was hers. I would appreciate it if you would take it."

"I shouldn't." Parker didn't really know what to say.

"Hey, she called me from this asking for help. And you are the one who answered the call."

The cell phone was the one she'd used to make her last call.

EPILOGUE

"**O**mar, you made the news again." The guard on death row at the United States Penitentiary liked to poke fun at prisoner number fifty-nine. He and the other fifty-eight prisoners were locked in single cells as members of the Special Confinement Unit. They shared the honor with a prior resident named Timothy McVeigh.

"What?"

"The Marine captain."

Omar barely remembered that night. He only recalled the man who threw him into the ground and pushed his face down into the mud. It wasn't the Marine captain.

"Yeah."

The guard stood at the steel door that separated the two.

"He's at the White House today getting the Medal of Honor."

Omar didn't sleep much anymore. It wasn't the sentence of death that kept him awake. The federal charge of use of a weapon of mass destruction allowed the

U.S. to move for death. A sealed federal indictment awaited him in Mobile. Alabama had its charges of murder as well. There was no doubt he was going to die. What bothered him were the sounds of the prison. They were endless. The metal clanking continued day and night. Sleep came like in combat, with a few minutes here and there.

Omar had been told the execution would be by lethal injection. It was scheduled for seven days from now.

"What do you want for the fly out?" The guard had made it clear that the death of the children and a pregnant police officer's wife made him a special prisoner. If Omar had been released to the general population neither the federal government nor the state of Alabama would have had their chance for the final word. Children-killers had a special place in the prison system and it was usually a blade just below the rib cage.

"Your buddy McVeigh had two pints of ice cream. Same cell. We call it the bad-luck cell, as the appeals just don't seem to slow things down for this one."

"Any word of my child?"

"No." The guard folded up the newspaper and walked away. "There's still no one on the visitation list."

The monsoon season ended early in Somalia that following year. The death toll from the meningitis had climbed, like that from Ebola, into the thousands. But slowly, as the rains stopped and the vaccinations from the new drug that Karen Stewart helped develop took effect, the tide turned. Now the medical camps were closing down.

However, Al Shabaab had a new leader and despite all that had happened, death would continue to follow the people of Somalia.

＊　＊　＊

William Parker stood at the grave on his farm the day of Omar's execution. The stone was marked with his father's name. He put the burned shell of a cell phone on the marker.

"This blood will wash off."

ACKNOWLEDGMENTS

I wish to thank many for their continued advice, help, and guidance with the stories of Will Parker and this novel in particular. Gary Goldstein had contributed immensely to the art of the thriller. He and the many at Kensington, including Karen Auerbach, Adeola Saul, Arthur Maisel, Vida Engstrand, and Alexandra Nicolajsen, are greatly appreciated.

John Talbot has been and continues to be a special advisor, counsel, and source of great knowledge in both creative writing and the publishing industry.

Jennifer Fisher is a most talented editor, and without her help, this novel would still be on page 100. I cannot express my appreciation enough for her guidance and talent.

The Public Affairs Office of the United States Marine Corps has contributed great insights on the continuing reshaping of the Marines: the units and the weaponry. I particularly appreciate the PAO and staff with the Marine Corps Forces Special Operations Command and also those who serve in the Special Operations Commands of the Army, Navy, and Air Force. I purposely do not mention names, for the nature of their continuing missions suggests that I should not; each of them, however, is greatly appreciated.

Also, I wish to thank my fellow writers from Charlotte who are all particularly talented, each in his or her own style. Nancy Nygard, Ellen Morris, and Linda Miller have served as good advisors.

Rick Sheehan is the electronics wizard who keeps the world informed of Parker stories. And I have always appreciated the advice of Meryl Moss, Deb Zipf, and M. J. Rose.

I particularly want to thank the USO for its continued support of the troops around the world and in making the original Operation Thriller occur. Mike Theiler served as the official photographer and worked late many a time, often with only a few hours sleep, to get the photos sent downrange.

Any mistakes are not to be attributed to anyone but the author. I greatly appreciate the readers who have supported these stories by their letters, e-mails, and comments. One kind person told me that my books allowed a relative to escape from the daily routine of chemotherapy. For that one reader, all of this has been worthwhile.